Adolescently
in love

Adolescently in love

NITHARSHA PRAKASH

PARTRIDGE
A Penguin Random House Company

To order additional copies of this book, contact
Partridge India
000 800 10062 62
orders.india@partridgepublishing.com

www.partridgepublishing.com/india

ACKNOWLEDGMENTS

Friends, family and well-wishers to every one of you who had
wished the best for me. To my mother for the guidance and
support towards for my interest in writing. To Mr Rajagopalan for
his editing skills. To my cousin who is an avid reader, who helped
me out for which I'm indebted. To my friends from college for all
their encouragement and the help they had given me with this
book which came in the most important of times. To the other
friends, who had in one way or another provided information and
knowledge that helped me to add value to the book. To the two
agents from Partridge. And also to anyone whom I might have
accidentally forgotten to mention.
THANK YOU

I am glad 'tis night, you do not look on me,
For I am much ashamed of my exchange:
But love is blind and lovers cannot see
The pretty follies that themselves commit;
For if they could, Cupid himself would blush
To see me thus transformed to a boy.
-William Shakespeare

Prologue

*T*HE BUS RAMBLED *on. There was no one beside him on the seat. He adjusted himself and moved towards the window and looked outside. There were dark clouds. Both sides of the road were strewn with trees that lashed out its branches forming an arch over the roads. He had a strange feeling that the road the bus was travelling seemed to head to a forest. The vegetation outside appeared to be wild. The road was totally unfamiliar to him. He'd never been here before.*

Rohit left the trees and the clouds to fly past and began examining the inside of the bus. He searched the bus for familiar faces. A few were. He saw a few juniors from his college. There were some faculty members from his college too. That was it. It should've been his college bus. But he couldn't figure out why his college bus was on such a road. His college was in the centre of the city and the bus never travelled beyond the city limits. There were also a few faces that he didn't recognize. He sensed that someone was watching him. He turned around.

A girl of his age, creamy-fair skin and thin eyebrows, dressed in a well-fitted blue salwar and white leggings sat in a seat just behind his. She looked unusually pretty. Rohit felt a peculiar tingling sensation within him. He had had that feeling before. But that was a long time back. There was no one sitting beside her. She was carrying nothing with her, no shoulder bag, no kerchief, and no mobile even. And the weirdest of them all was that she had her gaze intently fixed upon him. He ransacked his memories to identify her. Nothing. He remembered her tresses, the gaze, and the build. He had definitely seen her before, but couldn't recognize her. He tried to focus on who the girl was. His mind wasn't getting anywhere. He hoped the girl would soon turn away to avoid being caught looking, but she didn't. Instead her gaze was fixed upon him, frozen there.

"Um . . . . Where are we going?" he asked.

"It's to this place." She replied absent-mindedly. His question hadn't perturbed her still gaze. Her voice sounded familiar.

Still, Rohit didn't get the answer to his question. But he turned front and looked out again. As much he wanted to know the answer, he decided to not ask the question again. The bus jolted and a feeling of deja-vu crept through him.

"You look a bit tense." He heard her voice. He turned around again.

"Yeah, I have an interview . . . ." He had no clue what time or date it was. He took a glance at his watch. His watch was frozen. He just blurted out ". . . in the morning."

"So, you must want this job badly." She said

"Guess so." He replied.

It then hit him. He had no control over what was happening. Even his own tongue didn't seem to be under his control. 'Guess so' could never suffice how desperately he wanted this job. He had worked his ass off for the past three months to ace the interview. Everything around seemed to be a bit slow and confusing.

"You aren't bothered about anything around you. Are you? This interview must really be getting to your nerves. Tell me about it." It was the girl again. Here was a stranger talking to him and it kind of felt like he had known her for years. Worse still, she sounded like she too knew him well. He then decided to go with the flow and chat along to the girl. There was a sense of familiarity about her.

"It's a Microsoft interview; if I get the job I would be sent for a training program in the U.S. There are so many other perks. They keep making their interviews harder. That's what I guess I'm tensed about. But beyond that I don't know why I'm taking this job. Is this what I ever wanted out of life? I don't know how I'm supposed to find out." Rohit poured out, looking to find if she could offer comfort. It was weird. He was actually thinking aloud in front of this girl. It should probably be weirder for her. He hadn't confronted these questions earlier. He knew it lurked it in the corner of his mind. He had supressed it then.

"Always puzzling life is, isn't it? We have no idea where we are going, only to find ourselves in a destination we least expect. Those who can adapt win, others lose."

"Is anything you said really true? I always believed that life isn't what just happens, it's what you make it to happen." Rohit put in an argument.

"Seriously, what have you in your life? We all live under an impression that we have done so many things, but deep within us we know for damn sure that we have only made trivial achievements and the truth is a lot bitter. Most of us, just don't accept the truth."

"You like Moses?" Rohit questioned her. He completely diverted the conversation to a non-related topic.

"Ha! Nice man." Her face lit up. From then on the conversation went vague. It wasn't even a conversation anymore. They simply muttered sentences to each other. It was all incoherent.

The incoherent conversation lasted until the bus halted. In the middle of nowhere, the bus had stopped. 'The driver must have got down to go to the loo', he thought to himself. But the bus was parked in the middle of the road. Just then people began to vacate the bus. Rohit assumed, that the bus must have reached its destination. Whatever the destination was.

"Getting down, aren't we?" The girl asked.

"Yeah . . . Yes . . . . Sure." he blabbered as he got up from his seat and moved towards the exit.

Only when he got down he realized that the weather wasn't just cloudy but also very windy. The trees around were dancing to the wind. Something strange was happening. There was no bus stop there. Rohit realized that the bus had literally stopped in the middle of nowhere. All those who got down from the bus hadn't left at all. They just stood there as if they were getting some air while the bus was parked right in the middle of the deserted road. Rohit realized that he hadn't noticed any other vehicle along the road either. He went towards the front of the bus and noticed something very strange. There just wasn't anymore road. It was all rocks and mud and thick bushes. He turned towards the driver asked, "Hit the wrong road? Let's turn around."

"No. The road ends here." The conductor of the bus replied with a smirk. Suddenly everything began to lose its place. It seemed scary all of a sudden. Then the realization hit him, it was all a dream. He still did not know who the girl was.

"Do I know you?" he asked, trying to be polite.

"Of all the people in your life you don't know me?" she asked, sounding surprised.

"Just tell me. Will you?" He knew he didn't have much time.

"Sa-" And instantaneously, the dream crashed before she completed her name.

Rohit woke up with a start to find his phone was ringing beside him.

"Woke up?" came a voice he knew too well.

"Mmm." He asserted sleepily.

"Now only you are getting up huh? You remember that you have an interview right?" she continued.

"Yeah, yeah."

"You sound terrible. Are you feeling alright?" she was concerned.

"I'm all right. Just woke up from a nightmare." He replied with his thoughts over the dream he had woke up from.

"Fine, get ready and come to 'Green World'."

"No breakfast this morning." Rohit rejected her suggestion. Green World was the canteen where Rohit usually had his breakfast.

"What? Fine. But be on time." She hung up.

Rohit got out of his bed. He had always believed that dreams are the way of the subconscious mind sending a message to the conscious part of the mind. The subconscious mind that analyses things most logically and logically only, creates the dreams to suggest and warn against decisions and actions made by the conscious part of us that often gets clouded by emotions and prejudices. And dreams that are remembered, he considered them more significant. He had a dream journal. But with the interview at hand, he was in no mood to make an entry in the journal. He began recollecting the entire dream trying to decipher the message his brain was trying to convey. It had seemed like a normal pointless dream until the road ended. He had even mentioned the bizarre dream as a nightmare over the phone.

'So, what is this nightmare about? What is my brain is trying to warn me about?' He wondered, as he began to get dressed. He took out the Allen-Solly shirt and the Peter England pant he had ironed out and put it on carefully, trying not to damage the iron-creases. He pulled out his black tie and put a V-knot on it. He strapped on his Casio watch and looked at himself in his life-size mirror. His

black hair, combed and pressed with long, tapering side locks. He saw before himself a neatly dressed, 26 year old gentleman standing with a pair of bathroom slippers.

"Damn!" he cursed and pulled out his shoes from his shoe rack and began polishing them.

Inside the 'Jawahar' block, there were people pacing up and down. Rohit enquired from the information kiosk and discovered that his interview was on the eighth floor. He took the elevator and went into the conference hall there. A few students were already there and they were chatting amongst themselves. He was tensed, the feeling as if he was about to enter into an exam hall. Rohit took a seat in the second row from the front. The delegates from the company were already there. In just about fifteen minutes after he had come, the hall had filled up and a delegate began his speech.

"Good morning students. We are here to represent Microsoft Inc. And today we will be picking out a few of the best students in terms of . . . ." The delegate went on to explain the interview procedure for another half an hour. Rohit, rather than paying attention let his mind wander off. He really hadn't yet figured out what his dream was. The conductor's words kept ringing in the recesses of his brain.

"Here." He heard a voice. It was one of the assistants handing him the IQ test paper. He took it and trying to figure out what was supposed to happen. Once he realized that it was a question paper he began answering. He didn't find it difficult, it was challenging though. After an hour the papers were collected. Rohit just sat waiting for the results and in his mind, still processing the dream. All throughout the dream there was one solid question: *Where was I going?* He tried applying the same question to his own life. If he gets this Microsoft job, then he would soon be on a flight to U.S for his internship. That's what the delegates had promised during their speech. But that didn't seem like the end of it. If he didn't get this job, it would just be another MNC, hopefully. And, he had his girlfriend to marry. And it depended again on the job he was going to be placed in. That's the condition Lavanya's dad had set for him in order to win her hand in marriage. Suddenly his future, whatever it was, seemed so bleak, similar to the destination he had been pursuing in his dream.

Just then, the results of the Aptitude test were up on the screen and the murmurs of the students went up in volume. Rohit's results were among the top. The next round was that of the group discussion. He noticed that he had been assigned under a delegate and had to go to a class room where the group discussion was to be held. The group discussion generally comprised of two parts. The first half was the technical portion, where the discussion was based on engineering and the second half was a general discussion to assess the exposure level of the students. There were four students in the hall from his class. Hari, his class topper, dominated most of the discussion flaunting his academic store. But, to the delegates, smothering the discussion was considered negatively. Rohit managed to keep his speech short but very precise. The group discussion didn't let his thoughts wander off about the dream. But it was always there in the back of his mind, nagging him.

"We will announce the results of this level after lunch. Candidates still interested to get the job are asked to be at the hall where you had the pre-placement talk by 2p.m. That's all for now. Thank you." said the delegate at the end of the discussion. From the delegate's look Rohit could make out that he was clearly impressed by him. Everyone began to step out of the hall. Rohit too left for lunch.

The conference hall began to fill for the second time during the day. Of the students who had been selected for the interview, all but one were at their seat. Exactly at two o' clock, the delegate took the microphone and began,

"We analysed you students based on a number of criteria. And we have now narrowed it down based on the people who satisfy the criteria we are looking for. All of you here are young minds that have great potential, but sadly only a few have the potential that we require. So can I have the names of those who have been chosen for the interview?" he called out and the names flashed on the projector screen. 'Hari's name was the last and just before his was 'Rohit'. There were seventeen names together, and the students who were not selected slowly walked out, disheartened. The hall was almost empty now. The delegate left for the interview room. The seventeen names in the hall were arranged on the descending order of their performance so far.

Slowly, one by one the students walked out for their interview as and when their name was called. After about an hour only one chair in the room was occupied. The assistant called out, "Rohit."

Hari from his chair, turned around, "He isn't here." The assistant just left the room and returned in just a fling of a moment. "Hari, please follow." Rohit had missed his interview.

Within the same building, In the men's restroom at the ground floor, Rohit was. He had been here for the past one and a half hours. It wasn't a matter of urgency. It was his dream that had got him out of the interview hall. It was in his school he had met her, the girl from his dreams.

BOOK 1: SANJANA

BISON VALLEY

" **B** LESS MY FOOD that I'm about to eat, O Lord and give some to those who have none. All this I ask in your name. Amen." chanted the entire dining hall and sat down to eat. The morning's breakfast was *poori*. That was the menu on all Mondays at the mess in Bison Valley Higher Secondary School. Situated in Munnar, this school was one of the best in the district. The boarding facility and the cleanliness was something that was maintained, like no other school in town. The school was built on top of a hill near Munnar. The school entrance was guarded by wrought-iron gates. The gates had an antique appearance. Standing in front of the gate, the first thought that would cross a person's mind was as if it was the entrance to a haunted mansion. But, beyond the gate, there was no sign of the haunted-ness. It was a completely different scenery. The beautifully maintained orchard. A tar-road leading from there into the main campus. On either sides of the road were the trees lined in order, providing shade below and beauty around.

The school buildings were located beyond the end of the road. Till the end of the road, these buildings were completely hidden by the thick orchard. At the end of the road was a triangular junction and a ten-feet wall about fifteen yards away from the junction. On the wall was a plaque that read 'Bison Valley School, Munnar.' The school's crest was embedded into the wall and below it was a line in Latin *'Et disce ab illo vivamus.'*

Over the wall, in the higher ground rose the campus, standing majestically. It appeared as if the buildings were beaming with pride. The first time Rohit went into the school it was one of the best feeling he had. Had the background score been there it would have looked like the scene from Star Wars where the *Death Star* is revealed. For, some weird reason Rohit's mind drew comparison between his school and *Death Star*, the dangerous weapon from Star Wars.

The main building was a U-shaped one that housed the classes and the administration offices. There were two annex blocks parallel to the arms of the U-shaped building. The annex blocks housed more classrooms, exam halls, labs and the library. The gym and the indoor games rooms were there too. Behind the main campus, stood the hostel block, which rose higher than the three-story main building. Apparently, the hostel was situated on an even higher ground than the main campus. The space in front of the main building was the lawn. There were three flag poles planted at one end of the lawn. And there was a statue of the school's founder on the other end. The lawn was the main place of hangout during the recess period. It was also the place where the Morning Prayer services were held.

The moment the prayer in the mess ended, the students began filling their plates. At the corner of the men's dining hall was a table, like any other in that hall. Sitting in that table among the six of them, was a boy, tall and thin; with straight hair that hung over his forehead. He was the same age as the others.

"Guys, today the new chicks would be coming. Dibs on the hottest one." Chris distracted all eyes off the food.

"Yeah. Beware man; just because you called dibs, all are going to be so not-hot." said Vajish and the table erupted into laughter. The guy had finished applying his *Nutella* and took a bite of the slice. He then looked over to the conversation and joined in.

"You can only call dibs Chris, but you won't get the girl no matter what you do."

"You don't talk, alright? You hardly talk to girls in the class." Chris retorted.

"I do talk. Maybe not more than you, but I really do." Among teenage boys it was considered important to talk to girls. *'You ain't cool if you don't talk to chicks'.* It boosts the influence among the other guys. Sadly, for Rohit it wasn't his strength.

"Well, what was the last thing you spoke to a girl about?"

"It was . . . . Um . . . something personal." Rohit lied.

"I know what. The last thing you said was sorry. It literally was, 'sorry.' Don't say you spoke to a girl after that." It was Ajay.

"What? I didn't ask sorry to anyone." Apologising to a girl belonged in the lower end of the coolness scale amidst those teens.

"Yesterday, when the class ended, you said sorry to Sonya for having stepped on her foot or something. I'm dead sure you couldn't have spoken to a girl in the campus after that." Ajay recounted the episode of the previous day mimicking the way Rohit had said sorry to Sonya after having stepped on her foot.

"Fine. You can have your dibs. Don't eat me out. And asking sorry is a part of personal conversation." Belittling each other was what teenage boys always did. It was always so much fun. Rohit though on the receiving end of it, he too enjoyed the fun.

After the summer vacation, the school had just re-opened for them. As always the school had two different re-opening days, the earlier one for the students who had already been studying in the previous year and the later date for the new students. The old students upon the arrival of the new students conducted held a welcome party. The welcome party actually wasn't anything close to a party at all. It was actually just another of the morning's prayer service held at the lawn in front of the Founder's statue. The new students were usually given mementos as a symbol of acceptance into the school community. And today was the day the new students were coming in. And the thing that got these 11th grade guys excited was, as always, the new girls

After the meal the students filed out. The classes usually began at 9.00 am. The students had half an hour of recess period after the breakfast, until the class started. During the break, the junior students played their silly tag games running around in the grass-layered courtyard, while the more matured senior students gathered in groups and began chatting. Rohit came to the corridor and scanned the area. His class guys had gathered up where they always stood, in front of their classroom. They always referred to this spot as 'The Siren' The switch of the school siren was just outside their classroom. That's how the spot got its name. Their classroom was located in the ground floor in one of the arms of the U shaped building. Rohit joined along with them.

"Any news on how many new candidates?" asked Theo.

"No idea man. The attendance register is not yet prepared. So no clue."

"The good thing about these new students: we could while away some time with their introductions."

"Dude, but Robo won't let us have any introductions." Robo was the nickname of their class teacher Mr Venkatram. His stern, stringent and an inflexible insistence on maintenance of discipline had earned him that name. However strict and unfriendly to the students, he was an expert in his subject and as a teacher did his duty well. It was true that Robo would go about with the usual portions in the class regardless of anything.

"What if there are no hot girls in our batch man?"

"Don't jinx it, Vajish."

"Actually, there have been hot girls, neither in our class nor in our school, the ones we consider hot are the best-looking among all of the other not-good-looking girls around here." There was some murky laughter that rose. No teenage boys' conversation is complete without having something about anti-girls in it, although most of those stuff they say are simply juvenile. This conversation being about girls needn't be mentioned at all. The guys kept chatting, switching from topic to topic, once in a while hitting the 'anti-girls' zone. Finally the siren rang. Without another word everyone went into the classrooms.

From within the walls of XI A, the students sat looking outside the window. It was then that they saw what they had been waiting for the entire weekend. The girls' hostel in spite of being in close proximity to the boys' hostel, was well secluded. The hostel building was four-storeyed. It was an E-shaped building with the spine of the E being tangential to the curve portion of the U-shaped building. The middle spike in the E-shaped building consisted of the mess and some staff quarters. The other two ends were the students hostel, one for boys while the other for girls. The new guys who had joined had come to the hostel the previous evening and Rohit and the other boys had already got acquainted with them. But the girls, they had to wait, till now. In a single file the girls walked, towards the classrooms. The boys watched hoping that the most beautiful among them would walk into their class. The girls usually arrived in files in order of their classes. Rohit, too like everyone in the class, eagerly looked towards the direction of the girls, searching for the girls. The new girls, being intimidated by the new environment were among the last in the files usually. So once Rohit's eyes hit upon his class girls, he focused towards the end of the line, where the new girls would be. There were about thirteen of them, and closely behind them followed suit the 10th girls. The tenth grade girls came last among the girls because their classes were in the ground floor. He noticed that there were no new girls among the 10th grade girls

"Six are hot in the thirteen." He yelled out for the class to hear.

"Based on a guess, our class will have three girls, of which not more than two can be hot." Lokesh came up with his usual weird statistics. In no less than a second, the air was filled with noise.

"As always dibs on the hottest."

"Dibs on the second hottest." It turned out to be a chorus.

"If she's hot." A single voice came up. Laughter went up in the air.

"Dibs on the third one, if she is manageable." It was Guhan calling for the third girl and it again gained some cheering. The class was getting noisy. Chris put his hands up and waved them and signalled them to reduce the noise. The girls had reached the corridor, any more comments would be audible to them, but it was hard to keep the excitement down. The first class in the corridor was the XI A. At first the old-students entered and as soon as they entered, all eyes were fixed upon the door. Those thirteen new girls: one, two, three . . . twelve, thirteen; all of them, walked right past the class.

"What the fuck?" Chris cried out loud. The girls gave him a shocked look. Profanities are a common thing among teens, having learnt them newly, they try and frame sentences with those and end up using too much of them.

"Where are the new girls?"

"No new girls in our batch. They are 10th girls."

"What? Why?"

"Because the new students in the lasts year's 12th grade performed badly in exams. HM decided no more new students in 11th and 12th. The only two new guys in our batch have exceptionally good grades in their 10th. Otherwise even they wouldn't be here." Said Chris.

"You knew it all along."

"DC was saying man. Since when did we trust DC."

"So no new girls for us next year too, huh? This sucks"

"Shh. Robo. Robo." Rohit called out and the class fell silent as the class teacher stepped in.

The usual rituals followed: the prayer, the 'Good Morning Sir' and the attendance. Just as the guys had predicted, he didn't tarry his class to get to know the new comers, there wasn't need for any either. He began with the first chapter in the text book.

"So, last Saturday we completed Organic Acids and today we will start with Physical Chemistry. We will do a small chapter for the next three days." Just then he noticed the new faces in the classes,

"So how many new-comers?" the two guys rose up from their chair. One of them had unruly hair, a small tuft of hair at his chin and with broad shoulders, and his name was Anand; while the other fellow wore a typical school-going teen's look, was Badhri.

"No new girls huh?" the chemistry sir observed.

"At 'Bison Valley' there will always be time to get to know each other but time to learn your subjects, sadly very limited. Which school are you from?" he questioned the new comers.

"Chennai sir. JCES school." said Anand.

"Kanyakumari Matric School"

"Of all the things you learnt in your Chennai didn't you learn that there's something that people do once in a month, called haircut. Huh?" Anand looked down

"Get a haircut as early as possible; in here we don't entertain ponytails and braids among boys." There was some muffled laughter in the class from the girls' side. Rohit felt a bit sad that this guy's first day at a new school was going terrible.

"Do they teach 11th portions in that school of yours?"

"Yes sir. Three chapters in Organic chemistry."

"What about you?" he asked Badri.

"Four chapters in Physical Chemistry."

"Physical Chemistry is easy. Why did they start it off early?" Robo gave a mocking laugh. "Anyway, meet me later in my office both of you; I need to figure out how you are going to manage the portions that you missed." He added and continued with a chapter from Physical Chemistry. The class didn't end till 9:45. And when it ended, the next teacher was there. The students were allowed a sigh of relief at 10:30 when they got their 15 minutes break.

The students of the 11th gathered up at the Siren and began chatting.

"Why our batch, man? Why?" the guys complained over the fact that no new girls had been admitted.

"Because of those suckers who passed out last year. They screwed it up for us with their bad results." Said MJ. MJ was actually Surya's nickname. He had gotten it because he was a hard-core fan of Michael Jackson.

"Those thirteen of them, are they 10th?" asked Chris pointing to the direction where the 10th girls stood, at the opposite corridor.

"Which among the thirteen is the hottest?"

"What's with you? Those are our juniors." Commented Tanveer

"So what? It's only a statistical analysis. No harm in making an analysis dude."

"The girl wearing those frameless specs is hot." Some of them showed their agreement.

"There is a pair of twins' dude."

"What? Where?"

"See the two girls, identical height and identical everything, right next to that tallest chick." True enough, there was a pair of identical twins, they looked exactly alike. But to Rohit, one of the twin looked cuter than the other. He didn't know why but the twin on the left had something cute about her.

"They are also looking good right. They are actually better than the frameless one." Rohit expressed his opinion.

"No. No. No. The frameless is way better."

"Aw. Crap. Why did they have to be twins?" Lokesh sulked.

"What's your problem in them being twins da?" Vajish asked.

"Actually, it is an advantage. If two guys like something in one of them, one of the guys can just switch over to the other twin." MJ commented. But Lokesh just stood there awestruck and slightly disappointed. Everyone looked towards him. It was Jagdish who came up with an explanation for his weird expression.

"Oh my God! Actually, when the girls were coming towards the class, he seemed to be overwhelmed with feelings towards one of those twins. Now he isn't sure which of the two did he think looked good?" He explained and the group burst into laughter.

Just then, Rohit within the depths of his mind simply hoped that the twin that Lokesh liked wasn't the one on the left. The laughter continued for quite some time. Just then Rohit noticed Mr Jegan, his football coach peering over from the second floor corridor and smiling at him. He looked at him and returned the smile. The coach, waved at him. Rohit left his peers and began climbing the stairs. Just as he climbed a group of ninth grade girls walked past him. Rohit had known Mr Jegan from his sixth grade. He was the football coach in school and Rohit had played as the captain in the senior football team as a forward in the previous year. This year he belonged to the Super-senior category. By the time Rohit reached the top of the stairs, Mr Jegan was already waiting for him at the top of the stairs.

"Hello sir."

"When you returned, man? Didn't see you in the grounds"

"Sir, today only the new students have reported back sir. Only from tomorrow we will have games practice." Rohit said and moved towards the corridor parapet. His friends, at the siren, were still cracking up jokes. Everyone seemed to be laughing over something.

"Be there. Tell your other classmates also, okay? Only Vijay is there from the 12th this year. No one else plays football in their batch." It was true there were no one to play from the 12th but Vijay. He was a defender and he was never the guy to be a team captain. But, yet every year, it was the 12thgraders who captained the school teams. Vijay wasn't good when playing under pressure. Rohit knew Vijay would make a bad captain. That means he had to take up the responsibility. It also meant this could piss off the 12th graders. He had to deal with this captaincy issue delicately.

"Okay sir."

"So, your vacation went anywhere?" he meant to ask if Rohit had gone anywhere during his vacation. He wasn't as fluent with English as he was with the game. Rohit didn't mock it. When English came into India, the Indians had accepted it as a stylish language. And it was true that a lot of people were fluent with it. But, there were unseen misconceptions in many places. For instance, two synonyms mean the same to a lot of people although, it had lot of difference. Especially when it came to the usage, Rohit knew that he himself hadn't got it perfect yet. Luckily, the flexibility of the language masked his ignorance.

"No sir. Only to Kerala, I went."

"Okay, man. Go along. It's time for your next class." his coach said and walked off. Rohit took a glance towards his friends from the parapet of the first floor and saw that they were still on with their chat. He let his eyes stray off towards the 10th girls. For a moment he didn't know which of the two twins seemed cuter to him in the first place. Then he remembered that the cuter twin was on the left side. He spotted her. He realized that there was a complication, there was nothing that distinguished the one twin from the other. He was going to lose track of which twin seemed cuter if he didn't distinguish between the two, before the end of the recess period. He looked for something, and it glistened. On the ear of the other twin was an earring. The twin who stood on the left side had empty ears. He smiled within himself, for having spotted the difference. Just then, the bell rang. He began to run down the stairs to the class.

When he entered the class, everyone had already taken their seats. MJ was narrating Lokesh's dilemma Kavitha and Sonya, ". . . he doesn't know which one of the two he likes." The two girls burst into peals of laughter.

"The twins huh?" Rohit intervened the conversation. MJ nodded.

"Ranjana and Sanjana, from England, it seems. They are NRIs" said MJ to Rohit.

"Oh! You mean, British English." It was Rohit commented.

"Bollocks! They are so alike." said MJ mimicking British accent hoping to make a joke out of it.

"How do they distinguish each other? Sad fellow, Lokesh" Rohit asked out of his own curiosity, yet throwing the blame at Lokesh.

"Nothing that we know of so far. They are actually very very identical." said Kavitha

"Nothing huh? Then the earrings?" asked Rohit.

"What earrings?" Sonya asked, eyeing suspiciously.

"I noticed that the two were identical, so I was trying to see if there were any differences, and then I found that one of them wore earrings." Rohit revealed what he had noticed towards the end of the break.

"I don't know. Both of them weren't wearing any earrings, last evening. Their hair had some difference. This morning at breakfast, even that was identical. Seriously, you noticed an earring?" asked Sonya.

"Wait, that means Lokesh has a chance of finding out which of them was the one he likes?" said Rohit changing the direction of the conversation on Lokesh, he called out to him, "Aye, Lokesh did the twin you see this morning wear any earrings?" something inside Rohit hoped it was the girl with the earring.

"If only I had known she had a twin, I would have noticed all that."

"Does that even matter? Tell him to take another look and say which of them looks better." Said Jagdish.

"No, that's not conclusive. What exactly did you notice, Lokesh?" asked Rohit again contradicting Jagdish.

"I noticed her face. She looked nice. That's all."

"Then it's definitely the girl with the earring."

"How?" asked Sonya

"It's a guy-thing. You won't understand. Find out which of them isn't wearing the earring alright?" Rohit evaded her question. Some part of Rohit didn't want Lokesh to have liked the twin who wasn't wearing the earrings.

"Lokesh, I'll tell you after lunch, okay? Whichever girl that is?" Kavitha assured Lokesh but not before eyeing at Rohit as if he was up to something. Rohit gave a sigh of relief. So did Lokesh. Rohit didn't quite understand why he was so curious about the twin, but he didn't bother.

The next two periods were dull: Mathematics and Chemistry. Maths wasn't very bad. But Rohit grew restless during the Chemistry class, for he hardly understood the topic. He wanted it to end and when it did, he was just too glad. During the recess period after lunch, the guys were having an unimportant conversation until Haran turned up.

"We need to elect the Class Representatives" Haran said.

"What's the hurry with the CRs dude?" Yashan asked.

"No man. This time choosing the CRs will affect the captains who get chosen next year. So we need to manipulate it in the right way." The school had a weird way of electing captains. The management gave preferences to the academic toppers to be chosen as School Captain. The sports-oriented students came second in their preferences. The end result: timid book-worms getting elected into post that needed the ability to lead. The captains were chosen from the 11thgrade in the month of January and held their post till December, the time they have their farewell. Usually the 11thgrade CRs would never make it to be captains. The CRs wouldn't get chosen as they already had a post. That was the tradition.

"We have chosen Naresh in our class, the ACR is going be from the girls' side." Said Haran. Naresh had got the school first in the tenth grade and he was the school's choice for the captain.

"For our class we'll go with Theo huh?" one of them asked

"Yeah, he is another threat." Rohit agreed.

"You should become the ACR." It was MJ suggesting Rohit to take up a post.

"No way. It has to be girl right?" Rohit said. He hadn't thought of the possibility and he didn't want to be. At least not till then

"We should make Ajay the CR, else they will make him a captain of the Andromeda." Ajay was the best student in Rohit's section. He belonged to Andromeda, the blue house. Tanveer, also belonging to the same house always wanted to be the captain of it.

"No man, I want to be neither the CR nor a house captain. I need to focus on my studies. Even if I'm offered some post I'll openly refuse it. Make Rohit the CR. It's no way going to be me." Ajay spoke up expressing his disinterest. After some argument all of them decided upon Rohit as CR for one of the sections. They went debating about who should be the CRs till the break ended. It was Sanskrit period, for some reason Rohit was looking forward to it.

Few minutes after the bell, the girls too arrived in the class. Rohit noticed the twins inseparably walking towards their class. *Efficient method to avoid confusion, how canny of them?* he thought

14

sarcastically. The Sanskrit sir hadn't come yet. Rohit called out to Kavitha,

"Found out?"

"Found what?" she seemed puzzled.

"The twins, Lokesh asked, right?"

"Oh yea! The one with the earring is Ranjana. Sanjana wasn't wearing earrings during lunch. Why are you so curious about the girl?"

"Lokesh told me to ask you. That's why." He replied before she could begin guessing. Rohit turned towards the board. The Sanskrit teacher just walked in. He rose up to wish and sat down. Under his breath he muttered: 'Sanjana.' The Sanskrit professor began with a lesson from the recitals. Rohit didn't pay any attention. His thoughts drifted further and further away from the class.

After the day's round of classes the siren rang announcing the games period. Bison Valley School had one very large ground for almost all the games. Of all of them, Rohit knew and played only one game: football. The previous year he took his team to the quarterfinals round of the State Level tournaments. This year he had to play in the super-senior team. As Rohit entered the field he saw his coach standing with a beaming smile at him. He waved in return and walked up to him.

"Hi man." the coach greeted.

"Hello, sir."

"Listen, this year the tournaments are beginning early. I am asking the principal for special coaching."

"When is it, sir?"

"Districts is in July and the States is in August."

"Why so early, sir? Usually it is after November right."

"Don't know."

"Fine, sir. I'll tell all my batch mates to be there tomorrow evening."

"Good. This year also you are the captain." the coach said with a pat on Rohit's shoulder.

"Sir, But Vijay is there sir in 12th."

"I'll will talk at him." The coach replied in his own version of English.

"Sir, this year is going to be his last year at school and it will be probably be the last of his games. Let him be the captain. I have next year to be the captain."

"Go ahead and start warm up. Everyone has come. We'll decide on the captain later." His coach said.

The practice went for an hour and a half. Rohit wasn't at his best that day. Neither were the others. It had been two months since he had come in contact with a soccer ball. He fumbled here and there and his stamina had gone down to the drain. He had to begin his jogging right away to get in shape for the matches. The wake-up siren was at 7.30 in the morning according to the schedule. But students were allowed to wake up earlier and do a bit of studying or some jogging into the town. Rohit decided to set his first day target up to the botanical nursery, a mere 1km distance. At his high point he used to run up to Devikulam, a distance of 12km measuring both to and fro distance. From the misty mornings to the evening games, the life at school, nothing seemed changed, it was all familiar and what Rohit had gone through for the past eight years at Munnar.

An Impression

THE FINALS WAS scheduled at 7:00 pm. The victory in districts had given them a spot in the state-level. And after all the hard work, they had made it to the finals. The tournament was being hosted in Bison Valley. Hence all his friends would be there to see it. For some reason, he wanted Sanjana to be able to see the match. He had some kind of desire in him, to become friends with her. There seemed to be no apparent reason. But some part of him simply desired her acquaintance. He wanted her to know who he was. That a guy called Rohit exists and he plays awesome football. That was how he had decided to impress her. With his football. But Rohit didn't see anything more than making an impression on her. He decided that things will happen when it is supposed to.

Rohit spent the day watching the other games. Being the last day of the tournament, the matches were only the semi-finals and the finals. The most anticipated match was the Men's hockey finals which was played at 4:30pm. The match was between Bison Valley School of Munnar and Bethany's of Kochi. Bethany's was more of a sports school. Their teams usually excelled in all of the games. From Athletic and Aquatics all the way up to Fencing and Snooker, they had players. And they weren't just players; they were the winners too.

Although the Bethany's team had an edge over the Bison Valley team, Bison Valley scored the first basket. The second basket for their team came only after the opponents scored three baskets, of which one was a free-throw. Inspite the odds, the guys cheered for their school with all their might, hoping things will change. But nothing deterred the Bethany's players. The game ended with a score of 47-31. Right after the basketball match, began the handball finals. The match was once again between Bethany's and some other school. With the football finals an hour away, Rohit couldn't afford to watch the match. He went over to the football field to begin the warm-up session.

Left, Right Left, right . . . . Rohit was concentrating on his footsteps.

"Hey, Rohit" Rohit didn't turn. He wanted to focus on his footsteps and here was Lokesh distracting him. He heard Lokesh calling repeatedly and finally decided to turn lest anyone else gets distracted from their running.

"What's the time, man?" asked Lokesh

"Concentrate on your jogging."

"No man, it's just that our opponents aren't here yet."

Left, Rig . . . . It was of no use. Lokesh had successfully managed to distract him. He couldn't go back to his footsteps. He scanned the ground. There were very few people on the ground. The coach stood at the starting point, with his hands in pockets. The wind was making him shiver. The line umpires, referees and the other officials seemed to be getting things ready to organize the district-level finals. The team had almost completed another round through the field. Rohit called out to his coach,

"Sir, where are our opponents?" The coach too had hit upon the realization only just then. There were only fifteen minutes left for the match to begin. But the opponents were nowhere to be seen. He walked over to the officials' table and told them of the situation. They seemed to be too busy getting ready for a match where the players hadn't turned up.

The Bison Valley team continued their warm-up with the hope that their opponents wouldn't turn up at all. But that failed just five minutes prior to the start of the game. The Kottayam school team marched across the field, clad in their jerseys and boots.

They had lost the toss and the opponents, a school from Kottayam had chosen to take the kick-off. Rohit got to pick the side. He also had to decide the line-up for the game which his coach had told him to handle by himself. It was a reward for his performance in the semi-finals. He decided to go by the default set-up the team had. Right after the warm-up Mr Jegan had gone into the audience along with the other coaches. Mr Anirudh, a junior coach stood in the place of the coach as a dummy. The ground was filled with a huge crowd. Being the last match of the tournament, the entire school had gathered. There was a sofa laid out too. That should be for the chief guests. The girls had gathered. *Sanjana would be here,* Rohit thought. Something in him said that an ulterior motive in him had succeeded. It didn't matter to Rohit the end result. He wanted to perform extraordinarily in the finals.

After, the chief guest had wished the players, the match began. At the 11th minute, the match turned bad. The Kottayam School had scored. Gaurav stood, hands on his heads, embarrassed and disappointed for the goal he had conceded. But the 11th minute was too early for anything decisive to happen in a football match. The players didn't deter. The earlier they levelled the scores, the better it would do to the morale of the team. In spite of the opponents having a lead, there was their coach yelling at them as if they weren't playing good enough. The Bison Valley team wasn't being yelled at by anyone. All input and advice came from Rohit.

Rohit got two shots at the goal. Both were saved by the keeper. Kevin who played the left forward position lost three easy chances at the goal. End of first half, the players were worn out, but the scores were still 0-1. Rohit was yelling at his teammates for the mistakes that was, costing them the match. He thought of pulling out Kevin but it was too early for a substitution and the substitutes weren't fit enough to play an entire half.

Things weren't the same when the second half began. The opponent mid-fielder was having the ball in possession. He sent a through pass and the attacker had broken through the centre-defender. He was ahead. The moment his boots contacted the ball, he sent it flying down to the nets. Another goal for them. This was very bad. But then the celebration died down as early as it started. Rohit looked towards the side line. There was the line umpire with the flag raised. OFFSIDE. *'Thank God!' he thought.* The crowd erupted to know that the goal was not given.

"Vijay" Rohit called out and signalled him by waving his hand over his head. Vijay understood what he had to do. Vijay walked up to the other two defenders in the team.

"Naresh, you help him to cover the centre. Fred, you will pass the ball to me, ASAP." The two guys nodded in agreement. Playing what they had planned wasn't very easy. After a number of tackles, Vijay succeeded in getting the ball front. Rohit was ahead as he had planned. Only the keeper and a number of yards stood between him and the goal. He sprinted with all his might to score this. He noticed a defender running a few yards beside him. Just ahead of the defender was Fred. This was definitely a goal, if he didn't trip or get tackled. Luckily, no defender was in front of him. The goal keeper, well-alert stood with his arms stretched and knees bent, waiting to save. He moved a little in front towards the direction of Rohit. Rohit pushed the ball over to Anand just as he entered the penalty area. The keeper didn't see that one coming. And he was definitely going down. If the shot were to be taken from the place where Anand was, the keeper would have no chance of saving.

But the pass failed. A defender had got ahead and put his foot front and deflected the ball. Rohit managed to make a recovery from that pass and went for it. Thoroughly confused by the ball's alternating directions, the goal keeper failed the save and the ball had gotten past into the nets. The crowd roared. Rohit's eyes searched the crowd. Everyone had their hands up in the air, jumping and cheering. He searched and searched the crowd. Suddenly, a sweaty hug wrapped around him. The players had fallen over Rohit in an attempt to hug him. He too felt ecstatic. They were down a goal but now had drawn even. He knew there wasn't much time. But if he could pull off another goal, the cup was theirs. Rohit enquired the minutes left on the clock. Eight minutes. Tough one but they could still make it. The crowd was going wild. They were booing down the opponents more than cheering for their own team. It did work a little bit. The opponents missed shots, screwed up a few passes, it was getting to their head.

"Lokesh, enter. I want a header." He substituted Kevin's place. He wasn't the best player. But he was the tallest and had an advantage when it came to headers. He had to change the entire formation from 3-5-2 to 3-4-3 to bring him in. But at the position they were in, he didn't mind. He re-organized the team and gave them his new game plan. The opponents kicked off and the match was just a few passes and tackles. They didn't seem to be getting any advantage yet. The extra time card was up and 3 minutes were added to the clock. It meant they were probably in the 89th minute and had very less time to turn things around. The opponents were toying the ball around trying to find an opening. With the pressure high, nothing seemed to be happening. Until, Fred made a tackle and won the ball for the Bison Valley team. The crowd yelled in excitement. Rohit took the right wing position as he had decided. The ball was with the right mid-fielder and he had reached beyond the half-line, when he made the pass to Rohit. This was the final chance and Rohit knew it better than anybody else because it depended on him. This was what he had wanted. To be the one who nails the game for his team. This was the reason he had been working so hard. And now it was there. All that was left was netting the goal. He ran with all the stamina left towards the end of the field. The opponents had predicted what was going on. They moved into the penalty box. A defender was chasing him. Lokesh and Tanveer had taken positions; Lokesh at the middle of the post and Tanveer at the second post, behind all the defenders. The defenders were tugging and pulling Tanveer, having known that he was the better player. There was only one man covering Lokesh. Rohit crossed the ball. He had practiced this shot many number of times during practice and had perfected it. He knew this shot better than any other kick. But this attempt in the match, the moment the ball rose in the air he knew it wasn't the shot he had practiced it to be. In the anxiousness and pressure from the chasing defender he had panicked and twisted his leg and fell down. The ball was up into the air. His leg hurt badly. But it hardly mattered. Though he had messed up the kick, the attempt at goal wasn't messed up yet. There was a chance. He saw Lokesh push the defender and take a step front.

"JUMP" Rohit yelled at the top of his voice. Promptly, he jumped; with his height to aid him he managed to head the ball towards the post. The ball hit the post and deflected. But from nowhere, a kick was taken and immediately Rohit saw the ball reach home, into the goal posts. It was Tanveer. Rohit got up to run. No, his leg wouldn't help him. The pain in the leg was worse than he had expected. But he limped to Tanveer and hugged him; as hard he could. The crowd erupted into an endless roar. He let go of Vijay and ran to the centre of the ground and knelt down, tears streaming from his eyes. They had worked hard, but hadn't expected this kind of victory. His coach had come into the field and was hugging him. The entire crowd invaded the ground.

"Nice tactical change in the end. Bold of you."

"But it didn't work."

"True, it didn't get the goal you expected, but it was what got you the game you so badly wanted. If it wasn't for the substitution, the game would have ended at the 82nd minute. That change you made; it made the players feel like it was a different scenario ever since then. The team that had been struggling up to the 82nd minute was gone once you made that substitution. You gave an invisible hope to them." Mr Jegan replied with his face beaming with happiness. Suddenly, all hands were on Rohit, they lifted him up and began carrying him. His leg seared with pain. He groaned. The crowd was too ecstatic to notice. The school doctor had broken through the crowd and made them put him down.

"You were limping. Are you alright?" the doctor questioned.

"It's just pain. I should do fine."

"No, no. Come with me." The school doctor dragged him out of the jubilant crowd. "Go sit on those steps. I'll come back in a moment." Rohit limped up to the steps and sat down. He had never felt better in his life. *There can be no greater joy than this moment* he thought.

The girls, with their umbrellas, were coming in the direction of the steps. The umbrellas were not as a result of the weather. It was a rule, so that the girls didn't get wet if it rained unexpectedly; and in Munnar you never know when it is going to rain. They had to go to their hostel through the steps. He moved to the edge of the steps so as to make some way for them to pass by. Marie, the warden of the girls' hostel praised him and congratulated him and crossed by. Behind her followed the junior girls in lines of twos. They all glanced at the injured football captain who had just won the State-Level football tournament for them. All had smiles on their faces. He too simply smiled back at those little girls. The senior girls followed behind and didn't follow the line. They just walked past in clusters. Some of them smiled past. He too narrowed his smile and looked in the direction of the field, where stood a crowd still celebrating the victory. When his class girls walked past, they all muttered a word of congratulations at him. Sonya gave him a hi-fi. At the end, he noticed, the tenth girls walking in a group. The twins were there too. He tried to see which of the two Sanjana was. He couldn't distinguish. He just smiled. Both the twins smiled back as they walked past him. Whichever Sanjana was, he knew she had smiled at him. He let his eyes follow them, as they walked past. One of the twins turned around. On seeing him, she stopped in her tracks, turned around. With a double thumbs-up she slowly mouthed the words, "AWESOME." Rohit's face gleamed with a smile, a broad smile.

"Sanju, come fast di." It was Ranjana calling her sister to fall back in line. Rohit immediately realized the girl who had given him the thumbs-up. It was Sanjana. She promptly obeyed her sister and walked away. Rohit lied down on the steps, arms stretched and looked in their direction with his head rested on the ground. The entire world seemed upside down. He had a never-before feeling inside him. *Who was I kidding to tell there couldn't have been a better moment than now?* He again said to himself.

*   *   *

They weren't allowed to be there. They were, then breaking a dozen school rules. But none of it mattered to the victorious football team that was celebrating. The terrace of the classroom compound was always locked, but not for the coach, he had managed come with the key and a half a dozen pizzas from Dominoes and a bottle of beer. Rohit had spent two hours in the town hospital earlier that evening. His ankle had been sprained and he wore a flesh-tone bandage around it. The boys were merrily eating the pizza. A few of the boys had taken the beer and shared it among themselves.

"Rohit, you want beer?" Tanveer asked him.

"No, man."

"Why? It's a time to celebrate and it's only half a glass."

"There are a few things I have in my head now. I don't want that picture to get clouded by the beer."

"Oh! What is it?" Lokesh questioned.

"Huh? It's actually . . . the game we won. What a moment!"

"Who is that girl?" his coach whispered into his ear.

"No girl sir. Why?" he whispered back. Although he was in denial he didn't want anybody to know that even.

"Fine. I'm your teacher. I'll definitely find it out." His coach said with a grin.

"Sir." Rohit pulled his coach a little away from the rest of the team. "It's Sanjana, one of the twins. Don't say it to anyone please."

"Oh!" he dragged the word, teasing Rohit. Rohit's face went pink in the cold of the night. It seemed too good to be true. Deep within him, Rohit knew he wanted to be friends with Sanjana, for no reason though. He didn't know why he liked Sanjana more than her identical twin. The liking was just there. And it seemed to be too good that exactly Sanjana gave him the thumbs-up and not her sister or anyone else. Of all the girls who walked past him, she was the only one who showed him the thumbs-up. This was what he had wanted. Finally, his mind gave in to the truth: maybe he had played only to impress her and he had succeeded.

Embarrassed and Flustered

"ROHIT NOT GOING out huh?" asked Vajish. Sunday mornings were free time for the students at Bison Valley. The students were free to wake up anytime and that was the only time they were allowed to go outside the school campus, if they needed to buy anything.

"Dead-tired, man. I'm going to sleep all day." Rohit said and closed his eyes. But in a few minutes he was completely distracted by the noise of a rattling cupboard. Annoyed he opened his eyes. It was Jagdish, his bed was just next to Rohit's. He was getting ready. In a hurry

"What the hell? A little silently."

"Sorry, I'm excited about meeting Sonya at CCD."

"Today is the sixth of November." Rohit asked puzzled.

"So?"

"Isn't the girls outing supposed to be at the last Sunday of the month."

26

"I have no idea. I met her during the match and she told to come to the girl's point. Apparently, the girls are out this week and I'm not throwing away an opportunity."

"The girl's point."

"The what?"

"Café coffee Day. That's where the girls go to. So do all their boyfriends." Rohit shut his eyes once again to go back to sleep. But, sleep evaded him. His thoughts were in motion.

If I go I might get a chance to officially meet her at the café. We could have a cup of coffee and talk about may be the game or her London life.

But there wasn't any surety of that event happening.

What if she isn't interested? The whole school knows that the game was on me. Anyone would have appreciated for the game. Maybe she wasn't interested in me. It was probably just the game.

Even if it was only a game, there is a common interest: the game. So meeting up with her should have plentiful chances of meeting her going well.

If I go out there today and call her for a cup of coffee, the guys will start teasing. It will be a bigger embarrassment, if she rejects. And seriously, presence of other guys' there, is least helpful, let alone be it not disastrous.

She isn't going to turn you down. At least she will chat up even if she doesn't want to get to know you. From what she did yesterday, it's pretty sure that she will talk to you. Of all the hundred girls who walked past she was the only one who said 'Awesome' to him.

Rohit's heart leapt when he thought of that moment where she showed him the thumbs-up. He got out of his bed and got dressed. When Jagdish had asked him if he was going out he had said no. Now, he had to give an explanation why he was doing the alternative if Jagdish happens to ask him. Within his mind Rohit tried forming an explanation that was easily believable. In his excitement, it wasn't very easy to prepare a lie. His mind was torn between on deciding how to go up to Sanjana and how to lie at Jagdish.

He pulled Lokesh along with him to CCD. He didn't want rouse any suspicion on why he was headed to the coffee shop all by himself. They ordered a Brownie and an ice-cream. A group of girls entered the coffee shop a few minutes after the guys' order came. But Sanjana wasn't there. They all were their class girls. The girls waved at the boys and came to their table.

"So, what's up?" asked Kavi.

"Oh! Jagdish came to meet his girlfriend. We're company." He said, before the other guys could say anything. Jagdish got up and walked up to the other table where his girlfriend, Sonya had just taken a seat.

"Hey, where are the tenth girls?" Rohit asked.

"Why?" asked Kavi with a sly smile. She gave a look as if she was suspecting that these guys were up to something.

"Oh, it's for Lokesh here. He is curious about Ranjana."

"Why would she be here? It's 6th November." Said Kavi

"Exactly, my question. It's 6th November and how come you people are here?"

"It's for the Children's day program."

"Yeah right? I didn't know that the prep work had begun. What is our batch doing?"

"Fusion Dance. We girls are dancing for three songs and you guys for three songs. All together six songs" She looked at Lokesh and told him "So sad, that you were misled."

"I'm not here for her. It's only company." Defended Lokesh.

"Don't feel bad man." Rohit looked at him sympathetically, only in a moment, he continued, "If not today, you will see her another day." Both Rohit and Kavi began laughing hard.

"Urgh!"

"He is blushing." Rohit said pointing at Lokesh's flaring cheeks.

"Look at him. Disappointed that she isn't going to come? Aww . . . it's okay." Kavi teased. Lokesh sealed his lips so that he doesn't utter anything else that maybe used against him.

"By the way Kavi, what songs are the guys dancing for?" Rohit asked.

"No idea. Ask MJ. He is the one who is into all this right? Okay guys, got to go. See you in class." And Kavi left.

"This is why you need company huh? To tease and play."

"Yes. And always yes." Said Rohit between his laughter.

"Actually, why did you need company?" Rohit's laughter stopped.

"Jagdish asked me for company. But then I will have to be alone after he goes off with his girlfriend. So I wanted some company, and I got you. Don't worry man. Your ice-cream; it's on me."

"Wow! What's special about today?"

"It's for yesterday's match."

"Oh! Thanks. But if Tanveer hadn't returned the ball to the nets, would I still be enjoying this ice-cream?"

"Nope. I'm actually thinking of reconsidering even this ice-cream actually."

"What I took was a splendid header and I deserve this ice-cream. FYI . . . . We did it."

"WE DID IT." Joined in Rohit cheerily. The boys continued their talk.

"Lokesh, do you know anything about this dance prep?"

"Not much. Only two days back. They had started to work on it. We guys are doing three songs. That's all I heard. Why are you asking?"

"Thought I could actually give it a try." Said Rohit.

Rohit found that the thumbs-up was just a start. During the breaks, Sanjana would smile at him, sometimes even wave. He would return the gesture. And at rare instances, they would mutter a word or two. That was how he was getting to know her, in bits and pieces. It was a slow progress. The two would get together if they had an opportunity to talk. Rohit kept it a secret from his friends lest they start making fun of him. So he kept his talks with her on the absence of his classmates. They used to wave at each other, if they happened to see each other during the games. Sanjana was becoming a friend to him, just like he had wanted when he saw her the first time. He even met up with her in the café another day and had quite a detail chat with her.

Having his mind flooded with euphoric hormones over Sanjana, he had almost forgotten about the Children's day dance. There was about a month left for the Children's day. There was a lot of time in between. He didn't have any need to get into the dance right away.

But, before any of it could happen the Quarterly came. And Rohit performed badly.

When the results arrived in October, it was worse than he had expected it to be. He had failed in two subjects. Physics and Chemistry. His father wasn't going to be pleased. Once the results of the exam are ready, the class teachers, call up the parents and inform the progress of their child. The first-rank holder is given a medal during the prayer service. Rohit was afraid of what his class teacher might tell his dad about him. So he decided to confess his performance in a letter. He explained that he had failed in two subjects. He wrote about the glorious match. He also made a word of promise to do better in the next term. Rohit wasn't a guy who failed usually. It was the matches that had come up, which had thrown his exam performance out the window. The previous year, he got 11th rank in overall academic performance.

The letter didn't help in any way to please his dad. Two days later, Rohit got summoned from his class. He walked out. The peon led him to the 'The triangle.' Rohit saw a car that he recognised. And leaning on the car was a figure he knew too well, his dad. *Oh . . . my . . . God!* He said to himself. Rohit knew there was nothing he could have done to avoid this confrontation.

"What is this?" his dad asked. He was seeing his dad after six weeks. There are a lot of things, a man could ask his son from whom he had been away for six weeks. But all his dad started out was by asking about the failure.

"I come home from China, after a business trip and what do I hear? My son has failed in his exam."

"Dad, I know. I-" Rohit began.

"Let me finish." His dad cut him off. Rohit decided to keep his mouth sealed.

"Physics and Chemistry. You have failed in two subjects. Is that all you can fail in? Why did you pass Maths alone? You could have failed in that too, right?"

"I had matches, dad. Else I would have got a better score."

"Matches. I haven't said you not to play football. That is because it is your passion, a hobby. Yes. You should play football. I find no fault in that. I am not a dad who says his son not to play at all. I am not like the other dads. I want to be a cool dad. That's why I allow you to play football. I don't care about that part of your life. My concern is about your studies and studies only.

"Oh please! You aren't different from anybody else. You pretend to give me space to grow. Yet, you smother me with you advices." The thoughts ran through his mind.

"Dad, the exams were right after matches, so I didn't get time to prepare. That's all."

"Listen do not use your game as an excuse. You failed only because you didn't study well."

Just then the bell rang. It was recess period. Rohit did not want to be embarrassed in front of everyone. But then there wasn't going to be any escape.

"Okay, dad. Fine, I'll do well next time. I'm sorry." He apologized so that his father would stop scolding him. At least he could save his face in front of others.

"Sorry, isn't going to help. You are going to make a choice between football and studies. I tried to put up with your football practice. It's no harm in having a hobby, but you can't let that block your career. Even next year also you will have matches. Will you fail in your final year of school because you had matches?" His father did not seem to be stopping. This was something Rohit hoped his father would never say. But now he was saying the very same thing.

Worse still, the entire school was watching him getting scolded by his father. Of course, they wouldn't hear anything his father would say, but sure enough they would make out that he was receiving a draught of scolding from his father. Rohit scanned the courtyard. Quite a number of the students, both girls and boys had their eyes on him. Some of the teachers were looking in the direction. It seemed like almost everyone had nothing to do but stare at the teen receiving scolding from his father. Rohit was embarrassed. All these people will soon be asking him about what he had been talking. It was going to be uneasy to answer their questions.

He looked in the direction of his classmates. They too were looking at him and his father. But his classmates didn't make him uneasy. Rohit could make out what was going in his friends' head. They would understand the position Rohit would be in. In fact, they were the only people who could understand him right now. Rohit began feeling less uneasy as he looked in the direction of his friends. But there was something else he was curious to find out. He looked across at the opposite courtyard from where his classmates stood. Sanjana and Ranjana stood there. Both of them had the same look on their face. Staring eyes and sealed lips, their expression betrayed their emotion: disgust.

The uneasy feeling hit him once again like a strong wind. *Fuck! I tried so hard to impress her, and now because of my dad, my image is too damaged to resurrect.* He thought within himself. But from within him another voice lashed out, *why does it matter to impress her? And now why should I be bothered about what she judges me as?*

Certainly, a bad time for his superego and id to have a clash. Rohit cut the voices out, and tried to focus on what his dad was talking. He had no answer to the questions of his mind. Nor to the explanations his dad was demanding. His dad continued his lecture for about fifteen minutes after the recess had ended. He then took Rohit on a drive to Munnar town to go for a short round of shopping. But it didn't help Rohit at all. His peace seemed to have been perturbed ever since, Sanjana gave him her look of disgust. He wasn't interested to go shopping at all. He simply wanted to go back to his hostel and stay away from his dad, away from everyone else. But his dad didn't bid his bye until 4.30 in the evening.

After all the advice and embarrassment, Rohit was in no mood to go and play his regular football. His coach had told him to be there for the games, so that they could begin their preparation for the next tournaments. But Rohit decided to go to the hostel. When he went in, only Yashan was there. Yashan was there sitting idly and dreaming about something. Rohit reluctantly decided to open the conversation, rather than let Yashan ask him about what had happened that afternoon.

"Hey, what are you doing here, man?"

"Nothing. Just thinking, nothing else." He replied. He seemed to be in a daze.

"Skipping games huh? What are you thinking about? Who is that girl?" he teased him.

"Chi, no one dude. I was just, you know, trying to think of the purpose to our existence."

"What?" Rohit didn't understand what Yashan meant. This guy here, was wasting his games to dream some abstract stuff. He might rather do it any other time. Why waste the games time? The study time was always there to waste. But, this was whom Yashan was. A weirdo. He spoke quite less. He was always there as another guy in the class. But he wasn't known for anything in particular. He wasn't like Rohit in football, not influential like Chris, not even popular for having a girlfriend like Jagdish. But he was a nice guy. A nice guy. That was the label that Rohit had tagged on him.

"I was trying to see what the purpose of our entire life is? Money, fame, we all strive for so many things in our life. But all those stuff is very much trivial when compared to the stretch of eternity."

"So . . . . what is the purpose of our life?" Rohit still found it a bit stupid, to be thinking of such stuff. But at the same time he was intrigued what the answer might be. For two reasons: 1) he really cared for what the answer was. 2) If it was something stupid, it could be useful to laugh around during the breaks by making fun of it.

"The answer will be revealed to us in the course of time. All we have to do is evolve."

"What?" Rohit didn't understand the answer either.

"See, it is impossible for us to perceive the purpose of our life right now. Put yourself in the place of animals. They can't even think. So they can't question the purpose of their life. But they evolve. Evolution, I believe is not just to adapt to the environment, but also to help us find our future. Born into today's world the purpose of our life right now is to help the human race evolve. By one way or another, I think we are all a part of a chain reaction that will lead to evolution."

"So your point is?" Rohit hadn't understood a single thing from what he had said.

"That's all. All that is said so far is my point."

"Oh!" Rohit pretended to have understood Yashan's vague theory. *'Weird guy'* Rohit added the tag to Yashan.

"By the way, man. What was your dad telling you?" Yashan asked him the one question he hoped he wouldn't ask.

"My performance in the exam."

"You study well, right. What's the problem then?"

"I had the matches, right? So I flunked in two subjects. My dad can't tolerate failure. And worst thing, he didn't congratulate me for winning the states. People who don't know me and all wished that evening."

"Don't worry. It isn't just your dad. Lots of parents can't. My mom gets very grumpy if I screw up in any stuff."

"They are parents, dude. Obviously, they will be concerned. That is okay. You know what my dad does. If he doesn't want me to do something he can simply say that he doesn't want me to do it, right? But what he does is: tells me to do what he doesn't want me to do, pretends like he has no problem with it, then slowly puts limitations, telling that others won't see it as a good sign. So annoying. He was all like that even today. Worst part is that, he thinks embarrassing me like what happened today will help me out. What the hell, man!" Rohit didn't want to say anything more. He was already on the verge of tears. He didn't want to break down in front of Yashan.

"Have you ever got caught watching porn?" Yashan asked out of the blue.

"What?" Rohit was surprised with the drastic change of subject.

"Just answer. I'll tell you why."

"Not exactly. You?" Rohit questioned. It was weird to be answering. But, he didn't mind the conversation going in a direction away from his miserable afternoon.

"My sister found out. The computer in my house is on the first floor, actually. I shut the door, mute the volume and watch. If anyone opens the door, I will have enough time to pretend to be playing flash games on the net. Once, there was some dialogues in the video, so I put on my headphones like a dumb-ass." Rohit got the rest of the picture. He began to laugh out. Yashan went on. "Apparently, I didn't notice anyone. When I was done, I went down and my sister questioned me what I was doing. So I told that I was chatting. She asked me if it was a voice chat. I thought she might have seen. But, I stood with my lie. She didn't say anything else. I got intrigued and asked her what. She was like, "I'm just trying to figure out what that naked woman was doing on the screen." I was freaking embarrassed. Then she told me that if I ever wanted to watch porn ever again, take her laptop and do it in my room, to avoid getting caught. Luckily . . . ." Yashan stopped halfway.

"What?" Rohit asked, curious to know what had followed.

"Sorry, man. I was actually, trying to take your mind off the parents' pressure and the whole thing. You looked pretty devastated after telling me about your afternoon. That's why I led with porn. But I couldn't avoid relating it to family once again." Yashan said.

"It is okay, man. It did help. But seriously, why porn? You got no other less embarrassing topic to talk about, like some school gossip or something." Rohit replied. He didn't completely get the point, but he knew that Yashan was trying to be considerate to him. He added that to his label of Yashan.

"See, porn is considered vulgar and obscene. Parents, studies and God are considered opposite of it. Natural mentality will be to keep it as away from parents or God in your mind. You would neither want to think anything obscene with your parents around nor think of parents when your thoughts are something obscene." He explained to him.

"Whatever man. I think I might go and play now." Said Rohit and left the hostel.

Rohit had been always good in his studies. If he wanted he could get a very good score. But football hadn't given him time to study. But now football was over. He could focus on his studies to satisfy his dad. He didn't want the incident happening all over again. He had got the 11th rank in the previous year. Of the 10 students before him four had left the school. That put him in the 7th rank. Of the six of them left, only two were in the same group as he was. That gave him an easy shot at third rank and first if he put in enough hard work. Rohit decided to work for the first rank in his next mid-term exams. The first rank holders were given medal during the Morning Prayer. It would be an opportunity to repair his image that his father had damaged.

BIRTHDAY GIFT

OCTOBER 10TH. THE best day of the year. It was his birthday. Rohit's sixteenth birthday. He had been excited ever since he woke up from his bed. His friends had got him a cake early in the morning. They ate a part of the cake, the rest ended up on Rohit's face. He got his set of thrashings. It was all part of the celebrations He had got a box of *Twix* for his classmates. He also had a toffee for giving the teachers and other less important people. He had five Ferrero Rochers. They were pretty expensive. It was for the special people. One for himself, one for Mr Jegan, one for Chris, one for his computer teacher and the last one, he didn't know if it should be Yashan or Sanjana. After some thinking, he decided to give it to Sanjana.

Having been the football team captain, he was popular. Lots of juniors wished him. He was overwhelmed. But all the while, the only thing going on his mind was on how to give the chocolates to Sanjana. In the morning he saw only one of the twin in the corridor. He didn't know if it was Sanjana or Ranjana. He decided to wait for lunch. After lunch he noticed both the sisters standing and chatting along with other girls. He couldn't barge in. There were a lot of teachers around. And moreover, Sanjana might not even have known that it was his birthday. He had his box of toffees in his hand. But Sanjana didn't notice. Just then something came to Rohit's mind. He noticed his art teacher at the same corridor not far from where Sanjana was. He headed straight to his art teacher. Art was a subject that he wasn't very fond of. And the art periods were there only till ninth grade. Ever since then, Rohit had hardly said a word of hi to his once art teacher. But now he was the only way that he could get to let Sanjana know it was his birthday. He had a Ferrero Rocher in his hand. *Shall I just roll it down as I walk past her?*

No that will look bad. And I want her to wish. His thoughts were talking. He offered his art teacher the chocolates. Just as he was giving the chocolates, he looked at Sanjana. He had her full attention. She looked delighted. Rohit smiled. While returning, Rohit signalled her to come near the staff-room. He left the box of chocolates in his class and headed to the staffroom. He noticed that Sanjana had almost reached there. The staffroom was just behind the principal's office. And it was kind of in a secluded spot. That was where he had asked Sanjana to come. And she had.

"Happy, birthday." She said shaking his hand.

"Thank You." Rohit realized that she had slipped a piece of paper during the handshake. He immediately slid it in his pocket.

"Here. For you." He handed her the Ferrero Rocher.

"Oh! Sweet. Thanks. I knew it was your birthday only this morning. Else I would have made a card." She said smiling.

"This itself is enough."

"How old ar—shit! Priya Ma'am is coming?" she said and almost ran from there. Rohit looked in the direction. Priya Ma'am had her eyes on him. Rohit pretended not to have noticed her and turned away. If he had to leave, he definitely would have to cross Priya ma'am. *Had she seen me?* He decided to run into the staff-room. The staff-room had two rooms. One had cupboards while the others had desk. Rohit ran past the cupboard-room into the other room. Entry into the staff-room was strictly forbidden. Once, he and Fred tried see what was in there pretending to deliver some assignments to a teacher, but they had been stopped and asked to get out. And that was even before they set foot.

The tables had personal belongings of the respective person it belonged to. His chemistry Ma'am had a pen stand made out of Choco bar sticks. There was also a lip-stick on her table. The junior Maths teacher had a photo of himself and his wife. There was a box of snacks on another table. He realized why it was a forbidden zone. On the right wall was a window and it overlooked into another room. He didn't have time to figure out which room it was. There was a closet at the end of the room. He decided to hide there. Just then the bell rang for the classes to begin.

Oh my God! I'm trapped.

A few weeks back, two teachers had been caught whiling away their time by staying in the staff-room during classes. "I have caught a couple of students bunking classes and it was such an embarrassment. But when you catch two teachers bunking classes, it's such a shame." The principal had mentioned in the prayer meeting. And after that, the watchmen had been asked to lock the staff-room during the class hours. It were to be opened only during the breaks. That was why the staff-room was empty when he had come in. And now it should have probably been locked. Rohit stayed in the closet for what seemed like five minutes before he came out. The staff-room was empty. But he noticed someone watching him.

From the window on the right wall, the principal was staring at him. He was on the phone. This was worse than Priya Ma'am. The principal signalled him to come to his office. Rohit went and knocked at the locked staff-room door. The watch-man who was standing on the other side was puzzled to see the student in the staff-room.

The principal had asked him to stand near the flag-pole without even asking explanations. He knew what this meant. He had to probably stand there till late in the evening. Standing there wasn't the least of his worries. What was he going to tell when the principal asks him what he had been up to in the staff-room? *Punished on a birthday. How perfect!* He thought to himself. He decided to tell that he had been there to give chocolates to a teacher for his birthday. That would be the simplest lie he could say. He could offer his principal some chocolates too. It wasn't exactly a bribe. But nobody punishes a student on their birthday. He hoped it could help the principal to let him off.

Throughout the afternoon and during the sports hour, Rohit watched the students go about the routine from the flag-pole. Some of his friends questioned him. He told them that he had gone to give chocolates to Priya Ma'am and was caught for returning late to the class. His friends bought the lie. That was because they hadn't seen him emerging from the closet in the staffroom. To his luck, Sanjana hadn't seen him stand there. He didn't want her to feel guilty in any way. But it lasted only till the end of the sports hour.

Sanjana's class had a special class in the evening. The class room buildings were deserted by then. And she clearly knew why Rohit was standing there at that time of the day. But she hadn't been able to talk to him yet. She had to wait till dinner. Rohit hoped the principal would let him go before dinner. He was too embarrassed to talk to Sanjana about it. And moreover, he had underestimated the cold winds of Munnar. Standing in his white cotton shirt and the grey trousers, it was clearly not built for the cold weather. He hadn't worn his sweater as the morning was sunny. Now it was getting to him. His hair on his hands were straight up.

He stood, stood and stood on. And eventually it was time for dinner. Rohit didn't get to go to dinner either. He stood there starving. Now he understood, why the principal considered standing under the flag-pole as a punishment. When the dinner was over, Sanjana was returning to class. She couldn't directly come up and talk to him, but she approached him, yet stayed far enough.

"What happened?"

"Got caught." Rohit replied. She signalled him asking if it was because of her.

"No. After that." Rohit mouthed the words.

"Isn't it cold?" she asked.

"A bit, yes. But, I'm used to it." He told.

"Take my jacket." She said and tossed him the jacket that she was wearing. Luckily, it wasn't one of those girly jacket. Rohit thanked her and put it on. And it felt it really good to feel warm.

"I'll leave. Else I'll get caught." Sanjana continued. Rohit merely nodded smiling.

"Happy birthday, once again." She muttered and walked away. *This birthday couldn't get any better. Got the chance to talk to Sanjana twice on the same day. She gave me her jacket. And I am being punished. Well that is a bummer, but the bright side is way better.* Rohit stood there happily, replaying the memories of the day. She had earlier told him that she would have made him a card if she had known it was his birthday. *She would have made a card, not got one. That is so awesome.* He had been wrong to think that his image had been damaged when his dad yelled at him at him the other day. When his euphoria was at its zenith, the principal summoned him to his office.

Rohit put on a sorry face as he stepped into the principal's office. He offered the chocolates, before the principal could say anything.

"Birthday huh? How old are you?" the principal questioned him as he took the chocolates.

"Sixteen sir.

"What you did earlier, do you think it is an act of a sixteen year old?"

"Sir, I am sorry about that. I went to give chocolates to my teachers, that's all."

"First of all, the staff-room is out of bounds for the students anytime and any day and secondly I saw you emerging from the closet."

"Sir, Actually, I saw Priya ma'am entering the staff-room. I wanted to give the chocolates before the break was over. So I rushed there and called out. There was no response. I didn't notice ma'am leave, so I went in. Then the bell rang and I was locked. I panicked and ran into the closet. Only when I went inside I realized, that it was stupid. So I came out and . . . ." Rohit let his voice trial off to pretend that he was hesitant about narrating.

"Why are you wearing a jacket over the school uniform?"

"Sir, my friend gave it to me. It was cold."

"That was the whole point of making you stand there. As a principal, the only thing I ask of you people is to let me do something for the school. But all I ever get to do is such silly disciplinary actions which are over stupid mistakes. Do you think I have time to tolerate all this nonsense?" the principal scolded. Rohit merely looked down. "Only because it is your birthday today, I'm letting you go."

"*I have already served my punishment in the cold. How come you go blind to it?*" Rohit mocked within his mind. But on the surface, he said "Sorry, sir." He apologized and walked out of the principal's room.

PERFORMANCE

R OHIT ROSE FROM his bed and went towards the source of the music. It was his classmates practicing for the children's day performance. Rohit realized, that he had forgotten about the dance. His friends greeted him and he went in to watch them practice. Within his mind he was debating on if he should join with them. He had not danced on stage before. He had worked so hard to make an impression in front of Sanjana during the tournament. But his dad had ruined all of it. He needed to impress her once again.

That evening he asked Surya, who took the trouble of organising the practice, whether he could join. After, some negotiation, Surya agreed to take him, if he could do Michael Jackson's moon-walk. Rohit had never heard of moon-walk. To Rohit's mind, it struck him as a slow-motion step. *How hard pretending to walk in the moon be?*

The next day, he went to Mr Moses's room to check out the dance step from the internet. He was a Maths teacher and he was a good teacher. And by good teacher, it meant that he was lenient and approachable. He let the students use the internet in his room, if they needed it for any programme. On the contrary, he had a brother named Aaron. He was physics teacher. Unlike his brother,

Aaron was a strict teacher. He was one of the strictest teachers in the school. He wasn't a favourite among the students. Rohit sometimes wondered how two brothers can be so different. It made him think of Sanjana. He wondered if those two were as identical as they appeared to be.

After viewing the video, he realized that the dance wasn't going to be easy at all. And since he wasn't yet officially a part of the dance crew, he couldn't use the practice time allotted for those boys. He had to make his own time. And that meant practicing in the middle of the night in his hostel bathroom. He was losing sleep and he didn't care. He had purchased a pair of nylon socks during the weekend. The tiles in the bathroom floor were slippery. It provided him an easy platform to try the step. He had seen a few tutorial videos from YouTube. The step wasn't easy at all. And trying the same thing again and again, and not succeeding was annoying. But, Rohit' didn't deter. He took a break and got back at it. It was just this one step and he had about two weeks left.

The practice during the night was killing his sleep time. End result: he was dozing off in class. During a free period he had completely slept off. Luckily, Mr Moses didn't mind. It was Mr Moses. But Mr Aaron didn't take it lightly when he caught Rohit sleeping in his class.

"Go and stand in the last." he said. It didn't prevent Rohit from dozing off. Within five minutes he got caught again.

"I make you stand there and still you sleep. You and all won't change man. Thank God! I didn't make you to stand on the desk, else you would have slept, fallen down and hurt yourself." Rohit put his head down. Not in shame, but to avoid eye contact with the teacher. There was some laughter in the class.

"Are you sleeping again? Rohit." The teacher called to get his eye contact. When a teacher is yelling at you, eye contact is a bad thing. It makes them go on forever. Yet, Rohit looked up, making an expression of regret. But his teacher was too familiar with the expression coming from the students. He came up with a comment on that too. "Don't give me the 'I-regret-it-sincerely look'. You aren't regretting that you slept, but for having to be in my class." Mr Aaron yelled again. *Damn right you are* he back-answered the teacher within his thoughts. "Go wash your face and come." '*Bloody fucker*' he cursed the teacher within himself and walked out. As if the teacher had read his mind, he added, "Listen, go wash your face, but don't come back." Not wanting to hear any more insult, he left the class. Rohit washed his face and returned but the teacher yelled at him all the more and didn't permit him inside. Rohit sat down in the corridor behind the door. He took a position such that the teacher couldn't see what he was upto.

He had finally learnt the moon-walk. He was able to do it very well. In front of him stood, Mr Moses watching him do it. He had been practicing in the toilet when the Mr Moses had walked in. The teacher was appreciating him,

"So fluid-like."

"Let's see if you can do this." It was Tanveer. He threw a football at his feet. Rohit stopped the football and began to dribble it. The scene had changed. He saw a goal post. The very post that he practiced every day. But there was an unusual person guarding the post. It was Mr Aaron dressed in a football goalkeeper jersey. Rohit kicked as hard as he can. Mr Aaron cupped it easily in his hands. He had missed the goal. Suddenly, everyone around him were laughing. He hadn't realized the presence of others nearby until he heard their laughter. Mr Aaron was staring at him. And he threw the ball back at him. It came straight to his face.

Suddenly, the scene appeared different. The laughing people and Mr Aaron were still there. He felt something hit him. But, it didn't seem like a football, it was very much smaller. Rohit looked down. There was a piece of chalk. He was sitting down on his classroom corridor. Except for the location and the clothing of Mr Aaron nothing was different. Rohit realized what was happening. '*Shit*' he muttered and stood up with the same expression of regret. Mr Aaron face-palmed himself and walked away. He had sat down in the corridor and slept off. He even had had a dream. He looked around. There were a lot of people who had seen him and were laughing at him. He smiled back. From the other end of corridor, Sanjana was laughing uncontrollably. Rohit wondered if it was the good kind or the bad kind. His father had damaged his image, when he had come. Now by sleeping the corridor he had made a fool out of himself. And in schools, when you make a fool out of yourself, it is possible that you get to be made a hero by the peers. That's why he wasn't sure if it was good thing or bad. He looked up at the first floor. Mr Jegan stood there giving a thumbs-up with an expression that Rohit translated as *'Epic-shit, man.'* Rohit smiled back. Just then Chris came patted his back, "Fucking awesome, bro." It was a compliment.

The next few days, everyone asked him about this incident only. He hadn't attracted this much attention even when he had won the football tournament. Even Sanjana, when she passed by him, called him, "Sleepy-head." Within himself hormones surged, *Sleepy-head. What a cute nickname! Maybe I should keep one for her.*

Days passed by. Rohit's day dream of having mastered the moon-walk came true. He was so delighted to have done it finally. The next day the first thing he did was to show it Surya.

"I used to try it so many days and now I'm jealous that you can do it. Anyway you are in. Come to the stage this evening." Rohit managed to tell Sanjana during a break that he was dancing for Children's day. She wished him the best. Rohit was all excited. That evening Rohit had been given the role. It was easy and something just like he had wanted. It was a short one too. The last song they were dancing to, was a Michael Jackson song. During the song, everyone would freeze in their steps. That's when he had to do the moonwalk from one end of the stage to another. He should have to make sure he crosses the stage without missing the timing of the song. His moonwalk speed wasn't syncing with the music, yet. After he had crossed the stage, after two lines of the song, the dancers on stage would pause again. He had to do the moonwalk the second time. But with a slight difference. Rather than going across the stage right to the other end. He had to stop in the middle and join with the other dancers and do steps from the front. As long as he was on-stage the entire audience would have their attention on him. This was what he had just wanted, to impress Sanjana. The last few steps, the ones that Rohit had to do, Surya made sure it was easy enough for him.

Finally when the day came, Rohit was a little nervous before the programme. He was a little concerned if he would be able to pull it off. But when he did, it was an amazing feeling. The crowd cheered throughout the dance. But when the performers did a step that was hard to pull-off, the cheering went louder. And when Rohit did the moonwalk, he could hear so much of whistling and yelling. It gave him so much confidence. When he took the centre stage to perform the last few steps, he was so full of energy that he danced like it was going to be his last. When the curtains fell, the crowd roared a mighty applause. Behind the stage, everyone were hugging and congratulating each other. A lot of his friends seemed very much impressed by his good performance. Rohit decided to help Surya to take the props back to the prop room.

When the two of them returned Rohit spotted Sanjana in the back stage with other choir girls. Sanjana was a part of the choir for the evening. On seeing Rohit, she gave a 'no-way-you-could-have-done-better' expression and mouthed the words, "Damn Nice." Rohit smiled back and muttered a word of thanks.

"Program over?" he asked her.

"Yeah. They are setting up for the movie." She replied.

The children's day programme usually followed a movie screening at the auditorium. Movies were not a common thing in the Bison Valley School. Every year, only on special occasions movies were screened. And unfortunately, the school considered only three days of the year as special occasion and one such was the children's day.

The good thing about performing on-stage is that you get balcony seats for the movie. On climbing up he noticed a lot of empty chairs. He took an empty chair next to the wall, away from anybody else.

Moments later Sanjana came up the stairs along with the other girls. Rohit glanced at her and looked at the chair next to his. She understood it right away and signalled him to wait until the lights are out. He thanked the gods for the blessing. She took a chair in a row front of his, a little away from where he had been sitting. Rohit prayed for everything to go well tonight. They began switching off the lights. Just then, Sanjana moved from where she had been sitting to where he was.

"Hey." She said.

"Hi."

"Nice dance."

"Thanks, first time."

"So what movie for tonight?" she asked.

"I am not sure. You will know soon enough." Just then the stage lights came on.

"What's happening?" questioned Sanjana pointing at the stage. The principal was going up the stage. He took the mic and began,

"Dear friends. I have a grievous news to share with you tonight. Earlier this night, God Almighty had taken Mr Moses from us. He passed away in a car accident while he was driving back to school." The principal paused waiting for the message to sink in. Rohit was shocked. Mr Moses had been most helpful to him with the dance, letting him use the internet. "While he was here, he had been a great teacher, a good mentor to the pupils and a good friends to all my fellow colleagues. As much as it is a shock to hear his loss,

I am very sure that we all empathize for his brother Mr Aaron. So let's take a prayer of silence to express our condolences." The entire auditorium fell silent.

"It should have been Mr Aaron and not Mr Moses." Sanjana whispered.

"Chi. Don't say such stuff."

"Hey, it's just that he is so damn strict." She said. Rohit right away thought of the day he had been sent out for sleeping.

"Mr Aaron will be feeling so bad to have lost his brother."

"Mr Aaron is heartless." She whispered back to him.

"You have no idea, how tough it can be to lose a twin. Remember Fred and George from Harry Potter?" He said. Sanjana didn't reply. She had her eyes closed. Rohit wondered what had happened. When she opened her eyes, her eyes were wet. Rohit realized. Sanjana had a twin. Rohit's word must have made her think of Ranjana's death.

"I'm sorry." He apologized for bringing up such a gloomy topic. They remained silent for the rest of the time. After about three minutes, the headmaster broke the silence,

"And I'm sure with such grave news you aren't in any mood to watch a movie. So we will go to bed tonight."

"So much for my prayers. God has a crappy sense of timing." Rohit said.

"Damn it. Who doesn't want a movie now?" Sanjana expressed her disappointment.

"Too bad for us." Rohit said. The rest of the auditorium's light came on.

"Shit." Sanjana cried.

"What?"

"You forgot to leave before the lights. Your batch guys they must have noticed us together by now."

"Oh my!" Rohit panicked and got up from his seat. But just then a hand held him down. It was Sanjana. He sat down.

"What?" he questioned again.

"It's probably too late and your batch guys already know. So walk with me to the hostel." Sanjana pleaded. It was true. The guys must have noticed the two of them by now. Rohit didn't dare look in the face of direction of his friends because of embarrassment. He decided to join Sanjana.

After walking with Sanjana he returned to his hostel. The hostel had large rooms. Each room was shared by fourteen students. The moment he entered his room, the thirteen of them began coughing, to mock him.

"Where were you?" one of them asked. Rohit hid his embarrassment and didn't utter a word.

"Balcony."

"With?"

"With what?"

"I'm asking about the person you kissed in the balcony."

"I didn't kiss her, okay?" Rohit defended giving himself away.

"So you intended to kiss her, had they shown us that movie?" It was Vajish.

"No. I swear it, dude. We are just friends."

"Just friends. Is that a tone of regret I hear?"

"Ah! Please? Don't start teasing already man?"

"From tomorrow onwards it's Rohi-njana. Ugh! That doesn't sound very good. What is her full name?" he asked.

"I don't know."

"If you don't say her name it will be Rohi-njana. So you better say it."

"I swear I don't know."

"You hid this from us for so long."

"I didn't hide it. I just didn't tell you guys. That's all."

"That is also called hiding, you sly runt. For how long you have been loving her?"

"I told you, we are only friends now.

"You are only friends now? Now, you said. So you are planning on proposing later don't you?" It was Fred.

"No. I'm not." Rohit objected. He didn't know why he added now at the end of that sentence.

"See. Now you should have said 'never', but you didn't. So you have feelings for her."

"Look, I have no feelings for her. It would be silly of me to have so. And I will never ever propose to her. She is a good friend. That's all." Rohit said and walked away.

"He loves her, doesn't he?" said Vajish to Fredrick

"No he has a very big crush on her. It would do him good not to propose to her." Said Fredrick

FARE YOU WELL

THE DECEMBER NIGHT was gnashing cold. Luckily, Rohit had his blazers on, he felt warm within its shroud. *YES. NO. YES. NO. YES. NO.* His mind kept ringing within him. Rohit wasn't very sure if he should be proposing to her so soon. It had been two months only. He had been obsessed with Sanjana for the past two months and wanted to propose to her. But he had a fear of being turned down. He noticed Sanjana standing near the ice-cream counter with her hands close to her chest. *The cold must be getting to her*, he thought.

"Hey" he greeted walking up to her.

"Hi" she smiled.

"Want to go for a walk?"

"Yeah. Sure. I'll—I'll get my ice cream."

"Oh! Let me get that for you." He decided to help.

Being the organizing batch, he went behind the counter and managed 2 cones for the two of them.

"Oh thanks!"

"Privileges of organizing." The two of them began walking out of the courtyard.

"So, where to?" Sanjana asked

"I don't know. You suggest."

"The pitch."

"No, the cricket ground isn't exactly a nice place. I have one in mind."

"Oh! Is that why you asked me to suggest?" she had a sarcastic smile on her face.

"No, I got the idea, all of a sudden. Sorry. But it's an amazing spot. You'd love it."

"Alright man. Just pulling your leg." She laughed out.

"Just a moment." Said Rohit handing her his cone and sprinted off towards the teacher's food counter. He went over to his coach Mr Jegan. He seemed to be trying to convince the coach about something. And then in another few moments Rohit joined Sanjana once again.

"Hey, is there no difference between you and your sister?

"Of course, there is." Sanjana began to laugh. "It's just that you will not see it."

"Oh!" Rohit felt embarrassed to have asked it.

"How do I know it's you or your sister?"

"How do you know I'm Sanjana?"

"Actually . . . ." The realization hit him, he hadn't confirmed which of the sister he was talking to. His face went red in embarrassment. "Oh my God! I'm terribly sorry. Don't blame you. You two are identical. I mean—I should have checked. B-but I just forgot. I have known you—I mean—your sister—for only two months. I—just—didn't know." Rohit fumbled, lost for words. He could feel the blood rushing to his cheeks in embarrassment.

"Relax. I'm Sanjana. You have found the right girl."

His embarrassment disappeared. A new feeling crept into his brain. She had said that he had found 'the right girl'. Maybe he had. He had to propose. *Is that a cue to propose?* He wondered. *YES. YES. NO. YES. YES. NO. YES. YES. NO.* his mind began the quarrelling again, but he noticed the change. There seemed to be a decision in his mind. He only had to execute it. He decided to make the choice. To propose; but at the right moment and he decided to wait until the night was at its best.

"Hey, you guys did a nice farewell."

"Thanks. We gave them a farewell they deserved."

"Truly."

"What's your full name?" she asked him.

"Rohit Joseph."

"Catholic? I didn't know that part of it till now."

"Yea. What's yours?"

"Sanjana C Xavier. C for Charles"

"Xavier? You too Christian?"

"No, I'm a Hindu. Dad's a Christian. He named me with an Indian name so that, even if I had grown up in London, there would be a little bit of Indian in me." She explained.

"Three word names are very cool, because when you say the initials they are amazing, like those people you see in Harry Potter. Is your sister's full name Ranjana Charles Xavier?"

"Obviously." She replied.

"Oh! R.C.X and S . . . . Well, never mind." Rohit's voice faded away.

"What?"

"Nothing." He didn't want blurt out her initials. It sounded as 's.e.x'

"It's always been my name. Don't you think I wouldn't have realized it in the past 16 years of my life?"

"R.C.X and S.C.X" he said with a laugh. The S.C.X sounded like 'sex.' Sanjana too joined in the laughter.

"It does sound cool, although a bit unusable." He added.

The two of them had reached their classroom corridor. Rohit took her up the stairs, all the way up to the topmost stairs.

"The door is open." Rohit was surprised.

"Good for us. Isn't it?"

"No. It is supposed to be closed, that's why I got this key from Mr Jegan."

"Maybe, the watchmen had forgotten to lock it. Why would Mr Jegan have the key to the terrace?"

"Please don't tell anyone that you have been here. It's a lucky coincidence actually."

"Do explain." She asked him, as the two of them stepped into the terrace.

Rohit began narrating how they found the key when they needed the terrace for the celebration after winning the state level tournament. The breeze that was down in the grounds seemed to have gotten stronger and colder. Sanjana's hair flew up and brushed against his face. She excused herself and tucked it behind her ears. He asked her to follow her up the ladder near the clock tower. From the tower, it was a foot's gap and then they would be on the roof of the hostel. She seemed a bit nervous to cross that foot long gap. Down from there, she would crash on the roof of the toilets. She put away her fear and made the jump. It was hardly a jump. It was just a longer step. It would have been less scary if it wasn't about thirty foot off the ground. Rohit took her hand in hers. He took her to the end of the hostel roof, where it was closest to the tea estates.

"OH MY . . . It's freezing cold." Sanjana cried out, mesmerized by the beauty of the valley view at the same time at the harshness of the winter wind.

"Here, take the coat." Rohit offered his coat. Just then he remembered, he still had her jacket.

"Hey, you know, your jacket is still with me."

"Keep it. Let it be a birthday gift. The view from here is awesome." She said breathing in the cold chilly air. The school was situated on a hilltop and it overlooked the valley it was named after. The view from the terrace, provided them an exhilarating vision of the valley. Dotted in gold and silver amidst the darkness were the lights from the houses in the valley. Rohit watched on as Sanjana enjoyed the breath-taking view from there. The night couldn't have been more beautiful to Rohit.

But, all the while, the night wasn't anything like he had planned it to be. He hadn't talked to her anything that he had planned. It felt good to be having a natural conversation and not talking anything pre-planned. All the while, anything that he had wanted to say to her, he phrased it out in his mind, rehearsed the scenario how he would be telling and then say. But, now it was all happening by itself. He was a little concerned if he might say anything out of place. *YES. YES. YES. NO. YES. YES. YES. NO.* Within his mind the beat started again. It was so strong now he knew it was the time. He had to say those three words that would change everything between the two of them, either for good or for bad. Although, something bothered him. A small part of him hadn't changed its decision. Amidst the beat that rang within him a 'no' kept echoing.

He chose to ignore it. She had placed her hands on the parapet. He took a step front. Placed his hand over hers, as gently as he could, he opened his mouth,

"I hate you, Rohit" she said to him. Everything froze. He wasn't feeling dreamy anymore. It felt like someone had poured ice cold water over him *I haven't even proposed yet.* He thought within himself.

"What?" he was confused. He removed his hand from hers.

"You have known me for the past two and half months and you show me this lovely spot in our campus at the last night I get to spend here."

"Relax. I have been here for the past thirteen years in this place and I myself was here the first time just two and a half months ago, the night after the match. And on top of it, it's supposed to be out of bounds. So please don't tell anyone. If possible, not even your sister."

"Yeah, not your fault. Listen I wanted to say something. That's why I'm here now." Sanjana said. *She wants to say something. Please let it be 'I love you'. This night can't get any better.* Rohit's mind went into overdrive.

"I'm not coming back in January."

"What'd you mean?"

"Tomorrow, when we leave for the Christmas, I will be taking everything. I'm going to England."

"How?"

"I'm getting transfer certificate."

"Your board exams?" Rohit was confused.

"It doesn't matter. Actually it never mattered." Rohit was dumbstruck. She continued, "Me and my sister studied in a school in Chennai. There was an issue in my previous school. My father wanted to pull me out. At the same time we couldn't get admission anywhere in London. The principal there, being my father's friend got me a seat here temporarily. And my school starts on February 11ᵗʰ. So I won't be coming back. Probably, never again to India. I actually wanted to say goodbye to you. That's why I decided to join you tonight."

"You didn't tell me this any time before."

"No, Ranjana liked this place very much and asked me to convince my dad to allow us to stay here till we finish school. So I was hoping, maybe I might be here till 12ᵗʰ"

"Too bad you wouldn't be here."

"I hope I didn't mislead you in any way." She seemed very much guilt-ridden.

"No. No. Not at all. You were a nice friend to me. It was really nice to have known you. We had such good fun. I loved it."

"Sure we did. I can never forget that movie night." She had taken her hands off the parapet and was directly facing him.

"Yeah me neither. It's ironic that we didn't see any movie on the movie night."

"So, I'll get going. It's 10:20. Ten more minutes and we will have to go to our hostel."

"Yeah. Bye." Rohit said. He sounded terrible. It was like as if there was no sound in his voice.

"So, it's really a farewell tonight." she looked at him.

"Yep." Said Rohit and extended his hand. For a brief moment, they shook hands, there was no electric feeling this time. It was just cold. Rohit stood there trying to digest on how the night had gone. Sanjana descended down the steps and was gone. Nothing close to what he had planned. Nothing close to what he had wanted. Just then he heard a noise. For a second, he felt a scare, but then it should be nothing he thought. Only then he realized, he hadn't been alone.

New Year,

NEW FEELINGS

I T WAS THE first day of the new calendar year at school. The third term was an activity filled one and being the assistant class captain, Rohit had his plates full. But in spite of the bustling activity, something was missing. Those looks he would get from Sanjana during the breaks, the HI's they used to wave. Everything seemed very dull. With the sports day around the corner, intense preparations were going on. According to the school tradition, the sports day saw the handing over of the captain's post to the 11th grade prefects and the chosen captains for the next scholastic year. However, it was the 11th grade students who saw to the orderly organization of the years' sports day.

Earlier that morning, the principal had called in Vajish to be the house captain of Andromeda, the blue house. He was the one that the entire batch had wanted as the captain for Andromeda.

"I was going towards the office side to see the notice board. Just then the peon called me and told that the HM wanted to see. So I just stepped into the office. I had no time to even consider what I was being called for. I go in and he tells me that I have been chosen as the captain of Andromeda. I thanked him." Vajish was saying beaming with happiness.

"What about the other posts, man?" asked an anxious Theodore.

"The HM has the list in a file and he was looking at it, because I didn't realize what I was being called for I just went to his left side and stood. He held the file such a way that I couldn't see. Whoever gets called next should go and stand to the right side of him. Then they will be able to see the file. And one more amazing thing, if I'm not mistaken a new girl is joining our batch. She does look quite good. Let me put it this way. She would rank between Kavi and Sonya in terms of beauty."

The batch was excited that Vajish got to be the house captain and more importantly over the new girl. They decided not to jinx it by calling dibs. And the next day there was the new girl. Vajish also had been a competitor for the School captain post too. With him chosen as the Andromeda house captain; the school captain nominee from the students, Christopher had his line cleared to be chosen as the School captain. If only the management doesn't come up with crazy choices like they had done the previous year, the school captain would certainly be Christopher.

The next day Haran, got chosen to be house captain of the *Australe* house. Another choice, just the way the boys wanted. And the day after that, Rohit had to hand over to the Senior English Professor, Priya Ma'am; the list he had come up with for the Sports day M.C.s. He was waiting outside the staff-room for the ma'am to show up. His thoughts were over Sanjana. He was trying to recollect the times he had spent with her near the staff-room. There didn't seem to be anything much, actually.

"Rohit." He heard a voice. He turned around. It was the office peon. "The headmaster wants to see you." He said. Rohit followed the peon into the headmaster's office. The office by itself commanded respect and instilled fear into the students. The room had two large windows. The desk of the headmaster was exceptionally large and was filled with mementos that he had received all throughout the year. On the wall behind the table was a large school flag that was spread across. The cupboards were filled with folders, folders and more folders.

"Where are your manners, Rohit?" said the headmaster with a stern look on his face.

"Sir—Oh!—I'm sorry. I was here to meet the senior English professor when suddenly I was called in. Good morning, sir." Rohit fumbled.

"Oh! Okay, fine go and see your professor and then come and meet me."

"No, sir. It's alright. My professor can wait."

"Alright, so let's see what you are here for?" said the headmaster as he took an orange file into his hands. Rohit realized the reason he had been summoned and it wasn't good. He was going to be chosen as a captain. And it wasn't going to go well. The only reason he had agreed to be the assistant class rep was that he wouldn't be chosen as a captain. He tried to peek into the file to find out the other names in there.

"Rohit, you have been chosen as the Sirius house captain. Congratulations."

"Sir, but—Sir I don't want to be a captain." The principal's face turned shrewd.

"Oh! What are you talking? Hasn't this school ever taught you that you should make the best use of opportunities?"

"Sir. I'm actually honoured that I have been given this post. But I just can't."

"Give me a reason. A valid reason why you are not worth a penny?" The headmaster tried to insult to provoke him and make him take up the post. But Rohit knew better.

"Sir, I just can't be leader of a house. There are plenty of other guys who can do it better than me."

"Lame. Its' very lame. You led a team to victory in the state level tournaments. You are worried of being a bad leader. I don't think so"

"It was only a team of less than twenty. This about more than three hundred."

"Rohit, if a man can't lead twenty he will never be able to lead two hundred let alone three hundred plus."

"I'm very sorry, sir. I can't take up the offer."

"You, think I'm offering you something here. It's an assignment." The headmaster was looking frustrated, Rohit decided to be apologetic rather than openly refuse.

"I'm very sorry, sir. Please forgive me."

"Alright, you know what, I'll give you some more time to think about it, while I run through my work here. Wait outside and think wisely, I'll call you in."

"Thank you, sir." He said and left the office and stood outside. Rohit knew exactly what the principal was trying to do. It was the oldest trick in the principle's book. If the principal were to say, 'wait outside' nine out of ten times it usually meant that you are going to be there the next few hours. He would make him wait all day till Rohit gives in. Rohit decided to wait. If he takes up the offer, his teammate, Tanveer would be disappointed and offended. His entire class will be mad at him. He didn't want to be a captain if he had to lose his friends. Just as he had expected, the principal had made him wait the entire morning. Rohit was let go for and lunch and was asked to return after lunch. During the break he recounted the entire thing to his friends.

"Hey, I know it's tough. Just hold it. He will have to eventually give in." said Vajish.

"You know what, I can never give in, man. Only I know how much Tanveer wants to be the captain. He has told me. And I can never betray him with this stuff." Rohit replied.

"Rohit, you said you went to give names for M.C right? Who are the M.C.s." asked Naresh.

"It's Yamuna and Ajay, man."

"Hey. I didn't know you were choosing the M.C.s. I want a chance too. Is it too late?" asked Yashan.

"I think Ajay really wants to be the M.C, man." Rohit replied.

"Why don't they chuck the girl? She just came here two days ago and an M.C. already?" asked Vajish.

"No, her English is good and moreover it has to be one boy and one girl." replied Rohit.

"Rohit, just in case they decide on adding a third M.C. or if they want it as a two boys, I'm the one, alright." Said Yashan.

"Yeah, sure dude." Yashan had become Rohit's best friend recently. It seemed quite out-of-nature of Yashan to be wanting to be the M.C so bad. He had told him everything about Sanjana during the winter vacation. Rohit had something that needed to be addressed. But, he didn't know how to deal with it. He decided to confide it to Yashan and ask his opinion.

"Yashan, there's more to this captains issue than just me." Rohit told Yashan when they were alone.

"What is it?" Yashan questioned.

"I saw the list of other nominated captains. I didn't see the entire list though. But Ajay has been chosen as school captain. I didn't want everyone to know because if everyone tells him to refuse, he might feel insulted and do the opposite. He's very sensitive, you know right?"

"Don't worry. I'll break the bubble to him. And tell him to turn it down."

Rohit spent the entire afternoon and the evening outside the headmaster's office. Now and then he would be called and asked if he had made a decision, when he refused, he was sent back to waiting. And it continued the next day too. Rohit was missing his classes. To him, he was bunking his classes and he enjoyed it. The only bad part in the ordeal was that he had to stand outside the office doing nothing, literally idle.

Three days were almost over and nothing had changed. That evening when he returned to the hostel at night, the batch had made a decision; a decision to put Rohit out of the misery.

"Rohit, still no change?" Vajish asked him.

"Nope. That bastard, God I hate him." Cursed Rohit.

"Dude, take the post." Said Vajish.

"How can I?"

"You should." It was Tanveer. "He isn't going to give up. We all know the headmaster. Even if you continue another day or two eventually, you will have to be the captain."

"It may be a day or two that I stand in front of that office cursing that fuck in there. But you are going to regret this decision for the next whole year, maybe your entire life. I can't let that happen."

"I'll be the assistant class captain. Go ahead, dude. I'm serious."

"No." Rohit really felt bad. His friend was letting go of his important desire for his sake. If he had been emotionally weak, Rohit would have broken down on Tanveer's words. When he commands the house he will have to command over Tanveer too and it would be horrible for both of them. After a long argument and the approval from the entire batch, Rohit went and accepted the post as the house captain of Sirius. The headmaster simply mocked him for having wasted three days to make the decision.

The very next day, Prasad was chosen as the house captain of Aquila, the green house. And Tanveer got to be the School Vice-Captain. Everyone were happy for him too. He seemed content. But only Rohit knew that even the post of the School captain wouldn't elate him as much as the post of the house captain he had wanted so badly. All through the turmoil, there was one other thing that kept Rohit's mind preoccupied. It was Sanjana. She wasn't there, looking at him from the corridor of their floor and waving at him. If she had been here, he could have shared the fact that he had gotten the post of a house captain and she would said a word of wishes.

He convinced himself that he didn't love her but yet couldn't understand why he felt so miserable in her absence. He kept playing the moments he had shared with her over and over in his mind. And every time he returned to reality it felt worse. He vented his misery to his newfound best friend, Yashan.

"Life sucks, man." He said to Yashan as they sat on the parapet outside the volleyball court.

"You knew her for two months. Stop talking like she was your girlfriend."

"She is only a friend. It's just that I was hoping that I might have been able to become a very intimate friend to her. But I miss her."

"She didn't give you her contact or anything?"

"She sent a friend request on Orkut. I accepted. End of story."

"She sent a request?" asked Yashan.

"Fine, I sent a request. She accepted it. That doesn't matter. It used to be so much fun with her, you know. To think that I would be never be able to exchange another of those letters outside the English department. I have told you right; how the senior English professor almost caught us."

"Priya Ma'am, huh?"

"Who else do you think?"

"Did she almost catch you or caught you?"

"She noticed us. But she didn't mind, I think." There was a bit of silence. After some thought, Yashan questioned:

"Dude, do you remember what happened to Rahul and that Christy?" The two of them were Rohit's juniors.

"Yeah. Why?" asked Rohit. Yashan had realized something grave, Rohit couldn't figure it out yet. Yashan stood dumb. Rohit tried to connect the dots. Priya ma'am was very strict in general. She was the one who had caught Rahul and Christy when they were exchanging a love note during the Annual day. Rahul had been expelled from the school. He had also heard that the Christy girl was also taking T.C at the end of the scholastic year

"Sanjana gave a weird explanation for leaving the school don't you think?" said Yashan.

It was true. Nobody usually changes school before the board exam unless, they are expelled. And the question hit him. What if Priya ma'am was the one responsible for her leaving the school abruptly? That would make him partially responsible for the same. He was the cause she had to leave and she could have hid that from it so that he isn't guilty. It made sense to him. Rohit had been guilty the entire week over the fact that he had deprived Tanveer of his captaincy and now here was more guilt piling up. He felt terrible.

"OH! FUCKIN' CHRIST." He swore.

CHAPTER 1

"WE ARE DONE sir." Said Charan, the guy who had come along to aid them with the interviews. Mr Shri Venkat looked at his sheet. All names in the list had been ticked; all names but one. He called out,

"Charan."

"Yes, sir." The aide responded.

"Are you sure there is no one else in the hall. A candidate named Rohit hasn't attended yet."

"I don't know. But I'll check the hall once again." And Charan left the interview room to find out.

"It's alright, maybe the candidate wasn't interested in the job." Said a man sitting next to him.

"He aced the group discussion round. You remember the last guy we interviewed: Hari. This guy was better than this Hari whom we have now given the job. I have a very good feeling about that fellow." Said Mr Venkat. It was of no use. The other members of the panel were impatient and getting ready to go. Their work was done. He got up and walked out of the hall. He went to the hall, where the students had gathered. It was empty but for Charan, who was packing the projector and the computer, in the hall. Mr Shri Venkat, decided to let it go. He walked out of the hall and headed for the exit from the building. On the way, he noticed a signboard, indicating men's restroom. He needed to use it. He emptied his bladder and looked into the bathroom mirror. Reflected on the mirror, he noticed a movement in one of the stalls. The guy who had aced the group discussion was there bent down hands on his head.

"Excuse me." Mr Venkat tried to draw his attention. The young lad was startled and he got up from the toilet seat. He had been just sitting on it.

"Sir." He asked.

"Why didn't you come for the final round?"

"Sir, I'm having a severe headache."

"Oh! Is it a one-time thing? Or something more frequent?"

"Just now." The youngster replied.

"What's your name again?"

"Rohit Joseph, sir."

"Look Rohit, from what I made out earlier today, you have great potential. And we need people like you in our company. We can't lose you because of a silly headache. Go home, deal with this headache and then call this number, for your job." Said Mr Venkat and gave him his business card. Rohit took it and thanked him and walked out of the restroom.

Rohit glanced at his watch. It was almost twelve. His friends said they would be waiting for him outside the *'Jawahar Block'* where the campus interview was being held. He scanned the area for his friends, the moment he stepped out of that campus' main door. And they were there, both hoping the very best for him. Nishi and Yashan, his two best friends walked towards him. Rohit handed over his file to Yashan and adjusted his belt trying to build an air of suspense. Yashan and Nishi had their face drowned in eagerness. Rohit took a deep breath and said

"Sixer!!!"

"Bravo, man! The dream comes true." exulted Yashan hugging him. Nishi shook hands and patted over his back. The word 'dream' made Rohit think of the dream he had been pondering over.

"Call your mom, Mr Microsoft. She would be glad to know." Nishi reminded him.

"That can wait. No hurry."

"You call aunty now. Or I will." insisted Nishi.

"Fine; I will." replied Rohit with a tone of regret and pulled out his phone.

"I'll inform Lav. She is going to be so thrilled." said Nishi as if she was trying to cheer up some person who has failed an exam. Rohit began punching the numbers into his mobile.

"I'm supposed to meet her tonight right so, I'll surprise her." said Rohit as he kept his phone over his ear waiting for the call to connect.

"You're not elated. Are you?" questioned Yashan with a look of embezzlement.

"Lav is my girlfriend. We have known each other for three years, I took her out numerous times. It's not new to me. Going out for the nth time with her isn't going to excite me." defended Rohit.

"I'm not talking about your girlfriend, Rohit." said Yashan.

"Hold that thought. Mom on line." said Rohit. His mom had picked up the call. "Hello mom." He said over the phone and stepped a little away from his friends. It was not as if he wanted to hide anything from his friends. But it was just a habitual step-away that he did. The three friends were almost at the end of their MBA course. Rohit already had a degree in Computer Science. A bachelor's degree in technical field along with an MBA degree was the hottest choice of education. The campus interviews were going on. Being one of the toppers of the class, he had an interview on the first day itself. Nishi and Yashan had no interviews till the third day. The campus interview was spread over eleven days during which a number of companies sent their representatives.

Nishi had managed to ace her B.com before stepping up for MBA. Yashan too had a degree in Computer Science. Yashan and Rohit had been friends right from their school days. They did their college together as they both wished to be engineers and apparently in the same field. They had met Nishi when they joined Raguvarman College of Management. Even in the very first exam Rohit showed his excellence in the subjects. The Rohit who prepared for his exams in the last-minute had disappeared way back in his school days itself. Ever since he began his UG course, Rohit began focusing on his studies as he knew it would impact his career. Nishi was just a few ranks behind him. Of the students who topped the class Rohit was the only of the few from a non-commerce stream.

"So what are you guys doing tonight?" asked Rohit after informing his mother.

"I have some plans man. I don't know what Yashan's up to." said Nishi and looked at Yashan expectantly. Rohit too turned towards him.

"You, my friend are not happy about this job. I'm going to cheer you up." answered Yashan.

"What? Why would he be not happy?" said Nishi mocking Yashan's statement, she went on, "Microsoft's the dream job. Training in the U.S.A; that's what you guys always wanted. Didn't you, Ro-", she couldn't finish the sentence, she noticed Rohit eyes' fixed upon Yashan, not even slightly amused by Nishi's mocking. She realized that Yashan was right about it.

"It's not Microsoft. It's not about the job."

"Then?" asked Nishi open-mouthed.

"It's about what I'm going to do with my life."

"What do you mean?" Nishi asked.

"Look I don't know what you are thinking; but I do know that Microsoft is an amazing thing that can happen to you."

"Look where I'm in life. I got a job at Microsoft. I will soon get married to my girlfriend whom I have loved for three years. What happens then?" said Rohit with an unsatisfied expression. The other two seemed puzzled. It seemed like a perfect life.

"Dude, you're in the best place anyone can be in terms of life. Dream job and a dream girl, what else do you want. You have found the Happily-ever-after ending; its perfect." said Yashan offering an air of support.

"That's the end of story man. I always wanted life to be a little bit challenging and adventurous. Happily Ever After isn't my kind of ending. My life will suck to the core if this is the way it's going to go." He replied.

"It's that dream of yours, isn't it? It's just a dream." Yashan said. Rohit had told Yashan about the dream during the lunch time. "I knew it was eating your head, right when you told me."

"What dream? Nishi asked, trying to stay on the same page, as her friends.

"I had a dream, which made me question what I am doing in life. I always believed and wanted life to be an adventure. But the thought of settling down in life, makes me fear life will be not be boisterous and fun like I want it to be." He explained.

"Now, that's just fear of commitment. Everyone feels that way. Even after, you settle you will have adventure, man." Said Nishi, trying to help her confused friend.

"Hey, tell about the girl." Yashan provoked him.

"Which girl?" Nishi questioned impatiently.

"Sanjana was there in my dream. She didn't look like her although." Rohit said."

"What has the girl got to do with his career?"

"She was his first crush. Nobody can mess with your head as much as your first crush. He is not seeing it through." Yashan explained.

"Look, you may think I'm doing this out of fear of commitment. But only, I know deep down that I don't want this corporate life and a dream girl."

"Why now? Of all the time in your life, why did you make this decision now and not earlier?" Nishi questioned him.

"I—I—just don't know. Even I'm trying to figure out why." Rohit replied back, with a tone of disappointment.

"See, it's not going to be easy to convince him out of this. Yet, it is very important that we convince, before he goes on his date with his girlfriend." Yashan whispered to Nishi, making sure Rohit wouldn't hear them. Rohit eyed him suspiciously.

"What do you want then?" Nishi asked Rohit.

"I have to find out." Rohit explained.

"If you didn't want this job, you should have not attended the interview. Why did you take up the job offer?" Nishi asked.

"That is because, you couldn't let go of this job, even if some insane part of you craves crazy-ass adventure, like Bilbo Baggins." Yashan extrapolated from the question.

"All, through the interview, I sat trying to find out the meaning of my dream. When I was talking with him, I realized, that the girl was Sanjana. I tried to reason, why did it have to be her. I skipped the interview and went into a restroom and tried reasoning. The time of my life with Sanjana was the most adventurous part of my life, although a bit stupid, I liked it while it lasted and will treasure it forever. There I was thinking, that I had lost my shot at Microsoft, a man comes to pee and then he tells me I have some bloody potential that their company couldn't afford to waste. He gave me his card, to talk about my job placement." Rohit recounted what had happened.

"Interesting. It looks, like that man, must have had a dream. A dream which insisted him to give you his card." Yashan said, mockingly.

"Oh! Shut up. He must have taken in too much fluids and got his bladder filled. There's nothing more than that to it." Rohit said, clearly not being amused.

"Same thing with your dream too. It has-" Nishi was saying. But Rohit had interrupted.

"Don't try and convince me otherwise. I need to talk to Lav about this."

"No, don't tell Lav. Not tonight. Wait for another time." Yashan tried to make him procrastinate.

"You see, if I don't tell her now, I will have to say that I got the job. She will tell her dad and they will start talking about my marriage."

"I can't delay it any further."

"What'd you propose?"

"Breakup." Rohit said, firm on his decision.

"Well, that makes you are clinically insane." Said Yashan.

"You don't have to do this."

"I must. What are you doing in the evening?"

"I'm free, except for a little appointment. Very brief, actually." Said Yashan.

"I have got one major appointment. To try and stop you from ruining your life." Nishi added.

"I'm sorry, it's not happening. I'm going to go and get ready for my break-up date. It's at seven." Said Rohit.

"Rohit, how long will you take to break-up.?" questioned Yashan.

"Half an hour. Max. Why are you asking?"

"How about you treat us for getting the job? Listen, you aren't taking it, that's a different story, but you did get the job. It's an achievement. You should celebrate that."

"Yes. If we have the time. Thanks for supporting me." Said Rohit smiling, as he walked away.

"He is about to throw away his life, why are you supporting him?" asked Nishi after Rohit left. She seemed displeased, with what had been going on.

"I'm concerned for him, more than you are. I have known him more than you do. You can't talk him out of this. He should realize, the mistake in what he is about to do."

"It will be too late, by the time, he realizes. We have to talk to him." Nishi said.

"Talking won't do it. We need something to make him realize."

"What is it?"

"Even I have no idea. I'm trying to figure out. Something needs to happen to him that will change his mind. Best, if it happens before he breaks up with his girlfriend." said Yashan

"You mean an accident. How can we make sure it happens and yet he survives?"

"God! I meant something less fatal" said Yashan, giving her a creepy look as if she was plotting an evil scheme. "Actually, it should be an incident rather than an accident."

"You have anything in mind?" Nishi asked.

"I'm trying to see if I can. Could you please try and put your brain to good use, to aid me here? And by the way, get your phone. I need to check my Facebook." Yashan, made a sardonic comment.

CHAPTER 2

NISHI HAD REACHED Domino's pizza. Her plan had completely backfired. She hadn't expected it. She thought if Lavanya broke up with Rohit, before he did, it might make him reconsider, but things had gotten worse. She had returned to college to inform Yashan. Yashan had already found a table and was sitting down. She joined with him.

"What's happened? You look anxious." Yashan asked her.

"I came up with an idea to help out Rohit." She said.

"Cool, what is it?" Yashan got excited.

"There's no reason to get hyped with it, it failed."

"You did something about this, and didn't tell me." Yashan looked disappointed that his friend hadn't shared with him about her conspiracy to stop Rohit from ruining his life.

"I called Lav and told her to prank him by saying that she doesn't love him anymore. I thought Rohit will be piqued by the fact that he is getting dumped and might reconsider his recent thoughts. You know, out of his ego. I know it's a hard choice, but I didn't know better. But, from what I know, I had indirectly made it easier for him to break up with Lav. All I know is that Lav is heartbroken and wouldn't talk to me anymore." Nishi explained the complication she had created by her intervention.

"Shit! Why didn't you ask my opinion? You didn't make a hard choice. It was a wrong choice."

"There wasn't any time. I didn't see it coming." Nishi said. She looked like she had committed a sin.

"So, he broke up with her?" Yashan asked.

"From what I know, yes."

"Do you realize, how much harder have you made it now?"

"Soon Lavanya's dad is going to call Rohit's dad. And before we know it, it is going to be an issue." Said Yashan.

"What do we do now?"

"I have no clue, after you have messed it up so much."

"I was trying to help."

"See, he is having commitment issues. He is just afraid because, this job means a lot of commitment. It's just the pressure in his mind, that's making him to take the wrong decisions."

"Well, what do you suggest?"

"I'm working on that. Whatever idea you have, make sure it doesn't revolve directly around him. For example, Lavanya breaking up with him, was directly about him. But asking him help to break up someone else could be useful." After a pause Yashan added, "Your phone, please."

"Dude, you want to check FB now?" Nishi was surprised, that her friend was interested in trivial matters. Yashan didn't reply. He simply took her phone from her hand and opened the Facebook app. It was logged into her account. He was about to log out, but he noticed something. And strangely, the first post on her wall was a photo of Sanjana. Yashan was taken aback to see a photo of Sanjana on Nishi's wall. He read the post:

Sanjana Charles was tagged in a photo at Tarun's wedding reception, ECR, Pondicherry.

Below the post was the photo of Sanjana, standing beside a young man, probably the groom, Tarun.

"Who is Tarun?" Yashan asked Nishi.

"What? Why?" Nishi was startled. She had told her friends that she had had a boyfriend and had broken up with him. But she hadn't revealed any other details to her friends. She was surprised to hear Yashan mention his name.

"It says someone named Tarun is getting married today." Yashan explained, hoping that Nishi might have known whoever this Tarun guy was.

"Tarun's getting married?" Nishi was quite surprised. She never believed that Tarun had broken up with her. Even after he was long gone, she hoped he might come back to her someday. But he was now getting married. It meant that their relationship was over. Nishi took the phone back and stared into the screen.

"Oh my God!"

"Are you alright?" Yashan asked on seeing Nishi's face.

"No, what? Oh! Yes. I'm fine. It's just that he is my ex-boyfriend." Nishi said with a baffled look on her face.

"I have another plan. Sanjana is that friend of Rohit's right? He had a crush on her too." Nishi suggested after a minute of staring into her phone.

"Yes, it's her. What are you thinking? I hope it's better than the other one, which has failed terribly."

Just then, Yashan's phone rung. It was Rohit calling. The call interrupted Nishi from telling her idea

"Hey" Yashan answered the call.

"Where are you guys?" Rohit asked.

"At 'The Brown Cafe.' Where are you?"

"Yeah, I spotted you." Said Rohit and hung up. Yashan looked around. He noticed him enter the café waving at him.

"What's your idea?" Yashan asked Nishi as Rohit was approaching the table.

"No time to say now. Just make sure you show Rohit the Facebook post of Tarun's wedding. I'll explain the other stuff later." He walked up to their table and took a seat. Rohit glared at Nishi. She gave him a look attempting to comfort him. It wasn't any good.

"So what happened?" Yashan asked Rohit, who just took a seat.

"Good, actually better than I had expected. Let me tell you what happened. I go there with a feeling of guilt that I'm going to break her heart. I was feeling terrible. And I was looking how to say it in a way as to deal the least possible damage to her feelings. So, I decided to be honest because I had trusted her with everything for the past three years and hoped she would understand my feelings.

But before I could say anything to her, she said she wanted to break up with me. I was at first curious and wanted to know why, but then decided not to ask. I directly told her that I'm okay with it."

"That is how the two of you broke up?" Nishi was shocked. Because she was hoping her plan would save their relationship but it had gone exactly in the other way.

"No, not just yet. She looked surprised when I said her that. She asked me if I was joking. I said her that I would never joke on such stuff. Seriously, tell me guys, who jokes on 'break-up'? I mean isn't it one of the topics in life, you can never joke. It is like the other phrases 'I love you' 'I'm breaking up with you' or 'I'm going to die.' They are too serious to make a prank out of it." Rohit was saying.

"If people wanted to make a fool out of you, I think they would do it." Nishi tried hoping to find some justification so that what she had done might appear less terrible.

"No, it would be very lame to try anything. Let's say someone says that they are going to die. They usually mean they are in a tricky situation. You ask them what has happened and they explain their situation. They don't simply blurt out that they were trying to make you believe they were really going to die. You simply can't add a 'JK, just kidding.' at the end of these statements." Said Rohit mono-acting the lines.

"Screw it. Didn't you ask her why she wanted to break up with you?" Yashan asked.

"No, I just told her that I really meant a breakup and she was gone." After a short pause, Rohit opened his mouth as if he had realized something that he hadn't seen before, "Oh my-! Are you guys implying that she was 'just kidding' when she said it?"

"I think I'm quite sure that she was really joking about it." Nishi added.

"Oh crap!" said Rohit as he crashed on the table.

"You are such a moron." Said Yashan on how dumb his friend had been to breakup with a girl. He looked at Nishi. She was looking back at him. He mouthed the words at her, "You too."

"I didn't see it coming. I broke her heart, haven't I?" he asked with a guilt-ridden face.

"I don't understand how you could have done this. It is virtually impossible."

"You were a total jerk." Nishi added and looked away from Yashan.

"I was pre-occupied with my dream." Rohit said.

"Speaking of your dream, here is something you must see." Said Yashan and took Nishi's phone. The Facebook app was still open, he scrolled until he had found the post by Sanjana. He showed it to his friend. Rohit's face went pale.

"It's creepy. I dream of her. And the next day, she is three hours away from me. When did she come to India?" asked Rohit, his voice lowered.

"How am I supposed to know?" Yashan said.

"Rohit that is not the point of concern now. See the other half of the post." It was Nishi.

"Tagged in Tarun's wedding. Who is Tarun?"

"Her ex." Said Yashan.

"We never broke up. We simply drifted apart." She added.

"Is Sanjana marrying your ex?" Rohit wanted to clarify.

"No idiot, she is there at my ex's wedding. I have no idea how he could have known her." Nishi corrected him.

"So what is there to be concerned about him right now?"

"Look, I know I haven't told you guys anything about him. But I'm going to need you guys help. He dumped me and walked away. He never gave me a reason. And I want to know why he dumped me. I want to end the relationship we had left incomplete, so that I can move on." Nishi said, she hadn't finished. But Rohit took hold of her pause to interrupt.

"You want to abduct him?" He sounded excited.

"Yes, exactly." Nishi said.

"How?" Rohit asked.

"I and Yashan have made some basic scheming. It will take three hours to get to Pondy. But we want to know if you are okay with it? You had a hard day, too. Can you help me with this? We need your car." She asked looking at Rohit if he would agree. Yashan knew it was a part of Nishi's plan to divert Rohit's thoughts. But an abduction was too serious to be done. It was a felony. But he played along with Nishi hoping she wasn't being literal.

"You need my car?" Rohit opened his mouth wide out of excitement. I am going to come too. I and Yashan are the only people you hang around with, Nishi. Not even any of the girls. We will obviously help you get back at the guy."

"Thanks a lot, man." She said pretending to be genuine.

"So, when are you going to leave?"

"Now."

"Alright, I will go . . . . and get the car. When I get to the gate, I will text you. Come there." He said and rose up to leave. When he reached the café door, Yashan too got up and went after to him.

"Dude." He called out to his best friend. Rohit turned around.

"Nishi asked us if we could aid her in committing a felony. You don't even know the guy. Why did you agree? Really for Nishi's sake?" Yashan questioned.

"No, it isn't about Nishi. I just want to prove myself that my life can still be exciting and challenging."

"So . . . . You haven't chosen it because Sanjana is there?" Yashan questioned

"Dude, come on. It's eight-thirty now. By the time we get there. It would be almost midnight. She would have probably left by then."

"I'm sure your subconscious knows that if she would have probably left, there is also a probability of her not having left." Yashan said. Rohit realized what Yashan was hinting upon. An episode of embarrassment in Café coffee day back then. It had happened when he and Sanjana were in school. Maybe, he had agreed to go with Nishi and Yashan only because there was the small chance that Sanjana might have been there. It was dangerous, but his conscious told him that his best friend, Nishi needed help from him. It was the same conscious that knew the probability of her being there, using friendship to bend him to go to Pondy. Rohit was afraid to trust his own conscious when it was about Sanjana. He vividly remembered that cold night at the terrace. But, he chose otherwise.

"It's for Nishi, dude. And for myself, of course, but I won't desert you guys for Sanjana. And she mostly wouldn't be there."

"Alright, I'm coming for your sake, man." Yashan said and walked back to the table. He had realized that there was hope for the new plan Nishi had come up with although he didn't know what the plan was. Before he could sit down, Nishi asked him,

"What did he say?"

"Boys' talk." Yashan explicitly evaded the answer. "And, by the way, I have a feeling, this idea of yours may work."

"You still don't even know what my idea is."

"Yes, but I have a feeling."

"Oh! How did you feel about my previous idea then?"

"My insides were churning." Yashan laughed out. Nishi too joined in.

"Anyway, don't you want to know what my idea is?" She questioned.

"Yes, of course."

"We go there and attend the reception. We leave him in the hall, while we loiter around, pretending to be doing something about Tarun. When he sees the wedding procession, he will naturally tend to think of the joys of life in marriage. It could get him to change his mind."

"Are you that naïve?" Yashan asked.

"What is wrong in this plan? You said it sounded like it might work." Nishi questioned Yashan in return.

"It still could work, but not for the reason you suggest. Just because he sees a wedding he is not going to get interested in marriage. That won't happen. You have got to manipulate him into believing something. He needs to be scared."

"Look, he needs a pure moment, wherein he realizes what he needs to. This marriage might have the pure moment he needs."

"Please get this in your head. There is no pure moment in life. Every beautiful moment is a work of a thousand manipulation. You need to do something to create the pure moment you are talking about. And how are you planning to do that."

"Be patient and everything will happen on its own."

"No Nishi, that is wrong on every level. Nothing happens on its own in life. You have got to make it happen. I'll bet anything it won't work."

"A bet? Alright. My plan will work."

"Deal. It won't." Yashan challenged.

"So, in simple terms, if my plan gets Rohit back with Lav and Microsoft, I win?"

"Yep."

"Kay, what does the winner get?" Nishi pushed the bet further.

"The winner doesn't get anything. But, the loser has to kiss Lavanya. A very brief little peck on her lips."

"WHAT?" Nishi had expected cash. But this she couldn't agree to it at all. "No way." She rejected.

"Nishi, aren't you confident that you are going to win? You can change your plan anytime. That fact that you don't want to lose will drive you to win the bet"

"It makes sense. But, it's too gross at the same time. And you are making a bet, after I made this plan." Nishi didn't want the bet.

"Listen, I spoke to him, didn't I? From that, I'm actually quite confident that you have come up with the right thing by going to the wedding. The idea of abduction will remind him that his life is still challenging. And it is a marriage, it should remind him of the beauty of the commitment, like you said. It is the best thing that can happen to him right now. But it isn't going to be that which will help him."

"Then?"

"Look, he might have just said that he is coming to Pondy for your sake. But, subconsciously he isn't. It's to meet Sanjana."

"So he is going to meet Sanjana? And will that help really?"

"No, not directly alteast. It's one thing that this reception has people all night. But do you really think that Sanjana would still be here. It's late in the night. She would have returned home."

"So, he's not going to meet her." Nishi was trying to figure out what Yashan was explaining.

"No, but he will be hoping that he meets her." When he doesn't find her, he will realize that having hoped to find her there was stupid and he would extrapolate it all the way upto the interview."

"But won't he be feeling even depressed?" Nishi asked concerned.

"You see, now this is a hard choice. It's a risk that we have to take. I know this is pretty messed up. Trying to fix him by bending him even further. I don't know what else to do in short notice. And seriously. Are you considering abduction?

"No freaking way. You think I am someone who has the guts to kidnap a man?"

"No, but since the term abduction was getting repeated, I was starting to wonder . . ."

"No, no, no." said Nishi objecting him.

"So, you okay with the bet?"

"For Rohit's sake, yes." She said, nodding her head.

"Yay, it is on." Yashan said, excited like a kid that had won a video game.

"You sound juvenile."

"Yeah, I just realized it. We will reach the wedding by midnight. You still think people will be there?" Yashan wanted to confirm. It would be a total *bulb*, to go to a wedding that is over.

"Today, isn't *muhoortha naal*. It is actually tomorrow, so I'm expecting that people will be there tonight getting ready for the wedding. But only close family and friends would be there."

"Alright. It's okay. I hope, we don't face any other issue. It will work out just fine. Try and come up with the excuse on our way to Pondy." Yashan said to Nishi.

"What's taking him so long?" Nishi complained. But, just then Yashan's phone beeped. He looked into it. Rohit was ready at the gate. The two of them got up and left towards the place they had been asked to rendezvous.

"All set, guys?" Rohit asked as he turned on the engine. The car began to move out of the college campus and to Pondicherry, they were headed.

"Nishi, we are coming to help you out to deal with your ex. Don't you think we deserve to know what happened?" Rohit asked.

"It's okay, if you don't want to say" said Yashan.

"No, there's no reason that I have, to hide it. My story doesn't have any ending. So, I just chose not to tell anyone. That's all."

"Every tale is incomplete. When one thing ends there is always another thing." Said Yashan.

"No, mine isn't like that. I'll tell you guys and you actually deserve to know." She said and began recounting her memories. "It all began with my twelfth results. I got decent marks, but my dad didn't let me go to the college that I wanted. And that was why I had to meet him. Otherwise, I wouldn't have met that-"

"son of a bitch, right?" Rohit finished her sentence.

"No, he was actually nice guy. In a way, I don't regret that part. It's going to be a long story. So, please Rohit don't interrupt."

"Sorry, yaar. Proceed." Rohit apologized. He adjusted himself in the driver seat.

"As I was saying, my father broke a promise . . . ."

BOOK 2: TARUN

A BROKEN PROMISE

NISHI TWISTED AND turned around in her bed. Sleep evaded her. She had been trying every trick in the book to try and fall into sleep. But no, it wasn't being helpful, not at all. It is the most irritating thing; to try to sleep when you just can't. You lie down, doing nothing, your mind goes into an overdrive trying to process a lot of thoughts and all your focus is on those thoughts. She never liked that. She had always wished for a way to fall asleep the moment, she fell on her bed. But it hardly happened.

She gave up trying to fall asleep and put her hand under her pillow and pulled out her Nokia C4. In the dark, she fumbled. She searched for the unlock button. The clock in her mobile showed *2:11 am*. She let out a gasp within her mind. She had been trying to fall asleep for more than past two and a half hours now. And she hadn't succeeded.

She crawled out of her bed. She walked over to her bathroom and turned its light on. She looked herself in the mirror. Her hair was in a state of disarray. Yet she wasn't sleepy-eyed. In a matter of two minutes, she had stepped out of the bathroom and switched the light back off. No one would wake up in the house till 4:30 in the morning. She had two hours. She opened her cupboard. She stood there wondering what she could do. It wasn't going to be easy to pass the time. Whatever she did, she couldn't afford to do anything that will wake anyone in the house. She went back to her bed and took her phone and began punching a message to her best friend, Sharmila.

Wat u dng?

She wasn't expecting any reply from her friend. But there was a possibility of her friend replying and she pinned her hopes on it. She stepped out of her room, quietly shut the door behind her, not that there was anyone nearby, but she didn't want it to thump hard and disturb the silence of the night. Just next to her room were her brothers' rooms. Her two brothers, Vinayak and Adarsh, both elder to her were in college. Adarsh, did his Marine engineering course, while Vinayak was into Computer science. She climbed down the stairs into the dining hall.

She went into the kitchen and opened the fridge. She found some milk in a vessel, she took it out and placed it in the oven and heated it. In a matter of seconds, the milk had turned so hot that she had to cool it down by pouring it between two tumblers until it was safe enough for her to put it on her tongue. Slowly, sipping it, she walked back to her room. To her surprise and happiness, her mobile phone's screen was glowing. She looked at it. '1 New Message.' She opened her message:

AWAKE!! At dis time?

What r u dng?

Sharmila had every right to be surprised. Nishi had been friends with Sharmi for the past five years, ever since they met in school during their eighth grade. Not any time in that five years she had messaged her at this time of the night.

Drinking milk . . . couldnt sleep

Nishi had finished half of the milk. She clutched her phone in her hand and went down the stairs, she finished the last portion of her milk in a gulp and left the tumbler on the dining table. The light in that part of the house was from the lamp that was burning in the puja room. Her phone vibrated it hand.

```
Ohk. I was talkin to Anil
```

Anil was Sharmila's boyfriend. Having born into an orthodox family, Nishi knew better than anybody else that things such as boyfriend was explicitly a taboo in their family. Sharmila's boyfriend wasn't the same caste as Sharmila was. But her parents didn't mind it. But if Nishi were to do anything remotely close to that, they would disown and send her to the streets. In this family of hers, Honour was way thicker than blood.

She had known Sharmila from her school, The Gitashram School, Ooty. They had been classmates for five years. A place for children who had been born into posh families. Nishi's family wasn't one that could afford a place as good as The Gitashram. But it was her mother's brother, her uncle who had managed to persuade her parents to do all that it takes to put her there. Her uncle was very right in what he had said. To Nishi, it seemed her parents had been very sincere towards their duty as her parents, thanks to the advice of her *maamaa* (uncle). In many Indian families, the mother's brother assumed a role of a godfather. In any religious ceremony for his niece or nephew, the uncle was called upon for most of those rites.

Ooty was nothing like her orthodox home. In spite of being a traditional Hindu school, it was very modern in many of its notions. It was a girls-only school. But that never stopped girls like Sharmila from getting a boyfriend from the nearby boys' convents in the town. The school taught the Bhagavad Gita and many Hindu scriptures alongside the curriculum. But in there, she was exposed to girls from families that lived their lives nothing like her own family and half of her education she acquired in her school was from these friends of hers. The exposure that she faced never shook the values she had from home. It simply made her adaptable to the surroundings, and that, she always considered as the best lesson that her school had offered her.

With the conservative background from her home and the exposure from her school, she had grown to be a girl with a perfect blend of values and modern-ness, and was now maturing into the grasp of womanhood. Only when the phone vibrated again, she realised that she forgot to send a reply to her friend.

```
Are u awake becuz of tension?
```

Sharmi was very much right. It was her anxiety that was keeping her up so late. She entered into the puja room and looked at the gods who sat there. There was a paper before the foot of Lord Shiva. She wasn't supposed to touch it. She had to take it only after the sunrise and that too only after she had recited her mantras to Dhakshinamoorthy, the god of wisdom who took prayers as ransom to ensure you do well in studies. But she knew what that paper contained, for she was the one who had placed it there. It was a six-digit number: 467023. It was her Higher Secondary Exam Roll number. And that was the cause of her anxiety, for in a matter of about six hours the results were being announced.

```
Yea . . . I dont know wat i'll do, if don't
score well enuf.

My dad wont send me to college.
```

She texted back to her friend, pouring out her worries. She returned to her room and lay in the bed waiting for a reply. It soon came.

```
Don't worry. You will surely make it.

If I don't score well, my mom will make an
issue out of my bf . . . that my performance
was poor becuz of him . . . It happens to
all. :(
```

Sharmi was right. All of them, though it may be the different problem they faced, wanted a good result, because it definitely affected their tomorrows.

Her dad had promised her that she would be allowed to continue her further studies only if she scored satisfactorily, else all that their parents would do is shut her within the walls of her home, make her do household work and eventually find a groom and marry her off. At the age of 18, that could probably be the worst nightmare a girl like Nishi can actually have. Within the walls of the household, the women were meant to serve men and serve households. Nishi didn't just want to be a servant to some douchebag. She was ambitious and had dreams. A dream to pursue a career. Vinayak, the younger of the two brothers and her favourite person in the whole wide world had said to her that when he starts a firm in the future he would need a good administrator and he encouraged her sister to be that good administrator. And that was the dream of her life, inspired by her dear brother, all the efforts she had put into studies for the past one year was only for that reason.

How cum u r awake?

She sent a message to her friend. She had already guessed the answer, but she wanted to keep the conversation flowing lest she have nothing to do.

I'm pretty tensed up. Luckily I hav my bf to giv me company, we hav been texting all night long.☺

Came the reply to her message. She looked at the time in the mobile, it showed 3:18 am. Time was passing quicker than she had anticipated. She felt relieved. She continued texting her friend, until she heard a noise at the ground floor. She heard a click. Someone should have turned a switch on or off. She looked at the window. The first light of the day was already there. *Is it already 4:30? She wondered.* She was right. She went straightened out her hair and went down. The front door was open. She stepped out. There was her mom squatting down and drawing the *kolam*. Her hands were white with the powder that she had been using to lay the *kolam*. It was a 64 dot one.

"Awake so soon, Narmadha?" her mom asked.

"Yes."

"Couldn't sleep with the results releasing today huh?"

"Nothing like that. I slept well indeed."

"Oh! No wonder someone had drank the milk and left the tumbler on the table." Her mom said looking at her and smiling.

"I was just feeling hungry."

"Narmadha, I know you better than that. If you had been hungry, you would have taken a banana or the rice that was in the fridge. Not a cup of milk."

Narmadha was the name, her mom wanted her daughter to grow up with. But her husband didn't approve. So, her mother and Vinayak alone called her Narmadha and to the rest of the world she was Nishitha Pillai.

"Why have you become silent now? Anyway, take the buckets and go inside; switch on the motor. And don't walk around the house without washing your head." Her mom said. She picked up the buckets and left it in the washing area and switched on the motor switch. The growl of the motor engine starting wasn't there.

"Maa, there's no power." She yelled across the house. She went up to the room, and got ready for her bath.

She had taken her position at the computer in their home. She switched on the broadband modem and booted her system. Luckily the power had resumed in the area minutes before the results were supposed to be out. She typed the website and the page began loading. It seemed like it took forever. Her dad was just standing behind her watching the monitor. Finally, when the page loaded, she entered the six-digit roll number and in the next instant, on the screen were her marks. It was supposed to be a critical moment in every student's life. And here it was, before her eyes. Her eyes fixed on the total that she had scored. It was 1092/1200.

"Good work. Her dad hugged her from behind. It was a good result. It wasn't as if she had aced or obtained a distinction, but this was quite good. Soon, her mom too joined in. She looked at the marks hoping it was a little more. Yes, there is no satisfaction in these sort of things. No matter, what you achieve the mind tends to think what you have missed out. She hadn't got as she had expected in Economics.

"You should have put more effort into Sanskrit." Said her dad.

It was a curse. Nobody can be happy with the marks. Even the state rank holder, must have been concerned why he ended up with a 99 in one of the subjects and not elated that he had topped the entire state.

"So, what next?" her mom broke the silence.

"You apply for counselling. What you get in that, be satisfied with it? I can't afford to buy you a seat. You know that." Her father said. It seemed fair enough.

*   *   *

The bus had drawn into the town of Vellore. In a few more minutes the father and daughter would reach their home. They were returning from the college counselling. And Nishi had managed to get a seat in *Kunasekar College of Arts*. She got the B.Com course. The college was at a distance of 15km from her home. A bus travel of 45 minutes would get her there every day. She sat in the bus, wanting to get home as early as possible. She had her earphones in her ear and was deaf to the world around. Her dad sat beside her, looking out of the window. She hadn't talked to her dad since they boarded the bus. Finally, when the driver called out, 'Agraharam.' The two of them got down and walked into the streets. Nishi opened the door which was just closed and went in. An afternoon serial was running in the TV; her mother should have been watching it. She went into her room and closed the door with a bang.

Her mother who had gone to monitor the rice in the cooker, came running.

"You have returned. How did it go?" she asked to her husband. Lying down on her bed Nishi could hear the conversation going on in the living room.

"It went very well. Your daughter managed to get in KK College, in town itself. She also got the course she wanted."

"Very good for her. Where is she?"

"She went into her room." Her dad said.

Nishi heard the door open. The mother was quite surprised when her supposed-to-be-jubilant daughter was lying in the bed with her face covered. Her *duppatta* was lying on the floor.

"Narmadha." Her mother was full of happiness for her child that had grown and matured into a college student. There was no response from Nishi. She went and sat on the bed. She let her fingers comb through Nishi's plaited hair.

"What happened?" she questioned with a mild tone of concern in her voice. And then Nishi let out a sob.

"Are you alright?" she asked. Nishi couldn't control her sobbing. She shook her daughter hoping she would get up. Nishi turned around, with tears in her eyes. The mother's heart broke.

"Why are you crying? You got the degree you wanted, didn't you?" her mother asked sounding very much concerned.

"Ask daddy what happened. For my marks I had a merit seat in the best college in Chennai. Dad didn't allow me to study in Chennai. He put me in the hell-hole here."

"*Ennanga.*" Her mother called out to her dad. Her dad came into the room moment later, wiping his hands with a towel.

"Once she is out of college, she will marry someone and go to someplace unknown. Until then, I thought she could be here. Is it wrong of a father to want to be close to her daughter."

"If you wanted me to be close to you, why did you send me far away for my schooling? You could have kept me around your feet, couldn't you?" Nishi said amidst her flowing tears.

"A good school is a place where you get good exposure. I wanted you to have it. And college is a place where you experiment the exposure you have had. I wanted you to be safe when you do the experiment." Her dad said. Nishi was trying to make out what her dad had meant. From her mother's expression it was evident she wasn't even trying to make out. Her dad went on,

"As long as you were in school, you learned what is bad and what is good; but you never had the freedom to practice what you had come across. But college isn't like that, you have your freedom. You are young and may end up doing wrong things without knowing the consequences. I just want to be there to guide you in this part of your life, so that you don't do anything immoral." Nishi understood what her dad meant. He was just trying to be discreet about the whole concept of love and sex. Every parent in the Indian family does that. Nishi chose not to be discreet about it anymore.

"Dad, if you are afraid that I may fall in love with someone, you are being juvenile. I might have as well fallen in love with some guy in while I was at school. You put me in a girl school. What if I had turned out to be a lesbian after being there? I haven't told you, there were two lesbian girls in my own dorm. What is immoral to us will always be there everywhere, even in our own *agraharam*. I know what I should do and what I shouldn't." Nishi said. Her mother had a horrified expression on her face. She tried to silence her daughter.

"Just because you saw a girl touching another girl doesn't mean you have seen everything in this world. Anyway, there's nothing you and I can do to change your college. You will go there. No more change on that." Said her angered dad.

"Nothing I can do? That's what you think, huh? I would kill myself rather than go to that piece of thing you call college." Nishi lashed out. If her daughter wasn't upset and just angry her mother would have slapped her. The only thing that provokes the parent's mind apart from their children talking about sex, is their child talking about suicide. And thus, suicidal threat, has become the powerful weapon in the arsenal of teenagers threatening their parents. To picture, your child to be hanging from the ceiling fan itself is terrible enough.

Her dad walked out of the room, without a word and her mom sat by her to try and console her disheartened daughter.

NEW FACES

T HE NEW COLLEGE was nothing like Nishi had expected. It was neither bad nor good. But, Nishi felt like she had to hate the college. If only that college didn't exist she might have ended up in the college of her choice. It was a prejudice. At first, everything that was there, she felt like mocking it. Luckily, she didn't have to stay in the college hostel. All her hostel-ite classmates were narrating incidents of ragging during the break hours. Some of it sounded a bit ghastly and horrific. Nishi thanked her luck that she didn't have to stay in the hostel. But she knew it wasn't going to last too. The college rules had it that the final year students must stay in hostel.

Every time someone from her relatives asked her about how her college was, Nishi did nothing but grumble and complain about it. Her dad didn't seem to be happy about it. But Nishi didn't care anymore. Her father hadn't cared for what she had in her mind when they were choosing the college, why should she now?

"That place? You can't even call it a college." Nishi told her uncle who had come to her home. He had asked her how the college was.

"Why?" her uncle asked out of curiosity.

"That is because, she was saying it is just like how her school used to be." Her dad covered in for the question. But Nishi's answer was far from what her dad had said.

"Oh! Nice, nice. Glad to hear." Her ignorant uncle acknowledged. But Nishi knew too well that her uncle couldn't do anything to change her fate. Neither could her father. Nishi never stopped bitching about her college until Vinayak reprimanded her.

"Nishi listen. You have got to stop complaining about your college." Her brother told her.

"Why? Because dad doesn't like it." She back answered.

"See, Nishi. No matter how much you complain, there is nothing that you can do to change your college. There is no point in grumbling over this."

"So, you just want to tell me there is no escaping the sentence that I have received." Nishi questioned back, arrogantly. She knew she was being arrogant, and she wanted to be arrogant.

"What are you trying to do here? Do you think there is any use to what are you doing here? You know, Anjali. She wanted to do medicine and now she is stuck in a bad college. She tells me now that she has lost her interest in medicine." Her brother said.

"Yeah. Exactly. That is what is going to happen to me too. When I come out of the college, if you ask me to administer your business; I will curse you." Her brother fell silent. It seemed as though Vinayak saw that she had a point. After a few moments, her brother spoke again. But this time he wasn't trying to argue with her. It seemed like he was appealing to something, Nishi paid attention

"I know it was harsh of dad to have broken the promise and got you here. You deserved better. But, right now it is no more about our dad. Anything you do thinking that you are taking revenge on dad for having put you in this college, it will be a punishment against your own self. It is your life from now on. Your life has begun in a horrible place. But where you go from here is what will be your achievement. Just put up this once. You will get MBA admission in a good college. I will promise that you will go into a good MBA college."

Nishi didn't argue further with her brother. She had always looked up to him. She decided to let go of the entire thing and tried to get on with the new college.

Without her prejudice, there wasn't anything wrong with the college. It was a typical arts college. Built over a large area, with few buildings scattered here and there. Each of them labelled in such a way that the classes and the hostels were a like a mile away. No vehicles were allowed inside the campus. It was as though the college was trying to implement an inconspicuous campaign to promote walking. The hostellers had to walk for twenty minutes from their hostel to the class room. Luckily, the doors of the classes were at the rear of the lecture halls. All late-comers would simply slip in as they come to the class. This was the least of Nishi's concerns. Nishi didn't try and make any friends. Although she had stopped complaining about the college, there was still some prejudice left in her.

One. Two and three. Semester after semester passed. Nishi was the batch topper. She secured the first rank in almost all of the exams. Her parents were proud to simply see their daughter excel in college. But apart from books, Nishi never indulged herself in anything. She never stayed back in college any day after five. That was the time the college bus left in the evening. Even if she had something to go and refer from other books, she used her break time. She never stayed back. The cultural fests, sports events. No, Nishi wasn't involved in any of them. She used to take part in athletics in her school. By her third semester she couldn't remember how she used to take her position at the starting block. She had one goal, to get into a decent college for her MBA course. Apart from her B.com syllabus, she spent some time to study for those entrance exams that would get her admission for an MBA degree.

She hadn't made any new friends in her course. She pretty much stayed away from anyone at college. At the most, she would ask some of the girls if she had any doubts regarding the subject. Except that she kept to herself. She even forgot to keep in touch with her old friends from school. The number of times she called Sharmila went down. Even her best of friends suddenly weren't there. It was like as if she was all alone in her fight. But, eventually, Nishi got used to being alone. Loneliness became her friend.

At home, the father-daughter relationship had been severed ever since her dad had put her in this college. Nishi spent her time in the house, by studying or by herself. She hardly spent time in the living room where most of her family were. Life was pretty much boring. Only, when her brother came home for his vacation, he would take her out and the brother and sister would have a good time. Else it was just a mundane lifestyle Nishi had.

But it didn't always stay the same. Things changed with the fourth semester. The BBA students began to attend classes with the B.com students. The strength of the class had been hence doubled. And the classes weren't mere lectures. There were activities that had come in which made them to interact with each other. During the lectures, it was just an hour of a professor's talk. Nishi simply had to pay attention and take down notes. But with these activities, she had to talk to people. She struggled with it. Of all of them, the worst was an activity based on 'Business Organisation.' The entire batch was divided into groups of five. And the activity wasn't a one-time thing. It was a part of their weekly schedule and it were to last till the end of fourth semester. And before the semester exams, a presentation was scheduled wherein the groups should explain what they had achieved in the six months.

Nishi wasn't very comfortable with her group. The four of them in her group were complete strangers to her. Almost everyone in the batch was a stranger to her. She tried not to be bothered by it. But she couldn't. The five of them, when they got together they had to analyse and arrange the data they had got. Obviously, that didn't come without much of a discussion. She restricted her talk to the subject alone. But all five of them weren't the same. There was a girl named Usha. She seemed to be friendly towards Nishi. Although Nishi felt a bit good to have Usha for company, she didn't allow herself to get close. There was a talkative guy in their group named Tarun. He had shaggy hair that had never been combed. He was the one who diverted the topic away from the subject. Nishi wasn't very fond of him. She hoped that they could trade him for a more responsible person from another group. Also, she did know too well, that it would never happen. In her group, Nishi was easily the smartest. No one knew the subject as good as her. That's how it seemed to her.

The other two in her group was a guy named Hari and a girl named Raagini. They did their work, sometime involved in the small talk initiated by Tarun or asked a few doubts to Nishi. That was all these two did. And Hari seemed like an expert bunker. He wasn't there for half of these classes. This was what made up the fourth semester of the BBA and the B.Com students apart from the boring lectures. As the semester neared its end, the groups were busy deciding on which of them should do the presentation. Each group had been asked to select two of the five students to present it before the departments. It was the same argument that was going on in Nishi's group.

"How about Raagini and Hari?" asked Usha. Nishi was glad that she wasn't being suggested. But, she hid it, lest it might expose herself to getting chosen.

"No way." Hari objected.

"Why don't you and Tarun do it?" Raagini suggested towards Usha.

"Me huh? How about Nishi here? She is the one who should do it. She only knows the most about all this." Tarun said.

"What? No way. Why me? You do it, know?" Nishi was furious with Tarun for suggesting her name. She fired back. But Tarun had given a valid reason why she should be chosen. And that put her at a disadvantage.

"Hey, Nishi. You are the one who can do it best. You are the batch topper." It was Raagini. Soon everyone were trying to convince her. Nishi tried as much as she could to turn it back on Tarun.

"Look, I can't present and all. Tell him to do this. He talks the most." She explained pointing at Tarun.

"Fine. I'll do it." Tarun agreed, much to Nishi's relief and her disbelief. "But . . ." he continued "Nishi should be the other person doing it along with me." Nishi's relief disappeared. *Why did he chose me? What is he thinking? Me and him?*

"Nishi, now you can't say no. If you do, we will have two people who are up and willing to present." Usha said. Nishi couldn't do anything but accept. But she wasn't done with Tarun yet.

After the class she went up to him, "Why did you choose me to do along with you?"

"What? Oh . . . well, you are the batch topper."

"Why did you to do agree then?"

"You were the one who suggested my name. Now, you don't want me to do the presentation?" Tarun questioned back. Nishi had no reply. She walked away, leaving Tarun confused.

TARU(N)ISHI

THE DAY OF the presentations arrived. It was being held in the college auditorium. The entire commerce department was there. The students were called according to their roll numbers. At the end of one hour of the presentation, Nishi made calculations and found out that she and Tarun wouldn't be called until after three. She turned to Tarun who was sitting beside her,

"Tarun, if the proceedings go at the pace it is going right now. We won't be called until three in the afternoon. How about we do a little rehearsal just after lunch?" she suggested.

"Yeah, fine. But where?" he asked.

"You suggest." She let him suggest because she had no option in her mind.

"How about behind the auditorium. There will not be much people, to make us feel embarrassed. At the same time, if the things inside the auditorium speeds up a little, we will be able to dash in here." He suggested. She too agreed.

Their presentation went exceptionally well. The department staff seemed very pleased. Tarun's gang of friends were congratulating him. One or two of them, came up to Nishi too, to congratulate. She received them warmly. When she returned to her seat, Raagini and Usha looked at her and signalled that she did very well. The presentation lasted for another day. There was a prize for the best presentation and it was to be announced after the holidays.

Nishi proudly, called her mom to tell her that she had done a splendid presentation, however she decided to leave Tarun out of the description. The next day onwards the classes resumed. Nishi hadn't talked to Tarun after Monday. There was even no need for that. She, however did regret for judging him too early. She turned around and looked towards the last, bench where he always took seat, amidst his friends. It was the same shaggy fellow, she had seen a week ago. He wasn't paying attention to the class. He seemed to be looking at his mobile. He was wearing a black shirt. Black colour was a taboo on dress, according to her parents. They had not allowed her to buy any *salwar* which was more than quarter of area in black. They did however let her wear black bottoms for those light-coloured *salwars*. Not even her sandals were black. She looked down at her feet. Her mild-brown coloured sandals that they had bought for her a year ago. She noticed the toes of the girl sitting beside her, it had nail polish on it. The only thing that she had had so far to decorate her toe was some mehendi, and it never lasts.

Her family being orthodox Hindus, were very much adherent to the traditions. Nishi too liked keeping up to those traditions. In fact, she was even proud that she had traditions, unlike the modern hippie-kind of girls. It seemed like she was doing the right thing and the whole world had gone to the opposite. That's how the world seemed to her eyes. That's how it is in most people's eyes.

*   *   *

Nishi opened her eyes. It was Thursday. She turned around in her bed. Nishi never needed an alarm to wake up, as long as she went to bed on time. It was the way her body had been functioning all her life. She looked outside the window. It was too dark. She guessed, that she must have woken up too early. She put her hand under her pillow and pulled out her phone. It was 4:30am. She still had an hour and a half to sleep. She felt cold. In her sleep, she had pushed aside the blankets and it had fallen down on the floor. She rose up to grab her blankets. And instantaneously, her head hurt. It was like as if someone was trying to squeeze her skull. She put her hands to her head and bent as low as her knees. She got up. She felt the flavour of metal in her throat. She got out of the room and went towards the toilet. Her entire body was aching. She dragged herself, to the sink. She stood there for a moment or two looking at her own self. She threw up. She rinsed her mouth and came back, to bed, she lay down covered in her blankets, shivering. Nishi was having fever.

She spent the whole day, in her bed. Most, of the time she slept. Her mother made her some soup. Nishi tried to read something in the evening. Her mother insisted that she take rest. But Nishi ignored her. She wasn't able to concentrate for more than five minutes. She put her books down and went to sleep.

The fever didn't subside till the next day evening. She was alright by Saturday and returned to class. She didn't understand anything from the first session, because she had been absent for the previous day. The next class, turned out to be even worse.

"Roll no: 236. Why were you absent yesterday?" Nishi rose up from her chair with fear. As she did, she heard mention, of the word 'Tarun' from one end of the class. She had no idea why it was happening.

"Sir, I was not feeling well." She replied. The voices from the last row hadn't ceased. She looked in the direction. Tarun looked, embarrassed as he tried to make his friends shut up. Nishi understood what was going on. Tarun's friend were teasing her with him. She felt ashamed, as though she was being harassed.

"Oi, last row, there. What's going on?" the professor asked pointing towards the direction of Tarun and his friends. Everything went silent once again. The professor turned his attention towards Nishi,

"Not well for two consecutive days? Or you went out somewhere?"

"With Tarun." She heard an almost incoherent voice. The professor hadn't quite caught the voice. He ignored it. Nishi felt very bad. Her eyes were getting clouded with tears. One side was her teacher, blaming her for being absent, on the other side she was being teased.

"No, sir." She managed to tell, without breaking into a sob.

"Sit, sit. God knows from where you people come from?" the professor cursed and began the class. Nishi couldn't pay attention to that class. She was distracted about being teased by Tarun. She never should have agreed to do the presentation with him. Tarun never seemed a nice guy. She considered Tarun with disgust, for he was being friends with such imbeciles.

She had hidden everything about Tarun from her parents. If this were to complicate into an issue, what was she going to tell her dad. When, the class ended, she decided to leave the classroom as early as she could. But before she could Tarun had come up to her. She wanted to yell at him. But she told herself, it would be absurd. She decided to deal with the matter logically and try and escape out of it.

"Nishi, I have something to talk to you. Would you mind?" Tarun asked her. She looked back at him with a brave face, trying to hide the fact that she had almost cried.

"No, say." She almost ordered him.

"Look, I noticed that you were depressed about something in the class. And I'm guessing it is because of me. I wanted to apologize for it."

"What good it is?" she asked back.

"Look, I can see why you are mad. You are not very social and definitely you wouldn't fancy being teased. I understand. And I told my friends not to. But you see they won't stop. But, on the other hand, if you really want them to stop teasing you could try talking to them and say them you don't like it, they would stop teasing us. It would be useful for you and me." Tarun suggested.

Tarun was being apologetic. Nishi pictured herself trying to talk Tarun's friends out of teasing her. No, she couldn't go to a bunch of boys and girls and tell them to stop teasing her. They would simply claim that they were teasing their friend. She racked her brain for a better solution.

"I can't come and boss around your friends. It will be bad. I have a better idea. One that will definitely work."

"What?" Tarun was eager to hear it.

"They started teasing us, only because they saw us together. We gave them a chance to tease us. Hereafter, we will not be together, anywhere for any reason, whatsoever. Don't come and talk to me. I won't do the same. When we are apart, they won't have any reason to tease us."

"No, I don't think it-" Tarun appeared to be rejecting her proposal.

"It will work. Trust me. Another one week or something, they will stop teasing us. We might have to go together to accept the award, if we win the prize. But what are the chances that it's going to be us? It won't hurt. So got it? From now on don't talk to me." She said and walked away. She was delighted to have crafted out the brilliant plan. She felt proud of herself. She could not see how it could fail. And it wouldn't be so hard to do it either. They had nothing in common, except that assignment. What are the odds that she might have to work with him on assignments again? And thus it would be very easy for both of them to stay away from each other.

She had her lunch in the canteen. There was no one to disturb her. She sat there all by herself. She called up her brother and told him about the assignment. She mentioned to him that she had to work along with a guy named Tarun. It removed the nagging feeling that she had been hiding something. Now, if the teasing were to become an issue, her brother was there to help her.

*   *   *

Nishi was arranging her bed. She was moving into the hostel. She tucked the bedspread under the mattress. It was all part of what she had learnt in her school. It wasn't the first time she was in a hostel. She had been in one during her school days. She said her prayers to Vishnu and began to get her books into her college bag. The semester exams had got over just the same day and it was winter vacation. After the vacation, the final year of Nishi's B.Com course was set to begin. Once she had her B.Com degree, she could apply, for an M.B.A and when she graduates, she could administer her brother's firm, which he had been planning on setting up. The hostel wasn't as good as the one in her school, but she managed to adjust. She had two roommates and they were arrived there before her. Her roommates were a Ramya and Usha, the girl from her group. Nishi decided to leave her bags in the hostel before leaving for the vacation. She didn't want to be doing all that stuff when a new semester began. Nishi cursed the rule that said that the final-year students must stay in the hostel. As she was arranging, Ramya, one of the two roommates she had, entered into the room. She had just bathed. Her hair was drenched.

"Hey, Tarun." It was Ramya, teasing her. It startled her.

"What?" she asked back, putting her bag in the corner?

"Nothing. Nothing, Tarun." Her roommate teased her.

"What? No. You will not call me that."

"Why should we listen?" Usha told laughing.

"I don't like it."

"So, what? He likes you."

"What? He likes me? Who said that?" she questioned back.

"You both were doing something behind the auditorium before your presentation. You both looked very cute together."

"We were rehearsing for the presentation behind the auditorium hall. And I have no intention of being with him, any more than I had so far have been." She sounded as if Ramya and Usha were saying something reprehensible.

"Why? Don't you like him?" Ramya queried. Nishi knew this well. If she said that she had nothing against him, which was the truth, it would be used against her. She played dumb.

"Don't be so mad. We have no intention of teasing you. It's him we want to tease." Usha tried to cheer her up, thinking she was very upset.

"Even, he doesn't want to be teased by you." Nishi said, recollecting from the incident what had happened earlier.

"How do you know?" Usha asked back.

"He told me." She replied.

"Oh! What did he say you?" Usha questioned.

"He told he was sorry and that he told you people to stop, but you wouldn't stop it. So he asked me if I could persuade you people. I didn't see anything happening if I did that. So, I told him to stay away from me."

"Really? That's cold. What did he say?" Ramya, who was about to leave the room had stopped herself and questioned.

"Nothing. I came off."

"Oh my god! That's so bad."

"What's so wrong in it?"

"Don't you see it?" Ramya asked. Nishi didn't understand where she could have been wrong, she honestly gave a good suggestion. She simply shook her head.

"Look, if you normally don't like anyone teasing you. What you should do is that go up to the person and tell them to stop it. So you should have actually done what Tarun asked you to without himself asking, if you really didn't want us to tease you. And moreover, that guy apologized to you, about the whole thing. Saying 'sorry' means that the person is being nice. So, Tarun was being nice to you and what you told him was like as if you slammed a door on him. You indirectly told him to get out of your life. That's ruddy rude." Ramya looked unpleased.

"No, I wasn't being indirect, I directly meant that, he getting out of my life is better for him and me. What will he understand? It is a bigger issue for me. I'm a girl and he's a guy. I'm the one with the issue here." She shot back.

"You are the one who is being inconsiderate here. You tell a person to get out of your life, only if you hate them to the bones. You don't do it to a guy who is being nice. How come you don't know this and you are twenty years old" Ramya defended.

Nishi didn't understand what had she done that was making her roommates unpleasant.

"See, why do you hate Tarun?"

"I don't hate Tarun."

"Look, because you slammed him out of your life, he will be very disappointed." Said Usha.

"And the worst part is that, he will be blaming himself for what has happened. He will be feeling very guilty. You better apologize to him."

"Apologize? What wrong did I do?"

"Neither did he do anything wrong." Usha defended Tarun.

"Well, then neither of us will have to apologize then."

"You probably hurt him by asking him to get out of your life." Ramya said. She looked as mad as Nishi was.

"It was an honest idea, to solve the problem of people teasing me. There's nothing more to it." Nishi put her foot down on the matter.

Even after the vacation had begun, she couldn't get over it. He hadn't spoken anything to her ever since she told him to go away. There was no teasing after that day.

FLOWERS AND CANDIES

THE NEW SEMESTER had begun. She looked at Tarun during the class. He sat there, minding his own work. He hadn't spoken anything to her. There was no teasing, that she noticed. Her suggestion seemed to be working. She wondered why Ramya and Usha were so against it. But, there was a bit of sense to their suggestion. She shouldn't have pushed him out of her life. There was nothing that she saw so wrong with him. She was feeling very much out of place and he was considerate enough to adjust according to her wish. But then, now she had turned him down as if he had done all the wrong. This feeling had been with her all though her vacation. He was fidgeting his abnormally large-screen phone that he always had.

Nishi was curious about how he was doing this. Doing well in studies without paying attention to class. She was curious to find out. She went over to the library one day. She hadn't gone there to study, but to find if he was studying. He wasn't there, she spent an hour reading her lessons. When, she was returning she took a peek into the reading room, he wasn't there. She got back to her room, hoping her roommates would trigger an argument and she could ask them about him.

Her room was locked. She pulled out her keys and opened the room. Switching on the lights, she sat down and began to ponder over all that had happened from the time, she had first noticed him, in his green checked shirt. She was surprised to remember the details of that day.

That night sleep had evaded her. She was thinking about Tarun. It was very weird. She had never felt like this before. *Why was this guy causing so much confusion in her mind? Why is he in my mind in the first place?* She wished there was someone she could ask. It was taboo to talk to her parents about these. She had hid a part of it from her brother, Vinayak, she couldn't tell him that she had hidden something from him. Her brother would not trust her if she did. Her roommates were nothing more than roommates. She wasn't sure if they considered her as their friends. She had spent only a few days with them.

They did live together. They shared a few things, sometimes did group study. But no one trusted each other with their feelings. Nishi didn't feel that they were appropriate to share secrets. And suddenly, it seemed that she had been lonely, all these days. She wondered how she had managed so long without any real friends. She had her school friend, Sharmila. But they were drifting apart. Even Sharmila wouldn't have time to pay attention. In the first year of college, they talked about once in a week. During the second year, the gap extended to a month. And at the moment, Nishi couldn't remember, when the last time she ever spoke to her was. She felt slightly guilty that she had let her best friend go. But it wasn't her fault entirely. Even Sharmila didn't try to make any attempt to keep the friendship intact.

Sharmila, was doing medicine. All that she spoke of was how they pulled out the heart and sliced the brain of the dead bodies. She even had a fancy name for those dead bodies. Nishi couldn't remember it, it was 'cavadar' or something similar. Sharmila would tell it as if it was an achievement. It made Nishi repel out of disgust. The thought of those things they did to the dead made her feel nauseated.

Nishi realized her chain of thoughts drifting further and further from Tarun. It was like, as if Tarun was becoming less important. Once in a while, her mind reset her thoughts back to Tarun. She eventually fell asleep.

*   *   *

The awards for the presentation were to be given away. Nishi noticed Tarun sitting in the first row. He had his hair cut very short. It suited him rather than the usual shaggy appearance.

"The best presentation goes to Tarun Varadarajan and Nishitha Pillai." The announcer said. The H.O.D had the award in his hand. It was a certificate and a cash prize of rupees thousand five hundred. Nishi got up and walked to the front of the class. Tarun too did the same. There was a loud applause, for the duo. Nishi beamed with smile. She looked towards Tarun. He gave a calm smile as if he was pretending to be happy. When the class ended, a crowd of students had surrounded Tarun, congratulating. There were people who wished Nishi too. But, she had other plans in mind. She looked in the direction of Tarun. Once the other students, left him, she went towards Tarun, who was picking up his bag to leave the class.

"Tarun." She called out. Her voice was too faint. She called out once more. "Tarun." He turned around and stood. She walked up to him.

"Congrats." Nishi wished him.

"Same to you." He replied smiling.

"I'm sorry, that I told you to stop talking to me."

"Why? It's alright. Now, no one teases me."

"Yeah. Since, no one's teasing us now. I thought we could be friends." She was smiling, hoping he would agree. He too smiled back.

"Come along, will you?" he requested. Nishi followed him.

*   *   *

Nishi entered her room. She put down her bag. She had a bouquet in her other hand, the one that Tarun just had given her. She kept it on her study table.

"Oh! Who gave you flowers?" Ramya asked getting close to the flowers.

"Tarun did. They are nice, aren't they?"

"They are nice? They are very very romantic. God, you have a hell of a boyfriend." Usha too joined in. The two friends were admiring the flowers.

"Romantic? There's nothing romantic about this. His father had got it for being a chief guest in a college. Tarun didn't know where to put it. He asked if I could keep it in my vase that I had mentioned to him in a conversation. He isn't my boyfriend either." Nishi explained.

"Alright, let's put in the vase." Said Ramya and the girls began transferring the flowers one by one into the vase.

"What flowers are these?"

"They are called Anthuriums. They have heart shaped petals." Said Nishi to her friend.

"A red heart-shaped flower isn't romantic huh?" Ramya teased.

"Nishi, you have to look at this." It was Usha, starring into the basket where the flowers had been arranged. Nishi peeked. In the base of the basket, where little heart shaped candies, about fifty of them.

"Aww. This is so cute." Ramya was admiring the basket.

"CUTE? Why would you think that? It's absurd. Who would fill candies in a bouquet?" Nishi contradicted.

"You don't get it, do you? I don't believe this was given to Tarun's father anymore. But all the same, you are so lucky to get such a guy." Said Usha.

"This is the lamest thing he can do, if he is trying to express his love." Said Nishi.

"LAME?" it was Ramya's turn to contradict. "I am jealous of you. I wish I had a guy who would give me this bouquet."

"Seriously, what more could a girl ask for, more than chocolates and flowers." Said Usha. Nishi couldn't fathom any beauty or admiration towards Tarun's gesture.

"I am actually outraged, by this. If this is a symbol of affection, I'm going to chuck these candies on his face. Literally."

"What? Oh no! Don't break his heart. He seems to be very nice."

"Do you know what will happen if anyone in my house knows of this. They will slit my throat, worse my dad will LITERALLY kick me out of the house." She was almost in tears. The thought of her parents' reaction towards something like this had scared her bringing tears to her.

"Look, we are sorry. We didn't know you feel so bad." Said Ramya. For the first time, her roommate was being sympathetic towards her.

"But, if you are planning on doing what you had said. Don't do it. It is too much. Don't throw them on his face. Put the chocolates in a cover and return it. You can return the flowers too. Be angry. Talk to him and make it clear, that you don't have any such intention." Suggested Usha. At first, Nishi thought she should do what she had mentioned. But soon she realized, it wouldn't look too good to make a scene. She decided to make it a conversation rather than a confrontation. And she decided to get it over with that very evening.

"Ramya, can you ask Tarun to come to the cafeteria? Tell him, I said." She asked her roommate.

"Nishi, don't be rash. You be prepared before you confront him."

"I simply don't want him to be misled, not even for one more night. I can't stand it. Please call him." Said Nishi and began getting dressed, to go out and meet up with Tarun.

An hour and a half later Nishi returned to her room. Her roommates eagerly asked her what had happened and how it had gone. But Nishi had something else in mind. She desperately needed a person to talk to. A real friend. The confrontation had ended up nothing like she had expected it to be. It was her fault that the course of the conversation went not the way she wanted it to. She walked out of her room. The corridor was empty. She went to the end of the corridor and began punching numbers into her phone.

"Hello." A long forgotten voice came through the phone.

"Hey." She spoke back.

"How are you, girl? It's been so long." Her friend, Sharmila spoke back.

"I think I'm quite fine. It's all going good."

"What's up?"

"Oh! There's this one thing I want to say."

"Oh! Yeah, say."

"There is this guy in my coll-"

"Ah! Finally there's a guy in your life, huh? Unbelievable." Her friend interrupted.

"No, there's nothing like that. There is this guy. That's it."

"Okay, okay. I'm not interrupting. Carry on."

"He looks like any other guy from my place. Typical uncouth guy. But he gets amazing marks and performs very well in studies. Situations brought us together. And now he gave me a bouquet and chocolates."

"Wow. Nice boyfriend material I see there."

"Hey, no there's nothing like it. This evening I went to tell him that I have no interest in any such stuff. I was supposed to be angry at him. But he didn't give me any chance. It kind of looked like I had asked him for a date. I should have told him to get away. I could have done it anytime. But I didn't do it. I couldn't do it. I don't like all this. My parents would kill me if they find out. I don't know why I didn't stop him."

"Aww. You have a crush on him. Don't you?"

"I don't want to." Nishi said accepting the fact that she had a crush on him. She didn't like it. But denial wasn't going to help her get over it.

"Half the people, don't want to. Try escaping it, good luck."

"What do I do?"

"I wish I could help. But you are on your own. I have no idea who is that guy, what kind of places you people meet."

"I told you he is a typical Vellore guy. No posh lifestyle, but great in studies. Looks a bit uncouth. As far as the places, we meet, it's mostly classes, then outside the lecture hall, in the cafeteria." She tried to explain her situation.

"That will never give me the whole picture. You should have friends there, try asking them."

"I can't trust them."

Nishi continued to rant to her friend, to the last detail about Tarun. But her friend refused. The two friends had drifted apart. Nishi couldn't demand any help.

She was having a problem, she had to deal with it all by herself. It seemed liked the worst thing had happened in her life. She was having a crush on Tarun. It wasn't going to be easy for her.

*   *   *

A week after the prizes were given, the H.O.D of Economics department summoned Nishi. He was old, had grey hair and a silver French beard. The H.O.D always wore a white shirt. He had his ID badge around his neck. When Nishi stepped in, there was another guy there already. It was Tarun.

"Ah! Come on in." the HOD called out on seeing her at his door.

"Good morning sir." Nishi managed feebly. But, the HOD didn't respond to it.

"Listen Nishitha, You and him got the best prize of your presentation on Business Organization. Now, we want you to do it again for the Annual Expo." The annual Expo was an inter-college event. Nishi simply nodded her head to show her willingness.

"But, as this is the college Expo we need you both to do it a little differently. Now, tell me: you both prepared separately for the presentation, didn't you?"

"Yes sir. We divided the topics equally between us and got data on them separately." Tarun explained.

"I did half the work and he did half the work, sir." Nishi added.

"It's good to divide and complete it. I'm not saying it's wrong. But what you should have done is put the data together and integrated your presentation. That was lacking in your presentation. This time you both will sit together and arrange your data and present it well, alright?"

Yes, sir." Nishi and Tarun responded. When they walked out of the office, Nishi asked Tarun,

"The assignment-"

"Yeah. How about you meet me in the cafeteria at three in the afternoon? I'll run home and get my paperwork." He said.

"What? No. I'll meet you in the ledger database room." Nishi suggested. That was were those files were kept.

"Oh! If you don't know, the ledger room is closed on Saturday and Sunday."

"*Kadavule.*" She said calling out to God in agony.

"Don't panic. I have got a Xerox of the ledger assigned to us." Said Tarun.

"Alright, I'll meet you there."

"Can I have your number? I'll let you know when I reach and then you can come?"

"It's alright. I'll be there sharp by three." She said, not wanting to give her number to an acquaintance. He had got the work done. He seemed to be a nice guy, but he still appeared scary to her. That afternoon, she sat at the café at a table beside him. It wasn't the first time she was with him, but this time she felt a feeling: weirdness. Sharmila had told her that she had a crush on him. She was afraid if she really was. It was making it very uncomfortable for her.

"You want anything to eat or drink." He asked her.

"No, thanks." It was Saturday afternoon and quite a number of people were there. Nishi felt quite weird to be sitting with a guy. She had never done anything of this sort at all. She tried to focus on the work they had to complete.

"Do you have a laptop?" He asked her.

"I'll take notes." She said pulling out her notebook. He pulled his laptop. He had already done some of the work. She was copying down the notes. They spent three hours in the café doing their work. It wasn't anywhere closer to completion.

"Hey, let's take a break. We'll return here after an hour. I need a break. I'll be here at seven. Is it okay?"

"Yeah. Okay. But we will meet at seven thirty. I need to finish my dinner." She said and they parted. She headed straight to her room.

"God! I can't wait for this assignment to be over." She cried out.

"Why what's wrong?" Ramya asked.

"I had to sit with a guy in a café for three hours and I'm not done yet."

"So?"

"It's so awkward. I don't' know what my mom will say if she hears this."

"Then don't tell her."

"What? How can I?"

"Just tell her you did it by yourself."

"And one more thing that guy asked me for my number."

"And?" Ramya questioned.

"Isn't it wrong to ask a girl her private number? I turned him down."

"Hey, look, I understand you are not used to this. But that's not how you should behave. Tell me everything what happened."

"We were sitting in the café, alright. Imagine a boy and girl sitting in a café for three hours. It sounds so bad. What will the people who see us will think? He is inconsiderate about it. He is a guy, no problem for him."

"If you have a problem with the café, why don't you tell him, and go into a classroom. No one will see you both there. Moreover, you both already spent time when you returned his flowers and also he was in your group during fourth semester. You still uncomfortable with him?"

"You want me to be alone in a room with him? It isn't safe either. During the fourth semester he was just a colleague. But now he is the guy who gave me flowers. I'm just worried about that." Nishi complained. She didn't want to admit that it was because she might be having a crush on him. She couldn't understand why her roommates were coming up with silly suggestions.

"What else did you people talk about?"

"Nothing else. What'd you expect us to talk?"

"Listen, Nishi. As long as you are silent and do your work, you will feel that there is something weird even if nothing is there. Talk something to him. He will say something. When you pay attention to what you are talking, you will lose the weird feeling that exists between you."

"What will I talk to him about?"

"What to talk? Ask something randomly. Ask him how are the classes? What does he think about the weather? Talk to him about something in the surrounding."

"Alright. I'll try."

"When you ask him something, he will probably ask you back something, probably the same thing. Decide an answer for yourself beforehand. You both will have a goodtime?"

"Important: if he asks something that you don't wish to answer, don't say 'no'. Guys will be intrigued when you turn them down. Just evade the question." Usha suggested.

Nishi tried to keep all the tips from her roommates in mind. She had her dinner in the hostel mess. She took her bag and went to the cafeteria. It was much calmer then. Tarun was having a plate in front of him.

"I'm sorry. Five minutes, I'll be done with my dinner." He said, covering his mouth full of food. She simply nodded and sat down.

She decided to let him finish his dinner, before she started to ask him anything. He took out his computer, the two of them resumed their work. She began taking notes. She decided to ask him once she finished the page she was currently on. As she reached

133

the end of the page she got nervous. She decided to ask him about his classes. She thought of an answer in her mind. When the page ended, she turned over to a new page, looked up at him. He was, writing too.

"Tarun. Hey."

"Yes." He responded and looked back at her.

"How are your classes?" she asked nervously.

"What classes?" he asked back. She had expected a question in return. But not this. She had no response to it either. She simply decided to ask about classes because, her friend had told her so. She had no answer on her lips

"Oh! Never mind. Let's continue with our work." She blurted out. Tarun eyed at her, before resuming what they had been doing. Nishi felt all the more weird now. She shouldn't have asked. She decided against asking about the weather. *But maybe asking about something in the surrounding might help.* She thought.

"Did you notice, that waiters here are wearing a uniform?" It was a huge mistake, she realized it only when the words left her mouth. Tarun put his pen down.

"What exactly is your problem?" he asked. But he didn't seem annoyed, he appeared bemused.

"I'm sorry I thought, if I had something to talk about, I thought it might not feel as weird as it is right now." She told him

"What? Are you feeling weird? About what?"

"I don't know. Like, the fact that everyone around is watching us. I have not done this before. It is my first time."

"No. We have been together before." After a little pause, Tarun added, "Okay, that sounded wrong. This isn't the first time we are having a chat in the café. Remember the time you came to thank me for my bouquet."

"First of all, I came to return the bouquet. I'm thinking that I didn't explain myself well then, but about now. I don't know why. I just feel weird. Please." She begged of him to co-operate.

"You should have told me. A lot of people prefer the cafeteria for such work. I thought you would prefer the same. Had I known, we could have gone to the Reading rooms." Nishi hadn't thought of that. It was a better option, actually. She felt bad that she had been very judgemental about him.

"Alright, we will go there tomorrow." She said.

"Alright. We'll stay here for now. And to keep you from feeling weird I'll talk something, alright?" he suggested. She nodded. He began telling about himself, about his course. Nishi was paying attention to what he was telling. Slowly her inhibition disappeared and she too began to tell more about herself. A conversation was flowing between the two as they did their assignment.

The next day, as decided they went to the reading rooms to complete the remainder of their assignment. Nishi felt less awkward to be there. Moreover, their light conversation was fun and Nishi was enjoying it. With progression of days, Nishi began to enjoy his company. It wasn't weird anymore. At times she longed for it. Soon the day of the Expo came.

For the four days expo lasted, the two of them stayed together due to their presentation. From early in the morning to late in the evening, the two friends did everything together. Nishi within her mind marked him as a good friend. Tarun wasn't the scary guy from her group in Business Organization anymore. Nishi decided to get her meals in the cafeteria rather than in the hostel mess during the three days. This left the two of them to dine together.

Once the expo ended, the hangover was there. At first she tried to stay away from him. She had a crush on him, so her friend had said. Nishi didn't like the prospect of having a crush on anyone, neither did she know how unavoidable it was. She had promised herself to abstain from anything to deal with Tarun. But Tarun invited her to hang out with him and his gang. Nishi politely declined. But Tarun stressed,

"See, I know you are used to being alone. You will enjoy the company of people. You need to make some friends. It'll be so much fun." He promised her.

Nishi agreed, for the moment. But Tarun didn't seem to be allowing her to get away. During the break he caught Nishi's hand and almost dragged her to his friends. She cursed her ill-luck. Some part in her was elated. Another half of her revolted. Nishi pacified her thoughts. She pulled her hand away.

"I need to get some water." She lied, hoping to ditch him without being rude.

"Sure thing. So do I." Tarun said. The two of them walked to the water-tap and drank some water, before Tarun introduced her to the gang. There were eight of them including Tarun. Both, her roommates Ramya and Usha were there. Nishi smiled and pretended to laugh at their jokes during the rest of the break. Yet, some part of her was enjoying the company. She was hanging out with Tarun. *A bad idea this is; in spite of the good feeling*, she thought to herself. For the next few days, she found herself unconsciously hanging out with them. She became a real part of the gang, when one of them had their birthday. The nine of them went to a hotel for a meal. Nishi signed in the card that they had acquired. She was worried that if she stopped hanging out with them, it might come-off as a rude gesture. Something in her told, that the real reason she was hanging out with the gang was to enjoy Tarun's company. Nishi refused to accept that however. It wasn't the first time her thoughts were going hay-wire about Tarun.

Out of curiosity she would look at Tarun during the class. *What is he doing?* But even before she could turn the other part in her would object. *Don't turn around. You don't have a crush on him.* With the conflict from her super-ego, Nishi would abstain from turning around. And when the teacher walks to the back of the class, she would turn around to keep her eyes on the teacher. And just as she did that, she would let her sight slip for a second towards Tarun. Her conscience would swell within her: *You turned around. So you have turned around to look at him. You used the teacher as an excuse to turn around.* Nishi wondered if she was sane still. Yet, it was a good feeling.

Thus, with her deep-seated crush on Tarun that she was denying, Nishi had become a part of Tarun's gang. She was no more the one who spent the entire evening with her books. Every time, Ramya and Usha went out she too had to go. It was the peer pressure dragging her along. There were a couple of times she had to be alone with Tarun. At times Tarun's friends would tease her with Tarun.

Normally, Nishi would have objected. But she had seen Ramya react to getting teased with Daniel by just teasing back and taking the comment sportively. Nishi tried as hard as she could to take it sportively. But it wasn't easy. She felt embarrassed. She noticed Tarun make eye-contact with his friends signalling them to stop. His friends obeyed him instantly. Tarun seemed to have a lot of influence over the gang. He appeared to be the alpha-male of the whole lot. The new-found friendship lasted for the next four months.

REVELATIONS

THE SOUND OF her phone ringing was annoying. But it simply wouldn't stop. Nishi stretched out her arm and grabbed her phone. The call was from Tarun. And it was midnight. *What the hell does this guy want now?* she grumbled as she answered the call.

"Hello." She heard his voice, sounding jubilant and excited.

"Mm." Was all that she could manage to reply. Her brain was too tired to think of appropriate words. It just sent out a monosyllabic sound.

"Nishi?" The voice seemed to be in doubt. Nishi was in no mood to talk to him.

"No, I'm Nishi's sister. Nishi is asleep. Call her in the morning." She lied to him and hung up the call. *Idiot* she cursed within herself.

Only the next morning she realized why Tarun had called her. The realization hit her when Vinayak, her brother called her in the morning to wish her: Happy Birthday. Tarun too must have called to wish her. She lied to him that she was her own sister. Even by her standards that was rude. Tarun had been friendly to her ever since the presentation. And it was offensive of her to have done what she had done. However, she couldn't understand how Tarun had got his hands on her mobile number?

That day when she went to college, Tarun asked her if she had a few minutes to spare. Nishi agreed out of the guilt of the lie that she had told him. He had invited her over to the canteen. Nishi had been there with him previously. But she still felt a bit uncomfortable.

"Happy Birthday, Nishitha." He told her.

"Thank you man." She replied with a smile.

"You know? I called you last night to wish. Someone else picked up the phone."

"Oh! Sorry about that. That was my sister. I was sleeping."

"You have a sister too."

"A cousin actually." Nishi added onto her stupid lie that she had spun.

"Oh! With cousins at your house. They let you sleep before twelve on the eve of your birthday huh?"

"In our family, everyone goes to bed before 10.30 pm." She explained.

"Nishi there is something I want to tell you."

"Yes." *Does he know that I'm lying about my cousin? Is that what this whole thing is about?* the thoughts flooded Nishi's brain.

"You are a nice girl. I still remember how shy you were when we were here in this café the first time. Every statement you said was weird. We have known each other for the past ten months." Tarun was saying. *Wait. He is being nostalgic about some of the embarrassing moments of my life. What is his point really? Should I get up and walk away right now?* her thoughts were in a frenzy. Suddenly, Tarun stretched out his hand and took Nishi's in his.

"Through all this ten months I had been wanting to tell you that I love you." He finished. Normally her thoughts would have been, *Thank God! This whole thing was not about the lie that I said. He will never have to know.* But that moment all her mind was yelling was: *Wait. No. Did he just propose? Oh my God? A guy has proposed to me. What am I going to tell dad?* It was as though her mind would explode.

"Hey, Nishi. From your face I can make out that you neither thought about this nor expected me to do so. Listen, take time to think about it. You cannot make a decision such as this right away. Take a few days. Think over it and then let me know. If you are not comfortable telling it over my face, you have my number. Send me a message or tell it through someone if you have close friends." Tarun went on.

"Look Tarun. I don't know what to say." She hadn't finished yet, but Tarun interrupted her.

"See, that's why I'm saying you to take your time."

"No, no. It isn't that. My parents won't agree." She explained.

"Nishi, I do know that they don't support love in your house. All I am telling you is how I feel for you and that I'm interested to be in a relationship with you. Your parents don't have to know right now with whom you are in a relationship with. And importantly, your first reply to my proposal is about what your parents would say if this relationship happened. So some part of you believes that it might happen. Or you might be in love with me. Do pay attention to that voice in your head." Tarun replied.

"I'll let you know." Said Nishi and walked out of the café. This was one of the biggest things that had happened in her whole life.

The answer to a proposal would have been a clear no. But with Tarun things were a little different. For the past few months she had been having a crush on him and she had led that to build a friendship between them. Now a 'no' would put everything at stake. She didn't know whom to go for help. Her family would be the most unhelpful if she asked advice on love. She didn't know many people around. Her once best friend, Sharmi hadn't given any helpful advice the last time she spoke and it had been a long time Nishi had contacted her. She couldn't even believe herself that she was even considering a guy's proposal. Tarun had said to her "Your first reply to my proposal is about what your parents would say if this relationship happened." It bugged her. Her reply should have been a no. But the first thing that she considered was what would happen if she accepts her proposal. Maybe, some part of her had feelings towards him. Two days later, she had her decision. It was scary. But it was a 'yes' that she had decided. Tarun jumped with joy when she said her acceptance.

It felt like she too was supposed to jump in joy. But there was still a bit of fear looming in her that didn't allow her to leap out in excitement. Although Nishi had accepted the relationship offer, she was a bit sceptical about it. There was six more months of college. And then, she would graduate and what next? She wanted to do M.B.A at a fine institution and her college didn't qualify for a fine institution. She had no clue on what Tarun's plans were. As she spent time with Tarun she realized that he really didn't have any solid plan on what to do after graduation. But there were other parts of Tarun that Nishi really cared for. The more time the boyfriend and girlfriend spent time together the more intimate they became. Nishi found herself liking him more and more. At one point she told him, "I can't be sure if I loved you when I accepted your proposal. But after being with you, now I definitely am in love with you."

Like any other person in relationship the text messaging in the mobiles kept them close. Tarun would, like always send her a silly forward message. It would be lame sometimes. Yet, she would send a reply saying `nice message` He would send another message saying `that's why I decided to send it to u . . . BTW . . . wat r u doin?` And from that question, they will text each other for hours together. Tarun used the SMS shorthand always. Nishi wasn't fluent at all. He would send a weird bunch of letters like `lmao` or `gtg`. The first time she didn't know what it meant. She tried to pretend to know it and replied with an 'ok'. But once he sent her a `wtf` and she replied with a happy smiley face.

`Seriously, a happy face?` came a reply from. And she confessed how much the SMS shorthand meant to her. He sent another bunch of abbreviation, `rotfl . . . WTF stands for what the fish?` Even then, Nishi didn't understand what it meant. She decided to leave it at that.

Tarun listened to everything that she had to say. She didn't feel like there was nobody in her life anymore. If she wanted to talk to someone, he was there. He was the most and the only exciting part of her life. But, there was another thing Nishi was picking up from the relationship. As the duo went to places on dates, Nishi realized how drawn back were her principles. They were old and some seemed silly to her. She tried and adapted herself to the changes. The once conservative traditional homely girl had become like any other college-girl. All through the six months Nishi was worried for one thing. *What if my parents find out?* And eventually it happened.

* * *

It was Easter holidays. It wasn't a day of celebration in Nishi's house. Why would an orthodox Hindu family be celebrating a Christian festival? But the family was glad, that the government had declared Easter as a national holiday, for it meant, the family could get together and stay in the house. Nishi's brother Vinayak, had got his leave. But, Adarsh wasn't able to make it home. He was busy with his internship program in Kolkata. Nishi, sat on the couch, watching the special holiday programmes on her TV. Her mom and dad had gone over to her grandmothers'. Her brother, was up to something in his room. He had been reading a book, when she last took a peek in.

"Nishi, come here." She heard her brother's voice. It was from her room. She, wondered what her brother, had been doing in her room. She got up and went up. When she went, her brother was standing there ready to welcome his sister. Everything in the room was as she had left it. Her bags packed. She was taking the evening bus back to her college. There was no more classes for her. But she had her graduation the next day, a graduation to which, none from her home were going, except for her, of course. Nishi felt outraged. But she knew her parents couldn't come. It was the death anniversary of her paternal grandfather, a man she had never known. And to her dad, it mattered more than his daughter's graduation.

"Who is Tarun?" her brother asked her. Nishi was taken aback, when her brother asked her. She tried to fathom what made her brother ask this. She noticed her phone, lying on her study table. She had placed it for charging. Her brother must have looked into her messages and her contacts. This was headed for trouble.

"A class mate." She said.

"Only a class mate?" her brother asked doubtfully. Nishi had deleted all messages from Tarun, just before she came home and Tarun never messaged her when she was home. There was no way her brother could have found out she thought.

"Yes. Why?" she lied and tried to act naturally. So, she let her body loose and moved over to her mirror and adjusted her hair.

"What is this?" her brother asked. Nishi saw her brother through the mirror. He had brought his hands forward. And within the clutches of his hand, was a pink greeting card. Nishi looked at her brother's face in the mirror. There was a grin on his face. She turned around and went towards her brother.

"There was this guy who proposed to me in college. He gave me this card."

"And why is it in your cupboard?" Her brother didn't let her finish her sentence.

"I didn't want anyone in college to know that it happened. So I hid it in my bag, and brought it home to destroy it. Apparently, I forgot." Nishi was adding one lie unto another.

"If you had brought it here to destroy the card, why did you take it from your bag and place it in your cupboard and lock it?" Her brother had caught her lie. She knew that. Her brother must have found the key, on top of the cupboard, where she had always left.

"You don't have the permission to open my cupboard and take my personal belongings." Nishi was quite mad at her brother for invading her privacy.

"I'll show this to dad, and then we will know who is at a loss?" Vinayak replied. She was not having any advantage with it. She decided to play soft to her brother.

"Look, I'll explain. Please hear me." She pleaded. Phat! Her face stung. Her brother had slapped her across the cheek. Nishi broke down. She yelled at her brother to get out and she lied down on her bed in tears. Soon she felt a hand caressing her head. She looked up. It was her brother.

"Dad is not going to like this. I know he will kill me for this. Tarun is a nice guy. We had once been partners in an assignment. Then he tried to impress me, I turned him down. But at one point he was genuine. I decided to be just friends with him. Then I soon realized that I liked him every much. Let me tell you how special he is. Until I met him, I never knew what to think about, before going to bed. I will go lie down try falling asleep. I used to despise it very much. But from the time I liked him, he is the one I think about. I wasn't able to put him out of my mind. Trust me, I knew dad won't encourage and so I tried to stay away. But no, he is special."

"Listen to me, Nishi. I have had desires like this too. To spend time with some people. But they are your desire. You see, the society won't accept."

"I know the society won't accept. But, I don't think I can accept anything else. Please don't tell dad."

"I won't say dad. I understand. Even I hate some rules in the society. We all feel rebellious. But, you have to be little better than you are, or else like every rebellion you will be crushed." She didn't understand what her brother meant.

"I promise not to say to dad. But, don't keep any trace of him, here. I wasn't looking for your valentine's card. I accidently, found it. If the same thing happens with dad, you know you can't negotiate with him. He won't let you do MBA. He will try to get you married. You know that better than I do." Her brother continued his shower of advice.

"Thanks, Vinu." She said calling her brother, by his nickname.

"If you ever have a problem with this Tarun, I'm your guy. You have any photo of him? Show me, please." Her brother playfully asked. Nishi felt that at least there was someone on her side. And the best part of it was that it was her favourite brother, Vinayak. Her brother left the room.

Nishi lay in her bed thinking, of how useful Vinayak could be. She could use him for helping out with convincing their parents to accept Tarun. Just, then she heard the front door. Her parents must have returned. She got up and latched her room door. She decided to put the card in her bag and take it to her hostel. She looked at the card. She looked back at the moment he had proposed to him. There wasn't anything romantic about it. He proposed to her on her birthday. He didn't tell it to her either. It was something huge for her. She had decided to say 'yes'. It was all magic to her. After that, the two had been to a number of places. He had said that they were dating. Something, Nishi had never dreamt she would do. It wasn't easy for the conservative girl from an orthodox Hindu family to publicly hang around with the guy. It was too modern. Eventually, she got used to it. And the conservative girl existed no longer.

She suddenly, heard a noise, it seemed like an argument. It was her father's voice that she was able to make out clearly. She went towards to the balcony. Just below the balcony was the window of her father's bedroom. From the balcony, one could easily overhear the conversation from the room below. Nishi had often heard conversations, mostly arguments coming from her dad's room through her window. She stood near the balcony, to try and overhear what was going on. She clearly could make out what was going on.

"Tomorrow she is graduating and you tell me that she is in love with some wretched fellow in her class." Her father swore. Nishi went into a jolt, when she heard it. She knew what the conversation was on. It was about Tarun.

"Dad, take this a little calmly. It is not as big as you think."

"Not as big? You think, she will ever get married if the people of Vellore see her going around the town with a guy. They will say I have grown a whore in my house." Nishi was shocked to hear her father say that about his own daughter.

"Dad, Nishi never did anything wrong." Her brother convinced.

"Wrong? She is in love with a guy. Who knows what caste is he? Where is she?"

"She is packing in her room." Her brother said.

"*Avala . . .*" she heard her father.

"Dad, don't go in there."

"What?" her dad sounded outraged.

"You go tell her anything, she will never let go of this Tarun. We shouldn't say anything to her. Soon enough he will break up with her."

"I won't let some jerk break my daughter's heart?" her father still was angry. But Nishi saw concern in that voice.

"Look, I know everything. She has told me. I have seen a lot of people like this in my own college. You oppose, their love will become strong. Leave them be, soon she will return to us, bored of the Tarun. That's the kind of feeling it is nowadays."

"You are saying, Nishi is in love. And you ask me not to do anything."

"Dad, this is not any love and all. It is an infatuation and it will be gone soon." Nishi felt disgusted. Her brother had promised secrecy only about half an hour back. And now he had crept behind her back and told everything to her father. For, the first time she felt glad, that nobody from her family was coming for her graduation. She didn't want to stay there any longer. She had been excited about the graduation for the past entire week. It took her father and her favourite brother, an hour to ruin it. Nishi picked up her bags and went down.

She knocked at her dad's door. Her dad came out followed by her brother. Surprisingly, her mother also had been in the room all the while. She simply hadn't said anything. Women in the household never had a say.

"It's time. Goodbye. I'll see you day after." She said.

"So early?"

"I have to get my graduation gown and they told me to come early, so that I can get the right size." She weaved a lie.

"Alright. You want us to drop you at the bus stop." Her brother said pretending not to have stabbed his sister in the back.

"It's at the end of the road. I can take care." She said and left the house. She was regretting for having trusted her brother.

GRADUATE OUT

NISHI GOT OFF the stage. She had done it. She was now officially. Ms Nishi B.Com. And for her graduation, her parents weren't there. Not even did Vinayak, who had promised her that he would be there, hadn't come. She wasn't sure if she was going to be allowed to do an MBA as she had aspired, after what had happened at her house. Luckily, her dad hadn't brought the issue on her, at least not yet. That way she had been able to stay cheery for her graduation. Nishi took her seat beside her boyfriend. Tarun's friends congratulated her.

"Show, me the pics." She said to Tarun, who was holding his Canon Digital camera.

"Here you go, graduate." He said and showed her the photos. The two of them laughed over the pictures. Tarun's results weren't out yet. He had finished his exams just two days back. And as always the college took two weeks to bring out the results. Two weeks after the results would be the graduation. Tarun still had a month left in the college.

When the programme ended, Nishi went into the women's restroom and took off her graduation gown and hat. She stuffed into her bag. She adjusted her hair and re-joined with Tarun.

"So, we off then?" Tarun asked.

"Yes. Bring your bike." She said. Tarun had promised her to take her to his apartments on the last day of her college. Her parents, would be there the next day, to take their daughter out of the college. And it would probably, be the last time Nishi would be at the college. She had already taken her bags, when she had gone for the Easter holidays. There was her bed and a few more of her things left at the college. She had already packed them and kept, so that she could spend the evening with Tarun.

When, Tarun brought his Yamaha bike, she climbed on it and placed her hands on his shoulder. She took her *dupatta* and covered her face. Tarun had his helmet on. It was not the first time she was riding his bike. From the time he had proposed to her on her birthday, they had been going out a number of times and Nishi had gotten familiar with the bike-ride.

The Nishi who was very much intimidated by everything around, was long gone. She, knew it was not anything that was right according to her house-traditions. But, she convinced herself that her parents weren't and couldn't be always right. And after, what her brother had done to her the previous afternoon, she really didn't know if there was a single person that she could put her trust into.

The bike dragged past all the traffic, and they went into the compound. It was not a very large apartment.

"Take the *dupatta* off your face." Tarun said. She did as he said. Tarun had said that it housed sixteen apartments. One of them, belong to his parents. Tarun's mom was there with him during the weekends. Nishi wondered, why were the final year BBA students were allowed to stay outside the hostel, while B.com students weren't. Some, rules are always weird.

There was a small garden. A slide and a see-saw was there in the garden. But both looked, so bad that it must not have been used for long. A man, was watering the lawn. Apart from that, there was no movement in the apartments.

"Doesn't anybody else lives here?" she asked.

"It's afternoon time. The children will be in school, husbands in the offices while the housewives would probably be sleeping or watching mega serials." Tarun explained. The two of them took the lift. Every floor had four rooms. Tarun's portion was in the fourth floor. It was in a secluded corner. Nishi entered in.

The place seemed cosy. A living room with two doors leading from there. Nishi left her sandals in the shoe rack that was just next to the door. A small sofa was there in the living room. There was a table behind, the sofa. There were all kinds of stuff in the table: books, clothes, some fancy showpiece. Tarun went in and kept his helmet upon that same table. There was a flat screen TV too.

One of the doors, from the living room led into a kitchen. It was small, yet looked very much empty. There were hardly any vessels, around. Tarun must hardly be doing any cooking. The other door led to a bed-room. It had a single large bed. There was also a wardrobe and a desktop computer. The bed was too large for one person, but at the same time, it wouldn't be comfortable for two people to sleep. There was a door leading from the bedroom. Nishi guessed that it had to be the bathroom.

"Nice house." She complimented.

"Yes. Just perfect for my needs." He replied.

"So, what you have in mind for this evening?"

"How about we go to a restaurant? My friend told me about a place that would be good." Tarun suggested.

"I think I have a better idea." Nishi expressed.

"What?"

"We'll dine here."

"Here. Nice idea."

"So, what have you got in your kitchen?"

"Oh! Nothing much. I think there's some Coke and ice cream."

"Idiot, I'm talking about food, not snacks." She mocked at him.

"Alright, is there any place to buy stuff, near the compound?" Nishi continued.

"There's a mini-supermarket, not far from here."

"A mini-supermarket?" Nishi was puzzled.

"That's how they advertise."

"Alright. Drop me there. I'll buy stuff, get something to cook and eat, we'll watch a movie."

"How long are you planning to stay here?"

"Oh! I love this place. I think I might stay here." She said looking into his eyes. Tarun smiled back. She knew she was blushing. The two of them got off to prepare for the night. He dropped her at the mini-supermarket. Nishi bought a readymade chapatti pack and a gravy mix. Tarun soon picked her up and they returned to the apartment. Nishi began to cook. Tarun was setting up the player and the speakers for the movie.

"Hey, mail me the pictures that you took today." She asked of Tarun. Tarun simply agreed and went off into his room along with his Digital camera. About a few minutes later, he yelled from his room.

"Hey, I have mailed it." He said.

"Can you go into my mail and make sure it hasn't gone to my spam folder?" she asked back.

"Yes. But what is your password."

"Tarun245. No caps. No space." She replied. After a few minutes, Tarun entered into the kitchen.

"You were right. It had gone into the spam folder. I had to move into your inbox."

"Thanks." She said smiling and playfully sprinkled some water from her fingers on his face. Tarun just wiped it.

"I'll watch TV." He said and walked out.

"Hey, get back."

"What?"

"Typical male attitude: Relax in front of the TV when the women do the chores. I won't let you be like that." She feigned anger.

"What you want, ma'am?" Tarun was pretending to be submissive. They two of them joked around. Eventually, they sat down to eat. Tarun was full of compliments at Nishi's cooking. She modestly said that it were all nothing but, artificial mixes, that she had purchased. The taste that they relished were all from the artificial flavours that the manufacturer had added.

"Hey what happens, tomorrow?" Tarun asked. It was no ordinary question. It mattered very much. They had been together, till the end of their course. But what was to come?

"Your parents will never accept me, will they?" Tarun asked a second question, as Nishi was just being silent.

"Look, tomorrow is important and even more important to me is you. I trusted Vinayak very much and all he did was stab me in the back. There is only one thing I believe in this world right now, our love. And this is a beautiful evening in our love. Let's enjoy this moment, we will talk about it tomorrow morning." Nishi replied calmly. Beyond tomorrow, there was no guarantee, that she could see him. It was scary to her. She didn't want to confront it. She postponed it to the next day, she had to come up with something tomorrow. But, she did love Tarun. He was the only person she trusted in the world. She couldn't let him go. He was special.

To her relief, Tarun changed the topic. The fear went into a recess in her mind. They sat down to watch *Sarvam*. It was a recently released romantic movie. The reviews were looking good. She had been hoping to go to the theatre to watch it. But she had missed it. And now she got the chance to see it with her boyfriend at his place. The two of them sat together as the movie began. Arms entwined they got engrossed in the movie, passing comments now and then.

Halfway, through the movie, her phone rang. It was from her roommate, Ramya.

"No sense of timing." She cursed her roommate and hung it up. She sent her a text.

```
Having a special evening. Don't interrupt.
```

Tarun was distracted form the movie. He was looking into the phone. She locked the keypad and shoved it down her bag. She also took off her dupatta and shoved it into her bag. She didn't want her evening to be interrupted. She apologized to Tarun and sat down as they watched the movie.

When the movie ended, Tarun turned off the TV and the player with the remote. They were sitting on the sofa with locked hands. Nishi's hand was sweating, but she didn't want to leave Tarun's hand. He got up. She too did, without letting go of his hand. Even he was grasping her hand back. It seemed that even Tarun didn't want to let go of his girl. They both walked to the bedroom door. Nishi felt it, the sexual tension that loomed around. She understood how he felt. She too felt the same way. She had anticipated it already. But, she was too embarrassed to start it. The way they stood there was no way they could have started off without an awkward start. She was flustered. They looked at each other, for a moment and immediately she turned away out of guilt.

"We should get some sleep." He told her.

"Yes. How?" she followed his lead, asking where they should sleep. Tarun turned towards her, still holding her hand,

"You can take the bed." He said, his voice trailing off.

"Okay." She softly whispered, without raising her head. She looked towards his chest. He was so close, she could feel his breath. She slowly leaned against his bedroom door. The door moved and hit the wall. She adjusted herself, to the position of the door. He leaned forward. He sent his finger under her chin and lifted it up. Her soft chin pressed against his fingers. He placed his other hand into her tresses. They flowed in between them. He inched her head forward. She felt his warm breath on her face. His eyes were almost shut. She too closed her eyes. His lips pressed against hers. She parted hers to let his enter. He tucked his upper lip between her lips and sucked on her lower lip gently. Nishi, felt a surge of passion gush through her body. It was overwhelming.

Nishi had never expected that she would have sex out of her marriage, yet here she was making out with a guy whom her parents would never approve. But that seemed very much trivial to her passion-driven head. She placed her hand around Tarun's neck, entangling them. He pulled her closer. She wasn't leaning against the bedroom door anymore. She felt her breasts touch his shirt buttons, through her *salwar*. She inched more closely, letting them get caught in between the passion. It seemed like they were kissing forever. Tarun slightly broke the kiss and moved a little away. Nishi knew what Tarun was trying. He tried to take the action to the bed. She moved along, trying not to break the lip lock they had.

It seemed, like the distance between, the door and the bed was forever long. They moved until they collapsed on the bed. Tarun had crashed on his back. Nishi, fell right on top of him. Her entire body was resting on Tarun. Tarun was still holding her, but his hands had moved away from her tress. It had gone down to the level of her waist and was sliding lower. All, the while, the lips never ceased what they had been doing. Nishi spread her legs slightly to get herself more comfortable. Tarun took his hands off her back. He brought it up to his chest, slightly pushing her away. Their lips parted and she looked down at what Tarun's hands were trying to do. He was removing his buttons. Nishi, decided to help along. She pushed his hands away and undid the last two buttons off his shirt by herself. The shirt wouldn't come off completely, unless Tarun got up. She moved away, so that Tarun could get up and take off his shirt. She was kneeling on the bed, just beside Tarun's hip. Tarun got up. Nishi decided it was time, she too removed her clothes. She caught the lower end of her *salwar* and pulled it up to remove it off through her head. Halfway through, she felt a pair of hands over hers. She wasn't able to see the hands, with her *salwar* blocking her vision. She thought that it had to be Tarun wanting to disrobe her. She decided to let her boyfriend to go along with it. She lifted her hands, so that Tarun could remove her *salwar*. But, Tarun rather than pulling it out of her head. He put it back onto her body. She looked at him a bit surprised.

"No. I can't" Tarun said looking down.

"What's wrong?" Her voice sounded weird, after the passionate connection they had had. Tarun looked ashamed.

"We shouldn't do this." Tarun wasn't looking at her.

"Why?" she said trying to make eye contact with him.

"I'm feeling bad." Here was a guy refusing sex, with his girlfriend. Nishi wondered what was wrong. She realized, it must have been the conversation they had had earlier.

"Do you think I'm doing this because, my parents will agree to our marriage, when I say them that we have had sex? Don't even think of it that way. If I try and use this as an excuse for our love, my father will rip me into two pieces." She told him.

"No, it's nothing like that." Tarun said still evading her eyes.

"You love me?" She questioned. And immediately, Tarun's eyes caught hers.

"I do love you. I have never loved you more than I do right now. This evening was the best time of my life. I even enjoyed the little bit of sex that we had now. I loved it. And I want it. But I will never be able to forgive myself if I do it with you now." Tarun said looking into her eyes. He sounded genuine.

"I'm sorry if I had been the one who rushed this onto you. I had a hard time at home. I was feeling betrayed. I think it was all that acting up." Nishi apologized adjusting her dress. She didn't want Tarun to think the fault was on him.

"No, I knew there was every possibility that our relationship could get physical if I bring you here. I guessed. But please, let's not do it today." There was something going on within Tarun. Nishi decided not to ruin the night by trying to persuade him to come out with that. She decided to reserve it for later.

"We could snuggle to sleep." Tarun suggested, trying to make a smile. Nishi agreed. Tarun put on a t-shirt and a pant. Nishi had no other clothes. Wearing her *salwar*, she fell asleep in Tarun's arms.

CHAPTER 3

"IS THAT ALL?" Yashan asked.

"What?"

"It ended abruptly." Yashan said.

"Beyond that, it gets boring. And before I began I told you that it was incomplete, didn't I?"

"It's okay. We are interested." Rohit said, turning round from the steering wheel.

"No, I mean, things got worse. Anyone can guess what would have happened to a college couple, when I say it got worse. The usual stuff that you come across everywhere." Nishi said, indirectly trying to make them understand what happened.

"It got worse?" Rohit asked.

"Why wouldn't it? The same stuff happened to you guys. When all is well, something goes terribly wrong."

"Actually I was trying to figure out how it could have gotten worse." Yashan said.

"Did he break up with you?" It was Rohit being inquisitive into the last detail.

"They were having sex. Who would break up after sex? Her father should have found that she was in love with this guy. Maybe her father got angry and did something to split them up." Yashan made a guess.

"Only in your twisted mind, will such things happen?" Rohit mocked at his friend's explanation.

"Guys, guys. Both of you are right. He broke up with me and my father did find out about it and as a dad he did what he had to do to separate us further. And Yashan, I never had sex with him. We just made out. Don't say such stuff." Nishi explained. The guys fell silent.

"That should have been hard on you. I'm sorry." Rohit empathized with her. In the two years they had known each other, it was the first time she was sharing what had happened to her. Nishi had always, been a shy, secretive girl. She had only two friends in the college. They were Yashan and Rohit.

"No, I'll tell you guys exactly what happened: I woke up the next day, hugging a pillow. He was gone. I saw a lot number of messages and missed calls, most of them from my roommates, trying to warn me not to go to Tarun's apartment. The messages said that he proposed to me only because, it was a bet. A bet, to get into my pants. I didn't believe her. I went to the hostel, to vacate the college forever. And in the hostel, was my dad, waiting to ambush me. He had found out that I hadn't stayed in the hostel the previous night. A big drama he made. Blah. Blah. Blah. Luckily, Vinayak managed to convince my dad to allow me to do my MBA."

"God! What happened to Tarun?"

"The number you are trying to reach is currently not reachable." Nishi said mimicking the voice you get in the phone when a person is out of reception area. The guys didn't reply. After a few minutes, they saw a signpost

'PONDICHERRY WELCOMES YOU

KEEP THE CITY CLEAN'

"We are in Pondicherry." Rohit declared.

"Did you really take three solid hours to tell your incomplete story?"

"No, man. Remember we got off the topic completely when we saw that creepy looking cucumber vendor at the tollbooth on the way." Rohit said recollecting from his memory.

"Yeah, it got us diverted for quite some time." Nishi agreed.

"How are we going to find the exact marriage hall in the entire city?" asked Rohit doubtfully.

"Use Nishi's phone." Yashan suggested. The mobiles had evolved by leaps and bounds. The kind of phones, that let you only call and message, were long gone out of the market. The latest thing was something, everybody called it the Android. Half the people who owned Android phones did not know what exactly Android was. But, they simply boasted that their phone had Android. They thought it was a new feature, like Wi-Fi and Bluetooth. Half of them didn't realize that it was an Operating System, just like Windows was on all their PCs. Yashan knew this stuff better than his two other friends.

Nishi had a Sony smartphone. It was the new model and had all the cool specs.

"How are you going to find a marriage hall?"

"Sanjana tagged a photo of herself and had uploaded in Facebook. I'm pretty sure her location was tagged too. Her phone, which I'm quite sure is Android too, must have got checked in the Google Maps. So find, her current location, and I'm sure the closest marriage hall to her location is where we need to go." Yashan suggested.

"Seriously? You think, it will work. Technology is overrated, man." Rohit complained.

"Watch the magic." Yashan said, he took Nishi's phone from the dash board and fidgeted into it. After about five minutes, he cried out in despair,

"Aw, crap."

"What?" Nishi asked.

"Apparently, according to Google maps, Sanjana was standing over the Bay of Bengal, while she took the photo." Yashan explained.

"Ha! Screw technology. Ask a guy who is walking down the roadside. Best option." Said Rohit.

"C'mon Rohit. You can't ask go to a guy and ask him to direct us to Tarun's wedding. Nobody will know. We need an address." Nishi explained the stupidity of her idea.

"Moreover, this is a booze capital. Half of them would be drunkards staggering home. You want to rely on a drunk's direction, rather than Google's?" Yashan criticised Tarun's suggestion.

"What do we do?" Nishi questioned.

"We use a bit of common sense. Google might be a slightly wrong. The location it shows of Nishi is not far from here. Let's approximate Google's positioning. We will have the answer."

"What?" Rohit hardly understood, what his friend was trying to do.

"Let me see." Nishi said and plucked the phone from Yashan. Rohit slowed down the car to one side and parked it on the side of the road.

"Listen, according to my phone. Tarun's wedding is about 800m from The BeachView restaurant and 23km from the centre of Pondicherry. We just crossed the restaurant a few moments ago and the milestone up ahead says Pondicherry is 25km from here. I'm saying we are not far off. Now we ask a roadside guy, for a marriage hall in this neighbourhood and we have it." Nishi explained once again.

"That is exactly what I suggested." Yashan added in.

"I'll ask someone." Said Rohit and got down the car.

"Nishi, would you mind if I ask you something?" Yashan asked her, when Rohit had got out.

"No, what?"

"Did, Tarun dump you?"

"It was true, that he walked away. No information, whatsoever. Everyone, told so many things about him. But, our relationship never ended. He never dumped me, if you ask me. Why are you asking?" Nishi explained. It must have been hard on her, Yashan kept silence.

"By the way, what is the plan tonight?" Nishi asked Yashan.

"Hey, to come to Tarun's wedding was your idea. What are you asking me for the plan?" Yashan had been thinking, that Nishi had everything planned out.

"My idea is just a general one. Give him something to think of and he won't think of his blues. I need your help to keep him distracted, else he will find out."

"Then Sanjana." Nishi questioned.

"As I said earlier, she isn't going to be there. We'll leave him alone and he will definitely search for her. Umm . . . . I have nothing else. It'll work out. Shouldn't be that hard." Yashan answered.

"Hopefully, for Rohit's and my sake." Nishi said. Soon Rohit returned after enquiring about the hotel. He got into the car and started the engine.

"No luck. There are no marriage halls nearby. The closest is about ten kilometres from here."

"Really?" Nishi asked.

"Yes. Come up with some new strategy." Rohit told as they continued to drive past. They drove along trying to see if there was any sign of marriage around the area.

"Oh! This should be the hotel the guy said." Said Rohit as they drove past a resort. They were getting closer to Pondicherry.

"Hotel?"

"Yea. One dumb-fuck at a tea shop said that there was a hotel when I asked him for the marriage."

"Hold it." Nishi said aloud, signalling him to stop the car. "Are you guys sure the wedding is tonight?" Nishi asked.

"Sanjana's photo said she was at Tarun's wedding." Rohit said, recollecting from the post he had seen on the Facebook wall.

"Tarun's wedding could have been just the name of the event he had created on Facebook. Because today is not a *mukoortha naal* and tomorrow is one."

"Yes. No South Indian Hindu family conducts marriages on non-*mukoortha naal*" added in Rohit.

"So, it should have probably been a reception that, your friend had posted a pic of. The wedding must be scheduled for tomorrow. And it is a possibility that a reception could be at a hotel or the resort we just passed by."

"Okay, I didn't see that coming." Rohit said.

"Let's check the hotel, then."

The drove along the road and found the hotel. It was more of a beach resort than a hotel. There was a large granite plaque on the compound wall reading, 'FRANÇAIS BEACH RESORT'

Rohit, drove the car into the road, that led in. The road was flanked on both sides by coconut trees. There was a wooden cabin, amidst the trees. They parked the car, on the road and headed in.

The lady at the bell-desk smiled as they approached. She was a wearing a crimson sari. It wasn't like the sari any women in India wore. It was wrapped around her body tightly. Even the *pallu* was twisted around the hip and was neatly pinned on the other end of the hip.

"Good evening, sir. How may I help you?"

"We are here for a wedding." Yashan said.

"No, a reception." Nishi corrected.

"Mr Anand will help you." She said pointing right behind them. The three turned around. A man in an ivory-white shirt and a navy blue waistcoat that had a lighter shade of blue waves on it approached them,

"Good evening, ma'am and gentleman." Said the man in the waistcoat.

"We're here for the wed-, I mean the reception." Yashan corrected himself.

"Can I have your invitation?"

"No, we actually saw the event on Facebook."

"Oh! Give me your Facebook profile name, please." The man said.

"What?"

"Sir, the reception and the wedding is meant for people with invites only. To relatives, an invitation card had been given like the traditional style. They need to have their invites to enter. And with friends, most of them have been invited over Facebook."

"Oh!" Nishi said softly and turned around looking at her friends, who also had a similar reaction on their face.

"I'm Vignesh Kumar." Yashan cooked up a lie. The man looked into a list he had.

"I'm sorry, your name isn't there." The man, Mr Anand said. Yashan immediately let out a mocking laugh saying, "It must be a mistake. The three of us are his friends. I'm very sure at least one of our names are in there. This is Archana and he is Arun." Yashan tried to cover up his lie. But from the look on the man's face he knew his cover was blown.

"Look, sir. You might really be friends with Tarun, but I'm going to need proof." He said.

"I know it sounds bad. Look, we have come all the way from Chennai. Tarun is the one who will be disappointed if he finds out that we weren't allowed entry. We are really his friends. How else we could have known there was a reception to be held in this place."

"I'm afraid that I can't let you in. The orders are from Tarun's father. He is the one who pays me and I must follow his orders. But, if you will let me, I will-"

"What is going on here?" asked an old man. He was wearing a *pattu shirt and a pattu veshti*. He had a pair of thick glasses up his nose. His forearm and forehead were lined with wrinkles. He had grey sparse hair on his head.

"It's nothing, sir." Said the man, who had been refusing the three of them an entry. The man's voice sounded humble in front of the old man. Yashan realized that this man was working for the old man.

"Let me explain, sir. We are actually friends of Tarun." Yashan intervened.

"I'm Tarun's grandfather-in-law." He said with a smile.

"We had no idea, that there we would be asked for the invites. We have come from Chennai and now we are being asked to go away." Yashan explained.

"I'm very sorry." The old man apologized. "I told my son, not to have all this strict formalities, but he wouldn't listen. He didn't want any strangers coming in only to eat the food we have made for our dear ones. But, he is wrong. That is never the way of a Tamilian. We used to be known for our hospitality, but look at this, pushing out someone out of a marriage. I know it is rude and I'm sorry."

"Oh, no please, you don't have to apologize." Rohit said to the old man.

"I have to. Earlier, this evening there was a girl who had come without an invite. She had come alone and this chauffeur fellow is trying to chase her away. Then I had to personally take her inside." Said the old man and turned towards Anand, "Escort them to the reception." Anand tried to argue but the old man was his boss, he couldn't. Yashan had a guess on whom that lonely girl might be. He had got lucky. This old man was actually helping them the second time that night. But, neither Rohit nor Nishi knew that.

Anand, the guy in blue waistcoat, did as he was asked to. Rohit went off and parked his car. He put on his bag over his shoulders. The three of them were being led to the reception hall by Anand. He didn't seem happy. Yashan was beginning to feel something was wrong. The man who was escorting them wasn't taking them to any banquet hall. They were heading to the shore. Yashan decided to remain patient and pretend that he hadn't realized it yet. And when they reached the shore, there was a small boat stand. Three boats stood there. They were all motorised ones.

"Can you drive a motor boat?" Anand asked them.

"What? Where have you brought us?" Nishi asked.

"The wedding and the reception are held over there." said Anand pointing towards the sea. Rohit thought the man was playing a joke upon them, but when he looked there he sensed that he wasn't. Out in the sea, at the place where the horizon was, they saw a cruise. Its deck adorned in lights. Brightly beaming from the sea.

"What the hell?"

"Who conducts a marriage on a ship" exulted Yashan.

"The very person whom I work for." Anand said calmly.

"I don't think we can make it that far into the sea by our self."

"Yes we can." Rohit said excitedly and stepped into one of those motor boats. Nishi was shocked with Rohit's response. Seeing her expression, Rohit went up to her ear and whispered,

"We are here to teach Tarun a lesson, we would be better off without a waistcoat-wearing butler."

"Fine." Nishi said. It was her own idea that had led to this. She prayed to herself, that the situation wouldn't get bad. The three of them stepped into the boat and took off into the seas, towards the cruise. The man in the waistcoat still stood at the boat station as the boat was getting further and further.

"My God! I didn't think your boyfriend was filthy rich." Said Rohit.

"No, he wasn't. His family was only a well-to-do one."

"It must be the girl's side that's rich." Yashan said.

"Yashan, looks like my phone was correct about Sanjana's location." Nishi suggested.

"But, it was the old man who told us that there was a hotel here." Rohit objected.

"Oh! Please, don't give the credit to some old beggar that you met. This is not a hotel, either. It's a resort." Yashan grumbled.

CHAPTER 4

THE MOMENT THEY got onto the deck. There were two women adorned in costly silk sari. Their faces layered with makeup. He held their hands with the palms touching each other, signalling a *'vanakkam.'* They were actually in a room. They was only one other way leading out. They went through the door and found themselves in a corridor. They walked along and went into the first door that was open. It led into a large hall. The hall wasn't large like the marriage halls one sees in the cities, but it was grand. There were floral decorations along the ceiling. The entire decoration was themed to a teal blue probably to match the blue sea. It gave a hall a pleasant appearance. The three friends took a seat in the hall. The stage was placed exactly opposite to the entrance door. On the left side of the stage was a smaller stage. On the main stage, there was a music troop that was playing a classic *Ilayaraja* song. The three of them scanned around. There were few people seated here and there doing some chatting. None of the people there, were anyone they knew. Nor did those people notice them.

"So, what now?" Rohit asked them.

"Let's see." Said Yashan and began to wonder what they were going to lie to Rohit next. "The bride and the groom, both aren't anywhere around here."

"If tomorrow, is the marriage, tonight must be the stag party for Tarun."

"What will the girl be doing?" Rohit asked.

"Why are you asking? We have nothing to do with the girl. It's only Tarun we are going to deal with." Said Nishi.

"Oh, I don't know, just for an information I asked. Nothing else." Rohit explained.

"We have to ask around and find out, where is Tarun then?" Yashan suggested.

"I think he will be drunk if he is at a stag party." Said Rohit.

"I don't know. Listen, we will split up and work." Nishi had an idea, on how to get Rohit off their tails. "What we will do is, myself and Yashan will look out for Tarun and see what needs to be done. And how it has to be done. You, Rohit hang around in the hall. We might need you to create a distraction. In any case, I'll call you and say what to do, alright?" Nishi suggested to them. Yashan knew this was all part of Nishi's plan. But there was something telling him, not to trust Nishi with her scheme. But, he simply decided to nod his head. He decided to voice his thoughts in Rohit's absence.

"I'm okay with it. We are here for you. You call the shots." Rohit said.

"Fine, come along with me Yashan." She said and rose up from the chair. Yashan followed her. But, just then Rohit handed over his college bag to him.

"What is this for?" Yashan asked out of surprise. He had wanted to ask it earlier.

"Open it." Yashan opened it and sent his hand in to look to see if there was anything. There was a small packet, with some white powder in it. Yashan was shocked beyond words.

"Is this cocaine?" he almost yelled. Nishi shushed him. Some people around, were staring at the three of them. Yashan realized his stupidity.

"It is called GHB, a date-rape drug."

"What the FUCK is this for? Why did you bring it here" Yashan questioned.

"Calm down. Did the two of you come up with anything on how to get the guy out of here? It's for that purpose. In any ordinary marriage itself, it would be tough enough to get the groom or the bride outside. But this is a ship. We simply can't run away. There is a stretch of water. This will help you with it. I simply thought we might find it useful. Given, the circumstances I think it will be essential."

"What? ARE YOU NUTS?" Nishi hadn't expected Rohit would take the abduction so seriously. He had managed to smuggle illegal drugs from the state of Tamil Nadu to Pondicherry. If they had been caught at any of the toll booth, they all would have been in a load of trouble.

"Look, you simply have to mix it in his drink. And luckily, the groom should be at his stag party high on booze. I'm guessing he wouldn't notice you people slip stuff into his drink. My friend told it will take about fifteen minutes to knock him out. The effect lasts for from three to eight hours. It's the perfect stuff."

"Dude, such off-label drugs aren't safe. It's illegal to use it even. Abduction by itself is a crime. Possession of drugs is making it worse." Yashan said. He hadn't expected his friend to come up with something of such sort either. It was way out of their league.

"How did you get this?" Nishi asked.

"There is a guy for such stuff almost in every corner of the street. It was a guy in our college. I asked him and he gave me."

"Listen, get the bag." Said Yashan said pulling the bag away. He didn't want Rohit to do anything stupid with the stuff. "I'm going along with her and we will decide on what should be done and how it is going to be done. I realize that you very sensibly thought of this. But let's see what happens around here. You are only here to create a distraction. Don't do anything else in the name of help."

"*Thayavu seithu da,* don't screw us up here." Nishi pleaded. Rohit gave them an innocent look, as if he hadn't done anything. It was true, all that Rohit wanted to do was help his friend. He just didn't realize to what extreme he had gone to do it.

Yashan and Nishi decided to leave the hall to decide on what to do. There was a door at the left of the hall. From the doorstep, he took one look into the hall from where he stood. He saw Rohit rise up from his chair and head towards the corner of the hall. There were glasses of water placed over a table. He decided to leave Rohit and continued to walk with Nishi. They went through it and found themselves on the upper deck of the cruise. There was a lower level of the deck, wherein the food was placed. Yashan's mouth watered, but he silenced his hunger. There was more important things that needed attention than his stomach.

"Where is Tarun?" Nishi was asking a lady in a green sari.

"The stag party is actually two levels below." The lady replied.

"It's a stag party, I'm a girl I don't think I can go in there."

"No, no. You follow the corridor to the other side. You will find stairs. Descend down. You will find yourself in a corridor again. There will be two rooms. The one on the right is the room where the stag party is going on. The one on the left is an indoor games room. You will find Tarun there. He doesn't drink. I went down a few minutes ago, he was sitting by himself in the indoor games room." She said.

"Thanks aunty." Nishi said and the two of them drifted away from the lady. They stood near the railings.

"What are you thinking?" Yashan asked. Nishi returned a blank stare. "Why are you asking around where is Tarun? We are here tonight for Rohit's sake." Yashan tried explaining.

"Yes, Even I brought you guys for Rohit's sake only. But, what I said about myself and Tarun was also true. He hadn't given me an explanation at all. We simply drifted apart. I think I deserve to know."

"Look, you may want answers from Tarun. But don't mess it up for Rohit. We are here for him. We can't sail on two boats. We need to focus on one thing tonight. And it is going to be Rohit. Nothing else. You better agree." Yashan was starting to get annoyed.

"Look, I know tonight is about Rohit. I understand that it is a crucial moment of his life and we have to do what it takes to bring him to his senses. I suggested the whole thing so that we might get Rohit some peace, after all, it's a wedding here. And it's supposed to be a joyous occasion. But, please understand me, Yashan. Tonight is the last night of Tarun's bachelor life. It is the only time I have to end the relationship that we had. I must complete my story too. Else I will never be able to move on."

"I get it now. You brought us here, not for Rohit but for your own sake. You needed a mode of transport. You are simply using us. How can you do this to us, Nishi? I'm out of here." Yashan was almost yelling. He was furious with what Nishi was trying to do. Nishi broke down into tears.

"I am sorry. But, I swear I will never try to use you guys. You are the only friends that I have. How can I break your trust? Please believe me. I had no intention of talking to Tarun when we started off from Chennai. But looking back at those days telling you people those haunted memories, I just got desperate to know why we had broken up. Please trust me." She said sobbing.

"Look, I am sorry that I told you were using us. Of all the people in the world, you are a very nice person and I know you wouldn't do it to us. But, what I'm concerned about is the level of crime that we are indulging here. Rohit has smuggled drugs across borders. You are considering abduction." Yashan tried to reason.

A faint smile appeared on Nishi's lips, "Who said anything about an abduction? I only told that because it got Rohit excited. I know Rohit went over the limits by procuring the drugs. But I have no such intention. I just want to have a private word with Tarun. Nothing else." She explained. Yashan felt quite relieved when Nishi had told that she had no intention of abduction.

"I'm sorry. So, what are you going to do? What if someone sees you?" Yashan asked.

"I don't think, any elders will go down towards the stag party. I remember from college, that Tarun never drank alcohol. And that lady just mentioned the very same thing. So, he must still be in his proper senses. I will just go and try to see if I can have a word with him. If it isn't happening, I will give up." She said.

"Alright. Do not push the limits. Tonight it's still not your night." Yashan agreed. She at least had more sense than his friend Rohit.

*   *   *

Rohit's throat felt dry as a desert. He looked around. He saw the glass cups filled with water, placed on a table in a corner of the hall. He walked in the direction of the tumblers. He tried to think of what he could do to create a distraction. He had to do something that wouldn't draw too much attention upon him. That was the only way, he too could escape without getting caught. He glanced at his watch. It was 1:00 am. He had been through one hell of a mental turmoil, ever since he had the dream. It was in a way creepy. Only the previous night he had dreamt of her and she was not far away from him right now. She had told him that she probably will never ever return to India. And yet here she was in the same place. He hadn't spotted her anywhere in the wedding. Ever since he stepped into the restaurant, his mind had been distracted with the thoughts of meeting her, his eyes had been busy scanning the place for her. If Sanjana was here, probably Ranjana should be here too. So, there were two of them around. The chances of spotting her was doubled.

Every once and then his thoughts flew back to Lav, whom he had broken up with just a few hours back; his interview that he almost threw away, his friends whom he was on the verge of betraying. The reality that he had to face, was haunting. But, he didn't want to think about them. He decided to leave it temporarily without confronting the issues. He let his mind drown in the fantasy of meeting Sanjana tonight. Deep down, in his mind, he knew that he had agreed to help Nishi without any second thoughts only because Sanjana might be there.

He thought he was over Sanjana long time ago. He had dismissed her as just a crush and cast her away into his long-forgotten memories. But, the possibility of meeting her brought up emotions in his mind. Firstly he was curious how different she would be. It had been eight years. Secondly, he was interested to know what had become of her life. From the proud, football captain that he was back then, he knew he had become a man, filled with humility compared to the proud teenager he once was. She too must have changed from what she had been. He even tried to imagine how Sanjana would react if he met her.

Rohit picked up one of those glass cups he had seen from there. Only when he picked it up he realized it wasn't glass at all. It was those plastic cups that you get. It was all fogged up from the cold water that had been poured in. The fog in the cup gave it its glass appearance. He lifted and took it to his lips.

Just then, he noticed a pair of hands come from the behind and before he reacted, it covered his eyes. The hand felt very soft, like that of a woman. The touch of the hands radiated warmth into his eyes. Startled, Rohit spilt a little bit of the cold water over his T-shirt. And it trickled underneath and touched his chest, making him feel a chill shock across the midline of his chest. But, that wasn't bothering Rohit. His mind had been busy with the hands covering his vision. It wouldn't be Nishi or Yashan, because they were busy with their scheming. He knew that there was just one other person on board that he knew. And he very much wanted those hands to belong to the same person.

"Sanjana." He said and lifter her hands off his face. She immediately put her hands over her mouth. In front of him stood a woman. Her face with features resembling the girl whose name he had just blurted. Her hair looked different and longer. She appeared to be of the same height she had been when she was at school. It had been eight years. She was wearing a *chudithar*. It looked like it was a party wear. She was smiling at him. The smile hadn't changed at all. It was still the same smile that she had given him eight years ago.

*   *   *

Nishi walked along with Yashan, following the ladies' instructions. On the other side of the corridor. There was a flight of stairs. Nishi peered down.

"One sec. Just hold on." Yashan blurted and sprinted up the stairs. Nishi wondered where he was going. She was the one who had something to do and now Yashan had gone somewhere. She called out,

"Do I have to come?" he didn't respond. She decided to wait for him. But, Yashan didn't take more than a jiffy to return.

"Listen, I will wait for you up there. Go down and talk, when you are done come up." Yashan said to her.

"Alright. Fine." Nishi said and began descending down the stairs. She wondered how it was going to be when he faced her. She wondered what it would be like to see her ex-boyfriend again.

"Don't push the limits. If you can't get to talk to him. Do return. Do not risk anything. We are basically here for Rohit." Said Yashan disturbing her line of thoughts. Nishi simply nodded and continued her descent. The thoughts returned to her mind. Her love story had been incomplete. They might have broken up, but there was no proper explanation or reason. It was a complicated tale. But there was one thing she hoped for *'Will this night complete my love story? Or is there more to it?*

She noticed the two rooms. One was labelled as a 'Banquet Hall' while the other was labelled as 'Indoor Games room'. She went into the indoor games room hoping to find Tarun in there. The room was all lit. But it was empty. Tarun must have returned to the banquet hall. She tried to weigh the options: was it safe to enter a room of drunk men, to find Tarun. With the thought in her mind, she turned around to leave the indoor games room. Just then, she heard a door open. She turned around. It was the *Men's room* door. Out of it stepped a guy, in a denim blue shirt and a crème coloured cargo pants. He was adjusting the zipper on his pants. She recognized him. It was the one she had come all the way from Chennai for. Nishi tried to turn away.

"Nishi?" the voice called out. She turned around. She didn't say anything.

"Wow, I never expected you, here." At first Tarun sounded excited, but then it was like as if he tried to mask his excitement, his voice dulled down. Nishi's broken memories flashed through her

177

mind again. It had been four years. He looked almost the same guy she had been in love with. It was only the hair that had changed.

"I can't believe that you came." Tarun said. *'He can't believe that I'm here? So, was he hoping for me to come to the wedding?'* Nishi's thoughts raced.

"I was hoping you would come." Tarun added, as if he had read her mind. Nishi's inner voice panicked, *'Oh my God! Why did he want me to be here?'* She decided to voice her thoughts out.

"Why were you hoping for me to come?" she asked with a tone of suspicion.

*   *   *

Yashan walked along with Nishi, following the lady's instructions. They found the set of stairs on the other end of the corridor. Yashan looked up towards the set of stairs that were headed upwards. He saw the sky. It seemed to be leading to the upper deck.

"One sec. Just hold on." He said to Nishi and climbed up the stairs. He had guessed right. It was leading to the upper deck. He climbed down and returned to Nishi,

"Listen, I will wait for you up there. It's an open deck. I will be enjoying the view. Go down and talk, when you are done come up." He said to Nishi

"Alright. Fine." Nishi said and began descending down the stairs.

"Don't push the limits. If you can't get to talk to him. Do return. Do not risk anything. We are basically here for Rohit." Said Yashan with a tone of warning. Nishi simply nodded and continued her descent.

Yashan began to climb up those stairs. When he climbed onto the top of the balcony, cool breeze slapped across his face. He went and leaned over the railings that faced the back of the ship. From there he could see the lower deck. There were couple of people sitting on chairs arranged in a circle. They seemed to be having a good time. He could hear sounds of laughter from them. He decided to leave them there and decided to lean on the railings that faced the front of the cruise. Just then, he noticed that there was another set of stairs that led down from the stairs other than the one had climbed. He peered down, it looked similar to the other stairs. Yashan leaned against the railings. The light from the front of the ship had lit the waters up ahead. Below the ship the waters were swooshing. The wind sweeping his face was an amazing feeling. He stretched out his hand like Jack from Titanic. Sadly, he had no Rose.

Yashan was beginning to doubt how the night was going to end. He had formulated a plan to get Rohit out of his craziness. But, right now, there was something else he had to be concerned over. Nishi hadn't brought them to the wedding to take Rohit's mind off his troubles. It was also for her selfish reason: to confront Tarun. Yashan wasn't worried if her plan for Rohit might fail if her confrontation with Tarun goes wrong.

He felt a bit disappointed with what Nishi had done. She was a good friend to both of them, yet what she did was unfair. His instincts kept warning him that something was about get wrong. Yashan tried to push aside those fears and tried to focus his thoughts on something else. Just then, he heard the sound of anklets. The sound of anklets always reminded him of his once best friend, Yamuna. He looked in the direction of the sound. It was coming from the stairs. Someone was coming up. His line of thoughts which he was already struggling to focus got completely distracted. He cursed under his breath, *'You have got to be kidding me.'* Yashan decided to pretend like he never heard anything and concentrated on the scenery. He scanned the coastline. There were a few lights

Soon enough, a female figure emerged from the stairs. Instinctively, he turned around. He couldn't make out the details clearly. The deck wasn't brightly lit. He strained his eyes to see the person. She was wearing what appeared to be Prussian blue sari.

"Yash." A familiar voice erupted from the person who had just climbed up. Yashan was thrown aback. It could never be. There was no plausible reason as to why she would be here. He tried to see if there were any other explanation. She took a step closer and he recognised her.

"Yamuna?" he asked with a doubt. He knew he was quite sure that it was Yamuna. But, he said her name so slow, that it sounded like a question. A thousand memories came flooding back to him.

BOOK 3: YAMUNA

New Year,

NEW BEGINNINGS

IT HAD BEEN almost half an hour. Yashan couldn't make out what the voices were saying. He was squatting down on the top of the terrace over the classroom block in their school. He knew the two of them, who were standing on the terrace of the main building and talking between themselves. The two couldn't see him from there. It was only earlier this month he had come to know that they had something going on in between them. But he hadn't expected them to be here at this time. If he had known he would have never come to the terrace.

He had no intention of overhearing them either. The only reason, he decided upon lying down and pretending that he wasn't there was that, he didn't want to startle the two of them. It seemed like they were having a nice moment together. And he didn't want to be the one who ruined it for Rohit, whom he had known for the past seven years. He sat there for some time trying not to pay attention to what the two were talking. Then, he heard something he could make out.

"So, it's really a farewell, tonight." It was Sanjana. She was standing near the door of the terrace. He heard Rohit make a short reply. Then the distance between them grew and one of them had left. Yashan decided to wait for Rohit to leave too. But Rohit didn't seem to be leaving the terrace. He leaned against the parapet wall. Yashan got down from the higher terrace.

"What the fu-?" said a startled Rohit. Yashan knew his friend was going to be shocked.

"Sorry. I can explain. I had no intention, either to startle or interfere with your night. I didn't overhear anything. I am so sorry, I had no idea you would be here. I just wanted to be alone, so I came up, I swear. And I won't tell this to anyone."

"Where were you when I came up? And who gave you the keys?"

"The keys actually, I took it from the watchman." Said Yashan pulling out the bunch of keys he had managed to nick from the watchmen's stand. He added, "I heard a voice. I went and hid, thinking it was a watchman. By the time I realised it was you, I couldn't leave. If I had tried, you would have seen me and your moment would have been disturbed." Yashan decided to be apologetic.

"Look I swear not to talk about this to anyone." Yashan reassured Rohit while they climbed down the stairs.

"It's alright. I don't think it would matter really."

"No. I meant about this night man."

"Nothing will matter, dude." Rohit said. He seemed upset over something, something that was not discernable to Yashan.

"Why?"

"She's leaving."

"She's leaving? What'd you mean? She ditched you?"

"Nah. She's taking T.C"

"Don't worry man. There's time till March. You have got the sports day to spend with her." Yashan tried to lift Rohit's spirits.

"She isn't coming back after winter hols." Rohit explained. Yashan was confused. First of all, he didn't understand why anyone would change schools just before their board exams. The board exams were state level exams conducted in 10th standard and it was an important exam. He decided not to ask, because Rohit seemed troubled. When they went out into the grounds, Rohit headed to the hostel, Yashan had to replace the terrace keys. Just before the two of them parted, Rohit told him,

"Yashan, it doesn't matter, but still just don't say anything to anyone because I don't want everyone asking me about her. I'll tell you everything some other time."

"Definitely." Said Yashan and headed to the watchmen stand. There began a friendship between the two, with Rohit telling Yashan everything about Sanjana and all that he had been secretive about. From the football game till the night on the terrace. Rohit found Yashan to be the perfect outlet to share and trusted him with everything.

*   *   *

It was the first day of the new term and the first day of the calendar year that they were in school. January usually zoomed away with the sports day preparations. February was the time they had their practical classes and March had the end-of-year exams. The third term was a short and busy one. Yashan was excited to return to school. The creepy homesickness feeling that he always had wasn't there at all. During his first two years at Munnar, returning from home was always a dreadful experience for him. There were tears and sleepless nights. In time, his homesickness had diminished. The tears and insomnia were gone. There was just a little bit of moodiness. It was always there, no matter how much cheery he tried to be, the moody feeling always managed to creep in.

It was the lunch break and Vajish had something to share with his friends. Everyone were curious to know why he had been spotted outside the principal's office. They even had a guess on what it could be. January was the time the new set of captains were elected.

"I was going to towards the office side to see the notice board. Just then the peon called me and told that the HM wanted to see me. So I just stepped into the office. I had no time to even consider what I was being called for. I go in and he tells me that I have been chosen as the captain of Andromeda." Vajish was saying beaming with happiness that he had been made the captain of the blue house, Andromeda.

"What about the other posts, man?" asked Christopher anxiously. Chris was the guy whom the batch wanted to be the school captain. Even Chris desired the post.

"The HM has the list in a file and he was looking at it, because I didn't realize what I was being called for I just went to his left side and stood. He held the file such a way that I couldn't see. Whoever gets called next should go and stand to the right side of him. Then they will be able to see the file. And one more amazing thing, if I'm not mistaken a new girl is joining our batch. She does look quite good. Let me put it this way. She would rank between Kavi and Sonya in terms of beauty." Said Vajish.

The very next day, the new girl showed up in class. Yamuna, oval face, her shoulder length black hair pulled back and tied into a ponytail with a rubber band, a curl of the hair along hung over her face. Vajish had been right. The girl looked good. Her name was Yamuna and she went last in the attendance register right after

Yashan. She had taken the computer group. Every teacher that day spent a few minutes asking her to introduce and asked her whereabouts. She was from Pondicherry, and had previously studied there in a school that had a French name. It sounded incoherent to Yashan.

In the computer lab, where the students were given a computer according to their role number, Yashan had to shift to the next computer to give room for this new girl. He even did help her out with the standard procedures: where to save the files, where the assignment document in the system is kept. He even showed her how the archives of previous year's assignments that were done by their seniors weren't removed and how it can be used as their own assignments when asked for. With Yamuna at the immediate next role number, anything academic brought them close. It allowed him to get to know Yamuna a little better than the other girls too.

Every day, a classmate of theirs was getting designated as a captain and on the third day Rohit had been called. It was for the post of the captain of the Yellow house named as Sirius. Yashan knew he wouldn't take the post. Everyone wanted Tanveer to be the captain of Sirius. And moreover, although Rohit would make a good captain, he had no interest in it. His good friend spent the entire day in principal's office. Nobody knew what Rohit was going through except Yashan. Rohit had had a weird break-up kind of thing with the junior, Sanjana during the farewell. Although, they weren't committed to each other, Rohit was all gloomy these days. Now, he was going to have the captaincy issue on top of it.

During the break time, Rohit was recounting all that had happened the morning in principal's office. He even added too many trivial details, like how he had actually gone there to meet Priya ma'am about the Sports day M.C. While everyone were concerned over the captain's issue, Naresh was more concerned in the trivial details.

"Rohit, you said you went to give names for M.C right? Who are the M.C.s." asked Naresh.

"It's Yamuna and Ajay, man." Suddenly, it didn't seem so trivial for Yashan. Something felt heavy inside Yashan. It was as though it was eating him from the inside. He wasn't doing something right. It was Yamuna. Over the past two days, he had found Yamuna to be a nice and interesting person. The computer class gave him the opportunity to help her out and it seemed to pave way for a friendship. A hope had been building in him, a dream of a beautiful friendship between the two of them. It had been only two days since he had met her. But, he knew well, that he was excited for the next computer practicals. He had enjoyed her company the past two days. He knew two days were too short to evaluate his feeling. But, he had never been more eager to go to class in his lifetime. He had liked that and wanted it more. He realized that, if he could replace Ajay as the M.C., he would get ample opportunity to become a real friend of hers.

"Hey. I didn't know you were choosing the M.C.s. I want a chance too. Is it too late?" he asked, trying to find a gap.

"I think Ajay he really wants to be the M.C, man." Rohit replied.

"Why don't they chuck the girl? She just came here two days ago and an M.C. already?" asked Vajish. It was the anti-girl part of the conversation. Truly, no conversation is complete without it.

"No, her English is good and moreover it has to be one boy and one girl." replied Rohit.

"Rohit, just in case they decide on adding a third M.C. or if they want it as two boys I'm the one, alright." Said Yashan.

If he gets to be chosen as the M.C., he wondered: They would have loads of practice and in between those practices they would have the time to chat. Any funny stuff that happens during the practice they could laugh together. It would bring the two of them close. Yashan had no explanation why he wanted her company, but there was no stopping his mind. He wondered, '*Is this the feeling one gets when one is addicted to drugs?*' This was way better than the computer class. He didn't want to squander it. He wanted to try and get himself the role. Now it wasn't going to be easy.

When Rohit was done explaining about what had happened in the principal's office, Rohit said to Yashan that he had something important to share and needed an opinion. Yashan decided to help him out. When there was nobody over hearing, Rohit told him,

"Yashan, there's more to this captains issue than just me."

"What is it?" Yashan questioned.

"I saw the list of other nominated captains. I didn't see the entire list though. Ajay has been designated as school captain. I didn't want everyone to know because if everyone tells him to refuse, he might feel insulted and do the opposite. He's very sensitive, you know right?" Yashan didn't see the problem that Rohit was talking about. He realized there was something else here. A chance for him to be the sports day M.C. If that was to happen he had to take this into his hands,

"Don't worry. I'll break the bubble to him. And tell him to turn it down." Said Yashan offering support to his friend and within his mind, he was casting out his next step to make it to be the sports day M.C. If Ajay becomes the school captain, he wouldn't be able to be the M.C because as a school captain, he would have other work to do. But there was one another issue, Ajay wouldn't make a good school captain and the batch didn't favour it, although they had nothing against him. Hence, there was a dilemma for Yashan. If he had to help his friends and make Ajay turn down the post, he wouldn't make it to be the M.C. and at the same time if Ajay becomes the school captain, Yashan could get the M.C. role.

With the help of Rohit, he managed to get Ajay alone the next day, so that he could have a private word with him.

"You prepared for that class test on Monday?" Yashan asked. As Ajay was the academic topper, he decided to lead it with a studies-related question. There was nothing else that Yashan could think of that might interest Ajay either.

"Nope." Yashan didn't believe the answer.

"You heard the news, about the captains huh? Crazy stuff."

"Yeah. I didn't think Rohit would become a captain."

"Why?"

"He's the class rep, know?"

"Yeah. That's the reason we made the two of you class reps, so that you both don't get chosen as the house captains." said Yashan, hinting mockery in his voice. Ajay didn't reply.

"What'll happen if you become the school captain da?" asked Yashan again.

"Who knows?"

"We'll have to put up with your crap." said Yashan guffawing.

"I won't be that bad."

"You won't be very bad. But if you become the captain, our batch will forever be called as 'Ajay's batch. Yuck! That sounds horrible." Yashan paused. Ajay had nothing to say.

"Jokes apart. What'll you do if you are called upon to be the school captain? Will you refuse?"

"I guess, what else option do I have." said Ajay.

"He will make you stand outside his office till you give in. You know the headmaster."

"I won't make an ass out of myself by standing there all day. I'll tell him, 'fuck you' and walk away."

"You will say 'Fuck. You.' on the headmaster's face?" Yashan questioned. Ajay was falling for the bait. Yashan had already a statement against him.

"No, I don't know. I'll worry about if it happens. Anyway. I got to go." Said Ajay and hastened away. He didn't want to be made uncomfortable. Yashan knew he had done well. He had provoked Ajay. But Yashan knew that, when offered, Ajay would take the post of the school captain.

THE BAMBOOZLE

YASHAN FELT BAD for his friend who was spending his entire day waiting in front of the headmaster's office. There was nothing he could do either. And by the third day, the whole batch had decided that there was nothing they could do to make the headmaster change his mind about the Sirius house captain. They all persuaded Rohit to take up the captaincy and he eventually did. And in the following day, Prasad got chosen as captain of the Aquila, the blue house and Tanveer was made the School Vice-captain. Tanveer was more than elated on being designated.

And eventually, as Yashan expected, Ajay was called by the headmaster and he immediately took up the post of the school captain. The news had reached the batch even before Ajay returned to the class. Yashan saw to it that it turned out that way. As expected, nobody was happy with what Ajay had done; he had simply taken up the offer without any regard for Christopher. As soon as the principle was done informing him, Ajay went in search of his senior English professor to express his inability to be the M.C. A house captain has a lot of responsibilities and could never be the M.C. on the school Sports Day.

When Ajay returned, the guys decided to intervene him. An intervention as in the usual sense, wherein the friends of the guy gather to advise him on his behaviour that needs to be changed. And interventions are supposed to help the one receiving it. But when a bunch of teenagers do the intervention, it would be more appropriate to term it as an 'ambush' rather than an intervention. Because the person on the receiving end will never see it coming and he will not be advised as how the adults do, but riddled with questions that he wouldn't be able to answer. It is one of the worst thing a teenager can possibly go through. And in a hostel set-up like that of the school, they were in; it can make life very hard. Every turn you take, it is the same peers you will find. And to watch and wonder if they are still mad or not, it can simply drive one crazy. And if there was one person to be named for having setup this ambush: it was Christopher, the student's school captain nominee, who had lost his post.

The entire batch was sitting in the hostel study room. The boys' hostel was an L-shaped portion in the building. Every batch of students had a study room in the hostel where they were allotted desks and did their rounds of studies. The bedrooms were also located on the same floor. The 11th and 10th standard shared the first floor, while the ground floor was occupied by the twelfth. And the juniors had the upper floors. The wardens, four of them had their rooms in the part of the building above the mess. From the window of their study hall, they could see the door of the principal's office. The guys noticed, Ajay climbing the stairs to the hostel. He had just come out of the principal's office. The guys all sat down. It was study time and they acted normal. The only thing was that the supervisor wasn't there. They had convinced him that they were doing preparations for the sports day and had him leave. Christopher, sat in a desk that was close to the door. Yashan sat in his allotted desk at the last row, right beside his best friend, Rohit.

The moment Ajay walked in Christopher went up to him and shook hands

"Congratulations, Ajay. The school captain designate."

Ajay was surprised for a moment, but he realized, that somehow they must have come to know about this stuff. He asked back,

"Thanks. But how did you guys know? So soon?"

"You'll know." Christopher said with a smile and brought Ajay to the centre of the class. Ajay had no idea what was coming for him. That is the worst part of these ambushes: you never see it coming. Ajay signalled everyone to applaud. Everyone in the room clapped, trying to make the least noise possible, lest they let the noise reach the other floors and disturb the study. Chris went close to Ajay, the claps subsided, with his smile still unfazed he said,

"See, the question here is not how we came to know, and it is why the-" Chris took a little pause in his sentence and looked away for a moment, and returned his gaze to Ajay, this time there was no smile, "WHY THE FUCK DID YOU TAKE UP THE POST?" he yelled. Ajay looked stricken. He stuttered trying to explain. But Chris shushed him out,

"I don't know, Ajay. But on the day all the people in this class including your own fucking-self, voted on the next school captain, I heard my name being called. So I come up to the centre of the class, the very place you are fucking standing right now." Ajay tried to move a little, he was trembling. "And I ask the class, *'Does any of you have an objection?'* and there was a silence. Now I ask you, where your arm was shoved up back then?"

"Look, I can explain. It . . . ." he stuttered.

"We don't want any explanation now, you son of a . . ." yelled Tanveer. But before he could swear, Christopher cut him out.

"The school captain designate has something to explain and we will and must listen." Christopher mocked him and looked to Ajay to see if he had an explanation. Seeing his cue, Ajay began,

"I had no intention, actually. I wouldn't have done what I did now. We all know what happened to Rohit. He stood there for three days and . . . ." ". . . and made an ass out of myself, didn't I?" Rohit finished the sentence for him. Yashan had told him what had happened, when he tried to dissuade Ajay from taking up the post, with a little modifications.

"Look, I'm sorry. I didn't mean it that way, when I told it to Yashan. In fact, only because Yashan spoke to me that way, then, I decided to prove that I can be a good school captain. Else, none of this would have happen . . ."

"So, now you are blaming me? Not only you call him an ass, also you are holding me responsible for you taking up the post of the school captain. FUCK YOU." Yashan swore and banged on the desk with all his might, "OWWW." He yelped. He had hit the desk harder than he anticipated. He held his right wrist in his left palm and placed both his hands between his knees.

"You alright?" Rohit asked.

"Yeah." Yashan managed and decided to make his comeback at the accusation. The bang on the desk, gave him time to think of the comeback. The noise from the desk was so loud, it startled a number of them and some of them were shushing for silence. Yashan began,

"Guys, guys, I'll tell you what happened. Rohit managed to find out that Ajay has been designated. He told me and said he didn't know how to tell Ajay, because Ajay is a bit sensitive. So I told him that I will . . . ."

"Shush. The headmaster is coming." Fred announced. His desk was close to the window over-looking the principal's office. The entire room went silent.

Everyone, went back to their desks, even Ajay went and sat as if nothing had happened. "Guys, guys, guys, if headmaster asks what happened, say we accidently, dropped the desks." Said Christopher, coming up with a lie to cover up the noise.

"No, no, no, no, no, we say what happened here. We say that the school captain designate has resigned, haven't you?" Yashan said. Everyone were surprised, including Christopher. "If Christopher has to be made the captain, it's now or never." Yashan said. His plan had been going just perfect. Ajay had just declined the post of the M.C. It was the last part, which was left to execute. This final part, he decided to do it for the batch. Ajay nodded. There were smiles on a few faces, when they realized, what had just happened. "Look, don't talk anything. Just follow my lead and everything will be fine." They all sat down silently and waited for what was to happen next.

"What is the cause of the commotion going on here?" the headmaster, yelled as he entered the class. Everyone kept the mouths sealed.

"Is anyone going to tell or do I have to pull you up?" the headmaster questioned again.

"Sir, I accidently, pushed the desk while I was walking to the dustbin." It was Yashan, standing from his chair. Everyone looked at him, puzzled. Only minutes ago, he had them told not to give the lame desk-fell-down excuse and here he was giving the same thing.

"Please. I know you boys better than that. I heard more than a desk fall. Tell me what was going on here." Yashan looked at Ajay. Ajay was looking right back at him, in fact the entire class was looking at Yashan, for he was the one who had a plan. Yashan gave a slow inconspicuous nod.

"Sir, we were having a batch talk about my resignation." Ajay had got up from his seat. The eyes shifted their direction.

"What is the need for the batch talk?" asked the headmaster, completely ignoring the final part of Ajay's sentence.

"I wish to quit my post of the school captain."

"You are only a designate. You haven't been invested yet. And you can't quit now."

"I haven't been invested yet. That is why I have to quit now, sir." Said Ajay.

"You have to? What is the need may I ask?" asked the headmaster. Ajay looked in the direction of Yashan. Yashan who by then had sat down, whispered to Rohit,

"Say he has a problem with you."

"We both don't get along well sir. It has to be me or he, both of us can't work together, I definitely can't work under him." Said Rohit, he wouldn't have stopped his sentence if Yashan hadn't given the cue he was over-acting.

"Is that a reason even? This school is supposed to teach you to be diplomatic with people. And you should adjust and manage, after all he is your classmate. And Ajay, why didn't you tell me that when I called you to your office." asked the headmaster.

"I—don't—kn—know." Ajay had no other reply. He gave in. But to his luck, the headmaster had misinterpreted it.

"You didn't know? You didn't know that Rohit was made captain?" Yashan muffled a smile. He gave a cue to Rohit to intervene.

"No sir." Rohit immediately blabbed out.

"How come did he not know? Wasn't anyone curious why your friend here was in front of my office for the past two days?" the headmaster didn't seem to be getting it yet.

"*You and Ajay have a problem.*" Yashan whispered.

"I and Ajay had a misunderstanding."

"That's why you turned down the offer in the first place."

"That's why I refused to be the captain when you offered me the post, sir. I saw in the file that Ajay was the designate. I didn't tell anyone except Yashan. Yashan told to others and we had a batch talk about this now." Rohit had managed to improvise the rest of the explanation on his own. The headmaster had made out the chaos that was happening, but he wasn't interested in that. All he wanted was a solution, something which he would prefer. If he accepted Ajay's resignation, the batch would come up with the next designate and he didn't want that. At the same time, in the situation, he couldn't decline the resignation either. It was very important that the captains have nothing against each other. He couldn't ask Rohit to step down as he was the one who forced Rohit to take up the captaincy.

"Why is it you have to resign, Ajay?" asked the headmaster. And Rohit intervened before Ajay could say anything,

"Sir, I stood three days, hoping that you would accept my refusal; now you want me to resign?" asked Rohit, he looked furious.

"No, I was just looking to see if any other alternative is present. But since I see none here, I will take Ajay's resignation. And who is your designate?" the headmaster asked towards the class. Christopher rose from his desk, but before the headmaster noticed him, Yashan diverted his attention,

"Not yet chosen." Yashan told loud enough for the headmaster to hear.

"Alright. Make your choice by tonight." said the headmaster. Everyone kept silent, waiting for the headmaster to walk out of the earshot.

"Ten, nine, eight, seven" Yashan was softly whispering.

"What are you counting to?" asked Rohit

"To Chris hugging me."

"What?" he was puzzled. Just then everyone got up from their seats. It was almost dinner time. Christopher got up from his place and almost jogged up to Yashan. He opened his arms wide.

"Don't hug him." Rohit intervened.

"What?" Chris was confused.

"I'll give you fifty bucks if you don't hug him." Said Rohit.

"Go to hell." Christopher said and hugged Rohit hard. Rohit looked at Yashan and mouthed *"ZERO."*

"How the hell did you pull it off, man?" asked Chris extremely amazed with what Yashan had done. Yashan simply smiled.

"You are one hell of a bamboozler." Said Rohit patting Yashan. He thought he knew the entire plan of Yashan, but all he apparently knew was only one side of Yashan's plan. Everyone was amazed and at the same time surprised with what Yashan had done.

"Okay, okay, enough with me. I was improvising this, as events occurred. But there was this one guy who helped me very much to make this plan come through. I knew what I'm supposed to do, but he didn't even know he was playing his part in a plan, yet he played his role effectively."

"Who da?" asked Christopher.

"Before I tell who it is please, a silent applause for him." Everyone in the room clapped, trying to make minimal noise. When the claps ended, Rohit opened his mouth.

"It is Ajay." Everyone were very much stunned. Not twenty minutes ago, Christopher was swearing at him, only to realize now that he had something important to do with him getting to be the School captain. Ajay looked frozen. He couldn't understand if Yashan was being genuine or sarcastic.

"When he told that I provoked him to take up the captaincy, know? He was actually right about it. I intentionally did that, so that he would take up his post and it would come to this."

"You took so much risk? Why didn't you tell anyone of us? We could have helped you with this and even this sad fellow, Ajay, I yelled at him. I thought he might shit in his pants. Ajay, I'm so sorry, dude." Said Christopher. Ajay nodded smiling.

"Right now, when the headmaster was here, the only reason he asked for a valid reason for Ajay's resignation was to see if it was a something we were doing it for the sake of not wanting Ajay as the captain or if it was genuine. Ajay was little dull after the yelling, it made it look like there was a real problem here. And since both Rohit and Ajay were thinking a lot before saying each word, it seemed natural and he realized it wasn't any rehearsed dialogue. That was what the headmaster was looking to find. And moreover, if we had told your name now itself, then he might have rejected you. I see no reason why, but it's a possibility. So you join along with the other captains on Monday and become the official designate. Until then, don't let anyone outside our class know about the change in the designate." Yashan explained.

"You really are a Bamboozler." Tanveer added in.

"A what?"

"Bamboozler, a con artist." Tanveer explained.

"Artist . . . Ha! Nice. I like it." Yashan was smiling. Of course he had to smile. His con, as Tanveer had called, had worked out perfectly, up to the last step. He managed to get Chris as the school captain; he did that for the sake of his friends, but that was just secondary in his con. In the next two days Rohit managed to grab the role of the M.C for the Sports Day for him. Rohit had put in his recommendation about Yashan to Priya Ma'am on Friday and the very next day Yashan met his senior English professor and lied to her how Ajay had been made the school captain designate and will not be able to be the M.C and had got the script. Now it was safely, locked in his wardrobe. Somewhere not far off, in somebody else's wardrobe, the other half of the M.C script must be there. And Yashan knew too well, that the somebody, was Yamuna.

Practice and Malpractice

SHE HADN'T COME yet. She was supposed to be there half an hour earlier. With just five days left, for the Sports Day, the practice had become intense. Almost the entire day went in practice. They had just three classes every day. And all the practice time, Yashan had been spending with Yamuna, he was enjoying it very much. All thanks to the bamboozle that he had come up with. He did feel guilty a bit that he had to deprive Ajay of the role. *But Ajay didn't worry. He was totally okay with it. So what the hell?* He convinced his own conscience.

Out of the door, he saw his English professor returning to the office. She had gone out for some work, while making Yashan wait for Yamuna.

"She hasn't come yet?" she questioned as she entered.

"Fine, you start yours. Let her come." She didn't wait for Yashan to say anything.

"Ma'am, tomorrow we have the Physics Monthly test, I don't think she will be coming."

"What? She said that?"

"No ma'am. I think it is the reason she hasn't come yet. I don't think she will come any later." Within his mind, his thoughts ran unhindered, *Call the hostel and ask her to come for practice. We have only five days, ma'am. Just five more days I have got to make a lasting impression on her.*

"Oh! I see. Fine, you start with your role. If she doesn't come we will do it today without her." Said his teacher. Yashan cursed his luck and began reading. He stuttered and stammered.

"What are you reading, Yashan? You read very well, last evening. The life in you is missing."

"Sorry, ma'am. It's just that all the time, I was practicing with Yamuna, so I'm missing timing." Yashan tried to explain. He knew what he had to do get Yamuna there. Yashan tried to read again. He did better, but wasn't at his best.

"Ah! Where is this girl? I made a mistake of making her the M.C" said the teacher and she went towards the phone, in the staff room. She punched in the intercom number and waited for the line to connect.

In a few moments, Yashan learnt that Yamuna would be arriving soon. He resumed reciting his lines and when Yamuna came in, they did two rounds through the entire script before the ma'am allowed them to rest. Yashan's reading was flawless.

"Why were you late?" Yashan asked Yamuna casually.

"The warden didn't allow me to come. I was so happy that I could learn, then ma'am called me."

"You were learning huh?"

"No, man. I was about to learn. How do they expect us to study without giving us time?"

"This is nothing new for us. We are used to this stuff. That's how life here is." Yashan said. But the truth was different, it ran within his mind, *'We usually don't learn at all, then why give us the time?'*

"Mm . . . . That's there." Yamuna ended the conversation.

"How much have you finished studying?" Yashan asked. He didn't want the conversation to end.

"I finished up to 'projectiles'. You?" she asked him. Yashan had no clue what the topics were for the test. He hadn't even touched the book. And here was this girl so anxious, even after having completed a part of the portions. He had never been anxious or stressed to go to any test without learning. He was used to it. He hardly cared about the tests. But when time permits he would study, if there was no time, he just didn't complain.

"I don't study in the order. I go question-wise. I have finished the objectives and three marks. I still have five and ten marks." Yashan managed a reply by generalising the test topics. But, the truth was that he was simply lying about what he had learnt.

"You studied one marks huh? Do me a favour please, please, please?" she made a sad face and pleaded. Yashan couldn't avoid smiling. Her face seemed cute and innocent.

"Fine." He agreed.

"Thank You." Yamuna said, dragging the 'you' as if she was hugging an invisible teddy bear.

"What favour?" Yashan asked.

"Tell me the one marks. I will be sitting front of you. Just whisper the option into my ear."

"If it's possible, I will."

"No you have to. Please.

"Okay, as long as you are sitting front of me, I will able to." Yashan said guessing, the seating arrangements could differ. Yamuna happily agreed. When the practice ended, she bid her bye and reminded him once again of their deal for copying.

Yashan immediately, went up to the top floor of the west annex block. The exams were conducted on that floor. The doors were locked. Yashan peeked through the windows. The daylight fell, and showed him the desks neatly arranged for the next day's test. The desk that was closest to the window had a chalk figure on it, '11' and the desk just behind it had '12'. He counted the desk from 12 all the way up to 36, Yamuna's exam number. His desk was the third desk from the last and hers was just front of his. He wouldn't be able to evade. He had to help her. He decided to return to the hostel.

He opened his book and began studying. Luckily, he had the habit of paying attention in the classroom. He was able to grasp the subject easily. When he reached the 'projectiles' topic, the lesson got harder. For the next four pages, there were only derivations. And it needed calculus to solve it. Like many of his friends, Yashan hated calculus. He got stuck in 'projectiles' and couldn't study any further.

*   *   *

"Yashan, wake up, dude." He heard a voice. Yashan opened his eyes. It was Rohit. Then, Yashan realized: he had dozed off, studying. He had drooled over the book. He pulled out his handkerchief and wiped his face. Rohit had a disgusted look on his face. Yashan looked at his watch. It was 3:30pm.

"Oh! Crap!" he exclaimed.

"What happened Bamboozler?" Rohit asked.

"I slept for two and a half hours."

"Were you sitting and learning?"

"I tried to."

"You sly cunt. You were learning huh? We were all slogging in the fields with the practice. Here you are under the roof, preparing for tomorrow's test."

"No, dude. I need a big help. Tell me the one-marks alone know? Please." Yashan pleaded to his friend.

"What? I myself haven't learned yet, man. Why are you so into learning?" asked Rohit curious on why his friend was pretending to be a nerd.

"Yamuna. She asked for a help."

"And you can't say no to a crush, can you?" teased Rohit.

"She is not my crush. I would have said no to her. But I didn't see it coming." Said Yashan. He knew it was Rohit trying to have revenge for Yashan teasing him over Sanjana.

"Fine. We'll do it during the evening."

Yashan and Rohit did their group study that evening. They both read the chapter, whenever, Rohit came across a one-mark, he marked it on Yashan's textbook. Yashan read only the one-marks and nothing else. Next day, Yashan sat well-prepared for the exam. Well-prepared not to pass, but to be able to help Yamuna. As soon as Yamuna took the seat, she looked at him gave a smile. It was supposedly a reminder that he had to help her. He smiled back. Whenever, the invigilator was far off or turning away from them, Yamuna would lean back and Yashan would say the options, four at a time.

"*a, c, d, c.*" And the she bent forward and marked them. Once she was done, she again made sure that the sir was still far away and not looking and leaned back. "*a, b, b, a*" It took twenty minutes for them to complete the fifteen one marks on the paper. Yashan began, writing the next section in the paper. Yamuna bent down and she too did the same. Yashan had known 12 of the fifteen one-marks. But the other sections, he hardly knew anything.

He tried hard to remember, something from the classes and write. He wrote his own explanations and definitions. He wrote for another one hour. He looked up. Tanveer and Kunal had already finished their exam. Their pens were lying on the table with the lid closed. Yashan tied up his sheets. Yamuna, hadn't finished yet.

At the end of the two hours, the examiner collected back the papers and dispersed the hall. When, Yashan got up from his seat he noticed something on the ground. He picked it up. It was an eraser in the design of the cartoon *Tweety's* head. It should have fallen out of Yamuna's hand when she left. He decided to give it to her during the practice time. He flipped the rubber. On the other side of the rubber were written four letters with a gel pen: '*Thnx.*'

Two weeks later, the sports day had got over and the practices had ended. The only time Yashan got to talk to Yamuna was the computer period. He had returned the eraser that she had left for him.

*   *   *

It was the first time, they were going to do a program in C-language. Yashan looked at his assignment sheet. He had to do a basic program. The teacher had left the hall, because the principal had called him or something. He got on with it right away. Beside him, in the next computer Yamuna was sitting and typing the commands she had been asked to use in a programme.

"Why do I keep getting this error message?" she asked him.

"Change '*main*' to '*void main*'. It means there will not be any output. That's how your programme is designed to be." Yashan said after looking at her assignment sheet. Yamuna made the correction and it worked. There was a commotion going on behind them. The two of them turned around. Christopher was in the teacher's cabin. He was browsing sir's computer. The sir's computer always had unannounced mark-lists, the memos that were being circulated among the teachers. Some students had gathered there.

"Badri, what did he find?" Yashan called out.

"Physics Monthly test results. The one we wrote on the Monday before Sports day." Said Badri. Yashan was thinking he could ask someone standing in the teacher's cabin for the marks, but just then,

"Yashan, see my marks too." Asked Yamuna. Yashan rose up from his chair and went over to the computer. He came back to his seat.

"You got twenty two out of fifty." he said.

"You?" she asked.

"I got twenty out of fifty. Just pass. Both of us got twelve in the one-marks out of fifteen." Yashan told her. She smiled at him. Her capillaries in the cheeks got flushed with blood.

SOCIAL NETWORKING

FEBRUARY AND MARCH passed on. The exams didn't permit them to talk much after the results. They shared a few laughs and short dialogues between each other. As the annual exams approached, the number of practical classes dwindled, and the study hours increased. The study was separate for the girls and boys. Life had become pale and grey. Yashan was the happiest when the holidays came. He could have distractions at home that kept him from thinking about Yamuna and missing her. But three days into the holidays, he noticed a friend request from her on Orkut. With glee, he accepted it. He kept posting funny links on her wall. She too reciprocated with the same. One day, he was scrolling down his Orkut wall, there was a popup at the corner of the screen. It said:

Yamuna: hi

She had opened a chat conversation. The best thing about Orkut, the newly popular social website was that you can have private conversation with people for as long as you want. He decided to continue,

Yashan: hey

Yamuna: what are you doin?

Yashan: nothin much . . . what are you doin?

Yamuna: just surfin

They chatted on about each other, for over two hours and then the power went out in Yashan's house and he had to end the chat abruptly. He cursed the power and got up from the seat, he had been glued on for the past two hours. The next day, he found Yamuna online at around the same time. He thanked the Gods and opened up a chat conversation. The two friends stayed very much connected, during the holidays through Orkut, thanks to Google.

Eight weeks of vacation had zoomed past and Yashan's dad had made him to go to a tuition to prepare for the twelfth portions. Yashan, like any other boy of his age sulked, but went. He had tuitions in Physics, Chemistry and Mathematics. Luckily, his father didn't think he would need tuitions for Computer Science or Language. Amidst all his tuitions, he had made some time for chatting with Yamuna. That was the best part of the day. He had his video games, his friends from the neighbourhood, but the best of part of the day was when he got to chat with his best friend.

Yashan: what doin?

Yamuna: watchin movie with dad . . .

Yashan: kk what movie?

Yashan: Black

Yashan: doesn't ur dad have to go to office or someplace to work

Yamuna: he might go in the evenin.

Yashan: what does he do?

Yamuna: he owns a beach resort in pondy.

Yashan: so can I get a discount if I come?

Yamuna: u can come 4 free

Yashan: yay . . . thn I'll go n pack nw.

Yamuna: WHAT???

Yashan wasn't being serious, and the word 'what in caps, sounded like she was alarmed by what Yashan had sent. *Does she really think I was going to pack and go to her resort? He thought.*

Yashan: JK!

Yamuna: I thought so.

Yashan: am I disturbin u frm watchin the movie?

Yamuna: no . . . its a hindi movie. I don't know hindi. Im just givin company to my dad.

Yashan: so u are just chattin with me?

Yamuna: actually I was . . . . until Vajish started chattin with me.

She had been chatting with Vajish. It explained the reason why her responses were a little slow. Yashan opened his friends list and found Vajish online. Yashan decided to open a chat with Vajish.

Yashan: hi

Vajish: hey dude

Yashan: what doin?

Vajish: nothing

Yashan: nothin at all?

Vajish: lol . . . . no chattin with a friend

Yasan: anybody I know?

Vajish: nope a cousin actually

Yashan: u said friend?

Vajish: yea . . . a friend on Orkut, man

Yashan began to wonder, why is Vajish, hiding the fact that he is chatting with Yamuna. It intrigued him. But he couldn't ask. That would make it evident, that he had been chatting with Yamuna. Just when he was thinking. Yamuna's chat box was flashing. He clicked at it.

Yamuna: What happened? Silence?

Yashan: oh . . . mom asked for help. Went to get that.

Yamuna: kk

Yashan: what is Vajish askin you?

Yamuna: nothin

Yashan: how can u chat about nothin?

Yamuna: nothin important . . . i meant

```
Yashan: well, then why won't u say what u r
        talking about?

Yamuna: why should I?

Yashan: why shouldn't u?

Yamuna: what do u want?

Yashan: im intrigued about what u both are
        possibli chattin

Yamuna: why is it important to u?

Yashan: im ur friend, I have the right to ask

Yamuna: really? . . . . who said u r my
        friend?
```

[Yamuna has gone offline. You cannot send her messages now.]

Yashan was furious. She wouldn't disclose what they were talking and moreover, Vajish didn't even admit that he was chatting with her. Nothing makes a teenager more jealous than to see a girl he likes to enjoy the company of another guy. And Yashan was mad.

"How can you say I can't send her message right now, Orkut? I will send her messages whenever I want." He yelled at the computer screen and in fury he typed in the chat box,

```
Yashan: fuck you
```

[Yamuna has gone offline. You cannot send her messages now.]

Yashan banged his hand on the desk. He really couldn't do anything, not even overpower a computer website. He got up and lied down on his bed, looking up the ceiling. He had been very very stupid. He had never been stupider, when he was talking to anybody right on face. Here he was typing his words. He could have sensed his stupidity even before he hit the 'Enter' button on his keyboard. But he hadn't. Why did he lose all his sense?

He could have manipulated Vajish into telling him what he was chatting. Instead he acted like a possessive jerk. And the worst of all, Yamuna may not be his friend anymore at all. The possibility of it happening, suddenly filled his eyes with tears. He felt even angrier now. But this time at himself. He had been so stupid that he had even yelled at the computer. After all, what wrong did a website do?

The next day, he went online at the same time, hoping to find Yamuna online. He had decided to apologize for being stupid. But she wasn't there online. He spent another hour in the internet hoping she would come. Maybe she had decided never to talk with him. Or maybe she decided never to chat with him. Or even worse, she was upset. Every single possibility hurt Yashan and he ached to find out what happened to her. There was still one week to go to school. Yashan's tuition hours had decreased and he began packing his suitcases for school.

One afternoon, he found her online. He opened the chat box and sent her a 'hi' He waited for an hour and a half. She went offline without a reply. He decided not to give up and sat there waiting for a reply for the next half an hour, though she had gone offline. Then his mother called him for going out shopping, else he wouldn't have left that chair.

TWELFTH GRADE

THE SCHOOL REOPENED for the new scholastic year. It was Yashan's final year of school. From a kid, he was now a mature teenager. How much life had changed for him? He found a seat at the last row in the class, beside his best friend, Rohit. He had hardly talked to Rohit during the holidays. The two friends had much to talk about. Yashan told Rohit about the argument between him and Yamuna. Only the English teacher had changed. Priya Ma'am wasn't their English teacher anymore. All other teachers were same.

A new sir had been appointed. He was a new teacher in the school. His name was John Anthony. He was a young man, looked about the age of twenty-five. He was very jovial and when he taught his classes. His way of interaction was down to the student's level. The class liked his teaching too. His class was the only class that wasn't boring. Only two weeks of classes had been through and the teachers had begun conducting tests.

As far as Yamuna was concerned, she hadn't spoken a word to him ever since they returned. She tried as much as she could and avoided him. Yashan thought it was best if he didn't disturb her and Rohit had advised him to look out for an appropriate time to make up to her and to keep his trap shut till then. Yashan, always called by his friends as the 'Bamboozler' for his cons, didn't want to risk sabotaging his almost non-existent friendship with Yamuna. And he didn't want to try any of those con to make up with her.

And at the end of the week, the teachers had the results of the tests ready to be announced. It was the English period, just after the break. Mr Anthony came in with the papers in his hand. It was the first time the new teacher was evaluating their papers. The students were curious if his correction was going to be strict like others or not. It was a forty mark test. It had an essay-writing exercise and some comprehension and grammar exercises. English was a subject, the students wrote without preparations. The sir was distributing the papers, highlighting the common and silly mistakes which were there. The papers were arranged in random. The students had no way knowing who was going to be called next. Some of the mistakes the students had made were amazingly funny.

"8039" the sir called out. It was Yashan's roll number. He stood up to go and receive the paper.

"Please be seated, I have much to teach the students about what your paper has to tell." Said Mr Anthony and he picked up the chalk. Yashan sat down, he had performed neither badly or very well. He wondered what the sir found in his paper that was worth sharing.

"Every time a teacher corrects the paper, the students' way of writing reveals the understanding level of the student. But, your friend here, has gone beyond any other student by not only revealing his level of understanding the subject, but also has revealed how he had spent his holidays." The sir said. Yashan didn't know how he had revealed anything about his holidays.

"I will write the first three lines from his essay on the board. You will know what he has to reveal to us." Saying so, he began to write in on the board.

'He knows that the public are supportin Brutus, as Brutus has just given them a speech, so if he starts by accusin Brutus, no one would listen to him. He starts by embracin the public as 'Friends, Romans, and countrymen. And at the beginnin of his speech, Mark Antony praises Brutus by sayin that Brutus was "noble" and "honourable"*

Yashan understood his mistake. He was embarrassed. He had forgotten the 'g' at the end of the gerund forms of the verb. Before, he could explain, his teacher spoke,

"Now, tell us, Yashan. Who is this girl you have been chattin'?" the other students laughed, when the sir intentionally missed the 'g' in chatting.

"I wasn't chatting with anyone at all, sir"

"Oh! Were you then textin'? Did your dad get you a mobile?" said the teacher pulling his leg.

"No sir. It was accidental."

"Accidental in every word, now you are simply lyin'." The class roared with laughter. Even Yashan wanted to laugh he was gleaming back at the teacher, hiding his laughter. It was all as a result of chatting with Yamuna. He stood silent. The class was still laughing.

"Silence. Silence. Sorry, Yashan. I will not indulge in your personal affairs if you are not willin'." The sir mocked once again. Yashan couldn't control his laughter any longer, he let it out. His friends were laughing even harder, when the sir said 'willin'. The class continued till the bell, with the same momentum. But the highlight of the class was Yashan's answer sheets.

Immediately, after the class, everyone lined up for the computer class. It was the first practical they were going to have for that year. Yashan was quite hoping, she might talk to him. He decided to let her to make the first move. He had apologized through the social networking site, during the holidays itself. She hadn't replied anything. The students climbed up to the lab. The computer lab smelt of paint. They should have repainted it. Having come in the middle of the year, Yamuna, had the last computer. This year, with the roll numbers rearranged, she was placed after Vajish and before Yashan. However, she was still beside Yashan in the lab.

"Good morning, students." It was the Senior Computer Teacher, Mr Farooq.

"Good morning, sir." The students sang in a chorus.

"It's a new and the final year in this school." Well, you have board exams, but that wouldn't be a problem. Computer science, is easy to learn as it always has been. By the way, do you see any changes in the computer lab this year?"

"Paint." Some students answered.

"What has paint got do with computer students? I am talking about computer-related changes." Said the computer teacher. Everyone looked around, hoping to find some changes. Some of them looked into their screens hoping to find some answer. On the white board were two command lines written. Nothing else seemed different.

"Sir, there is Firefox installed newly." Said Kunal.

"There is internet connection, sir." Said Fred.

"Yes, correct. We have installed internet connection. It will not give you the browsing speed you get in internet cafes, but you will be able to send and receive mails. Speaking of mails, how many of you have mail Ids?" the sir asked. About six or seven hands went up into the air. The rest of the students were too lazy to raise their hands.

"Very few." The teacher commented. He pointed to Fred, who had his hands up in the air and questioned him, "What do you use your mail-ID for?"

"I use it for Orkut-ting. My dad created one for me, when he created one for his business." he said, little bit flustered to have admitted that it was only a futile ID.

"Not bad. At least you have one. Today's exercise is going to be creating an E-mail ID for each of yourself. Emails have a bright future. Ten years from now, postal letters would be outdated. Emails are quick and don't get lost. That's the power of emails. You all are going to create a Yahoo email ID for each of yourself and you will send mail to each other.

This is how you will go about: First go into the Yahoo! Website, then sign up there, and create an account. Once you have done it successfully, open command prompt and type in the command you see on the board, only the first line of the command. And in the place of 'email ID', you will type in your email ID that you have created. After you finish all this; type in the second command that you see on the board into command prompt and it will open a notepad file, with all the email IDs that you have uploaded into it. And from there you can mail your friends. Anywhere you get stuck, ask me." The sir explained what they had to do that class. Everyone got busy, trying to create an email ID. It wasn't easy with the network being slow. Finally he created one mail ID for himself and he entered into the command prompt. When the notepad opened, he found that about fifteen names were already there. He found Rohit's name too. He decided to send his best friend his first email.

```
Hey Rohit,

Can't quite believe communication has come
to this level and even more unbelievable is
that we are using it. Here comes my first
mail. WE ARE BLOODY USING NEXT GENERATION
```

COMMUNICATION SYSTEM. It sounded very cool when sir said, 'THIS IS THE FUTURE' . . . . LOL we are in the future.

Relax I'm being sarcastic. Emails are old, even I know it. Sir sounded ridiculous. With the latest social networks needing emails for logging in how does he think that we won't have email ids man?

Yashan

This was Yashan's third email-ID. The internet was a good thing in the school campus, they shouldn't make it sound so ridiculous by acting as if they own the future, Yashan thought to himself. His friend had replied, he opened it,

You Buffoon,

You are such an idiot. Send an email to Yamuna and try and make up with her. This is your best chance. She was in peals of laughter when Anthony read your essay.

Rohit

Then, it hit upon Yashan. He hadn't thought of it. Maybe he was a good bamboozler, but bad at genuine acts of goodness. He began typing an apology into his computer. He had typed for about one entire page. He read it once. It sounded weird to him. He decided against sending the mail the same way to Yamuna too, not after what had happened. He erased everything and retyped it and sent it. After hitting the 'send' button he glanced at Yamuna's screen, waiting for it to popup in her screen. And when it did, she glared at him. He looked at her. She immediately turned away and opened the mail. It opened and his mail was on her monitor. From his chair, he could see the mail he had sent, it had two letters, just two letters:

```
Hi
```

That was he had sent, after ruminating upon that the one-page mail was sounded weird. She once again glared at him. She opened a new page to reply. He turned away from her screen as to give her some privacy in typing a mail. And in no time, the popup arrived. He opened it. She had sent a reply that was equivalent to his mail. Her reply had three letters. He was quite shocked. It wasn't even three letters actually. It read:

```
???
```

He typed in a reply.

```
Sorry . . . :(
```

And her reply arrived,

```
Fine
```

She had accepted, his apology, although she hadn't told if they were still friends, she had forgiven him. It was a start. He didn't know what to reply. He just typed in a single letter reply:

```
k . . .
```

And she retorted to that one letter mail.

```
For God's sake, this is email, not a chat.
So, do send, more than just a few letters.
And don't do ur English papers with these few
letters, nxt time sir reads out such things,
I will definitely die of laughter.
```

Yashan, was happy. She had forgiven him. He felt lighter all of a sudden as if a heavy block of stone had been removed from the top of him. This mail was all that he had wanted. He felt happier than he had been in the past two weeks. In excitement, he hit on the computer table and the mouse fell down, drawing everyone's attention. Yamuna began to laugh out again. Regaining composure, Yashan looked over to his best friend. Rohit was showing him a thumbs-up. Yashan smiled back. He decided to give a proper explanation to Yamuna.

```
Hey

I'm sorry that I was bein possessive, the
other day. It was my bad. The fact that u
were hidin something was what got me to act
that way. I promise not to do it again.
```

He hit 'enter' and the mail got sent to her. Soon, enough she had sent a reply.

```
Im also sorry. Partially it was my fault,
I shouldn't have tried to hide anything.
You were my friend. And actually, I thought
of doing it only for fun until things got a
bit serious. I actually wasn't chatting with
Vajish at all. Sorry.

Yamuna
```

Yashan read it. He realised how that chat had been actually over nothing. He realized, Vajish must have told him the truth, when he asked about it. Yashan felt stupid. He just looked and smiled at her, glad that the tension between them was over. She too smiled back.

"Please turn off your computer." Said Mr Farooq. The class was over. The forty five minutes seemed to have been over too fast.

New Interests

THAT AFTERNOON, YASHAN was sitting among his friends and just enjoying the flow of conversation. Everything seemed amusing to him, after Yamuna had accepted his apology. One fine evening, as always the friends had gathered at the siren to chat. Vajish called him out of the gang, to have a private word.

"Hey, Bambooz, can I have a word?" asked Vajish.

"Hey, what's up man?"

"You and Yamuna are friends, right?" asked Vajish. Yashan couldn't understand, why Vajish would ask about Yamuna. The entire class knew that the two were friends. He simply nodded as an answer.

"Look, don't get me wrong. But I think I like Yamuna." Vajish said. *'What the hell?'* Yashan thought to himself. But he didn't let his feelings surface. He simply said, "Ok." Intending Vajish to proceed.

"I think . . . I'm interested in getting to know her."

"Sure."

"But I don't know, how to do it." Yashan had become good friends with Yamuna. He very much liked her friendship, but there was a part inside him, that had a crush for her, that had motivated him to come up with the con to get to know her, a part that had got angry, when it thought she was hiding something, and Yashan could sense, that little part inside him was outraged. On the surface, Yashan kept his cool.

"And?"

"Since, you are her friend. You know her too. Can you help me and moreover, you are one hell of a bamboozler, so, if you can come up with something so that I can impress her; that would be great."

"Hey, I have known you for seven years. I'm definitely going to help you." said Yashan only with the intention of being nice and had no intent to help him really. He continued, "But, look at the situation here. There is no way I will be able to help you. You need something in common with her."

"We have Volleyball. She is the captain of the girls' volleyball team. She plays amazing. I see her every day at the court. From there only, I started liking her." Vajish interrupted him. '*What the fuck? He is ogling at her during the evening games. How dare he do that?*' the little part in him was furious.

"Fine, but from what I know of Yamuna, she likes people who are genuine. You don't want a con of mine, a trick to become friends with her. If she ever finds out she will be very mad. I don't think any bamboozles will do the job here. And one last thing, it all comes down this, I can play your position in volleyball, but not in your game of love. If you want to impress her you are the one who should come up with the idea. I mean, I have no idea, what kind of scenario it will be like, to try and befriend her in the court. So, I don't think, I can be of any help. I really would like to though." said Yashan faking an apologetic tone.

"Hey. If you know, what kind of atmosphere, it is in the court, will you be able to help me?" Asked Vajish. '*What is this guy thinking? Does he expect me to come to the court, just to help him get Yamuna?*' Yashan thought.

"What?" Yashan questioned back.

"You know, Ravindran has left, so we need a new substitute and you could try to fill up his shoes. That way, you will not only be playing, but also helping me out, because you too will be on the court. You can try and work out things for me from there." Yashan wanted to yell a 'no' at him. But then, something else dawned on him. Vajish was the captain of the boys' team, while Yamuna was the captain for the girls' team. Both of them being captains, should give Vajish bountiful chances to make an impression on Yamuna. If he uses his common sense, he could actually manage it without Yashan's help and that might work and end in ways he didn't want it to. But if he were there, he could keep check on Vajish's attempts to impress Yamuna. And one more thing was that, there was no coach for volleyball. The previous coach Mr Jeyabal had left. Everything was under Vajish's control. Another advantage for Vajish. Yashan chose to agree.

That evening, Yashan was putting on the knee-cap he had borrowed from Duke. Just then, the girl's team came for practice. The volleyball team had no person to coach. Yamuna, directly walked up to Yashan

"Hey, *Bambooz*." Yamuna teased him.

"Since, when did you call me that?"

"Don't worry. Just for fun. You will be 'Yash' to me always." She said. And Vajish joined in, hoping that there might be something in the conversation for him.

"Anyway, what are you doing here?" she inquired.

"Ask the caps." Yashan said pointing at Vajish, who stood there.

"Oh! Right. *Bambooz* is the new player, in for Ravindran."

"Wow! Nice of you." Yamuna said to Vajish and walked into the dressing room. When she had gone, Vajish said to Yashan,

"Nice of me? You had been here for half an hour and you are already helping. You are definitely in the team." Vajish was elated at Yamuna's comment. He hugged Yashan with gratitude. Yashan simply smiled.

That evening, Vajish had boasted to everyone about what had happened in the volleyball court. He even told them how Yashan, was the one helping him. Unlike Rohit, he wasn't very secretive about his personal affairs. And Rohit, who knew about how Yashan felt for Yamuna was surprised,

"You are helping Vajish to impress her?" he was surprised.

"Yep."

"I thought you liked her"

"Yes I do."

"Then?"

"I didn't want to be possessive."

"Don't give me that bullshit. You have a crush on Yamuna."

"Shut the fuck up, okay? I don't have a crush on Yamuna." Yashan almost yelled. His friend apologised. It annoyed Yashan, every time Rohit mentioned Yamuna as his crush. Rohit defined Yamuna as a crush because Yashan had no rational explanation for why he had done what he did to become the Sports Day M.C. Yashan too didn't have a reason inside him. It had just happened back then. He really liked the friendship that he had with Yamuna. He was afraid to lose it by surrendering to his confusing emotions. And he didn't want anything more than that. It scared him.

"To impress any girl, the only thing that matters is what you do, I don't think any girl is going to be impressed on a guy by someone else's work. That's why I agreed to help Vajish."

"You think Vajish won't succeed?"

"I know Vajish won't succeed."

"Why?"

"He won't as long as I'm there in the court."

"How?" Rohit didn't understand.

"Why do we look for new friends? It is when the ones that we already have, aren't there around us. Why would she be looking for a new friendship when her good friend, I, am there?"

"It seems logical. But I don't know how you are this confident."

"I'm his Bamboozler. I have to give him suggestions and all I will be throwing at him are crappy ones, that'll get him nowhere."

"Hey, I think you should tell him that you can't help him."

"I help a lot of people, how can I refuse this alone? Won't the question be raised, why I am refusing this alone?" said Rohit.

"You are misleading him. He is going to be devastated."

"He will be happy that he tried and failed rather than not trying which he would be doing, hadn't he come to me?" Yashan argued back.

"Look, I think you like her and if you say so, I'll do all that I can to help you win her. I'm on your side about Yamuna. But here, I think you are being evil."

"He is trying to take away Yamuna."

"You told me you don't want to be possessive."

"Possessive, my ass. Which guy would like to see a girl he likes with another guy?" Yashan seemed displeased. Rohit got the point, but he had a nagging feeling, his friend was doing something wrong. "Dude?" he was trying to pull him back out of what he was doing.

"Every time, I'm up to something. You are against it. How did you become my best friend?" Yashan said laughing. Rohit tried hard and faked a laugh at his friend's comment.

*   *   *

The tournaments were a week away. Yashan had become a permanent part of the Volleyball team reserves. He was still a beginner in the game. He didn't deserve to be a part of the team. He was there because Vajish thought he needed him. He did create moments where Vajish was able to interact with Yamuna, and work to impress her. But, Vajish didn't seem to be making any actual progress, apart from becoming a casual friend. *How much harm can that be?* He thought to himself.

There was a boys vs. girls practice match underway. Yashan was sitting outside, waiting for his substitution. On the court, Vajish was heading the boys' team and Yamuna was leading the girls. It had just begun. The boys' team were much stronger than the girls. But that was the kind of practice, the girls' team needed. To compete against a tougher opponent. Point after point, it was only the boys' scoring and Yamuna, was getting sour with every point that they lost. She began yelling at everyone, for their mistakes. Yashan told Vajish to ask her to control her temper, which Vajish told at a very wrong moment, thus fuelling her anger even further. The set ended 4-25.

"With a week, from the tournaments, is this what we can do? I cannot lead such a team." She yelled and walked out of the court and sat on the corner of the field. Everyone looked at her, shocked with her anger. They hadn't expected such temperament from Yamuna.

"Girls, take your positions, we are clinching this set." Said Sonya, the vice-captain of the team. She substituted in an eleventh grade girl and the next set began. Yashan, too was surprised with the way, Yamuna acted. He decided to talk to her. He got up from where he was sitting, walked up and sat beside her. She was sitting with her head in between her knees, sobbing.

The girls had a team for volleyball, they were quite good and had a standard game. There was nothing of splendour. As always, they were expected to represent the school, win one or two matches, make it to the semis or quarters was all that they were expected to achieve and they did just that every year. They never practiced with an aim to win the tournament, but just to play a few decent games.

"Hey." Yashan said. She didn't look up. But the sobbing stopped. He rubbed her back and said, "It's going to be okay. You guys are good." She didn't mind his hand. But Yashan felt it was weird. He withdrew his hand back as soon as he had finished his sentence. She lifted her head up and wiped her tears.

"You aren't crying about the game. Are you?" Yashan asked. She simply shook her head, signifying that her tears were about something else.

"I thought so." He added.

"Look, you are a very good friend to me. If it's anything, you think I might be able to help with you with feel free to let me know." Yashan said hoping she might open up.

"You are proud to be called *Bambooz* aren't you?" she asked him.

"What?—Why are you asking that?" Yashan couldn't understand how, why his nickname had something to do with her being upset.

"Say yes or no." she said, wiping her cheeks with the back of her hand. Yashan shrugged, like as if it didn't matter what he was called by.

"In my old school, I was called '*Catwoman.*'" She looked at him. Yashan saw no connection in what she was saying. "*Catwoman,* implying, a black cat, the bringer of bad luck. If at all, I was involved in anything, it failed. When I came to this place, I hoped I might get to be someone other than a black ill-fated cat. I have no intention of winning the volleyball tournaments, I just wanted not to be a black cat. I don't care if the team loses the first round. But, here I am leading the team and if I don't win, I'm afraid that I might really be the black cat." Yashan found it a bit absurd. Nobody, would ever think of her that way, even if they lose the first round. She had never been referred in anyway similar as far as he knew.

"Look, I feel sorry that your previous school was filled with stupid fucks. This place is nothing like that. You see all the people you call as your batch mates, they are your brothers and sisters. You have been here for just six months, yet you are and will be one of us. That is how we live. You never have to be afraid of that black cat."

"Yashan, I'm not trying to prove the point to you people. I know how you consider me. From day one, never have I felt as a stranger in this school. It's my conscience that keeps itching over this black cat thing and I'm trying to silence it by winning the tournament. It's my own self that I'm fighting against." She said, her tears still rolling down.

"For the past eight years, a volleyball team has represented this school. They never practiced. All of a sudden, a group of girls will go and simply play a few matches. Out of luck they would win one or two matches. But this year you are leading them, not to represent but also to win; it's a big thing by itself. You are doing something that nobody has ever tried. And remember, what I said, how that we are your brother and sisters. We will always stand by you, even if the whole world roots against you, and even if your own bloody conscience roots against you." She smiled through her tears. Yashan meant every word that he said. The next set of the practice game ended, 19-25. And the whole week, went with such practices, not one of the match, the girls did win. But Yamuna remained confident with the team she was leading.

Unlike last year, this year their school didn't host the tournaments. It was to be conducted in a school at Idukki. The volleyball and the throw ball matches, were being conducted in a different school in Idukki altogether. The school had sent Mr Farooq, the senior Computer teacher as the team manager, for the Volleyball teams. As a team manager, he was actually being asked to supervise and make sure the students remain safe. It was almost like the job of a study supervisor, except that there was no study to supervise.

The *Bison Valley's* girls' team were better than most other teams. Their practice with the boys had made them trained for a higher level of volleyball, which the opponents couldn't match. One by one the opponents fell, and they had managed to qualify for the semis. They had a tough line-up in the semis. The girls knew well enough, that the semis was going to be their final game in the tournament. But they decided to do their best. They geared up for the matches. The boys' team not having any match at the same time, decided to be present to cheer up the girls.

To their luck, the umpire for the girls' match was none other than their former coach, Mr Jeyabal. The boys immediately went and greeted their coach and enquired about him. He had joined as the volleyball coach, in a school in Idukki. And thanks to the partial umpiring of their former coach, the girls' team grabbed a win. He gave a few 'tapes' that the opponents hadn't made and ignored a few that the *Bison's* made. The opponents sulked and the *Bison Valley* team made it to the finals. It was the first time a girls' team from *Bison Valley* was reaching the finals. And all the girls were very much happy. Yashan told Yamuna,

"Thanks to your luck. You got Mr Jeyabal to umpire. See you are not a black cat." She smiled. Eventually the finals followed.

14-16 was the score in the first set. Yashan had missed the start of the match because he was busy with the game they were playing. There was quite a crowd watching the game. Mr Farooq stood on the other side of the court, close to the bench, where the substitutes were sitting. The *Bison Valley* team was trailing by two points. Yashan realised it only when they lost another point. The score was 14-17 now. Soon, the other guys also had come. They joined together and began cheering for the girls. The scores improved and they went onto win the opponents in the first set. It ended 26-24.

Yashan signalled Vajish to go and give advice. They had no coach and Vajish was one of the best players. The girls' team gathered around Vajish and Chris. The two boys were making new strategy for the girl's team. The plans worked very well and the second set ended, 25-17. The opponents were getting pressurized. The *Bison Valley* team used the pressure to build their game.

The next set didn't go well for the *Bison Valley* girls. The opponents had brought in some substitutions to change the game. It worked for them. The third set went in the opponents favour, with 25-22. The girls didn't panic just yet. They had a set lead. In the fourth set, the *Bison Valley* picked up an early lead of seven points and had reached 23-17. They were two points from victory. And the serve was in the opponents hands. The girl who was playing the post position took up the serve. Her serve came on too fast and the *Bison Valley* players missed it. One. Two. Three . . . They took five straight points and narrowed the lead. No one was able to take up the serve. It was so fast, that it hurt to face it. Kavi dropped one of them out of fear itself. The *Bison Valley* team called for a time-out. Vajish tried telling them something to make them get the final two points. Just as they were getting ready to get back into the court, Yashan called Yamuna aside and told,

"You will never be able to take her service. Make eye contact with her. Give her an I'm-going-to-screw-you-look."

"What?"

"Distract her." He explained. He knew, that she hadn't understood him. But the referee blew the whistle. "Shoelace." He told to Yamuna. She looked down at her laces. They were tied up perfectly. Both the teams took up their positions. Yashan sincerely hoped Yamuna would understand what he meant, atleast by the time she bends down from tying the shoelace. The referee threw the ball to the opponent to serve. She walked up to the line. Just as she was about to serve, Yamuna called out to the umpire,

"Sir, sir." The whole audience looked at her. She pointed down at her shoes indicating she had to tie her laces. The referee asked the server to wait. Yamuna bent down and tied her laces. The entire crowd was glancing at the girl who had bent down to tie her shoe lace. The opponent server too was looking at her opponent who was bent down tying her shoelace. The plan was working.

And just as she got up, the expression on the face of the server changed. Yamuna had an indescribable expression on her face. The referee gave the signal to serve. And the serve came straight to Yamuna. She put her left foot back and stretched out her forearm. The ball bounced on her forearm. It hurt, but the ball was up in the air. Kavi took it up and she gave it to the post for a shot. The ball hit the mud in the opponent's court. They had the point and they had the broken the serve. The team celebrated.

"Yamuna, take the serve." Vajish called out from outside. She came and stood at the service line. Yashan was just a yard away from her. She looked at him smiling.

"Left side of number seven." Yashan said to her. She understood it immediately. And she sent the ball spinning into the opponent's court just to the left of the girl wearing a No.7 jersey. And the ball hit the ground. The point was theirs. They were a point away from winning the District Level tournaments. Yashan had asked her to repeat the same serve and for the second time too it worked.

The entire team was celebrating. The girls gathered together in a group hug. She looked at Vajish who had guided her to this victory and smiled at him in elation. Yashan saw Vajish's face light up too. Yashan had let Vajish make an attempt to impress Yamuna, thinking that he might fail, but Vajish, in the most unexpected way had impressed her. From now on, he had to take it a bit seriously. After a little while, the girls broke their hug and immediately, Yamuna ran towards him and threw around a hug. Yashan kept his hands at his side; not wanting to return the hug with a number of people watching, including his computer teacher, Mr Farooq. Sensing Yashan's hesitation, Yamuna too pulled away immediately. With one hand in her hair, her face flustered in bright red, she said,

"Ooops." She then went and gave a hi-five to Vajish. Her palms were as sweaty as her t-shirt. Yashan felt confident. Vajish might have gotten ahead with impressing her; that hug made him understand that he was way ahead of Vajish.

"You are all sweaty." Yashan said.

"Yeah. I have to change my t-shirt. Come with me till the restroom na?" she suggested. She ran to the substitution bench. There was one large air-bag there. She pulled out her track shirt and re-joined him. Yashan swung his backpack over his shoulder and walked along with her.

"You are no more a black cat." Yashan said.

"Yeah, I am not. See, no matter how big this victory might be, it is actually very trivial in front of my conscience. All that mattered so much to me was to prove myself that I am someone." She said.

"Good for you." Yashan replied to her philosophy. She seemed really happy. But, her happiness wasn't over the victory they had been struggling over. It was something within her mind. Yashan didn't understand it completely. He decided to let it go. Yamuna disappeared into the women's restroom while Yashan stood outside, waiting for her to return. She returned in a jiffy, with her track shirt on. She handed over her sweaty jersey to Yashan.

"Keep it in your bag, for now. I will take it back when we leave."

"Alright." Said Yashan shoving the t-shirt into his bag. The stickiness stuck to his fingers. Something transpired between them in that instant. A level of intimacy between the two. Something was brewing within Yashan's mind. He didn't like it. *It was a very casual gesture.*' he reassured himself. Body contact always meant a level of intimacy among boys.

The price-giving ceremony was in the other school. The volleyball and hockey teams went over there for the ceremony and to join with the other teams. Rohit's football team had won the finals. Rohit was jubilant over the victory. Tanveer had sneaked a camera and they were taking photos.

For, the girls' volleyball team, Yamuna went to the stage and collected the trophy. The entire girls' team took photos with the trophy. Yamuna got Yashan to stand with her along with the trophy and took a photo.

"Great game." Yashan.

"Thanks to you, Yash. Speaking of which, you really are a Bamboozler. How did you think she will flop her serve?"

"She didn't flop her service, you drew her attention and she served it to you."

"Then?" Yamuna was surprised. She had thought at first it was a trick that Yashan had done there

"I knew you will take her serve and that only you will take her serve. She served it to you and eventually lost." It was no trick that Yashan, the bambooz had come up with, and he had just put in some confidence in her.

"You have no idea, how much you mean to me at this moment. I am so glad that we met. Thank you so much." Yamuna said. It was the one thing, she should have never said. That small part of him that said that she was meant to be more than a friend was aroused. With Vajish too trying to impress Yamuna, that little animal in him will not be quenched. It began twisting his thoughts, corrupting his emotions into thinking that she loved him.

"You won the trophy. No need to thank me and all."

"For having been my best friend."

"I will be forever."

"Do a pinkie swear?" she said pointing out her little finger.

"What swear?" Yashan hadn't heard of anything like that. Yamuna explained. Yashan declined to swear because it sounded too girly. But, deep within him it felt like he had declined it for some other reason.

"Alright. Let's take an oath, over this victory."

"Fine. Oath on?" Yashan questioned.

"You and I, best friends forever."

"Forever we will be." Yashan said. Then the two friends kissed on either side of the cup. Rohit managed to take a photo of the two kissing the cup.

With the tournaments drawing to an end, the classes resumed its burden. Yashan's mind had been stirred. *Was that a casual gesture?*

It had her sweat. It was in contact with her body and she handed it over to him very casually. Was their friendship that intimate? Or was it friendship at all? Yashan's mind hadn't forgotten the minutest detail from the tournaments. She had handed over to him her sweaty jersey. He had it for only a short while. But, it had disturbed him.

Did she love him? He liked her very much. She would make a very good lover. He analysed everything that happened from that day on to see if she loved him. On Sunday afternoons, when he was idle, he would sit in the volleyball court, fantasizing her proposing to him. *How should I react? Should I say a yes or a no?*

No way, I can't think of her that way. She is a good friend. But, they had known each other for about six months. Was it just friendship still?'

Yashan was losing control of his thoughts. No matter where they originate it diverted towards Yamuna. He relived all those memories that he had of her. His life had changed very much from the January she had entered. All through these months there was one major thought that ran in his mind always. He realized it when he was conversing with Rohit

"She gave me a sweaty t-shirt. What do you make of that?"

"Seriously, is that what is running in your head, *Bambooz*?" Rohit asked looking puzzled.

"Why? What's wrong in it?" Yashan questioned confused by what Rohit was trying to say.

"Nothing's wrong. Before and all, anytime I come and ask you what is running in your mind, you will be having some weird explanation about the purpose of our life. But, for the past few months, the only thing you talk to me is about Yamuna. She has really done something to you." Rohit explained.

"It sounds cheesy and lame. Doesn't it? God! When did I become like this?"

"No. I didn't mean it like that. I understand how you are feeling. This summer hols I went to Pondicherry, didn't I? All I was hoping was to meet Sanjana."

"But you said she was going back to England."

"Yes. I knew that better than you. I just hoped for the impossible. It's her native and maybe she could have come for her summer holidays. I was fantasizing that during my entire holidays. It just never came to pass and will never. She changed a lot of things in my life." Rohit said, recollecting his fantasy.

Yashan analysed how much he himself had changed. The trickery that he did to make himself as the M.C. in order to be with her, made him to be known in the batch as the 'Bambooz.' Eventually, he had found himself getting involved in every manipulation that was there to be done. Postponing weekly tests, reducing the homework load, getting the supervisor to let them sleep in the study, for all of those stuff, he was the guy. Ever since she had come into his life, he had become somebody in the batch. Everyone looked to him for help. He was gaining influence amongst his friends. That mattered very much to every teen, to have a good influence among the peers.

VIRUS IN THE LAB

TESTS AFTER TESTS were being conducted. That was the 12th grade. Marks were everything. Without the necessary marks, you would never be able to make your way into the college of your choice, unless you had money. And money meant, loads and loads of money. With the burden of studies on him, Yashan hardly got time to talk to Yamuna. Only the computer classes gave them that freedom. There were being tests added. Only about once in two weeks, they had the chance to go to the lab. And when they did, Yashan tried to maximise the quality time he got to share with Yamuna. At one time, when he was talking to Yamuna, the sir had spotted him. Yashan immediately, but conspicuously turned away and tried to focus on the screen. Yashan knew it was too late. Mr Farooq was coming straight towards him. Yashan immediately erased the browser history and closed Firefox.

"What are you doing?" Mr Farooq asked. Mr Farooq knew too well that the two had something in between them. He had also watched the two of them share a brief hug, during the tournaments.

"Nothing, sir." Yashan replied. He turned and asked the same question to Yamuna. She simply shook her head.

"Yashan, open your inbox." The sir demanded.

"Sir?" Yashan was surprised.

"Open your damn mail, I said" his voice got louder. The other students turned around.

"Why sir? It's private." Yashan back answered.

"It's private? I know what you just did. I can take you to the principal. Are you going to open it or not?"

"Sir, I forgot my password. And moreover, I deleted all my mails." He lied.

"This is it. I'm taking you both to principal." His teacher threatened. Yashan couldn't let this happen. He was also putting Yamuna at risk. The school didn't mind casual boy-girl interaction. But, if anything more than casual was suspected it was considered a serious offence.

"Sir, I have the password written in my diary and the diary is in the hostel." Yashan interrupted before his sir could say anything.

"Go take it and come." Yashan got up and walked out. The whole class was looking at him. Yamuna seemed anxious. Yashan came out of the lab. He had no password written down in his diary. He knew it by heart. He couldn't let his teacher see his mail, it would mean bad news for both himself and Yamuna. He tried to think of something, to cover up the issue. *Could I just go and hide myself in the toilet until the class was over? No, that is just lame. Moreover, sir will ask in the next class for the password.* And then an idea entered in. He went to the administrative office and into the reception.

"Excuse me Ma'am, Farooq sir has asked me to check a mail for him. Can I do it?" He asked the receptionist. The reception had a computer and an internet connection. If he could delete his mails that he had sent and received he would be safe. Definitely, the sir wouldn't check Yamuna's mail. The teachers, especially the gents' staff, maintained a safe distance from the girls. Hence hopefully, he wouldn't check Yamuna's inbox.

"What? Is there no internet connection in the computer lab?"

"Ma'am it is there. All computers there use the same network, it could be easily hacked. So sir wanted me to check the mail from a different network."

"Why did sir want you to check the mail? Can't he do it himself during the break?"

"He said it's urgent."

"Okay fine." She said and gave Yashan the access to the keyboard. He opened the browser and typed in the URL

"Ma'am I have to type the password. Can you look away?" Yashan asked politely.

"He trusted a student with an e-mail password and you don't think he would mind telling me what the password is?" the receptionist sounded suspicious.

"Ma'am being a student. I don't have easy access to email. So by the time he changes his password, the likelihood of me opening his mail is non-existent. But, on the other hand, you have access to it, all the time." The receptionist knew that the student had a point, although she didn't like it. Without saying a word, she got up and moved to the other side of the table. Yashan took advantage by sitting down and he typed in the password.

"Done." She asked.

"Wait ma'am. I have typed it wrong and the page is reloading." He told.

He hadn't made any mistake with the password. But if he had said that he had entered the password, she would return to look into the computer. With her not looking, he deleted all his mails in a click and logged out. And three minutes later, he was in front of his allotted computer, at the computer lab, punching in the password. His mailbox came up on the screen.

"It is empty." Mr Farooq observed.

"I told you that before you sent me out, sir." Yashan replied. Yamuna breathed a sigh. Mr Farooq knew that the two had been chatting. He didn't have any evidence against them. He looked enraged.

"Follow me. I'm going to allot you a new computer." He said. Yashan followed him. He told Yashan to use the system he himself was using in his cabin. Yashan was suspicious why would sir give him his own system. Then Yashan noticed. Among the installed programmes, there was also a programme that tracked the key presses. Yashan could not open his mail in from this system. To add to the disadvantage, it was far off from Yamuna. He couldn't even talk to her directly. He was facing in a different direction altogether. And that cost Yashan dearly.

The Quarterly exams were approaching. Yashan hadn't been able to stay much in touch. They hardly were able to talk. Being in 12th they didn't have the privilege of any distractions from the daily routine. Yashan was missing her. But, he believed it was all for good. With her away, the part of him that said that he was in love with Yamuna was silenced. The nearer he got to her, the louder were his feelings. At one point, Yashan himself thought it was most right to propose to her. But then decided against it, moments later. Yashan knew that he wouldn't be able to keep the feelings within reins for long. He had to deal with them, somehow without sabotaging his friendship.

If he stayed away from Yamuna, he would be less tempted to propose to her. Yashan felt that the sane part in him, didn't want him to propose. But the more he stayed away, Vajish was closing in on her. He couldn't bear the thought of Vajish taking her away from him.

The holidays finally began and Yashan couldn't be happier. The first day he got home, he began chatting with Yamuna. On the first day, the two of them chatted for almost seven hours. Mostly, bitching about Mr Farooq, then talking about how they had missed each other. It felt like they had been together all the time. Yashan didn't miss her anymore. They tried to contrive a plan to stay nearer than they had been, when they return for their second term.

And every now and then, Yamuna mentioned Vajish. And every time she did, it hurt him. Yashan tried to not be hurt by it. But something inside him, felt like it was on fire. He had known Vajish for seven years. Vajish was a good friend and he never had any dislike for him. He tried to be happy for Vajish. But no. It wasn't happening.

Eventually Yashan found a way they could go back to mailing in school. He had found a workaround software for the key press tracker. He had been so engrossed about this workaround, he had forgotten a very important opportunity to spend time with Yamuna. It was the annual exhibition. Without realizing this, he along with Rohit had given his name to the department of English. But, Yamuna, hoping to find Yashan, there in the computer department had given her name there. Vajish too had given his name in the computer science department. This had allowed Vajish to spend time with Yamuna. Yashan was disappointed. His mind was being torn into a war, considering whether to fall in love or not.

ANOTHER FAREWELL

I T WAS THE farewell night once again in Bison Valley. The December breeze was playing in. Yashan had his hands in his pockets. And in his right hand that was in his pocket, he was clutching the little gift he had bought. It was a parting gift, he had decided to buy for his best friend. In his mind, he had more than just the gift in plan. The girls were doing a dance programme. It was a classical and nobody was interested. Yashan took out the little gift wrapped package and showed it to Rohit, who sat beside him.

"A parting gift for Yamuna?" he asked.

"Yes, but there's more to it. I'm going to take her on a walk to the computer lab corridor and I'm going to propose"

"Prop—What? You are going to? Really?" Rohit's eyes were almost falling out. He didn't seem to be believing it.

"Yes."

"As your best friend, there are hundred good dialogues, I want to say right now. But I'm going to let it pass, and just say, I'm happy for you, man." Rohit said, smiling at his friend.

"Thanks, bro." Yashan told his best friend.

"My god, I can't believe this is happening. When you did all that stuff, to get to know her during Sports day, I knew this girl meant something to you. But tell me, how long this has been going on." Rohit said with joy.

"Ever since the volleyball game, my mind had been twisting and turning over it."

"I never expected this from you, *Bambooz*."

"What are you doing, tonight?" Yashan asked.

"Remember, previous farewell. With Sanjana. I still miss her. I'm going to the roof of this building and look back at my memories."

"That's just sad, dude."

"No, it isn't really bad, man. She was actually just a crush, I don't know why I had never been able to admit it when she was there. But to look at it from now, she was my first crush and I don't regret it. She is special." Yashan didn't have anything to say. His friend wasn't disappointed or gloomy over Sanjana. And he didn't mind. The programme was longer than the previous years. It was quite good.

At the announcement that the dinner had begun, long queues began forming in front of the counter. The 12th students had a special counter and it let them get their food quick. Yashan was thinking and rehearsing on how to say it to Yamuna. Out of his nervousness, he didn't want to spend the dinner along with his other batch guys. Rohit was nowhere to be seen. Yashan was talking to a few junior boys when, Chris came up to him,

"Dude, can you come along? There's something for you."

With his hands toying with the gift package in his pocket, he didn't try and wonder why Chris must have called him. His focus was on how Yamuna will take it. *Will she say a yes?* He still remembered the kiss they had planted on the Volleyball trophy. They had taken an oath. *Am I breaking the oath by proposing to her?* He was full of doubts. Chris had brought to him the place where, all the other guys and even a few girls were there.

"Yashan, I have something to tell you." It was Vajish. Yashan nodded his head to signal that he was paying attention.

"Look, I don't know what you are going to say about this. But let me tell you. If you have any objection I will comply according to you."

"What?" Yashan hadn't expected anything vague like this. He didn't understand it either.

"Dude, I think I'm in love with Yamuna." Vajish paused as if he was waiting for Yashan to take it in. Yashan was completely taken aback, *I am bloody going to propose to the same girl and he is telling it to me now? This evening, she is mine.* Had Rohit told them already about his plan of proposing tonight?

"I'm planning to propose to her tonight." Vajish was talking a bit slowly. He showed to Yashan a gift wrapped package, a little larger than the one in his own pocket.

"Look, all that I know is that you and she were like best friends. That is what she had told me once. I probably should have asked you this earlier. But, do you have anything against me proposing to her. See, you tell me that you don't want me to propose, or that you love her, I will throw away this gift. I just want to know if you are okay. And I remember well, when I came to you for help, you put her aside for my sake, because you had known me for seven years." Yashan was processing everything. Yashan was slightly guilty that he had tried to mislead Vajish. Yashan had his hands still in his pocket, clutching the gift he had purchased. Everybody was waiting for a response from him. *I could confess my love and Vajish will drop his plan. Will he really do that? Even if he throws away the gift, what of his feelings?*

"Dude, do you have something to say?" It was Christopher. Yashan took his hands out of his pockets and threw them around Vajish pulling him into a hug.

"There are hundred good dialogues, I want to say right now. But I'm going to let it pass, and just say, I'm happy for you, man" he repeated the same thing that Rohit had said to him earlier in the evening.

"Thanks, bro." said Vajish. The two friends pulled away from each other.

"Look, it was nice of you to have told me this, because I was planning on taking her for a walk, but right now, your moment is more important. And good luck." Said Yashan as he let all his plans that he had built, crash. But there was something else he saw as the result of the outcome.

Yashan walked out from among his friends. He wasn't yet fully convinced why he had said yes to Vajish. But, he saw many things in it. For the past two and a half months, the part of him that had decided to propose to her had caused the other part of him to take a plunge into guilt. He had been feeling bad that he had destroyed the beautiful friendship that he and Yamuna had with the confused aspects of love. And once a thought takes root in your mind, there is no eradicating it. With Vajish's proposal, if Yamuna accepts, his mind would be at peace. He wouldn't think of proposing to her and at the same time he could be friends with her. That's how he saw it.

He searched the crowds for Yamuna. She was standing with Sonya and Kavi, wearing her white *salwar*. She looked beautiful in it. She was having an ice-cream and chatting with her friends. And then she caught his eye. She looked back at him. Just, as she looked, she smiled at him and in an instant she bent down. Their eye-contact had been perturbed by a junior who handed over something to her. Yashan kept looking in her direction. It was a tiny bit of paper that she unfurled and read. She mumbled something to her friends, the three friends looked up into the sky. Yashan wondered why the hell they were looking up at the sky. Then she spoke something to the junior. He must have been second or third grade. The boy, pointed towards a far corner of the courtyard. Yashan's eyes followed the direction. It was his batch mates, they had been standing there the whole dinner time. Then, something hit upon Yashan's mind. It told him to join with his batch mates. He quickly walked up to his batch mates, who had gathered in a tight circle around something. Yashan peeked in,

"What's happening, guys?" He saw Vajish squatting on the ground. "Whoa! What are you doing, Vajish?" Yashan asked. Jagdish came up from behind and told him,

"Don't look immediately. But if you see to the right side of the stage, you will notice Yamuna talking to a junior." Yashan didn't have to turn to know what Yamuna was doing.

"Yes?" he said

"Vajish had sent her a message telling her to come to the terrace. Now, when she goes up there he is going to surprise and propose her."

"Very romantic." Yashan said. But Jagdish had turned away his attention to Yamuna. Yashan saw Yamuna set her plate down to climb up. There was one thing only Yashan knew. He had to go to the terrace. No matter what happens, he should go there before Yamuna or Vajish. Yashan, guessing Yamuna to take the steps behind the principal's office, the one that was closest to her. Vajish would take the steps that they usually took to reach the class. Yashan decided to take the flight of stairs that was near their 11th grade classes. Just as he was about to climb up, someone caught him. It was the same junior who was delivering the letter to Yamuna.

"Anna, one *akka* is waiting for you behind principal's office." The boy told Yashan. Yashan knew it must be Yamuna. But he didn't realize why. He went there to find her waiting for him.

"Yash, Vajish is planning to-"

"I know." He cut her mid-sentence.

"You know?" she was surprised that her friend hadn't told her.

"Just few minutes ago."

"What should I say?"

"You are asking me?" Yashan almost laughed out. It seemed funny to him. It was the second time he was given the control over the same thing. *First, Vajish asks me if he should propose. Now she is asking me how she should react. Why am I being given the remote-control from both sides? Is the universe trying to say something? Are we destined for each other? Am I supposed to manipulate the whole thing?*

"You are my best friend and you have known him for a number of years. What's your take on this?"

"This is not a movie, to ask my opinion. It's your life. It should be your decision."

"I need some help, man." She said. Yashan knew he still had a chance to propose to her. She might agree or may not. If she was intending on agreeing to Vajish, she would definitely accept his proposal. All he had to do was pull out the gift that he had brought. But something held him back. That would be stabbing Vajish behind the back. But Yashan knew too well, how much it would burn to watch Yamuna with Vajish. He had once almost destroyed the friendship because of his jealousy. He could manipulate everything and make him look clean, yet win Yamuna. But he didn't want to dirty his conscience with betrayal. And there was one more thing.

"You want help? Here it is. Go to the ladies room. Do some touch-up on your makeup and go up there and confront him."

"Chee. *Poda.* I asked you for advice." She said expressing mock regret for having called him. Saying this this she went into the restroom.

Once out of sight Yashan sprinted up, skipping steps to get on top as early as he could. And when he reached the terrace, it was empty. He looked around. Rohit was sitting there with a lot of ice-cream on his plate.

"What are you doing here?" Rohit asked.

"We have got to get down from here." He said.

"Is the watchman coming?" Rohit asked, not aware of what was about to happen. He picked up his plate and slowly rose up. Just then, they heard the jingling of Yamuna's anklets. Yashan knew it was too late.

"Hide." He told Rohit and the two best friends climbed over the clock tower and into the hostel terrace. Yamuna had come up, she walked around the terrace once and then went and leaned near the parapet wall.

"Oh! Change of plans, huh? Go ahead, surprise her. I won't overhear anything. Just like you did last year." whispered Rohit to Yashan with his smile wide apart.

"Shut up, will you?" Yashan wasn't very happy. If he was found there, it would be totally weird.

"Sorry, sorry." His friend apologized. Soon they heard another set of footsteps. They waited in silence.

"Hey, Yamuna." They heard a familiar voice. It was the Andromeda house captain, Vajish.

"What is he doing here?" Rohit whispered. Yashan explained the sudden turn of events.

"Why did you do that?" Rohit looked upset that his friend had given up.

"We are friends. What if she considered me as a friend?" Yashan put back a question.

"Dude. You have got to be kidding me. You love her. You will regret this decision for the rest of your life."

"No Rohit. I won't. I was simply afraid that I might lose her friendship, because within my mind the doubts of love had begun. Now, with her being Vajish's girlfriend, I won't have any such doubts. That will save our friendship." He replied.

"Bullshit." His friend said, trying to express his annoyance without making any noise.

"You and I have been good friends and we will have to part now." Yamuna was saying to Vajish. They could overhear the conversation, the two of them had moved closer to the tank.

"What if we don't have to?" it was Vajish.

"What?"

"I love you, Yamuna." Said Vajish. There was a silence between the two of them. The music played from the courtyard was soft and it provided the perfect ambience for the night. And in that perfect moment, Yashan heard those dreaded words that he had desired to have been meant for him.

"I—I love you too."

A part of him cried in agony. His whole body felt like it was being crushed by an invisible object. A part of his mind wanted to get out there and push Vajish off the terrace, but Yashan didn't move. He pulled out his gift.

Rohit looked at his friend. He was toying with the gift he had bought for Yamuna. He threw it out of his hands, into the tea estate, that was there outside the fences.

"It's time to let go." He said. There was complete silence. They guessed that the two of them must have gone down. Yashan slightly lifted his head to confirm his guess. He was wrong. Vajish was still there, with his lips perched on Yamuna's. The two had their eyes closed in passion.

Yashan crouched down again. After about five minutes, they heard their footsteps travelling the stairs. The two friends came down from where they had been hiding. From the parapet on the inner side, Yashan looked down, Vajish was excitedly conveying the news to everyone. Yamuna too seemed excited.

"You are a freaking Bamboozler, why did you let this happen?"

"That is why." He said. Yashan looked confused.

"Every person has an identity, me a bamboozler. She was the one who made me the bamboozler. Till the sports day, I was just another guy in the batch. But, ever since she came, I became a somebody. I had an identity of my own. I want this identity. You yourself told that you never expected me to fall in love with her. You see, I am not the one who should be falling in love. That is so not-me."

"What are you talking? How would falling in love change the fact that you are a bamboozler? You will always be one. And you think that by letting her go you will lose your identity, but let me tell you. By letting her go you are losing the person, who gave you the identity."

"It may not be possible for you to understand. See, no matter how big the fact that I gave away Yamuna might seem, it is actually very trivial in front of my conscience. All that mattered so much to me was to prove myself that I am someone. Look, it may not be easy for you to understand. I am at peace."

"You gave up your love, so that you could be called a bamboozler? Dude, you will regret this choice."

"Funny, isn't it? What do you think is love, Rohit? It is only a feeling that is usually misconceived. It is a choice: to love or not to love. If you choose yes, every part of you, lives for that girl. Else, nothing would change. Love exists only till the desire to do so does." He replied, looking down at the people.

"You should have twisted everything, lied to everyone and should have proposed to her. But instead, you gave up on what you desired. That is the one thing the bamboozler never did. After all, looks like you have lost your identity, Mr Bambooz." Said Rohit and went down the stairs. Yashan didn't have anything to say either. He had given her up. But he had no idea, if he had done the right thing. Something inside him was at peace. The animal that craved for the love was gone. There was probably no going back. To go back on what he had done would mean, stabbing his friend at the back. Yashan could never do that. Tears were rolling down his eyes.

The winter vacation had begun. Yashan went into his chat messenger. He found her there. Like nothing had changed, he opened a chat box and sent a 'hi'. He believed, nothing had changed at all, they were friends, but he was far from realizing it. She replied back, and the two good friends chatted for hours. They did chat for some time. Yashan was glad that things had gone the way he had made it to. At first it felt like it was all the same. But with the progression of time, he realized that it wasn't as good as it used to be. He found it weird every time their chat touched upon Vajish. They didn't chat as they used to previously, it was only once in two days. And when the holidays ended, the last few days at school had begun. The clocks were ticking down. The exams were approaching. And everyone were engrossed in studies. The classes were almost non-existent. The teachers had finished the portions by December itself. It was just revision study, and tests. Both offered very little time for Yashan to talk to Yamuna. The computer teacher stopped taking them to the computer hall.

"Who is the creator of C++" *Yashan sat thinking.* He had studied, but he had forgot. Yashan, not able to recollect, decided to go with the next and the last question on his paper. It was the day of his final exam. It was computer science. The biology and the commerce students had already left. It sucked to have them not there. It was very depressing, that after having been together for so long they had to depart early. He knew the answer to it. He immediately wrote it down and looked back at the previous question trying to figure out what it was. He sat thinking on it for a long time.

"Tie up your papers." The invigilator said. Yashan decided to give up on answering it and tied up his paper. Drew lines here and there to make his paper look neat. He read through the programmes that he had written to make sure there were no mistakes. And when the bell rang, the teacher, collected the papers. He got up and walked out. Vajish, who had come out, before Yashan stood near the hall without leaving. Yashan had wanted to say a proper goodbye to Yamuna, who had been a very good friend to him during the year. She came out and went straight towards Vajish. He saw the two of them talk something. They were bidding their byes too. Yashan decided he shouldn't interrupt. He decided to stand a little away and wait for her. Just then, Rohit came. Yashan pulled him near as an excuse for standing near the exam hall.

"Hey, how was your exam?" Rohit asked.

"Good." Yashan replied without taking his eyes off Yamuna.

"Oh! Going to say goodbye to her, huh?" he said.

"Hey, what's the answer to the second last objective question?" he asked his friend.

"Oh! It's option (A)." Yashan replied.

"Shit. I thought it was, but marked (D)" Yashan regretted. Just then, Yamuna was stepping away from Vajish, waving her hand. The other girls had already left. To avoid trouble, she took to her heels, in the direction of her hostel, before Yashan could stop her.

"Goodbye, Yamuna." Yashan whispered to himself. He had once said to his best friend that he had let her go in order to save the identity he had gained. He decided to stay the 'Bamboozler.' That's how it all seemed to him then. And within himself he knew it wasn't the true reason he let Yamuna away. He had managed to evade his thoughts. But now it came back to him. He looked into his thoughts. The real reason was there. He simply didn't want the beautiful friendship to have been destroyed by the prospects of love. Or in simpler terms, he was afraid to propose, for fear of rejection. That was the reason why his conscience didn't let him pull out his gift that night, under the stairs. And now, she was gone. Forever.

CHAPTER 5

J UST THEN, HE noticed a pair of hands come from the behind and before he reacted, it covered his eyes. The hand felt very soft, like that of a woman. The touch of the hands radiated warmth into his eyes. Startled, Rohit spilt a little bit of the cold water over his T-shirt. And it trickled underneath and touched his chest, making him feel a chill shock across the midline of his chest. But, that wasn't bothering Rohit. His mind had been busy with the hands covering his vision. It wouldn't be Nishi or Yashan, because they were busy with their scheming. He knew that there was just one other person on board that he knew. And he very much wanted those hands to belong to the same person.

"Sanjana." He said and lifter her hands off his face. She immediately covered her mouth in elation. In front of him stood a woman. Her face with features resembling the girl whom he had just mentioned. Her hair looked different and longer. She appeared to be of the same height she had been when she was at school. It had been eight years. She was wearing a *chudithar*. It looked like it was a party wear. She was smiling at him. The smile hadn't changed at all. It was still the same smile that she had given him eight years ago.

"Hey, sleepy head." She greeted him. Rohit couldn't believe his excitement. It was the same feeling he had had when she appreciated his dance. It hadn't changed. Neither had she. She looked very different from the Sanjana he had seen in her dream. She seemed pretty much the same girl, she was at school.

"What are you doing here?" he questioned her. He meant what she was doing in India, when she had told him that she might never return.

"With friends. I came here for a function. Then some old friends asked them to join along for the wedding. You?" She explained.

"Similar story." Rohit answered.

"So what are you doing now, man?" she asked.

"Going to graduate. Then job and all that stuff."

"Marriage?"

"Yeah! But I don't think right away."

"Nice spot for a wedding? Isn't it?" she commented on the cruise.

"Yes. The families must be filthy rich."

"But, it's kind of boring here. The bride is only a friend of a friend. So I don't know anyone here and it sucks."

"Yeah, same thing for me too. My friend's friend is the groom. She came to wish. Just for company I and a friend of mine came along. You remember Yashan from my class? He is here."

"Oh! So you are bored here?" she questioned. Rohit had an idea. He could ask her to go out. It was late in the night. So what?

"Yep. You know any place we can go nearby?" he asked making an indirect request to her to join with him.

"There's a Café coffee day nearby. Shall we go there? It'll be like old times. My friend's *Scooty* is here." Rohit readily agreed to her suggestion. But he was going to have to ditch his friends. Rohit had known that this was bound to happen. He left a message to Nishi and got on the *Scooty*. The two of them were on the ECR, headed to the cafe.

Having a date with Sanjana in a CCD at Pondicherry had been the thing he had fantasized during the summer vacations after Sanjana left. And right now a dream and a fantasy seemed to be coming true.

CHAPTER 6

"YASH." A FAMILIAR voice erupted from the person who had just climbed up. Yashan was thrown aback. It could never be. There was no plausible reason as to why she would be here. He tried to see if there were any other explanation. She took a step closer and it was really her.

"Yamuna?" he asked with a doubt. He knew he was quite sure that it was Yamuna. But, he said her name so slow, that it sounded like a question.

"How come that you are here?" Yamuna said with her face filled with joy.

"Who asked you to come here?" he asked sounding paranoid.

"What?" she asked with a puzzled look. The happiness on her face was still there.

"No, I meant, what are you doing here?" he asked her. '*This is too cool to happen for real. Tarun is Nishi's first crush. Sanjana is Tarun's first crush. Yamuna is my first cru-, no good friend. And all the six are on the same boat?*' he thought within himself. His mind hadn't let him label Yamuna as a crush all of a sudden. Only earlier this evening he had mentioned that she was a crush. And yet his mind refused to label her now. Yamuna was laughing violently,

"What am I doing here? What are YOU doing, man?" she questioned him. Yashan didn't see anything as funny as it seemed to Yamuna.

"I'm here with friends." He said with a blatant face.

"For?"

"One, of my friends; he knows the groom." He said. Something in him, didn't let him mention that his friend who knew the groom was a 'she'

"Oh! You mean bastard. You're not here for me? Do you know who I am?"

"You're Yamuna. And I still don't understand what you're here for." He said. She laughed again.

"Idiot. I am the bride." She asserted. Yashan felt a jolt. '*I am at Yamuna's wedding. I am at the wedding of my once best friend whom I was in love with. The girl I loved once is getting married to a jerk who dumped my other best friend. Is there no karma anymore? What the hell?*' Yashan's thoughts were racing.

"You look petrified." She added. Yashan returned to the reality.

"I just didn't know you were getting married." He said to her.

"Answer that now. You aren't here for me? How dare you?" she said throwing a fake punch into his arm. That fake punch, it made him feel like as if they had never been separated at all. As though nothing had changed. Yet, there was a gap of seven years, the two hadn't met any time after school. They hardly stayed in touch.

"This is unbelievable. I didn't expect you to be here. Don't get me wrong, I'm actually glad you're here. I don't even understand how this is even remotely possible." She added. Yashan had no idea of what to reply. Nishi was all excited.

"I'm the one who doesn't understand. We leave school and you don't turn up online for any chat. Yes, our lives have been busy, true. But, not even an e-mail? I thought you forgot me. And you didn't even invite me?" Yashan questioned.

"Don't ask me what happened after school? Sorry, for not inviting, but how did you get here if you didn't have an invite." Yashan questioned.

"Funny thing. I tried to fake another name. It failed. Then, Tarun's grandfather-in-law, I mean your granddad." He said.

"I meant why did you come here? You know, without even knowing it was my wedding?" She questioned him.

"As I said, I came with friends. A friend of mine knows Tarun. And when did Tarun come into your life?" Yashan asked.

"Do you know him?" she asked.

"No, I don't know."

"We found each other through Online Matrimony website." She said.

"How did you agree to marry him?" Yashan said with a tone of disgust. During, his UG Yashan had designed a prototype for a dating website. He knew what algorithms went into the programme. The fact that in arranged marriages, the choice is made by almost the whole family was horrible enough. To think that some computer gibberish created by a software engineer in his cubicle deciding a partner for your life, was a nightmare.

"What are you implying?" she asked, looking suspicious. For the first time, that night, the happiness seemed to have drained of her face. Yashan realized the stupidity of his question. It was alright from his perspective. But from her point of view, it was so wrong and awkward. It sounded like he was doubting the wedding.

"I didn't mean anything by it. It sounded very awkward. I simply asked, have you both talked to each other?"

"Obviously, yes. We went out a couple of time and got to know each other. He is a nice guy. Like you, man." Yamuna said.

"My god! You are going out with people. You are getting married. Times have changed, haven't they?" Yashan said with a sigh, thinking on how much life had changed ever since they had left school. She noticed Yamuna looked way more mature and grownup in her Prussian blue sari, her hair longer than when she was school. It was plaited. Her hands were decorated with mehendi. She was no more the girl he had befriended, she was a woman now, ready to start a family.

"Yeah, man. You know, when I was in school, I used to dream how my future will be. There was one thing that I was afraid of, my marriage. You know, why? I used to fantasize myself becoming this, that and lots of things. I was able to imagine myself becoming great. But, marriage no. I used to think life ends in marriage. Because, I was able to imagine anything except life in marriage. You see it's different for guys, but a girl. She has no idea, who the guy is going to be. What his family will be like. Will she ever be what she wanted to be after marriage? It used to terrify me, you know." Said Yamuna.

"Yeah." Yamuna was sharing her teenage philosophy. There was no point in objecting them. So he simply acknowledged. "What happened between you and Vajish?" Yashan questioned shifting the topic again.

"Ah! We broke up. You thought that teenage love will work out huh?" Yamuna laughingly said. It was like as if Vajish was a joke in her life. She went on, "Actually, I was hoping you would propose to me that night. That's why I called you under the stairs. But, you didn't say anything. I felt guilty that I had been in love, while you considered me as good friend. To avoid that guilt eating me, I agreed to Vajish's proposal. And I realized that staying in touch with you might make me feel bad, so I distanced myself away from you. It was hard. But I had to. That's why I didn't make an effort to stay in touch. I'm sorry. I broke the pact that we made." She said. This was something Yashan had never dreamt of. She had made a huge confession. May be it wasn't so big to her, but it was, to him.

"You said teenage love doesn't work out, didn't you? Then we would have broken up too sooner or later if I had proposed. Is that what you wanted?"

"You are not the same as Vajish, man. I won't say that we definitely could have been together. But if it had been you, everything in my life would have different. We might have broken up even, but it's you. I don't know, things could have got better or something. Remember the volleyball trophy that we swore on? I have never done any such thing with Vajish or anyone else in my life." She said. Yashan had a strange euphoric feeling inside him. The only time he had the same feeling was when Yamuna handed over her sweaty jersey to him. Nothing was going to change because of what she had just said. It would be terrible to try and change anything now. But, the fact she too had once been in love with him. He had a feeling like his story was complete. He had never considered it incomplete, like Nishi did. But, that moment it felt more complete than ever. Somewhere, in the far corner of his mind, it began to tick. A plan was taking shape within the recess of his brain.

*   *   *

"Nishi?" the voice called out. She turned around. She didn't say anything.

"Wow, I never expected you, here." At first Tarun sounded excited, but then it was like as if he tried to mask his excitement, his voice dulled down. Nishi's broken memories flashed through her mind again. It had been four years. He looked almost the same guy she had been in love with. It was only the hair that had changed.

"I can't believe that you came." Tarun said. *'He can't believe that I'm here? So, was he hoping for me to come to the wedding?'* Nishi's thoughts raced.

"I was hoping you would come." Tarun added, as if he had read her mind. Nishi's inner voice panicked, *'Oh my God! Why did he want me to be here?'* She decided to voice her thoughts out.

"Why were you hoping for me to come?" she asked with a tone of suspicion.

"Just to know that you are okay." He said.

"Okay about what?" she asked.

"The e-mail. I know it wasn't a proper way to say goodbye. But, I had to. I was too ashamed to face you." Tarun explained. But, Nishi couldn't make head or tail out of it.

"What mail? I don't understand. All you left was a note saying *'goodbye'*. What are you talking about?"

"I sent a mail to you the next day. It explained why I had left. And everything else." He told. It seemed like Tarun was equally confused.

"Oh! I remember. I got a mail. But, I never opened it. I was afraid that you might have broken up with me. So, you didn't break up with me?" Nishi was slightly elated to hear that her incomplete story wasn't over yet.

"No, no, no. That mail actually explained why I was breaking up with you." Nishi's elation hit the ground.

"Why did you break up with me?"

"Listen, shall we talk about this elsewhere?" Tarun asked.

"Where?"

"We'll go to the hotel."

"Back to the shore?" Nishi was surprised that Tarun didn't want to explain it to her then and there.

"Yes."

"See, I came with some friends, I can't abandon them."

"Listen, we will go and return in a moment. Please. I need to know you are okay before I get married." He said. Nishi couldn't make sense of half of what he was intending. But, she may not have time, she just played along.

"Won't anyone think wrong? If they see you going to the shore with a girl, just the night before your marriage."

"That is my concern. I think I can risk that." Tarun told, still trying to convince her. Nishi too wanted to know the ending to her college love. That was the reason she had come, but Tarun might be risking something here. She was worried if anything goes wrong. On one side, she didn't want anything to go wrong with Tarun's wedding because of her. On the other hand, she was anxious if Rohit might do something stupid.

"I know it's your problem. But, just because of that I can't bear you take this risk for probably nothing."

"Listen, most of them are asleep. Only my family is sitting in the lower deck of the ship. We will take a boat from the front side of the boat. No one will see us slip away. Trust me. My friend in the other room will cover for me. He is the one who is supposed to be responsible for me. It's my stag party, no one in my family will disturb.

"Alright." Nishi agreed. She was not sure if it was the right decision she was making. She had sworn to her parents that she will never see Tarun ever again. Yet, here she was ready to ride out with him. It was 1:30 am. It felt terribly wrong.

CHAPTER 7

"SIR, WHAT ARE you doing here?" the guy in the waistcoat asked, as soon as Nishi and Tarun docked their ship.

"Anand, do me a favour. This girl here, is a friend of mine. She needs a room for tonight."

"Sir, all rooms in this hotel have been filled." The guy replied back.

"Listen, she is a lady and she can't go back home all by herself. I don't know where you will go but just, go outside and find a safe hotel for her to stay."

"Sir, but then who will be here at the dock."

"No one will come here at this time of the night, man." Tarun tried to convince the guy.

"Sir, you see there is a boat coming. I have to be here to make sure it's docked safely." The guy said pointing to a boat that was headed in the direction of the resort. Tarun and Nishi looked into the sea. There was a boat and there appeared to be one man on the boat.

"He will know how to park the boat. Now do what I say. And once you find the place, just inform Rajiv." Tarun said with a sterner tone. Immediately the guy obliged. He left the boathouse. Tarun took a look at the boat that was headed towards the boat house. Then he along with Nishi headed to the parking lot.

Nishi saw the *Figo* in the parking lot. She felt guilty for ditching her friends. She decided that she would send a text to Rohit and Yashan from Whatsapp. It was then, she realized, Yashan must be waiting on the upper deck for her.

Tarun revved the bike. It wasn't the old Yamaha bike that Tarun had taken her in, during their college. It was a new one. She climbed on it and placed her hands on the back of the seat for the support. In college, she used to place it over Tarun's shoulders. But Tarun was no more hers.

"What do you want to know?" Tarun asked, as they left the resort gate. They were on the ECR.

"Where are we going?" she asked.

"Actually, I asked about the break-up. Anyways, we are going to get my suit?"

"This time of the day? Which tailor works at 2 am?" Nishi asked.

"That's what the guy told me. That he will work late night. I can come and take it anytime of the night." He said.

"Why were you wishing to see me in the wedding?"

"Ever since, we broke up, I believe I have changed a lot. I was an irresponsible idiot back then."

"An irresponsible idiot who topped the class."

"I did that for you. Let me explain. My point is that. That part of my life, the BBA was the darkest one. I don't mean it because of you. It was just that I was a brash, mean dude. I was irresponsible and adventurous, maybe. It was during those days I had the most fun. I wanted a complete closure on that part of my life. And the only one who can give me that is you. I need to know that you are okay about the relationship that we had once. I have to know if you aren't broken. That you have moved on."

"Alright, if you want to know that, I need to know why you broke up with me in the first place. I need a closure on our relationship first." she said. Tarun turned into a street that had a signpost for a *Natarajar* temple.

"I have explained it in the mail. You didn't read it?" Tarun replied.

"No." Nishi asked. She had no clue.

"I was too ashamed to talk to you after that night. So I sent a mail to you. You are saying that you never got it?" Tarun seemed a bit disappointed.

"Actually I got it. But I was too scared to read it. I had flagged it and left it unread itself. I was too scared to accept that you had broken up. I was afraid that I won't be able to handle the fact that you are gone. My roommates told me that I was better off without you. I don't know when, but when I picked up the courage to open my mail. I had forgotten the password. I know I could have recovered it, but I thought it was fate asking me to stay away and I did. And I completely forgot about it eventually." Nishi explained how she had left the mail unread in her inbox.

"Fine, go and read that. You will know what happened back then." Tarun said.

"Listen, screw the email. I have no clue what the password is for the account. There's no way that I can access it hereafter. I hardly used it then, and haven't used it after B.com. You have to tell me now." Nishi said.

"Tarun245. No caps. No space. That is your password." Tarun said recollecting from his memory.

"When did I say you my password?"

"Our last night together." Tarun said. "We have reached the tailor" Tarun added.

Tarun, slowed the bike. Nishi got down. There was a small hut. There was no board even advertising the presence of a tailor anywhere close by. Nishi wouldn't have dared to come out to such a place in the late of the night with any guy. Not even with Rohit or Yashan. She tried to reason why had she agreed to come along with Tarun. Eventually, convinced herself, that she must have agreed because, Tarun was a groom whose marriage was next day. Nishi told herself that was nothing to worry about. Soon, Tarun returned with the suit.

"You gave your costly wedding suit to a guy who can't even afford to put up a signboard huh?" she asked Tarun.

"No, no. Actually, his tailor shop is in the town. He told me he will finish the work and get it here by midnight and that I can collect it after that." Tarun explained turning on the bike.

"So, we are headed back to the cruise?" Nishi asked. She actually was intending to suggest.

"No, we will go to the beach, nearby. We are not going back until I know your answer. Even if you are not going to be okay with it, I want to just know it. I swear that I'll take you back even if you say you are not okay with the whole thing." Tarun said. They were heading to the beach. Nishi was beginning to get annoyed. She had no clue what was the question that Tarun was posing on her, yet he was asking for an answer.

"First, tell me why you broke up with me, else I can't give you an honest answer." Nishi said sounding pissed off.

"Alright, I'll say you. But it is very embarrassing. And I'm a little worried if you will take it well." He said. They had reached the beach. Tarun turned off his bike engine.

"What is that?" Nishi asked seeing something out of place near the beach.

"A temple." Said to her. *A temple? No way. He must have gotten it wrong. A red pyramid in the sands. Is this Egypt?* Nishi wondered on seeing the tapering pyramid. Then she saw a temple *gopuram* outline in the background. Maybe, Tarun had said it wrongly, she wondered.

"I'm asking about the pyramid here, not the *gopuram*." She said

"This also is a temple. That one is another temple. You should have seen that temple on our way up here." Tarun explained her confusion. Nishi couldn't remember seeing any temple. She decided to get back to their actual topic of conversation.

"Okay, back to the breakup." Nishi reminded. The two of them got off the bike. The beach was covered with coconut trees. There were houses nearby that prevented them from having a panoramic view of the shoreline. On their right was what seemed to be an abandoned beach house. It must have been beautiful once, but now it was a deserted chunk of wood.

"But, I won't go to the details, I am too much ashamed of what I had done." Tarun said as the two of them walked towards the abandoned house.

"Just tell it." Nishi said.

NITHARSHA PRAKASH

"Look, I had no interest towards you. You were one of the, forgive me; hottest girls in the batch that year. So, I got into a bet with a guy that I will get you to fall in love with me. Don't be mad. Like I said I was jerk back then. So I did all that I could to impress you. Eventually, you developed a crush on me. Everybody knew that, everyone except you. Even your roommates, Ramya and Usha knew this. I used the crush you had on me to get you fall in love with me. But, there was one thing that was beautiful about you. You were genuine in everything that you did. Every girl will buy her boyfriend a birthday gift. Because it was expected of her. But, you did it because you were happy for me on my birthday. Every little thing in you was genuine. You never did anything just because we were in love. You did everything out of the love you had. I always wanted a girl like you to be my girlfriend. But, I had been cheap to have made that bet and it cost me your true love. I did not deserve the love you had for me. I knew I had to break up with you. I simply kept procrastinating, until it went too far. We ended up making out in my apartment. And then I couldn't stand it any longer. I decided to leave. I threw away the bet. It seemed trivial before the genuine affection that you showered. And I was riddled with guilt" Tarun said. But, Nishi still couldn't understand why Tarun thought that she was supposed to get mad.

"Look, I don't know if I get the whole thing about what you say. But it does seem a little bit clearer than it had been. And I don't know why you think I should be angry with you. I was a reserved girl, when I fell in love with you. But that one year, everything changed. I discovered a lot about myself. I do have to thank you for all that good you had contributed to." Nishi explained.

"So you have your closure on our relationship? You aren't telling this just so that I will get you back to the resort, are you?" Tarun asked.

"No, I really mean it. It was nice to have known you. And now I wish you a happy married life. That's all I can say. About our relationship, either I didn't understand everything that you said or you left out something" Nishi said.

"Alright Nishi, I'll say it. The bet wasn't to get you to fall in love with me. It was a challenge. To get into your pants. Do let me finish now. Your roommates, Ramya and Usha they were better friends with me than you. So they helped me, in indirect ways. But we guys told them that the bet was just to get you to fall in love. That's why they agreed. You remember that presentation. We did win it. At the same time I asked all my BBA friends to do it in a simple way, so that they don't end up as our competition. Because that was the only way I saw to get us closer. I wasn't a good guy back then. I'm sorry that you had to be a victim of him." Tarun confessed.

"That pretty much explains it." Nishi said sounding sceptical.

"Listen, Nishi. The only reason I didn't tell it in the first place was because, I'm embarrassed and moreover, you know your mail password now. Definitely you will go and read the mail."

"Let's talk about something else, for now . . . Tell me, Tarun. Who is the lucky girl you happen to be marrying?" The two of them continued their walk. There was no need to rush back to the resort. Nishi knew that she was supposed to be angry with Tarun, but she wasn't. It seemed like she had no stores of anger in her. Hence, she evaded to change the topic of discussion.

"Her name is Yamuna. She is from Pondicherry, the town." Tarun too let go of the past they had been talking about. Tarun was a little surprised that Nishi had no reaction to the explanation of his.

"Yamuna?" Nishi questioned. It rang a bell in her mind, Nishi wasn't sure where she had heard it.

"Yeah. You know her?"

"No, man. Name sounds familiar, that's all." She explained.

"Her dad owns the resort where the wedding is going on."

"Oh! Sweet. I'm just asking this, okay? Have you told this girl about us? I mean about how we used to be."

"I did tell her. I wasn't a very nice person back then. I had to tell her that and that I didn't have a good past history. You were a part of it. Even before coming here, I texted her that I'm taking you out to get closure on my brash days of youth. She is okay with it. She is a cool girl."

"She seems to be a nice girl. How many boyfriends has she had?" Nishi questioned to keep the conversation going.

"Only one. Even that was one-sided, it seems. A guy named Yashaan from her school." Nishi realized that Tarun had mispronounced the guy's name. She managed to recollect who Yamuna was too. She knew what had happened between Yashan and Yamuna. There were so many bells that went off in her head. They all seemed to be signalling one thing. DANGER!

*   *   *

The two of them had finished their juice. They had been standing on the deck and talking until Yamuna complained that she was feeling drowsy. Assuming it to be the sea-sickness, the two of them came down from the top deck.

"I think I'll go to my cottage. It isn't helping. Come along with me?" Yamuna suggested.

"Sure. No problem."

"Thanks. I'll just tell my mom and return." Saying Yamuna walked away. Yashan stood there waiting. There was a sense of uneasiness. The heist he had in his mind, had seemed simple enough inside his mind. But, now with the plan in motion, he was afraid. His fear disappeared when Yamuna returned, it re-doubled when he learnt that Yamuna's cousin was accompanying them to the shore.

"Don't mind her. Apparently, mom doesn't want her adorable bride to be alone. So she asked my cousin to come along." Said Yamuna pointing at her cousin. After introductions, the trio got into a boat and left for the shore. All along Yashan's uneasiness kept surfacing. Yashan didn't say a word. They travelled in silence. Once they docked,

"Listen Ara, I'll talk to my friend here and join you. You go to the room." Yamuna said to her cousin.

"It's okay, *anni*. I'll wait." Her cousin didn't realize that she wanted a moment of privacy. Yamuna pulled her cousin away from Yashan and whispered to her, "Look, he is a friend. I will talk to him for a few minutes and come. You go to the room, okay. If you want to babysit me, you are going to have to wait for another twenty minutes. I'll be in the room in twenty minutes. Until then, we will be sitting by that garden." Her cousin knew better than to argue. She immediately agreed and left.

"Sorry about her. Let's go the garden over there." Said Yamuna.

"No problem. Sure." said Yashan and followed her. They sat on a bench in the garden.

"My head is still hurting. I guess the Bay of Bengal is very unfriendly at night." Yamuna commented and leaned on Yashan for support. It felt awkward all of a sudden for him.

"SO how is your life, man? Any girlfriends?"

"Chacha! No. I'm always single. I'm going to complete my MBA. After that I'm thinking of going to Hyderabad. You see, get a job, live independently for a year or something. Then probably return to my dad's place to take over his business."

"Nice, man. Marriage?"

"It'll happen when it has to."

"Yea. You're a guy. You can get married whenever you want to." Yamuna said it as if she hated the fact that she couldn't have that freedom.

"So tell me about Tarun?"

"Very sweet person. He works in Toronto. We're going to settle there."

"You're going to America? When?"

"Well, technically, Toronto is in Canada. Just after our honeymoon."

"A very sweet life you have got up ahead of you. Congratulations."

"I know. But, you know I am a little scared, like any other bride, if it will be the way I liked it. I studied in Bison Valley for just a year. That year was the best in my life so far. Ever since then, my life had been missing excitement. I hope it changes for the better in Toronto." After a pause, Nishi questioned "Hey, I'm really drowsy, do you mind if I lie down on your lap."

"Sure. Uh-Yes. No. No problem. And don't worry. Your life is about to get amazing."

"What makes you say it?"

"Trust me. I know it. It will."

"Ha! Thanks for coming, tonight. I think you made my wedding perfect." Yamuna said with her voice fading out. Yashan stayed silent for a minute. Then he bent down and softly whispered her name into her ear. No response. She had fallen asleep.

Chapter 8

NISHI STOPPED IN her tracks. "Tarun, we have to return immediately." She told and began walking to the bike. He followed her. But not without asking questions.

"What's wrong?"

"Tarun. You shouldn't be here now."

"Look, I told my fiancée that I'm out here. No one will misunderstand what I'm doing here."

"No, you don't get it. You have been tricked man. I have been tricked. Worse still, I have been tricked into tricking you."

"What do you mean?" Tarun asked. They had reached the bike. But Tarun didn't get on it. He wanted to know what was going on before getting on the bike.

"I'll tell you, man. But none of this is my fault. Please don't be mad at me."

"Just say it. Will you?" Tarun was starting to get annoyed.

"I came here along with two friends, alright. Both guys. One of the guy's crush is actually at your wedding."

"Please don't tell me that his crush is Yamuna." Tarun interrupted.

"Not exactly." Nishi began to explain. Tarun almost breathed sigh. But she wasn't done yet, "This is actually a little more twisted, but technically speaking, the guy who was once in love with your Yamuna is here."

"You brought a guy who was in love with Yamuna here?" Tarun complained. He seemed very much annoyed.

"No Tarun. That wouldn't get me as concerned as this. You see, it's more complicated than that. I didn't bring him. The guy who was once in love with your Yamuna brought me here." Nishi explained.

"WHAT?"

"Listen, I'm sorry. I had no clue. He manipulated me into thinking that I might get closure on our relationship if I were to talk to you. He brought me here so that I could distract you, while he—well I don't know what he has planned to do about Yamuna. Like I said, he tricked me. His nickname is bamboozler. It means a manipulative person or something like that. Shit! I should have known." Nishi apologized.

"Bamboo—what?"

"Listen, Tarun. I'll help you get things straight. But as of right now. We have no idea, what has happened to him. So let's just hope that he hasn't done anything stupid."

"Nishi. This is crazy." Tarun yelled. Nishi pulled out her phone. She punched in Yashan's number. The voice on the other end said *'The subscriber you are trying to reach is outside the service area. Please*

278

call later.' Tarun by then had placed a call for Yamuna. The rings kept going and no one picked up.

"Let's get to the cruise. We'll know what's going on if we get there." Nishi suggested. In no time, the bike was back in highway speeding towards the resort. Nishi explained in detail how and why the three of them had got there.

CHAPTER 9

YASHAN COULDN'T QUITE believe he had done it. It was as if someone was controlling him through means of a voodoo doll. All that he had warned his friends not to screw up with, he had done the very same thing. He was sitting in the driver's seat of Rohit's car. He had no idea of what to do next. He had no idea where he was headed even. He simply drove on.

The thoughts and the rekindled feelings in him had led to it. It all went wrong when Yamuna innocently confessed that she had loved him once. His mind got torn apart, between to-do and not-to-do. He had asked her for the whereabouts of the kitchen in the mini-cruise so that he could get some juice. Nishi had given him the directions.

Back in the cruise, when he got a juice, Yashan, got a glass of juice for Yamuna, too. Within a few minutes of her having drunk it, she complained of giddiness. Yashan convinced her that it was the sea and that she had to get off the cruise and have some rest in the hotel. She agreed and asked Yashan to accompany her till the shore lest she faints. Just as Yashan had expected the drug in her juice knocked her out, while they were chatting in the garden.

After Yamuna, fell asleep in the resort garden, Yashan headed straight for the parking lot. He had Rohit's car keys in his pocket. It all seemed fine when it happened. But from the car, when he thought of what he had done, it all seemed stupid to Yashan. He had warned to Rohit that it might have side-effects, yet he ended up drugging his once best friend, the girl who loved him once, the girl he loved once and still had feelings for. It was the very dumb of him. It was true that he had manipulated a lot of people to become friends with her in the first place. But what he had done now was nothing good. It was criminal.

Yashan found a road that led off from the highway, on his left. He took the road. It seemed like he was driving into a small village. There was a government primary school. A sign board said that the area was called as *Anumanthai*. There were no lights to light up the road. The only thing he saw ahead was what was lit up by the headlights. There was a temple nearby. He drove past all that. He heard the ocean waves. He must be nearing the shore. The neighbourhood seemed to be a poor neighbourhood. All that was there were small huts with thatched roofs. Some of them had tiled roofs. There was a small elevated platform. It must be a kind of stage for conducting any festivities. The area seemed deserted. There were rows of those small houses all around. Soon, the houses diminished and there were a few coconut trees.

The car stopped moving. Yashan snapped back to reality. It was all exciting when he was getting Yamuna from the boat into the car. Now it was simply haunting. He looked what was ahead. He hadn't concentrated on the road. In fact, there was no road even. The car had reached the beach. The tires must have got stuck in the sand. He stepped out of the Ford *Figo*. He looked around. He had reached the beach. The beach was empty except for the catamarans and the small fishing boats that were parked on the shore. He was able to see the mini-cruise from the shore. His friends must be there, probably searching him. He was surprised that he hadn't gotten any call yet. Yamuna's fiancé must be having a bachelor party while his bride was lying unconscious in a Ford *Figo*.

Yashan walked around and opened the backseat door of the Figo. In there, lay a figure, unconscious, draped in a deep blue sari. He had abducted Yamuna. *'You fucking son of a bitch'* Yashan cursed himself. There was a part of him that was disgusted and angered by what he had done. There was another part of him that told him that the wheels are in motion and he has to worry of the consequences. Yashan heeded to the latter. *How am I going to explain to Yamuna, why she is waking up in a car? Is there any way of getting her back to the ship?* Yashan racked his brain to come up with an explanation. Vexed with the entire evening, he sat down on the sand and leaned against the *Figo*. It was supposed to be just another evening for him. Yet, now all that can go wrong had gone so. He tried to work on what to do next. But, his guilt kept dragging him down. His phone vibrated. His friends, they must have begun searching for him. He pulled it out. He had a missed call from Nishi. *Best option* he thought to himself. He punched in Nishi's number.

*   *   *

As soon as they reached the resort, the first thing Nishi looked for was if the *Figo* was still in the parking lot. It wasn't there. Nishi felt a jolt in her. *Where in the world is Yashan?* She wondered. But she decided to keep quiet until she was very sure. They got on the boat and headed to the cruise.

"Nishi, you came here with two guys, right?"

"Yeah."

"Did you try calling the other guy? By any chance, is it possible that the two have planned this together?"

"No, Rohit is far more responsible than that. They are friends from school. But I think he couldn't have been a part of this." Nishi defended Rohit.

"But . . ." Tarun seemed unsure about something.

"What?"

"No, it's just that if Rohit is a responsible guy, as you said, why did he throw away his job, dump his girlfriend?"

"Tarun, like I said. I'm not sure which part of the last evening was manipulation and which was real. Maybe Rohit doing all that irresponsible shit was also a part of the manipulation." Nishi explained. She knew there was a flaw in what she had said. Tarun exploited it right away.

"See, now you said it yourself. So, either Rohit did what he did out of his own wish, which means he isn't responsible enough to abstain from Yashan's scheming, or even losing the job and girlfriend was a part of the plan to get you here, which already shows that he could have been a part of Yashan's plan."

"I'll call him." She said and pulled out her phone. She had no signal. She decided to call him once they return ashore. Nishi couldn't still quite accept the possibility that Yashan could have done this. *What if Yashan hadn't planned anything at all? Was it all a simple coincidence and nothing more?* Nishi wondered, as the boat cruised along. Nishi's fears proved worse when the two of them got to the cruise. Tarun asked one of Yamuna's relative where Yamuna was. She introduced Nishi as one of Yamuna's friends. The lady, the relative of Yamuna, had no clue. Yamuna wasn't in her room. She had left her mobile in there. They met Tarun's brother, Varun on the deck. He had the room keys that Tarun had asked the guy in the waistcoat to get. Nishi thanked Varun. Nishi and Tarun searched through the decks for another ten minutes, before returning to the resort. Tarun looked very much pissed. When they parked the boat at the shore, the guy with the waistcoat was there. He greeted them once more.

"Sir, you are leaving again? Got the wrong suit?" the guy asked implying a second meaning.

"No, no . . . Actually . . . um . . ." Tarun stuttered.

"Where are the keys that I asked for?" Nishi improvised.

"I gave it to his brother, Varun." The guy replied.

"No, he didn't have it. He told me that you had given it in the reception. And at the reception, I was told that you didn't give it to them." Tarun yelled back. He wasn't feigning anger to get the waistcoat guy walk away. Not wanting to get yelled at by Tarun, Yamuna placed the call to Yashan right away. But before the call connected, she had an incoming call from Yashan. She attended it.

"Hey, it's me." Yashan's voice came over.

"Where the hell are you?" Nishi asked.

"Hey, sorry. There are things I need to say. I'm at a beach. There is a temple with a large statue nearby. I'm not sure where I am exactly. Can you come out of the resort?" he said. His voice seemed to be a little down.

"Come out of the resort? Where? I don't know where is it you are talking about? How do I get there?" Nishi questioned. She didn't want to share her revelations and arise any doubt.

"Look, I'll tell you. Do you remember Sanjana, Rohit's first crush? She is at the wedding. She must have brought a vehicle or something. Can you take that and come? It's important." Yashan instructed.

"Wait, wait. How'd you know Sanjana brought a vehicle. Where is Rohit in the first place? He isn't here. Isn't he with you?" Nishi questioned back.

"Oh yeah! I forgot. Rohit and Sanjana are at Café coffee day. So you won't have a vehicle."

"Wait. What are they doing there? And why are you at a beach. We are here for Rohit, remember. The whole point of bringing him here was to make him be at a wedding. Why is he on a date at this time of the night?"

"Listen, Nishi. I remember that. I didn't tell you this before. I brought us here, so that Rohit could meet up with Sanjana. I'll elaborate it later. If you can, get a vehicle and come to this place, know?"

"What is it you are not telling me, man? How can I come there? It isn't safe to take an auto now. What'd you suggest? Why don't you return to the resort?"

"You see, I can't come there. If you can find a way, fine, be here. Else, I'll come back in an hour."

"Why can't you come here? You guys brought me here. You are responsible for my return to college." Nishi sounded angry. She had given him enough time and Yashan wasn't it telling it yet. Standing beside her, Tarun was growing impatient.

"There is a small situation. I'll explain it to you in person. Just give me an hour. I'll return to the resort." Yashan pleaded.

"Fine. Stay there. I'll see if I can come. But if it takes more than an hour, you better return, Yashan. I don't like this." Nishi said and hung up the call. Tarun was looking at her for an explanation.

"It's worse than I had imagined it." Nishi said.

"Just tell me where in the damn world is Yamuna? That's all I care for." Tarun said sounding impatient.

"He told he is at a beach nearby. He didn't mention that she is with him. He told me that there is a situation and that he can't come back to the resort. So I strongly think he has her. There is a temple with very large statue not far from where he is."

"*Hanumaan* statue." Tarun questioned back.

"He just told me that it's a very large statue, nothing else." Nishi answered.

"I think I know it. Let's get going." He said and the two began to walk towards the car.

"Is your other friend with him? If that's the case. I'm taking my brother along." Tarun said.

"No, that guy is on a date. I have to call him."

"A date-?" Tarun asked as he revved the engine on.

"That's where I'd told you that it has been worse that I had imagined." Nishi said.

"Like I already said, we all set out to help out our friend. The guy who is on the date. He was supposed to be in the wedding hall. I had an intention to meet you, which I will admit was a bit selfish on my part. But I made sure, my intentions didn't override anybody else. But Yashan, as I think, had manipulated me into coming here and also setup a date for the other guy."

"So, he worked alone and managed to abduct Yamuna? How did he do that? It doesn't make any sense. Why ditch you guys? Hasn't Yamuna found a way out of Yashan's scheming? Or did Yamuna go with him willingly?" Tarun asked sounding melodramatic.

"Listen, even I don't get the whole picture yet. Yashan had done something to meddle with your wedding. Until he tells us what he has done, we are not going to know. And don't confuse yourself now. Yamuna and Yashan hadn't seen each other, ever since school. He wasn't in touch with her, anytime I had known him. Just one thing. I know you must be furious at him. But please don't make things physical." Nishi ended with the request. For a moment Tarun didn't reply. After a while he said, "That is entirely up to your friend."

CHAPTER 10

S O FAR, THE evening had been going good for Rohit. He had come to Pondicherry with the hopes of meeting Sanjana and it had happened. Only the previous night, he had dreamt of her and now she was, there with him, sitting in the café, living something he had fantasized long back. Sanjana had apparently come to India to attend a function. He was living a long-forgotten fantasy. He was sitting with his first crush. They had been talking about the old times, sharing nostalgic memories. Rohit didn't go into the details of his interview and about his girlfriend. He had shared his feelings to the Sanjana who appeared in his dream, but he didn't tell her. Something was holding him back. There was something about her that was different. He guessed it should be that things have changed after the years they had been apart. Yet, he didn't want this to end. It suddenly seemed like nothing else existed beyond the coffee shop.

Until, he was pulled out of his dreamy state by his phone ringing. The reality came back to him. His screwed up interview, broken relationship, and uncertain tomorrow. The call was from Nishi. It brought back to his mind, how he was supposed to be there in the cruise to help and aid Nishi to get to Tarun. That was what he had been asked to do. But he had abandoned her and

Yashan at the cruise, to be on a date with Sanjana. Rohit wasn't sure if they were on a date, given the time of the day. He had asked Sanjana, if she was interested to hang out someplace and she had responded by suggesting the café.

"Hello Nishi." Rohit answered the call unsure of what he was going to receive. He got up from the chair and moved a few feet away not wanting to reveal to Sanjana that he wasn't supposed to be there.

"Rohit. Where are you, man?" Nishi questioned. She didn't sound annoyed or displeased. She seemed to be in a car. *Have they already decided to leave for Chennai? Has Nishi already completed talking to Tarun? Without any help?* Rohit wondered

"Sorry, Nishi. I met Sanjana here. So we are at this Café Coffee Day nearby."

"You need to come back right now." she replied.

"What happened? It will take time for me to get there. Can't Yashan help?" he questioned back unwilling to go back.

"Yashan for help? Yashan is the problem now."

"Why? What happened to him?"

"Listen, you remember Yamuna?"

"Yamuna? Are you talking about the girl from my class?" Rohit asked.

"Yes. She is Tarun's fiancée. And Yashan has kidnapped her."

"Oh! You mean to say that the plan is changed from kidnapping Tarun to Yamuna."

"No, you idiot. I had no intention of kidnapping Tarun. We came here to for your sake, everything else was part of an act."

"What do you mean?" Rohit was stunned to hear that. He had been having a very good time so far. *This is how this night should have exactly been. What was this act? What's gone wrong in it? What had Yashan done?* His thoughts raced.

"Look, actually I and Yashan decided to bring you here to get you out of your commitment issue that you are having. You, turning down the job, you girlfriend, and all this stuff. But apparently, Yashan had come here for another reason."

"The Bamboozler is here for Yamuna, isn't he?" the realisation hit him.

"Yes. He. Is."

"Nishi, but seriously, do I have to come? I'm having a good time right now. I'm with Sanjana now." Rohit didn't want to lose this chance he had got. He just wanted to be there with her, at least for the time-being.

"You better be joking? Rohit, you are his best friend. Haven't you figured out yet that Sanjana is also there because of Yashan? Yashan told me just now that he had asked her to come. I'm sorry, but she is playing you." Rohit felt like as if a beautiful cosy bubble had just burst. He had been having an awesome night, not because it was happening, but because it was forced to happen by his best friend.

"Where are you?" Rohit questioned back.

"I'm headed to where Yashan is. Come there, know?" Nishi pleaded once more.

"Yeah. But where is Yashan?"

"Oh! Just one second." Nishi said. She seemed to be asking directions to someone else. Rohit couldn't fathom who she was talking to. At the moment, he wasn't interested to ask."

"Listen." Nishi spoke again, "You're at CCD right?"

"Yes, I am."

"You remember that check post that we drove past on our way here. There is a *hanuman* temple near there. Near the check post will be a small township, there will be a road there towards the temple. Sanjana might know." Nishi instructed.

"Alright I'll be there." Rohit promised.

"Hurry please." Nishi made the request and hung up.

Rohit looked around. The night wasn't the same anymore. The beautiful dreamy state was gone. Yashan cursed himself.

"Is something wrong?" Sanjana questioned.

"I think so. We need to head back right away. Can you finish your ice-cream fast?"

"Sure." Said Sanjana and tried to finish the ice-cream as fast as she could. The paid the bills and stepped out into the cold night. Rohit gave her the directions and the two them headed to the beach.

"What's wrong, may I ask?" Sanjana asked.

"You don't know?" Rohit questioned back.

"What? No." she pretended as if it was natural.

"What are you doing at this wedding?" Rohit asked.

"I told you, I came here for a function. Then some fri-" Sanjana repeated the same reason. This time Rohit knew it was a lie.

"Yashan asked you to be."

"What?"

"Yashan asked you to be here, didn't he?" Rohit said it again for her.

"Yes." Sanjana gave in. She turned around taking her eyes of the road. She was the one who was driving.

"I asked you out. And you had agreed. We were, sorry I was having an amazing night. Only to know that it was all manipulated piece of crap."

"Listen. Who told you this?"

"Yashan told Nishi and Nishi told me."

"It's not what you are thinking. Yashan told me about your job and girlfriend. That' why he sent me here. To make you change your decision. You are throwing away your life." Sanjana revealed her true purpose of being there.

"Please, Sanjana. Don't give me advice now. Yashan and Nishi had done that already this evening and I also know that you are here to distract me not save my job or girlfriend."

"What am I distracting you from?" she asked.

"Whatever Yashan had planned to do at the wedding."

"Look, I don't know what you are talking about. All that Yashan told me was that I need to get you out of your dilemma." Sanjana explained.

"I am Yashan's best friend. He didn't even tell me the truth about why he was here, why would he tell you. You are just a set-up." Rohit said. But as soon as the words left his mouth, he regretted it. Set-up was sometimes used as an abusive word. It refers to a person who is having an affair. In the tone, he had said it sounded very abusive. Sanjana turned around with her face filled with rage,

"How dare you?" Just as she said the scooter jolted. The vehicle had gotten slightly off the road.

"Just turn around. I'm sorry. Lo-" Rohit didn't get to finish the sentence. It was too late. The vehicle was out of control and both of them lost their balance.

Chapter 11

YASHAN STOOD OUTSIDE the *Figo* watching the waves. He wasn't enjoying the sound of the waves crashing at the shore. His mind was wondering on what was going to happen. What was he going to tell Yamuna? What will he do if Yamuna wakes up? He had been standing alone there, in the dark. There was nothing that moved except the waves. The shore was dead silent. Behind the beach was a little village. There were a number of coconut tress all around. And in the direction of the village, he could see a tall statue of a god from the temple that stood there.

And then he heard a vehicle sound from his right. It should be Nishi, he hoped. He couldn't see the vehicle though. It was masked behind the trees and huts. He walked towards the source of the noise. Just as he came into view of the vehicle, he saw Nishi dismount. But she wasn't alone, someone else was with her. *Rohit is also here. Good* he thought. But as the two figures approached him. From the posture, he made out Nishi, but the other person wasn't Rohit. He had the figure of someone else. He was able to make out their face only when the two of them, came close to him.

"Hey." Nishi greeted him.

"You must be . . ." Yashan looked at the other guy.

"Tarun." He said extending his hand.

"I'm Yashan." Yashan reciprocated.

"I guessed so." Tarun said. *Does he have any clue that his fiancée is in the back of my van?* Yashan's thoughts mocked. He looked over in the direction of his car. He couldn't see his car. He shouldn't let Tarun near the car.

"If you don't mind, I need a moment alone with Nishi." Yashan said and tugged Nishi away.

"I asked you to come. Why'd you bring him?" Yashan asked. Things would have been simpler, if Tarun wasn't around. He could have explained everything right away. But now it was going to be different.

"You expect me to walk the whole distance?" Nishi questioned back at him.

"I told to get Sanjana's vehicle, right?"

"She is at a café with Rohit."

"Oh! Right. I forgot."

"You knew that they were in the café? We brought Rohit here to get over his commitment issues. He was supposed to stay in the cruise, remember? It was my idea."

"Yeah. I do. My bad." Yashan apologized. Tarun was leaning against his bike and fidgeting his mobile.

"Look, I can tell you now. But it won't matter if I say it now or later. But there is something else you should see." Yashan added, thinking it was not the time for explanations. There was work to be done.

"What is it?" he asked.

"Come along." He said and took her to the car.

"What are you doing here?" Nishi asked. Yashan froze when he saw that the rear door of the car was open. He glanced inside. Nobody was there. This was getting out of his hand. *Where did she go now?* he wondered, looking down. Under his feet, the beach sand lay. But there were more than grains of sand. There were footprints. He looked around the car for more footprints, to deduce the direction it led to. Nishi was standing beside him, asking,

"What are you looking for?" he pushed to look for footprints around her. And then he noticed a number of footprints. It literally were footprints, not boot-prints too. *Had I brought Yamuna barefoot?* He couldn't remember. He followed them. As he followed them, he realized, there appeared to be more than one set of footprints. The footprints disappeared where a cement road began. He looked ahead. There were a bunch of men, dressed in lungi. They were carrying something. And then they rounded a corner and disappeared behind a house.

A shiver ran across Yashan's spine. He realized what they were carrying. He covered his mouth in horror. He walked back with his hands still over his mouth.

"What is happening?" asked Nishi. Apparently, she had seen what Yashan had.

"What was in their hands?" Nishi asked another question.

But, Yashan couldn't answer. He was responsible for what had just happened. If Tarun were to understand what had just happened, he would be enraged beyond words. Yashan couldn't tell it aloud. For, Tarun had followed them, but maintained a distance. He was now standing about a few feet away from the car. Nishi looked at Tarun. Tarun, sensing something was wrong began closing in.

"Yashan" Nishi hesitated.

"What is going on?" Tarun said without any emotions.

"Is that her?" Nishi questioned. Yashan wanted to ask her back how she had guessed it. But he couldn't utter a word. He simply nodded his head, meaning a 'yes'

"Tarun, I'm afraid . . . . Yamuna . . . . has been kidnapped . . . ." Nishi said breaking up at her sentence. Tarun stared at Yashan. It looked like he was trying to burn Yashan by just staring.

". . . for . . . the . . . second time." Nishi added. Tarun looked towards Nishi. He didn't get the last part.

"WHAT?" This time Tarun sounded grave.

"It was Yamuna." Nishi repeated.

"Some drunks just kidnapped her." Yashan said. There was no way he was getting out of the mess he was in. And now there was a complication in it.

"Why did you bring her here?" Tarun didn't look pleased anymore.

"She was sleeping." Nishi said trying to save her friend from Tarun's wrath.

"I abducted her." Yashan said. He knew that Nishi had come up with a sensible reason. But Yashan didn't want to lie any further. He was afraid if he might push things further, if it was in his advantage. He confessed.

"WHATHA-?" Tarun swore.

"I abdu-." Yashan didn't get to finish the sentence. He was on the ground. Tarun had landed a blow right on his cheek bone. Yashan had one of his hand across his face, nursing his cheek.

"I'm sorry." Yashan cried. But, Tarun wasn't done yet. He raised his leg to kick him. Reflexively, Yashan hit Tarun's other foot. Tarun too crashed on the sand beside him. Yashan knew well the fault was on him. But some part of him, considered Tarun to be vile. Yashan yelled back in anger,

"Why are you so pissed? You are the jerk who broke Nishi's heart. Yamuna deserves better than you. I gave her up to a good friend of mine. Not a jerk like you." Tarun wasted no more time on the ground. He immediately was on top of Yashan with his hands at Yashan's throat.

"You bloody kidnap my fiancée and label 'me' as the bad Guy. Tell me? Am I the bad guy?" Asked Tarun rhetorically not taking his hands off Yashan's neck. Yashan was writhing violently. Tarun had overpowered him. Nishi had panicked. She could see Yashan's failing efforts to get free. She tried to pull Tarun away from Yashan. She tried, but it was futile. In one moment, she bent down, and threw a handful of sand into Tarun's eyes. At once, he got off Yashan. He stooped down, trying to get the sand off his eyes.

"*Thev-*" Tarun was about to swear once again. But he stopped midway. Yashan rose up from the ground beating the sand off. He was coughing. Yashan wasn't done with Tarun yet. He rammed into Tarun and tackled him. With the sand in his eyes, Tarun couldn't do anything. Nishi ran towards the waves. She had a coconut shell in her hands. But, the two boys were too busy with their tussle to notice anything beyond each other.

"Look, Tarun. You are not the bad guy here, but you are definitely not the hero here too. Has she ever told you about me? About the friendship that I and she had shared? You know what your fiancée told me this evening on the cruise? She told she had loved me when we were together in school. You met her on an online matrimonial site. But Yamuna and I were together in school. We had a beautiful friendship between us. I deserve her more than you do. Do you have any idea what kind of feeling it is?" Yashan was saying. Just then, Yamuna poured water on Tarun's face to wash off the sand. Tarun took a wild swing at Yashan's face. Yashan dodged it. He let go off Tarun.

"I have no intention to hurt you. But you should understand my feelings." Yashan yelled at Tarun, not wanting another bout of brawl.

Tarun didn't reply. Nishi yelled at the two of them.

"If both of you love her, why isn't anyone of you'll trying to save her? You guys are idiots. Yamuna has been kidnapped. You are fighting over a girl you both may not get." She chucked the coconut on the ground. Both the guys looked at her.

"Alright, what'd you suggest?" Yashan responded after a moment of silence.

"You stay the hell away from my fiancée, you bastard." Tarun yelled at him. He had one of his hand on his right eye.

"I think, there were five drunk, who carried away Yamuna. I am sure that even the combined efforts of the three of us will not succeed." Nishi said. She had a point. The two guys in spite of their difference, had to work together.

"Call the police." Tarun suggested.

"Tarun, then everyone will question about how you and Yamuna ended up here." It was Yashan objecting. He had abducted her. It was a criminal act. Within his mind, there was a worry if calling the police would get him in trouble.

"Listen, before it's too late we need to find out where they have taken her. So, immediately we split up and search for her. We'll decided what to do next, when we find those drunkards." Nishi said.

"We'll split up and search. They headed that way we'll see where it leads." Said Nishi.

"Just for a safety, silence your mobile." Added Yashan. Tarun headed off in a direction, while Nishi and Yashan stuck together. As, Nishi and Yashan reached the car, she began,

"What is wrong with you? Why did you do all this?" Nishi asked him.

"I didn't see it coming."

"What were you planning to do with Yamuna?" Nishi questioned after thinking for some time.

"No idea."

"You planned every intricate detail of this evening except the main part? Your confrontation with Yamuna?" Nishi asked.

"I didn't plan anything. As I said, I never saw this coming."

"You didn't plan anything? Then why are you here?" Nishi asked. She was annoyed that Yashan wasn't letting go of his plan yet. *Is there more to it? Is that the reason he is hiding it still? Maybe his plans haven't fallen apart? Or even this was a part of his plan? Is he planning to let the blame fall on the drunkards and come clean?* Nishi tried to figure out what else Yashan might have included in his twisted plan.

"What are you thinking of? I just came here to hang out, while Rohit gets his mind cleared?"

"You mean his date with Sanjana?"

"It's not a d-" Yashan began saying. But Nishi finished it for her.

"It's not a date when it is a part of some manipulated vile plan."

"Nishi, I'm not sure why you are mad? I set Sanjana up to clear his mind. That's all. We had a bet remember? You decided to show him a wedding to get him alright. I decided to show him his crush. Only thing, I didn't tell you until now."

"So, it was an honest attempt to rescue Rohit?" Nishi asked doubtfully.

"Yes. It damn was."

"But what did that had to do with you and Yamuna?"

"What are you talking? I don't get it." Yashan complained.

"Why did you come here?" Nishi continued her enquiry.

"My friends Nishi and Rohit wanted to be here. I'm here to give you company."

"Well, then, where did kidnapping Yamuna come from?"

"For the love of God, I didn't see it coming." Yashan was getting annoyed. The two of them weren't making any progress in finding Yamuna. They were simply walking from one street to another. In the village, it wasn't a street even. It was just a path.

"You didn't see it coming?" Nishi questioned him for the nth time. It seemed like her doubts were increasing with every question Yashan answered.

"Yes. I had no idea she was here. I saw Tarun's wedding. I know that Tarun was your ex. Although only today you told the details of your relationship, I guessed that you might be interested to go. So I made you come here and asked Sanjana to come here and convince Rohit to change his mind about Lavanya and everything else."

"You didn't know it was Yamuna's wedding?" Nishi cried as if she had heard a blasphemy.

"No, I didn't. If I had known, I would sulked at the thought. But I wouldn't have come here, definitely."

"So, you came here only to help Rohit?" Nishi asked in the same tone of her previous question."

"Wait, you did something here, didn't you?" It was Yashan turn to question. Nishi had her hands over her head.

"I thought, everything that was happening tonight was a twisted plan of yours to get Yamuna."

"I had a chance to do that in my twelfth grade. Tonight isn't my night."

"Ah! Crap!" Nishi cursed. Yashan hadn't heard her curse much. He realized that there was more. "I thought, you set up Sanjana only to distract him."

"No way. I wouldn't do that. That is a bad idea, however. If I was here for Yamuna, Rohit would be at my side helping me." Yashan suggested.

"I called Rohit and told him that you set up Sanjana, so that you can get Yamuna."

"WHAT?" Yashan cried out worse than Nishi. "You realize what you did here? You ruined the night for all of us. Now there is no true purpose to what we are doing here."

"You shouldn't have abducted Yamuna. Else none of this would have happened."

"Nishi, this night has been going not very well, for me. Now don't blame me for more and get me started. I'm going to call Rohit now. All other stuff later."

"We should search for Yamuna first. Nishi explained. He decided to let go of it for now. There were more pressing matters indeed. After a few minutes of silence, Yashan began to explain,

"Back then, in school, there was a choice. I could have proposed to her. But, I held back because of a promise. And when Yamuna told me that she was expecting me to propose to her in school, my emotions went haywire. So, I began to think why did she had to marry a jerk who broke up with you." Yashan explained.

"He wasn't a jerk." Nishi defended Tarun.

"I never thought I will put Yamuna into trouble." Yashan said.

"You know something, Yashan: You seem to be having a crush on Yamuna. And that is the reason you are not the right person for her. You can never be the right person for her. No matter how much she loves you. She could take too much advantage of you. You will forget your life and will live for her sake alone. That is why crushes should be kept far." Said Nishi.

"I had a crush on her when we were in school. That's all. And Yamuna wouldn't take advantage of me" Said Yashan.

"There is no such thing as 'had a crush'. Your feelings disappear when you drift away from them. It gets rekindled when you get closer. The feelings will always be there. Look what happened tonight. This might be hard to accept. You told that, back in your school, you let her go, because you wanted to be the bamboozler, for your personal gain. Tonight you abducted her for your personal gain again. Both the times you didn't give a thought what she wanted. You really think you have true feeling for her? Don't you see why you need to be away from her?" Nishi said. The two of them came to a T-shaped junction.

"Alright, I think we need to split up. Just in case, be careful, Nishi." Said Yashan. Just when they were about to walk off in different directions, Nishi felt her phone vibrate. Apparently, Tarun had found where the drunks had gone. The two of them headed to where Tarun had asked them be.

Tarun showed them. There were the not five but six men sitting under a thatched roof and they were getting drunk. They could hear a harsh voice. They didn't make out what the voice was saying.

"Where's Yamuna?" Yashan asked Tarun.

"She's behind that blue house, under that tree. You can't see her from here actually. You have to go past a few more houses. They must have decided not to leave her in plain sight." From where these men sat drinking, they couldn't see the tree. These men were getting drunk at the front of the blue house, while they had hidden her in the back. It meant, there was an easy chance to save Yamuna.

"What'd we do?" Yashan asked.

"Call the police." Tarun said.

"Hey, we can't risk it. The police might take too long." Yashan warned.

"My dad knows an inspector here. He is a family friend. I'll call him." Tarun replied.

"But-"

"Look, I know you don't want police here just because you don't want to go to jail. I'm sorry but I just can't risk putting my fiancée at any more risk."

"Listen. It's not-"

"Don't bother. I'm calling him." Tarun pulled out his phone and made the call.

"Damn!" Tarun cursed in anger. "No signal. Nishi can you give your phone?"

"My phone has no balance." Nishi lied. It was right on her face that she was lying. She was a bad liar

"Here. You are right. I have no intention of going to jail, but right now it's not about me." Yashan said and handed over his phone. Tarun placed the call from Yashan's phone.

"No luck, man. The person isn't picking it up." Tarun said handing back the phone. "Listen, Yashan. I'm still mad at for what you have done here. But, I know the inspector. So we might be able to manage to get you out of it." Tarun added.

"So, what do we do now?"

"I actually have an idea." Said Yashan and explained to them how they might be able to save Yamuna by re-kidnapping her from those drunks without their knowledge. "We'll take my car. Go around and come behind the blue house. They won't be able to see us. We can just put her in the car and disappear."

"Alright." Tarun agreed.

"But, what if these people finish drinking before we return?" Nishi questioned.

"I'll go ahead behind the house and keep an eye. You guys get the car and come. It's still open." Yashan suggested.

CHAPTER 12

WITH THE ESCAPE plan, set in motion Yashan approached the blue house after taking a wide detour. He couldn't reach where Yamuna was, right away. If he did, he would have no visual on these drunks. As of right now, he had to make sure that they weren't getting any close to Yamuna. He hid in the darkness near a house that was straight opposite to the blue house. He watched those men, waiting for Tarun to return.

Tarun surveyed the surrounding. The housing in the area was in rural standards. There was no order to how the houses were arranged. There were a few cement roads. The rest was just the sand-paths that had been paved by constant use. The blue house stood one side of the road. Its front door, wasn't facing the road though. On its porch sat the drunkards. And at the back of the house was where they had laid down Yamuna. From what Yashan could make out he was to the east of the blue house. Apart from the cement road that lay between the house behind which Yashan hid and the blue house there were no roads on the east of the house. That meant, that Tarun and Nishi would be approaching from the west of the house and also that he had approached from the wrong side. But now was too late to make amends. He would have to go around further in order to re-join with Tarun and Nishi once they save Yamuna. He wouldn't be able to cross this cement road without being spotted. This was one hell of a mess that he was entangled in.

Tarun had already called his police family friend. It put him in the risk of getting landed in jail. He hoped that he could get out of this mess before the police respond. The last time he had put himself and Yamuna at such grave risk was in Mr Farooq's class, the time he had almost got caught for e-mailing her. He succeeded then by a slight manipulation. This time, it seemed like he didn't have much control. He had to play along with Tarun. Just then, his phone began to vibrate.

"Hello, Yashan. I think we have reached close to the house. But we can't come any closer because there is no road." Nishi explained.

"Actually don't. Park the car. If you come too close with the car, they might hear you. Just come in the direction of the house until you see a cement road. You will be able to spot the house, easily. You are going to have to carry her to the car, I think." Yashan told them the exact situation.

"Fine. Where are you?"

"I'm opposite the blue house. I won't be able to join you directly. I'll come around and we'll meet on the outskirts of the village.

"Don't hang up. If anything changes, we need to know." After a minute of pause, Nishi's voice came again. We found a place to park the car closer. We can see you from here." Yashan looked around. On the end of the cement road, stood the car. From it both Tarun and Nishi had gotten out and they stealthily walked towards the blue house. Yashan gave them a thumbs-up indicating, 'All clear, proceed.'

In no time, Nishi and Tarun began carrying the unconscious Yamuna from there. *Hasn't she been too unconscious for far too long? Isn't something wrong in*—his thoughts were perturbed by the clanking of bottles. He noticed the drunks, slowly getting up, they were finished with their liquor. Nishi and Tarun hadn't made much distance with Yamuna. If they didn't move quicker, they would be spotted. And worse still, Yashan hadn't yet figured a way how he could get into the car without drawing attention. There was one option, which he had. He could run up to the two of them and help them carry Yamuna to the car. It would make it quicker to reach the car, but also it would reduce the time they had before they were spotted. That was because the moment Yashan steps out of his cover, the drunks would be alerted. But at least, this one got him to the car. And once he is in the car he can make his escape. *Three . . . . Two . . . . One . . . .*

Yashan counted within himself, and sprinted up to the two of them. He put his efforts and lifted Yamuna up further and they moved quicker.

"They are coming. We have no time. They are going to see us soon. Rush. Tarun, go and get the car started." Yashan suggested. Leaving the weight bearing to the other two, Tarun rushed to the car. The two of them hurried along as fast they could.

"Yaaruda athu? Oye!" the heard a voice from behind them. *Who's there?*

Luckily, they had managed to make it to the car. Nishi got into the back seat after, placing Yamuna there. Yashan had to run around the car, to reach the front seat. By then, they started hurling stones at the car. Yashan, pulled the door, it didn't budge. Apparently, it was locked from inside.

"Hurry, open." Yashan yelled in haste at Tarun. But Tarun did something else.

"Take my bike." Saying he flung his bike key, towards Yashan. Before, it was too late, Yashan picked up the bike key and sprinted away from there lest he is followed. He heard the car engine start and drive away. In the panic, Yashan had forgotten the directions. Without stopping, he made a wild guess and ran hoping to find Tarun' bike. To his luck, it was in the same place still and he wasn't being followed. But he didn't want to risk another moment in the area. He started the bike and began to drive it from there. As fast as he could.

Yashan was furious. All other emotions had vanished from his memories. Tarun had retorted for what he had done. Of course, he did deserve it, but not at the moment. If it weren't for his presence of mind, he might not have made it. *That son of a bitch is going to have to pay for what he did.* His mind was boiling in anger. He had reached the ECR. The resort wasn't far away.

Against the winds on his face, he felt his phone vibrate in his pocket. *It should be them. Now concerned if I'm alive, huh? To hell with him. I'll show him that I'm alive on his face when I go to the resort.* Rohit sped on the highway. As soon as he reached the resort, he left the bike on the porch of the lobby. There was a crowd at the lobby. It probably, should be Tarun's family. He had to be there. He went up to them. The entire group was looking back at him, as if a murderer was approaching them. He scanned the crowd. Tarun wasn't there.

"Where the fuck is your groom?" he questioned in anger. He spotted the old man who had helped them get in among the crowd. Even Anand was there.

"He is the guy." He heard a voice from the crowd. It was the cousin who had accompanied him and Yamuna in the boat. He realized that Nishi too wasn't there. He felt a hand behind his back. Before he could respond, he felt something tighten around his wrists. He was handcuffed. A man pushed him down on one of the sofa.

"I am a police. Now, where is Yamuna?" he questioned.

"Wha—What?" Rohit stuttered. His phone began to vibrate in his jeans again. Against his tight jean, the vibrations made an audible noise. The policeman, pulled out the phone.

"Nishi. Hmm." He observed on looking at the vibrating phone.

CHAPTER 13

A FALL LIKE that, Rohit had imagined, to be very dramatic. From the off-balance *Scooty* to the mud Rohit had expected it would take forever to crash. But, in reality it wasn't anything he had expected. In a flash of a moment, he was whining on the ground, with abrasions over his limbs that hurt. He whined but didn't get up from there. He couldn't. It felt like as if he was stuck to the ground. First the beautiful night had crashed, by Nishi's revelations on why Sanjana was with him, then it was the vehicle they were on that crashed. He heard someone come over him. It was Sanjana. She appeared like as if she hadn't been hurt at all. She caught hold of his shoulders and tried lifting him.

"Rohit. Rohit." He heard her voice. "God has a crappy sense of timing." He cried out. His arm was hurt. There were abrasions over his elbow.

"You okay man?" Sanjana asked being concerned about his silence.

"Yeah. From not a great day to an amazing evening to a screwed up night." He rose up and sat.

"Mmm. I need to call Rohit and Yashan." He realized.

"Don't worry the wedding is not far from here." Sanjana assured. She went on, "Rohit, about the evening . . ."

"It' okay. You don't have to explain. It's usual of Yashan. I have been with him for a number of years. He was the guy who manipulated people to get what he always wanted. A Bamboozler." Rohit stopped her.

"No. It isn't what you think." She took hold of his hand. "Yashan did ask me to do this as a favour. He had found out that I was here. So he asked this of only as a favour. Then he told me about what you did at the interview. He also told me about your dream. I was there in it, wasn't I? I was the one responsible for you throwing away your wedding. It is my responsibility to fix this."

"No, it wasn't. Even though you were in my dream, it was my own conscience that asked me to do it. Not your fault."

"No, it isn't like that. You have got to deal with it. You happily decided to come here, because you wanted to get away from reality, you are afraid to confront it." Nishi had stopped. She was waiting for him to say something.

Rohit knew Nishi was right about what she was telling. All the dreamy state he had been enjoying with her, was because he was afraid to confront reality. Even now, Yashan and Nishi must probably be searching for him.

"You are right, I just came here to escape my real problems temporarily. But this isn't the first time. Whenever I wanted to escape from reality, I fantasized this kind of a date. Where we would sip coffee and talk about our life. Every time I fantasized, the conversations were different. Interestingly, I never completed the fantasy. I mean, I don't remember how it ends. I just hope this is not how it ends."

"It doesn't' have to. You deserve better." She was looking into his eyes. In the depths of eye, it seems like he could see her remorse, for his mistake. He didn't want to let go. Sanjana bent down and tucked her hair behind her ears. It made him think back of the night on top of the terrace. Rohit leaned forward and placed his lips over hers.

At first, he could feel the warm moisture. But it disappeared immediately. Sanjana had pulled back and turned her face away. With her hand she wiped her mouth. There was guilt on her face. Rohit realized his mistake.

"I'm sorry. Very sorry. I just had been through a trauma. I guess that got me all confused. I'm very sorry." He began to apologize. He was worried she might begin to cry.

"I'm sorry Rohit." She said. He didn't understand what she was apologizing for. He just wanted her to not cry at the moment. If he doesn't apologize it's going to leave a guilty voice in his head. He didn't want that.

"What are you apologizing for? It's okay. No problem at all." He tried comforting her.

"Who am I to try and take her place?" she said. He didn't understand what she was saying. She had been trying to comfort him until he leaned forward to kiss her, after that the roles seemed to have switched. Normally, he would have patted her shoulder to console her. But after his attempt to kiss, it wouldn't be the right thing to do.

"Are you alright?" he asked her.

"I am. She isn't." she said still crying.

"Who?"

"Sanjana. I am not Sanjana. I'm Ranjana."

"WHAT?" It had been bad enough for Rohit to know that the wonderful date he had been having was something already planned. It was already what his friends called *'getting the bulb.'* But to know that he was dating the wrong person. It was like getting the brightest of the bulbs. To narrate to anyone it would be total embarrassment. But it didn't matter now, what his friends would think. *Why is Ranjana here?* Suddenly, his sorry feeling for Ranjana had changed, she had made a fool of him. He wasn't angry though. But he felt that he had to be angry.

"I was in London. Sanjana had got married five months back." *Sanjana is married? I never got to know that. Should be a London dork.* "She married an Indian and settled down in Coimbatore." *An Indian dork then,* his mind abused the guy, whoever he was. "Last month, she . . . met with an accident. And she didn't make it out safe. She passed away." Ranjana's voice broke down. *Sanjana IS DEAD. NO FUCKING WAY,* his mind panicked. She was only a year younger than him. It seemed impossible to believe. That girl who used to wave at him in school, who chatted with him in the café was not alive. Till then, Sanjana was there in his best of his memories and to think that she was not there alive, Rohit could feel the blood draining off his face.

"I said I came for a function, right? It was for her final rites." She began to cry uncontrollably. Yashan didn't know if he had to comfort her or cry for Sanjana. He kept his mouth shut and his expression blank. He hoped there was more explanation that Sanjana had.

"I'm sorry for your loss, Ranjana. I'm terribly sorry. It should be very hard." He said after a minute or so.

"She used to tell me everything. She told me everything about you also. Every single word that she you had ever said to her. That's why I thought I could come. Losing a twin is much harder than losing anybody else. And I never came to advice you at all. Yashan did tell me about your issues with job. But I didn't care for it. You came here with two other friends, didn't you? Nishi had come to talk to Tarun. From what you told me when we left the café, I presume Yashan is here for Yamuna more than anything else. You too are supposed to be in the cruise. You ditched your friends to come with me. All of you had been selfish in some way tonight. So was me. I came only to see what it was like to be Sanjana for one more time. Probably, the one last time. I am damn sorry. I know you are having a hard time with your job prospects and all. But . . . It was selfish." Ranjana had said. He didn't know how to react. Maybe he should think about getting back from here. His friends would be searching for him. Rohit picked up the *Scooty*. It wasn't starting.

"I'll call my friends." said Rohit and pulled out his phone. His phone's screen was shattered. The phone didn't turn on either. Sanjana didn't have anyone she could call. She didn't want to wake up her family to pick her up from the highway. They were stranded.

"We should have to get a lift. Or can you call someone?" Rohit asked.

"Rohit." She said getting up. "Like, I already said, I don't care for the issues in your life. But from what Yashan told me it sounded like you are throwing away your life. Just as you throw your life away, do remember that there are people who don't have a life to live. Like my sister." she said and walked towards the road. Rohit's eyes became moist. It seemed like he had done nothing wrong, yet he was feeling guilty, for a reason he never knew what. He had to get back to his friends now. To back to his usual life. He wasn't sure he had one. He had to explain about his job to his parents. What was to follow? He had no clue. This is what he had wanted. But, he wasn't so sure anymore.

CHAPTER 14

YASHAN WASN'T PICKING up his phone. It was starting to make Nishi anxious. *Had he successfully made it out of there? Did he get caught by the drunkards? Should we return back there now?* The thoughts raised her anxiousness. Just then, the car slowed down.

"What's happening?" she questioned.

"We'll wake up Yamuna. It isn't going to look good to carry her unconscious." Saying Tarun took the water from the car and went over to the back seat. He sprinkled it over Yamuna and tried waking her up. Nishi didn't put her phone down, she kept redialling Yashan hoping he would pick up. The line kept going. There was no response from the other end at all.

"Nishi . . ." it was Tarun. She turned around. "She isn't waking up." Yamuna lay there unconscious and unresponsive. Nishi got down from and she too went over the back seat.

"I think she OD'd." Nishi placed her hand over Yamuna's breast and felt for a heartbeat. There was nothing she could feel. She hoped that she was doing it wrong. She put her finger in front of

Yamuna's nostrils. She felt a very faint breath on her finger. Again she wasn't sure if that was supposed to be happening.

"I can feel her breath very softly." She declared after comparing the same thing with her own breathing.

"Do you know to check for her pulse?" Tarun asked.

"No . . . but." Nishi caught hold of Yamuna's wrist in an attempt to feel for her wrist.

"Isn't it felt at the neck."

"I don't know." Nishi place her hands over Yamuna's neck. She could feel a soft pulsatile movement under Yamuna's neck.

"She is alive. But something is wrong. I think."

"Let's get her to a hospital." Tarun suggested.

"Where? At this time of the night?"

"There is a medical college very close." Tarun replied. Nishi this time got into the rear seat and placed Yamuna's head over her lap. Tarun turned around the car and headed to the hospital. Nishi's anxiousness had gone up. But not over Yashan, this time it was Yamuna. *How serious is she? Did I feel correctly? What if . . . ?* She had to force herself to avoid herself from thinking tragic thoughts. She tried to focus herself by looking outside. The scenic ECR was brightly lit by the moonlight. And it reflected on the Bay of Bengal's waters. The car turned into a smaller road next to a bar. Contrary to the moonlit ECR, the road was almost pitch black. Even the car's headlight was hardly helping to shove away the darkness. In no time, the car pulled into the ER of the hospital. It then hit Nishi, she had forgotten to inform Yashan. She called him again.

"Hello." came Yashan's voice.

"Dude, we had to come to a hospital. Yamuna isn't getting up."

"Where?"

"Come towards Pondicherry, a road will go on your right next to a bar. There's a medical college."

There was no response.

"Hello."

Still no response. The call had got cut. Before she could redial, Tarun had opened the door for her. There was a ward-boy with a stretcher behind her.

*   *   *

"There's a car coming. Ask for lift." Ranjana told him. Rohit waved his hand, hoping the car would stop. It did. It was a police jeep. A man in plain clothes got down.

"What are you doing here? Who are you?" the police asked. A girl and a boy in the middle of the night on a highway was a bad impression to anybody. Rohit didn't want the police to think what it looked like.

"We were here for a wedding. When we were returning, the vehicle, slipped it's not starting." Rohit explained.

"Where are you coming from? What's your name?" the policeman seems all the more suspicious.

"I'm from Pondicherry. Sanjana."

"Rohit. Chennai."

"Where were you going to?"

"There is a wedding going on nearby. We are returning there."

"Whose wedding?"

"Friend. We know the groom."

"Do you know where the groom is?"

"Where else would he be? He is at the resort, where the wedding is going to be held."

"Oh!" the police inspector after a pause continued, "Okay, get in. I'll drop you. Sanjana, isn't that your name? You get in the front."

"Thank you, sir." The two of them muttered and climbed into the vehicle. Rohit went to the rear of the vehicle and opened the rear door. And instantly, his pupils dilated. There was a person there already. And the worst part was that Rohit recognized the figure in the darkness. He wished he hadn't.

CHAPTER 15

"THERE, THE POLICE itself is here. Consider yourself lucky." Said the M.O. The two of them turned around. Nishi wasn't quite sure if they were lucky or unlucky. A police jeep drove into the hospital and it stopped at the front of the emergency block. The door opened and a man got out. He wasn't in uniform, he was wearing plain clothes. And his appearance was intimidating.

"Ah!" Tarun sighed as if it was a good sign. "He is the family friend, whom I had been trying to call." Nishi understood his reason was sighing. And right after him, the rear door opened and a girl got down. She was wearing a party wear. *Do I know her?* Nishi wondered. Then just behind her someone else got down. And then it came to Nishi's mind, '*This girl has to be Sanjana, because the one who was getting down after her was Rohit. But what are they doing with this police guy? Were they arrested? Did they call him? What is going on?*' Nishi couldn't take a guess to any of those questions.

But, just then something happened that made her heart almost stop. A fourth person got down from the jeep. The fourth person didn't make her heart stop though, it was the fact that he was in handcuffs'. *Oh God! Please tell me what's going on here?* She prayed. Yashan after having gotten down, surveyed the surroundings. The moment, he spotted Nishi, Nishi was expecting a smile, instead he frowned. And he came straight towards them.

In spite of the handcuffs, limiting his hands, Yashan caught hold of Tarun's collar.

"What the fuck were trying to pull off there, man? Ditching me to deal with the drunks? Is that your revenge? Do you know what happens when a revenge fails? You get hit harder. So hard that you can't even think of a revenge." Yashan yelled into Tarun's face.

"Get off him." Said the police and pushed Yashan away. Tarun stared back in silence. "I shouldn't have let you out of the car. Taken you straight to custody."

"Why?" Tarun questioned.

"Why else? For kidnapping Yamuna."

"No, you are mistaken, uncle. He didn't kidnap." Tarun said laughing as if it the prospect of Yashan kidnapping Yamuna sounded absurd. Nishi was surprised. *Was Tarun defending* Rohit? *That is too good to be true.*

"Then?"

"Yamuna and he were having a talk. It was at that time, she got kidnapped. He informed me first. So we all went together to rescue her. Actually, I called you first, you didn't pick up the call, and so we went by ourselves." Tarun changed the whole story. Yashan was astounded. The one thing he feared that the night might lead to, he was out of it now.

"But, then he came to the resort?"

"Yeah, I didn't inform him that we came here. That's why he is mad at me. And by the way we really need your help now."

"What?"

"The kidnappers, they drugged her or something. The doctors are telling that we need police approval because of the drug use. Else they won't discharge her."

"Yeah. Don't worry. I know the C.M.O here. I'll take care of it. You people wait here."

"Sir." Yashan called out showing his handcuffed hands.

"Yea. I'm sorry about that." saying the cop un-cuffed Rohit.

"So what happens now?" Nishi questioned.

"I'm going home." Ranjana said.

"How will you get home?" Rohit asked out of concern.

"I will take an auto and go my way. Don't worry." She said and headed to an auto that stood in the parking lot. Rohit decided to join along with her.

"Ranjana, I'm sorry for all that I have put you through." Rohit apologized.

"It's alright. You don't have to be. Both of us had a crazy night with the accident. I realized that stepping into my sister's shoes isn't as easy as I expected it to be. And you realized, well that m—my sister is n—no more."

"I think I have realized a lot more than that. Thanks to you."

"Like what?"

"About stuff, that's all." Rohit said.

"*Anna, Pondy poganum.*" Nishi instructed the auto-driver and she got in. "Rohit, I'm sorry that I tried to manipulate you. I hardly know anything about the woes of your life, but just let me tell you, Unlike Sanjana, you have a life that you are throwing away. Lavanya and Microsoft may sound scary now, but trust me, they will be your best decisions one day."

"I'm not being rude. But I already know what I need to do. You don't have to tell." Rohit said smiling.

"Okay, bye." Ranjana said. Rohit stood watching the auto leave the hospital gate.

*   *   *

"So what happens now?" Nishi questioned.

"I'm going home." Ranjana said.

"How will you get home?" Rohit asked out of concern.

"I will take an auto and go my way. Don't worry." She said and headed to an auto that stood in the parking lot. Rohit began to walk along with her.

"Can we leave? I mean, your family friend, he wanted us to wait. But we really have to go." Yashan said.

"You have to leave. I don't want you here when Yamuna wakes up." Tarun said. It was rude of Tarun to say that. But Yashan knew it was best if he leave. Moreover, he already wanted to leave as soon as possible, to avoid any more trouble. He hadn't realized until then that he was probably never going to see her in his life ever again. But he was too ashamed to face her. He had to leave.

"Tarun. You could have said the truth and had me arrested for all that I had done. But you didn't. I am not going to ask you why. But thanks."

"You could have very well hid your phone and prevented me from calling my uncle, at the beach. You didn't either. You made a choice for Yamuna's sake. Neither am I going to ask why. This was just my way of saying thanks for that." Tarun replied.

"Nishi was right. Yamuna is a crush and I have to let go. I mean, I was 16 then, I couldn't have been more wrong. And about you and her, there are a hundred things I could say to you right now. But I'm going to let them pass and simply say, I'm happy for you, bro." Yashan said to Tarun and went to get the car. Nishi and Tarun stood in silence.

"You asked me if I can be okay with the fact that you had broken up with me. I am still not sure what you mean by that. I will read that mail. But there was a Tarun that I knew in my B.Com course. He was doing his BBA. I loved that guy then. I actually had a crush on him. I never wanted to. I was so furious with myself, when I found that I had a crush on him. No matter how much I tried, my mind was obsessed with him. He was my first crush. He was a special person in my life. And today he is getting married. And I want him to be happy, so I am going to say, no matter what you had done then, I am okay with it. We both have moved past all that."

"Thanks a lot, Nishi. Ever since, then I thought it was too late to get over what I did to you. But I guess, nothing is too late in life. You added to making my marriage a perfect one." Said Tarun smiling.

"So, Tarun, how will you return if we leave?"

"The police vehicle is here. Or I'll call my cousins. Don't worry. I'll take care."

"Fine. Bye. Happy Married Life." Saying Nishi walked towards the car. Rohit and Yashan were already there. It was almost dawn. The first light of the day was already there.

The radio in the car was playing a classic Tamil number. Nishi had her eyes closed and was hearing her thoughts within her mind. *Life isn't in black and white. But in shades of grey.* She had heard that from somewhere. She had hoped that meeting Tarun would bring about a closure with Tarun. But she didn't really feel the way she had expected to be. He was getting married. Well, soon would she be too. Starting a life with another guy, raising a family, that's what her life had for her. Tarun had referred to his college life as an adventurous and irresponsible phase of his life. And he had mentioned that it was his best phase in life. *But I never had an irresponsible phase? I never did anything because I wanted to do. I did what I was supposed to do. Did I miss out the best part in my life?* Maybe she had. She realized that she has to do something about it. *Was it too late in life to do that? Or as Tarun had said nothing is too late in life.* She could move to someplace and get a job. Probably work there for a year or two before settling down with marriage. It sounded scary and thrilling. Her parents would never let her do it. That meant an ugly argument with her dad to let her go. For the first time in many years, Nishi felt as though there was a whole deal of life left for her to live.

"Hey Yashan, you okay?" she heard Rohit ask.

"Yeah." Yashan replied. But his voice sounded different. Something was wrong.

"Hey, you can tell now. Nishi is asleep." Rohit tried persuading. Apparently, Rohit didn't know that Nishi was just having her eyes closed. Nishi decided to stay so.

"When Tarun asked me, I said that letting Yamuna go is the right thing. But in school I thought the same thing and let her go with Vajish. In the cruise, I realized that I was wrong then. I'm just scared that what if I might have been wrong again. I am scared of making the same mistake again. And I'm worried that I have already made it." Yashan broke down in tears. Nishi wanted to stop pretending and comfort Yashan, but that might make him more uncomfortable.

"Look, you can never know if what you did is right or wrong. You know why? Because there is no right and wrong. Life isn't a canvas of black and white, but of different shades of grey. Letting her go will change your life, hopefully for the better. One day, you will laugh at the silly crush you had on her."

"I do know this shades of grey talk. But it's easier to say something, than to go through it. I let her go because that is socially the right thing. A part in me still thinks that I should win her back. What do you say for that?"

"Have you ever got caught watching porn?" Rohit asked Yashan.

"What?"

"I have a friend. Once he was watching porn in his system and his sister saw him. This idiot didn't notice his sister. Later his sister put him to embarrassment by asking about it and offered her laptop for him to watch porn. He has a cool sister, doesn't' he?" Rohit narrated. Nishi didn't understand what Rohit was talking about. *Boys talk?* She wondered. She tried to peek between her eyelids. But then, she heard a muffled laughter from Yashan.

"Was it easy for you to let go, Rohit? You met Sanjana tonight, didn't you?"

"My problem wasn't about letting go. It was about holding on. All that havoc I began there, I'm starting to think it was because I was just scared about the interview. The interview was my life's dream. If I were to not get the job, it kind of seemed that my whole dream might be gone. I know it wouldn't, but still. There was too much pressure and I panicked over a silly dream."

"Glad to know. Look, I'm sorry that I tried manipulating you. I just did it for your good. Nishi told me she had blabbered it out to you that how I was the one who got Sanjana there."

"Listen, Yashan. I actually thought of not telling you this. Your whole plan didn't go really well."

"I know. Nishi told you."

"No, your plan didn't even come together."

"What'd you mean?"

"Sanjana didn't come, actually. In the café, I realized that something was different. Then, I thought it was just that I was meeting her after a long time. But when Nishi told me I thought it seemed like Sanjana was intentionally forcing all the conversation about me. We were sitting by the side of the road, we were talking and . . . . . I kissed her."

"Oh!"

"She pulled away immediately and confessed that she was Ranjana. Sanjana—she passed away in an accident.

"Shit! Dude?"

"Yep. Even I was shocked."

"I'm sorry, man."

"It's alright, man. You plan didn't work, but what you are getting what you wanted. I'm going to take the job."

"Really? I'm—just happy. And I'm not going to ask any further questions although I'm curious to know."

"And I need your handiwork to convince my father-in law too. Convince Lavanya that it was a mistake."

"Sure."

"The one sad thing though, there had been a question that I had been meaning to ask Sanjana if I ever got to meet her. When I thought Ranjana was Sanjana, I decided to ask it just before she leaves. Well, I'm never going to know the answer to it."

"What were you planning to ask?" Yashan questioned. The conversation seemed to be going over something important. Nishi tried to listen carefully.

"Well, you once told me that she might have been dismissed because Priya ma'am had possibly seen us. I just wanted to know if that was the real reason she left? I always felt guilty about that. If it had been that why she had to leave, well I deserved to be dismissed too. I felt bad for her. I'll never find out."

"Oh my God!" Yashan exclaimed. He could partly remember what Rohit was talking about. But it had been his fault, the whole time.

"What dude?"

"Look, I have had the explanation to it all along. You may not like it. But here it is. I don't remember the details. You remember the thing that I pulled off to be the sports day M.C back then. Telling you that, was part of my plan. I don't know why I said it. But it was a lie that I fabricated. Nothing more."

"So I wasn't responsible for her dismissal."

"Not even remotely. As she told you, she wasn't even dismissed. She withdrew from school."

"You son of a-. I had this thing for all these years and now you tell me this."

"I'm glad you asked atleast now."

"Go to hell, man." Rohit cursed. Nishi didn't really understand the final part of their conversation. But the real reason why they had come to the wedding was fulfilled. Nishi was excited, but she continued to pretend to sleep.

"But what kind of ending is this? It was a great night. I won't deny that. But I came to the wedding with the hopes of abducting Tarun. At one point, I was on a date with Sanjana, or that's what I knew then. You had Yamuna with you. Nishi was with Tarun. The three of us met someone important in each of our lives. But nobody got to ride home with their girl or boy for the instance." Rohit said.

"You know what? It is true that we didn't get to ride home with the girl or guy. But the thing is the right girl went home with the right guy. It's a happy ending, just not for us. And that too, only because tonight is not when it ends for us. We have got way to go" said Yashan.

"We're here. Wake Nishi up." She heard Rohit say. Nishi felt Yashan shaking her up. She pretended to have had her sleep disturbed.

"You guys you'll get down and head to hostel I'll go park the car." Said Rohit and headed to the parking lot.

"Well, this evening wasn't a waste after all. Rohit has agreed to change his mind." Yashan told Nishi.

"So, the bet?" Nishi questioned out of the pride that she had won.

"Yeah. You have to pay up. Kiss Lavanya."

"What? Why do I have to kiss her? You lost the bet."

"See, you don't the whole picture right? Please explain how you won the bet."

"I suggested we go to Pondy and taking him to the marriage. Seeing that will change his mind and I guess it worked."

"Technically Nishi, Yashan didn't see any marriage. Moreover he hardly stayed on that cruise for twenty minutes. So your plan failed."

"Okay. Fine. Your plan didn't work either. I accidentally destroyed it. And moreover Ra-." Nishi argued. She almost blurted out what she had overheard. If nobody had won it no one had to pay up. Nishi didn't have problem with it as long as she didn't have to kiss a girl.

"You thought you destroyed my plan. Apparently my plan is stronger. And you see my plan is more complicated. The post I told you about, I actually saw it earlier. I called Sanjana."

"But it was Ranjana who came."

"Yes. I called Sanjana and then there was no response. So I called Ranjana and told her to inform Sanjana. She told she would, but then she came there herself. Had she told me about Sanjana, I might have considered something else."

"Wait. That means you made the plan, before the bet. That's cheating."

"It's smartness. You agreed. No backing out now."

"No way."

"First of all, Ranjana was the reason he changed his mind. And why was Ranjana there? Because I called her. Moreover, you made a plan and executed it, didn't you? Technically, making you to make a plan and make a bet out of it and to win the bet even before you make the bet was all part of my plan. If you see, I actually won on so many levels? I began winning the bet, right when you agreed to make the bet. Moreover, the whole point was to get him to take the job. You heard him mention in the car and that I'm responsible for it indirectly. So suck it up and fulfil the deed."

"What did he say in car? I was sleeping." Nishi pretended.

"Pretending to sleep."

"How did you know?"

"Your eyelids were moving, because you were trying to peek."

"Damn it. Fine. Let's go to the hostel. I'm sleepy now."

"Yes. You are going to kiss a girl." Yashan teased. The two of them began walking towards their hostel. Halfway through Nishi stopped Yashan.

"Wait, you called Sanjana as early as you told me earlier?"

"Yes. If you don't believe see my dialled calls in my mobile." Said Yashan pulling out his phone.

"No, no. It's not that. Rohit agreed to go to Pondy after we made the bet. If you had called as early as you say, it means you knew damn well that I would choose to go to Pondy and that Rohit would agree too. How did you know that?" Sanjana was puzzled. Yashan smiled back.

"Oh! Tell me. There was no guarantee we would go there. Yet you made a call."

"You see, Nishi. There's a reason they call me the Bamboozler." Yashan said beaming with pride and joy over his victory.

EPILOGUE

*T*HE BUS RAMBLED *on. There was no one beside him on the seat. He adjusted himself and moved towards the window and looked outside. There were dark clouds. Both sides of the road were strewn with trees that lashed out its branches forming an arch over the roads. He had a strange feeling that the road the bus was travelling seemed to head to a forest. The vegetation outside appeared to be wild. The road was totally unfamiliar to him. He'd never been here before.*

Rohit left the trees and the clouds to fly past and began examining the inside of the bus. He searched the bus for familiar faces. A few were. He saw a few juniors from his college. There were some faculty members from his college too. That was it. It should've been his college bus. But he couldn't figure out why his college bus was on such a road. His college was in the centre of the city and the bus never travelled beyond the city limits. There were also a few faces that he didn't recognize. He sensed that someone was watching him. He turned around.

A girl of his age, creamy-fair skin and thin eyebrows, dressed in a well-fitted blue salwar and white leggings sat in a seat just behind his. She looked unusually beautiful. Rohit felt a peculiar tingling sensation within him. He had had that feeling before. But that was a long time back. There was no one sitting beside her. She was carrying nothing with her, no shoulder bag, no kerchief, and no mobile even. And the weirdest of them all was that she had her gaze intently fixed upon him. He ransacked his memories to identify her. He remembered those tresses, the gaze, and the build. Yet, his mind couldn't place her. It had to be either of the two persons. One, it was a girl he had kissed in a hospital garden, five months back. Or it has to be her dead twin sister.

"You look a bit tense." He heard her voice. He turned around.

"I have been here, already haven't I?" he asked her.

"Then, why are you here again?" she asked. It then hit him. It was a dream. He had had the same dream five months ago. Why was the same dream recurring again? Last time he had the dream, he . . . The dream didn't last any longer, it crashed.

Rohit woke up with a start. His phone was ringing beside him. He answered the call.

"Woke up?" came a voice he knew too well.

"Mmm." He asserted sheepishly.

"Now only you are getting up huh? You know what day it is?" she continued.

"Yeah, yeah." Remembering why the day was important.

"You sound terrible. Are you feeling alright?" she was concerned.

"I'm all right. Just woke up from a . . . never mind. I'll be there." He hung up the call. He had had a dream. He had a faint recollection of having a dream. He tried to remember what it was. There were trees, some people. There was a conversation too. But he couldn't remember anything else. He could visualise the atmosphere of his dream, but not what its contents were. He had a feeling his dream had been left incomplete. He decided to get ready.

An unremembered dream has trivial meaning, he told himself. It itched his mind to not be able to remember this dream, he didn't know why. He had a hot water bath. The water washed away all thoughts of the dream and his mind filled itself with thoughts on the important day ahead. When he returned the LED notification light on his new smartphone flashed a pink light. Pink light meant a *Whatsapp* message in his phone. He checked it out. It was from Lavanya. *"Look, what your friend did . . ."* And the next message was a photograph. Repulsed by the photo, Yashan mockingly kicked Rohit, who was asleep on a mattress on the floor. Yashan slowly slumbered out of bed. By the time Yashan was out of bed. Rohit was trying as hard as he could to comb his hair. Once, Yashan was out of bed, Rohit showed the photo that Lavanya had sent. Yashan looked into it.

It was a picture of Nishi and Lavanya. Nishi had her lips on Lavanya. Lavanya seemed to be not interested in the smooch.

"Well, that is so unfair. She should have done it in front of me. But still, I think I will accept that the bet is sealed. And don't delete the photo." Yashan said with a snorting laughter. Rohit didn't understand, but he was in no mood to inquire into it. Nishi had promised to take care of the bridal night while Rohit was responsible for the bachelor party. Rohit never expected Nishi to have placed her lips over his fiancée's. He put on his *sherwani*. It suited him perfectly. It was the day of his marriage. He was marrying his girlfriend, Lavanya. *Dream come true.*